"A refreshingly different and intriguing story of mid-life relationships. The equivalent of Bridget Jones several years later, and on horseback."

Nicola Saxton

"The kind of book that makes you laugh, smile and occasionally gasp. Whether you ride either a horse or motorbikes (and there are more similarities than you would first think), this is the book for you."

Rachel Lee

"Kick-Start was compulsive reading."

Lesley Morrison

"Such an accurate portrayal of speed – on horseback, on motorbikes, and on the dating scene … strap yourself in!"

R Wright

KICK-START

Lorna Roth

Matador
9 Priory Business Park,
Wistow Road, Kibworth Beauchamp,
Leicestershire. LE8 0RX
Tel: 0116 279 2299
Email: books@troubador.co.uk
Web: www.troubador.co.uk/matador
Twitter: @matadorbooks

ISBN 978 1800463 219

British Library Cataloguing in Publication Data.
A catalogue record for this book is available from the British Library.

Printed and bound in the UK by TJ Books Ltd, Padstow, Cornwall
Typeset in 11pt Adobe Garamond Pro by Troubador Publishing Ltd, Leicester, UK

Matador is an imprint of Troubador Publishing Ltd

For Rachel
A best friend: always ready to
top up our glasses with laughter.

Chapter 1

"Spill the beans, Lizzie. Which is more hazardous? A horse? Or online dating?"

Judith's high-pitched question is shouted into the air, but the words are left behind as swiftly as they are thrown. They mingle and swirl with steam, in a vacuum of space through which three horses flash. No answer arrives above the rhythmic pounding of hooves. Each stride is gaining momentum, scattering frost, digging deep into a cushion of turf.

Three women and their equine counterparts are whooping and squealing with delight. They thunder along the track, totally focused, swept up in sensory overload, borne along within the zigzag maze that is Thetford Forest. Three pairs of human eyes hawkishly searching in a fleeting instant for any rut or hidden rabbit hole, a predestined but much dreaded appointment with terra firma. Three pairs of equine eyes locked onto a beckoning stretch of unfenced heaven. Three sets of quadruped legs stretching, lifting, leaping, landing, joyous and unfettered. Three pairs of female arms, biceps straining, fists taut. Autonomous parts, all streaming as one entity. Occasionally a ruddy cheek is turned hurriedly, an instruction hurled over a shoulder:

"Steady up, there's a dip on the left," or, "Caroline. Shift over, for Christ's sake. If Tarquin puts in another buck, I'll hit the deck."

At the front, Judith drops her eyes to her hands, quickly snatches her reins in a bit shorter. She looks up too late, cannot swerve the low-hanging branch in her path. She frantically calls, "Watch out. Ah, shit," hears the ragged smack of the birch hitting her hat, finishes the sentence, "that was close."

Laughing, she brings her body upright again, turns to check her friends are still on board. Lizzie and Caroline are both crouched in a classic racing position, feet wedged firmly into stirrups, bottoms raised above the seat of their saddles, elbows bent, maintaining the balance between holding half a ton of wilful flesh and muscle and the far lesser strength of female frames. Judith feels the ache in her knuckles, the burn in her wrists, knows she has limits. She finds her own voice annoyingly plaintive when she speaks.

"I'm slowing down girls. Need a breather."

As they settle into a walk, Judith flips a stray lock of black mane hairs across Rommel's neck. She stares at the spaces around her in the forest, untarnished, the trappings of civilised living expelled. She savours the fluidity of it all, the season-changing shades of green and brown. The stillness of the trees, the criss-cross of an occasional track, brimming with potential, tantalising in its promise of yet more avenues, just out of sight. When they reach the next junction in the lines of trees, Judith stops Rommel, holds her hand up to halt the other two women. Her head is tilted. Every now and then, the breeze brings the fleeting whine of engines.

She asks, "Can I hear motorbikes?"

A throaty drone plays in and out for thirty seconds, no more, before the density of the trees swallows up the sound again. The quickening of her heart is exactly that. Not a bile-inducing bang,

bang, bang of abject fear, simply a vague but irritating pattering. A team of mice scuttling up the stairs inside her chest. Tarquin fidgets sideways making Lizzie chirp up impatiently.

"Stop fretting, Jude. We'll be fine, they're nowhere near close to us."

Judith opens her mouth to speak, but Lizzie's sceptical expression squashes her hesitancy. She sees the sudden flash of Tarquin's bay leg kicking out behind him, knows it mimics the impatience of his rider. Judith concedes.

"OK, OK. Come on. Let's open 'em up a bit. Who's gonna get mud in her face? We can pull up at the top of the slope."

Caroline's kick-start is sharper than Judith's. From a standstill, her horse, Flint, has already lurched two strides into a canter before Judith and Lizzie get a chance to point their mounts in the same direction. Judith waves a friendly fist at Caroline's back, calls out.

"You cheated. False start," but she's grinning as small clods of loose grass and soil fly up in Flint's wake.

* * *

Running parallel only 400 metres to their right, another forest track is taking the imprint of speed. Their tyres gripping into the sandy soil beneath the patchy turf, four off-road motorbikes growl up the incline. Regimentally spaced eight metres apart, equidistant to perfection. Visors dropped, the four men are in the zone. They left early in the certainty that the forest would be theirs and theirs alone. They squeeze up the throttles to 45mph. Looking ahead to the brow of the hill, the lead biker sees an outer perimeter fence running along the horizon. Carefully, he releases his left hand from the handlebars, quietly praying he doesn't hit a rut, and points his whole arm out to the left. The four bikers slow only fractionally, torsos stiffen in anticipation of the sharp turn, clutches grind, booted feet are lifted from the pedals to stretch straight forward, soles skirting the grass briefly.

Now travelling at a right angle to their original course, the lead biker is upright again and momentarily dares to turn his neck and check that his mates are all following. He knows this area well; his favourite hook right is coming up fast and he's itching to put Jerry in his place. The wind whips away his words:

"Let's test your metal, Jerry. Bloody ex-officer. It's time for you to eat some dirt."

Luc starts counting down the metres in his head in anticipation of reaching the intersection of tracks. Now twenty metres away, he cuts off the throttle, stands high on the pedals, braces his arms, grips his fists ready to take the full weight of the bike. The bright morning sun reflects briefly off his visor.

"Fuck it, I can't see."

* * *

Judith registers the air rushing past her face; it mixes with the echo beat of the hooves. The trees conspire to hog the sound and create a cabin effect – muffled as if she is cruising in an aeroplane. Caroline is still in front; she twists around while in full flight. Judith can barely make out her words.

"I can hear motorbikes."

Replying, Judith gasps, "Where? I can't see any?"

Ahead of them by a mere six metres, the first bike roars into their path, cutting straight across from the avenue to their right.

Caroline screams, "Noooooooooo," as she flings her shoulders back, her feet forward, her arms rigid, frantically attempting to stop Flint in his tracks. Judith sees the biker's head lift as his focus is suddenly wrenched from peering at the handlebars. He's caught sight of a chestnut mound of horseflesh on a collision course with his own fragile human body parts and his survival reaction hurls him sideways at the ground on the corner.

The air that shoots, fast and furious, into Judith's lungs comes with a split-second panic – there isn't enough space to stop, it's far too late! Flint is a big horse and Caroline a seriously quick-witted, sharp individual. Her brain processes, her body reacts, her hands lift, taking the reins and the spontaneous instincts of her steed with her. Flint's hocks gather under him, the motorbike is sliding crossways before him. His head and neck follow the urgent upward motion of Caroline's hands and he rises high above the threat below him. The biker squints in disbelief – a hairy underbelly, iron-clad hooves and sand all flying over him in a nightmare of meat and mass. No single anatomical part of Flint actually touches the throbbing monster beneath, save a green dollop of descending dung. It splatters swiftly through the gap between polycotton and helmet, into the gulley beneath the biker's chin.

Judith grasps feverishly at the two or three extra seconds she has to realise what's happening. Another motorbike dramatically hurls into the scene. She cannot quiet the roar between her ears, the certainty – this is it. He'll smash into Rommel's legs. She yells.

"*Lizzie, watch out…*"

She drops the right rein completely, frantically grasps for the left rein only and in one long motion she hauls at Rommel's head. She thinks… *There, can I make it through the gap, down the side between the flattened motorbike and the pines? Is it wide enough?* Rommel's front legs hit the small bank running along the edge of the trees. He stumbles. Judith's head flings forward, catapulting her face into Rommel's neck as he all but comes to a halt, then panics, and squeezes his bulk past the bike. Her knee is rammed through the protruding spikes of a tree branch then miraculously she is past. The third and fourth motorbikes grind to a halt metres from the carnage.

Judith rams her fist into Rommel's neck to stop him careering off again in panic; she witnesses Lizzie and Tarquin come to a dramatic sliding halt well before the motorbikes. Tarquin is grabbing at the reins, plunging his head forward towards the ground, spinning in circles, his equine instinct impelling him to catch up with and follow the herd when being attacked. He throws his head skyward and whinnies in vain, spins on the spot and stops abruptly. Lizzie is caught totally off balance, hanging half off Tarquin's saddle as he unhelpfully scurries backwards. Lizzie leaps rather than falls the rest of the way, landing feet first square on the ground, one hand still holding the reins as Tarquin continues in reverse gear.

"Whoa, Tarcky, whoa. It's OK, my little man. Whoa."

All engines are now miraculously still. Breathing. All that Judith can hear is a steady melody of breathing. A mini snort from Flint, now standing neck arched, ears flicking back and forth, back and forth, tense, ready to flee. Caroline has shock written across her jawline. Judith looks down at Rommel's bent neck. *Bloody hell, my hold on this rein, it's rigid! The bit slewed in his mouth, it will bruise, but dare I let it out a tad? Will he throw his might into bolting off?* His nostrils, a frightened testament, are flaring – in, out, in, out. Leaking a gelatinous stream of hot snot.

A deep lung-filling inhale of breath surges through the lips of the prone biker. There is a bare whisper of a hiss from the hot exhaust pipe forced into damp grass, the wind surreptitiously adding its own personal dimension to that fragment of eerie lack of noise. She runs her tongue around each cheek, grimaces at the sour reflux taste in the back of her throat. She wonders – breakfast eaten too fast or regurgitated fear? Disbelief hangs cloudy in the air. Not for long. Lizzie's neck and cheeks have coloured into sunset red. Her angry bellow shatters the air – a voice low and strangely manly.

"You lunatic bunch of morons. You nearly killed all of us."

The thoroughbred in Tarquin means his 'flight' mode is now on emergency alert. He quickly drags Lizzie, tripping over tussocks of grass, to stand wild-eyed close to Rommel. Once all three horses come together, Judith feels a comfort arrive, a reassurance in each other's closeness. Both riders and horses bunched up, shoulder rubbing shoulder. Completely engrossed, she pictures her crooning words, streaming mercurial through her arm, leaving her palm, soothing into his neck. Her bottom lip seems bulbous, tender. Lizzie, not yet daring enough to remount Tarquin, looks up at Judith.

"You look like you've been in a street fight. Show me your teeth. Are they OK?"

* * *

The pungent aroma of horse shit launches into Luc's sense of smell. He is pinned on his side, aware of the weight of his bike crushing his knee and yet his hand manages an involuntary movement towards his own throat. He feels the stickiness on his fingers and grimaces as he realises the offending green stuff has splattered everywhere. He twists and stretches, sliding away from the dollop beside his shoulder. The world still appears to be running in numbing slow motion, so he begins fumbling with the clip on his chin strap. He tugs off his helmet. Suddenly, clear sound and perception floods in and Isaac's stubbly face appears upside down as it pops into his line of vision.

"That was a close shave, mate. Don't try to move for a minute. I'll lift the bike for you."

Finally released, Luc is still clutching a steadying hand on Isaac's arm when Jeremy's unruffled voice breaks the spell:

"I assure you that none of us is at fault or to blame for what's just happened. We have as much right to be riding in this forest as you do. In fact, it covers over 40,000 acres so I am struggling to understand why you had to choose an area where you may bump into a motorbike. May I recommend that in future you read a map and don't ride your horses anywhere near where the Green Lane route crosses."

The rider on the winged Pegasus is leaning forward over her saddle in order to come down to eye level with Jeremy and she spits out her words:

"A map, with this maze of tracks. Bloody impossible! I shall be reporting this whole incident to the Forestry Commission first thing on Monday morning. You and your friends are completely irresponsible to travel at those speeds in a public place. Green Lane or otherwise! I want your name and mobile number right now." Jeremy valiantly summons a polite throat-clearing noise followed by a measured:

"Pot. Kettle. Black. Springs to mind."

Luc watches him make a point of fiddling about in both pockets of his jacket before smiling up at the rider in mock angelic fashion and sarcastically replying,

"Oh dear, I don't appear to have a pen on me. And yes, if you insist on taking my name, I am perfectly happy to provide it. But, as you can see, the only person here who is possibly injured is my friend over there. It's not every day of the week that an enormous beast like yours flies over his head."

Luc studies the blonde rider as she hurriedly gathers up her reins, shoves her booted foot into the stirrup and swings her leg expertly over the saddle. She joins in irritably.

"Oh, leave it, Caroline. We're all fine, aren't we? Judith, is your leg OK? I saw you hit the tree." The dark-haired rider glances down to her left knee, a patch of torn fabric gaping open, but only a minor graze glares back at her, so she replies,

"No problem with me, Lizzie, and the horses are all good. Let's just get going."

He sees the softening in her eyes as the rider called Judith speaks with genuine concern:

"Will you lot be able to get back OK? Will that bike start, do you think?" But within seconds the blonde is spinning her horse around and blurting words at Jeremy's open mouth:

"Oh, come on, Judith, for goodness' sake. They're grown men. Let them sodding well look after themselves."

Luc stops leaning on Isaac. The tingling rush of circulation in his thigh has settled. Still quiet, all four men watch the receding scene – a collection of tails, one black, one grey, one chestnut, jigging and bobbing from side to side. The blonde rider, Lizzie, is occasionally throwing out an arm or turning in her saddle to point back at the bikes. Snippets of grumbling conversation keep drifting back. Luc notices Isaac unstiffen his neck from its strange angle then let rip with his boot into a bank of grass. As Isaac lifts his chin in defiance, he stares at the group of receding backs and curses in his best Irish accent.

"Bunch of shittin', four-legged eedjits."

Chapter 2

Judith

This is our second foray into staying at Keeper's End. A gem of a discovery, it sits half a mile into the heart of Thetford Forest. Originally a hotchpotch selection of decaying farm buildings, the Petersons have grafted year on year adding, fixing and improving to create accommodation for forty-two equines of every shape and size imaginable. The biggest guests get the five-star touch – rows of spacious, modern stables complete with wash-down/shower area, and the incredibly sandy soil is a bonus for any four-legged holidaymakers. No heavy mud to stick in chunks to hairy legs, a quick dandy-brush will knock off any residue from a horse with a tendency to wallow. The main drive is a swathe of compacted sand; here and there it reveals a path or track leading off to sun-speckled rides. It ends at the two flint stone cottages and 110 acres of paradise cocooned by the surrounding woodland. The Crittall windows in the picture-postcard cottages gaze out onto huge paddocks in every direction. The hub of a thriving holiday let business and local livery.

As I amble into the main living area of cabin number three, I consciously take in a roving view of the interior and smile. I've been anticipating this break for months. A pair of jodhpurs is hanging over the back of a dining chair, grubby footwear is lined up by the door, a packet of spaghetti, three cheesecakes, several bottles of tonic, some Hendricks gin and a bowl of fruit are squeezed onto the tiny kitchen surface. Lizzie is holding her palms up towards the warmth of the gas log burner and our merry foursome is now complete; Emma has joined us. She is in full flow, apologising for her late arrival.

"I know it's not a new Iveco, but I bought it from a reputable dealer. Sodding typical that it refused to start this morning. Just when I needed to be here with you lot for 9.30am! I'm so pissed off I missed the first ride."

A knowing look passes, unnoticed by Emma, between Caroline, Lizzie and me. Her absence on our morning ride had enabled us to let loose, uninhibited by her slightly timorous attitude to any pace faster than a sedate canter. Emma continues babbling as, in fits and starts, she pulls sundry riding kit from a large sports bag.

"Can't wait for all of you to see Rocket. He's a midget at 14.2 hands, but I already love him to bits. He's going to look tiny next to Flint, Caroline."

Caroline reaches across and places a reassuring hand on Emma's elbow.

"With your diminutive frame, Emma, you're more like a feather than a rider. Nothing wrong whatsoever with having a pony rather than a lolloping great lump of a horse like mine." Emma blushes a little at the compliment, manages a small appreciative smile.

"Ooh, do I smell your spag bol cooking, Caroline? I can see Judith has brought her usual supply of cheesecake. How many different flavours this trip?"

I am concentrating on jamming one foot into a trainer but I know, without looking, that the girls are making bulging hamster faces out of view. There is no hesitation in my V-shape two-fingered reaction shoved behind my back in their direction or the mock pout of my bottom lip as I turn to face them. I wail forlornly.

"I shall seek solace with the only friend I have who doesn't ridicule my foibles," and exit the cabin with a dramatic flourish. The diminishing sound of laughter follows me along the path.

Blinking from the glare of the bare overhead lightbulb, I slide back the bolt on Rommel's stable door and step inside. The acrid stench of fresh urine is mingling with the summer-meadow smell of crisp hay. My hair falls heavy and irritating across my face. I rake it back where it belongs, behind my ears. When I squat down beside Rommel's shoulder, a tender tightness pulls through my bruised thigh muscles. I wince.

"Let's have one last look at you, just in case."

I cup the palm of my hand and my fingers firmly around Rommel's near-fore, starting at his knee, feeling for any trace of excess heat or swelling, slowly running it all the way down to his hoof.

"Thank God it's my knee that's damaged and not yours, boy-oh."

Rommel's other foreleg receives the same process of concentrated scrutiny from me. Straightening up, I leave the warmth of the stable and bolt the door behind me.

"Night, night, boy-oh. Don't let the bed bugs bite."

An involuntary shiver runs around my shoulders in the chill of the March evening. In the distance a full moon is rising from behind a bank of ominous clouds. I pick my way gingerly across the uneven yard, resort to a childish rush through the tenebrous area at the end of the huge Dutch barn, take a breath again when I reach the row of wooden sheds. As I emerge around the corner, there are squares of light escaping through the windows of the log cabin and landing in pockets on the surrounding scene. My feet crunch on the cinders of the path underfoot; the sound is barely audible, overshadowed by the raucous male voices and guttural laughter piercing the night air from the next cabin fifteen metres further on to the right. There are only seven cabins, plus a large caravan for paying customers at Keeper's End; three in a cluster here; the rest dotted about at strategic quiet spots around the premises, enabling any occupants to have a modicum of privacy. A low hedge of laurels has been planted between and behind each cabin in the hope of creating a visual screen, but the plants are still barely two and a half feet high.

The lid of the boot bin by the cabin door clatters as I wedge it down firmly – there is rain forecast and the mood of the night, the essence of its latent darkness, halts me in my tracks. My thoughts begin wandering, quiescent, so I wait, staring at the turbulent clouds.

Do I love it or do I hate it? This sky, today, now? Cold and dim. Angry wind pushing pockets of tumbling grey. Is this sky a mirror of how I am to be? A tumbling mass of emotional distrust. How can I rid myself of the knowledge – that I am simply 'just not good enough'? My (supposedly doting) husband claimed he had, 'fallen out of love'. No rowing, no dramatic outbursts, just 'I no longer find you attractive. You've become a workaholic frump'. An affair would have been easy to stomach, but ambivalence! I am tired of being angry. Even Mother has chastised me, told me to 'Move on, Judith. Let it go. Four years is long enough.' I need some warmth in my world.

A distant pocket of diaphanous light appears for a few moments, far off, unearthly. I try to relax my shoulders, lean against the cabin, inhale the faint hint of pine. The distant beam is still there. *Such a cliché, 'Ray of Hope'. But it's true, that's what I must find.*

The cabin door creaks open and Lizzie steps out. I feel no urge to move, simply pipe up, "Fag break?" The roots of an established friendship do not need a constant watering with superfluous words. Lizzie waits till the end of the cigarette is glowing, continues the long, slow drag before speaking.

"Don't start, Jude. I've been incredibly good, considering."

A *ping, ping* sound from my coat makes me frantically search for the phone in my pocket. I prod in the code, spot two notifications in my emails from First Glance, but as suddenly as it arrived, the signal is gone again. I look quizzically at Lizzie, blurt out:

"I wonder if that chap called One Man Band will reply by the time I get home on Friday? He ticks *so* many boxes on my Superman wish list. Seriously sexy eyes, too. Doubt I shall get a second call from Steven – his voice gave him away. Ice; I kept seeing ice cubes in a tumbler all the way through our phone call. Couldn't quite put my finger on it, the nub of his problem, that is."

The cabin door creaks again. Emma leans out, squinting into the gloom, her strawberry-blonde locks, as always, scraped back tight into a ponytail. I raise my hand in an impatient wave.

"We'll be in in a minute."

The door shuts again. I continue in a hushed voice:

"Why the hell did I follow your lead? You've already been internet-dating for a whole year and you take it in your stride as if it's an everyday part of life. But did I choose the right site in the end? There are so many? Who knows? The choice is endless: Elite. com, Ourtime, E Harmony, Zoosk or Match.com? Should I have gone with a specialist site, perhaps Muddy Matches or Fitness Singles?"

Lizzie's head nods up and down in time to the flailing of my hands. She claims that I only ever do it when I'm getting agitated. I crash on.

"The shift in the traditional front lines of etiquette, they're all blown out of the window with internet dating. *You* treat the whole process like a job interview, phoning a man you've never met face to face. I struggle to make small talk, delve into someone's lifestyle, his family history, his profession. Even if I'm brave or stupid enough to actually meet a chap, it won't be anything like the normal way of the world. I won't have had a chance to associate him with a certain set of friends, note his taste in clothes or hear his jokes. You seem to be able to laugh it off whenever you regale me with your escapades. You see the light side of it all. Not sure that I can – it's just a friggin' lottery. Am I doing the right thing?"

Our eyes are suddenly drawn to the tiny patch of light, way off in the distant heavens, as it begins flickering, becomes uncertain. I slump against the cabin wall, dejected, direct my final comment at my own feet rather than Lizzie.

"Hope. It's such a horribly precarious emotion."

* * *

Luxuriating in the piping hot stream of water coursing down my back, the intermittent trembling which had beset my body since the dramas of the morning begins to subside. But I cannot quite eradicate the hallucinations – a moving picture of sharp chrome cutting into Rommel's chest like a steak knife into beef; strips of skin peeling from his knees; white ligaments and bone exposed. Through the hum of the power shower, an indistinct voice breaks my torment. I ignore it. More insistent, and pitching her voice an octave higher, Emma repeats the question through the dulling effect of the bathroom door.

"Oy, cloth ears. How long are you going to be, Jude? I said –

do you want a gin and tonic first? Or will you dive straight into the prosecco?"

Emma is the timid, petite, completely understated member of our group, but also a consummate mischief. A jet of earth-chilled water suddenly batters my bare shoulders and I yell.

"Ah, that's not fair. Shit. That's cold." I sidestep the harsh stream, grasp for the shower head and unhook it from its fitting high above my head. When I fling open the flimsy shower curtain, Emma is caught red-handed, her nail-bitten fingers still resting on the wall switch. I aim haphazardly at her chest, soaking her top. Emma jumps backwards allowing water to flow down glass and tiles then quickly caves into erratic screeching.

"OK, OK. White flag. I give up."

Stark naked, dripping wet, any modesty in me has evaporated.

"Definitely gin and tonic. I'll only be another five minutes."

On entering the lounge, an indisputably garlicky aroma hits my nostrils. The girls are in various states of female ease. Lizzie is clad in soft pink Little Mermaid pyjamas and a pair of incongruously large oven gloves. She is carefully placing a baking tray of steaming French sticks in the centre of the dining table. Emma's choice of dry garb is no less bizarre. The left ear on her white rabbit onesie is flopping over her eye as she neatly lays out the cutlery, piece by piece, right angle to right angle. Caroline, the consummate classy bird of our merry equestrian quartet, is reclining on the sofa, propped up by copious cushions. Her skin-tight shiny black leggings hug every contour of her strong, toned thighs. No wonder she bagged a moneyed City suit while men still regularly appear to fall at her feet, drooling. She proffers an outstretched glass in my direction then looks up hopefully.

"You're on your feet. Please be a darling and top me up."

Seriously well-endowed in the cup-size department, the loose blouse she is wearing falls open and I get an eyeful of her braless curves. My instinct is to look away briefly, but my stare reverts again in the direction of the cleavage. When I reach forward to clutch the glass, I cannot disguise the frown creasing my eyebrows or the curtness which slips into the tone of my reply.

"For goodness sake, Caroline – put them away, will you?"

Caroline's expression lights up. Pouting fuchsia-pink lipstick, she places a hand each side of her breasts to squeeze them into double-D cup formation.

"Oops, chill out, Jude. Don't be such a prudy-wudy. I only ever get to really relax when I'm with you lot. Emma, quickly. Prudy-wudy Jude needs loosening up."

Emma rushes to pick up the half-pint glass of gin and tonic waiting patiently on the kitchen unit. The tip of her fluffy rabbit ear plops into the clear liquid as she pivots on her heel and aims a question in Lizzie's direction.

"You're the medical expert here, Lizzie. Would you recommend that I administer intravenous gin and tonic immediately to Jude?"

My thumb and forefinger have parted in glass-width anticipation when I spy the slow osmosis of juniper-infused liquid as it climbs the rabbit ear. Emma pauses, her gaze drawn to follow my own stare. Like a shot, she whips the offending material upwards, pinches it with verve, her face triumphant as three small drips return to the drink.

"Waste not, want not Jude. I know that's your motto."

Graciously I take the G&T, smile brightly and plant puckered lips on her cheek.

"Thank you so much, Emma. You are the epitome of generos—"

But Emma cuts an urgent question across the unfinished sentence.

"Right, come on, girls. You haven't filled me in yet. Exactly what happened on your ride this morning?"

Her eager, round face is still within huffing distance of mine. She waits, the silence lasts only briefly till her simple question detonates like a mini incendiary in our midst. Within thirty seconds I have to resort to raising both my hands to shush them. I begin with a succinct description of the factual sequence of events. Caroline, however, cannot help but boast:

"Of course, it's all the hours, days, weeks and months of training I've put in with Flint. It paid off. He had the trust in me and in a split second the physical ability to treat that biker as if he was an upright gate at Stratford Hills Horse Trials."

Lizzie, on the other hand, comments:

"Why *do* most men get so damned excited by the size of an engine, for Christ's sake? Is it the sound? Is it the speed? Or perhaps it's all of the above? Is it a primal thing – the further his roar travels, the more powerful he feels and the more females will look his way?"

At this point, I cannot stop myself from jumping in.

"No, Lizzie. No man-bashing allowed; I won't have it. The roar of a V8 is fantastic. Just not if it's anywhere near me and my horse!"

Chapter 3

Alone in the dimly lit confines of the cosy bedroom, one by one Lucas Stockdale pulled on individual items of clothing. He felt justified in congratulating himself on his own misgivings. *Why the hell did I allow myself to get conned into thinking three days away like this could work? Why did I let Isaac talk me into it? A cabin in Thetford Forest, for fuck's sake. With Jeremy! No escape each evening. I left the army to get away from the likes of him.*

Belatedly, he felt his body reacting to the day, particularly the pressing tension that lurked behind his eyeballs. His memories of the morning were flooding back. A tidal wave of flashbacks swirled around, unannounced and uninvited – the satisfying growl of his Honda, the brightness of light, the panicky intake of breath into lungs. Only they insisted on doing loop-the-loops with his other memories. Eleven years since his fateful accident, but sometimes Luc couldn't stop the bilious reminders.

He reclined on the bed, pulled out a pillow and plonked it full-length across his head, wrapping the soft fabric tight around his ears. The fragments of sight and smell kept coming, crashing in on his conscious perception. The petrol fumes; his bike heading forward; his face pivoting to the left; the sand spraying... *but no,* he thought, *the tyre is screeching on tarmac – sand, tarmac, sand, tarmac. Which is it? Which is real, which is not?* Luc's confused mix of time persisted in churning, marching on and on. The pictures flitted; a golden, hairy horse hurtling at him; the sand; the shit; the roundabout; the blue 4 x 4 hitting him full on; enormous above him. The worst part was always prefixed by the silence of his motorbike. Then, he remembered the weight, the crushing, the pain. *I want the siren to stop. Why is everyone shouting?* He pushed the pillow aside, dropped his hand to his thigh, pinched a lump of skin. He sighed into the sensation, the squeeze, the knowledge that it was OK. His fingers came up to his temples and began a gentle, circular motion. He made a decision. *No thank you.*

Jerking himself upright, Luc's fist thumped the unyielding surface of the bedside table. He stared vacantly at the wall for a few seconds, spoke to a vertical line in the wood panelling. "Damn it, I am *not* going to let this happen."

A few more moments passed until a smirk initiated a loosening of his rigid jaw.

A little pick-me-up – that's what you need, Luc. He turned to leave, carefully squeezed the handle of the bedroom door, peered to the left and the right, then swiftly entered the adjoining bedroom. Jerry's favourite and, as he often reminded them, ridiculously expensive aftershave beckoned from the windowsill. Luc tipped the rich green bottle deftly upside down on his index finger and dabbed the Polo Eau de Cologne two or three times under his chin. He mused to himself. *It wouldn't be a fair society if us lesser mortals were denied an occasional luxury, would it? May have less worldly cash than Robert, a smaller pile of bricks and mortar than Jeremy, but what the heck. Besides, those two would make mincemeat out of Isaac if I wasn't here to be his wingman. Blame it all on Isaac and The Gardeners' Arms. Beer and bikes brought us all together. Beer, beer.* Luc registered his teeth, dry against his tongue.

His partners in crime were already well lubricated when he strolled into the cosy lounge area of the log cabin. He mustered a plastic smile but he had always felt an outsider, a Northerner. When he joined the army as a naïve eighteen-year-old, he was desperate to escape the dull stone Yorkshire town his extended family called home. Initially, he had revelled in the gruelling physical discipline and ribald camaraderie. His quick-witted reactions and innate ability to bond and communicate easily meant he had risen to captain in record time, but the realities of several overseas postings in quick succession had returned him disillusioned and generally distrustful of humankind. His farewell to his army career was also a fitting end for his pile of fatigues – a bonfire. The new framework to his foothold in civvy life became his carpentry.

His one true friend, he knew, was standing in front of him and was the only reason he tolerated spending time with Robert and Jeremy. And, he conceded, their occasional day trips to explore out-of-the-way Green Lane routes had thrown up some cracking rides in recent months.

"Oy, mate. Earth to Luc."

Isaac thrust a chilled bitter into Luc's outstretched hand and winked.

"A whole weekend away from the lovely ladies – time to party."

This all spoken with an exaggerated Irish lilt. The fact that Isaac's parents were originally from the Emerald Isle was a legitimate excuse, as far as he was concerned, to retain an Irish accent, his upbringing in Suffolk being completely irrelevant. Robert, the oldest and heaviest member of the foursome, slapped the meagre layer of hair populating his scalp before pointing his index finger first at Luc, then over to the cooker at Jeremy.

"It's all right for you two single lotharios. Some of us have

21

responsibilities and families to think about. We're not free to cast our net elsewhere."

Isaac reached for his smartphone on the table, frantically swiped the screen backwards and forwards several times.

"Right, Luc, what website is it that you use? It's about time we got Jeremy sorted out with someone classy, don't you think?"

Robert leant over the back of the sofa, pressed his fist into his stomach and feigned a retching heave.

"Don't be daft. I've heard so many tales about dating websites. No way would there be anyone in Jeremy's league."

Standing just an arm's length from Jeremy, Luc spotted a telltale pinking of the flesh around his cheeks and butted in:

"You'd be surprised, Robert. There are sites to suit everyone's taste, class and pocket. You just have to know where and how to look. I could certainly point him—"

But before he could finish, Jeremy swung around on his heels to face the room.

"Grub. Need some grub. Let's get started."

Whenever Luc looked at Jeremy's military-spec haircut, square jawline and general air of confined physical power, he felt that he could see the army still present in him – sitting on the man's shoulders, dictating the style of his walk, the order of his day. Adnams in hand, Luc approached the cooker, one eyebrow arched for dramatic effect as he mockingly rounded his vowels and held Jeremy's eyes with his own.

"Oh, I saaaaay, Sergeant Major. What dooooo we have on the menu this evening? Is it perhaps foie gras for starters, followed by lobster thermidor and, of course, something sophisticated to follow? Crème brûlée perhaps?"

Jeremy squared up his torso and returned the eyeball-to-eyeball stare, revelling in reverting to his role of superior officer.

"Right. Sort yourself out, soldier. But before you do that, I order you to get this damn cooker working. I'm starving."

Shoulder to shoulder, they both grew their backbones taller, holding the eye contact. Neither of them blinked and Luc warmed to the smug recognition – a vital extra three inches in height! He found himself sucking his top lip into his mouth, laughter simmering in his stomach, concentrated his attention on the bushiness of Jeremy's eyebrows.

"Might help if you flick this big bugger of a switch on, sir!" And he relished a particular delight in the act of bringing his right hand up in an efficient salute before he leant to one side and deftly knocked the cooker switch halfway up the wall to 'ON'. Luc also registered with uncertainty the slipping of Jeremy's Sandhurst demeanour, and took it in his stride as an accurately placed, but less than mock, thump from Jeremy landed in his ribs. He sensed that the mirth in Jeremy's words was genuine.

"Right, that settles it. I've never been any good at driving a bloody cooker! You're in charge of tucker, Luc. You're better at it than me."

"Yes, *sir*. Absolutely, *sir*. At once, *sir*."

Without any hesitation, Luc raised his beer bottle. Clink, clink, glass to glass with Jeremy. Then Robert – clink, clink. Then Isaac – clink, clink. In fact, Luc noticed that the whole evening quickly descended into a predictable repetition of glass on glass – swig, swig.

When Luc accidentally flipped a piece of steak onto the floor, he cast a sneaky wink behind Isaac's back, retrieved the errant meat onto a plate, jested, "Good for the immune system," and clink, clink – his glass met Robert's.

Robert then visualised himself as Rod Stewart and tried to sing a rasping baritone version of 'Maggie May'. Oddly, it worked quite well and clink, clink – all glasses met.

What began as a jesting, macho discussion on 'finding a nice lady for Jeremy' sent him to noisily load the dishwasher while the others agreed it to be a worthy challenge and… clink, clink.

Luc noted that, strangely for this group of confirmed petrolheads, the only time they touched on the subject of motorbikes was when, out of the blue, Isaac chipped in with,

"Jeremy, do you think those women will phone the Forestry Commission? Hope you gave them a false number?"

Stern-faced, Luc knew in his own mind that he must be pissed when he found himself springing to answer on Jeremy's behalf.

"Of course, he gave them the right number. I heard him. And anyway, even if we do get a reprimand, they were travelling just as fast as us. In fact, thank God I didn't listen to you lot and buy a bigger bike. A 550cc like yours, Robert, would have busted my leg for sure."

Isaac quickly put his arm around his best friend; his head wobbled a little as he gave Luc an Adnams-scented kiss on the cheek.

"Fair comment. I still think you would get a kick out of an Enfield, though. We could all do a road trip."

Luc's reply was laboured.

"Same old, same old – tired of this argument." But he gave Isaac a bear hug anyway. "Speed doesn't turn me on anymore. I'm perfectly happy with my nifty 400cc, thank you."

And there they were again – clink clinking and yelling at the ceiling. "Here's to 400ccs."

Chapter 4

Judith

Our evening continues to move forward in a gluttonous succession of food, wine, gossip, mickey-taking, more wine, chocolates and more chatter. Steady, heavy rainfall has been drumming on the roof throughout dinner and by the time the wall clock is ticking its way towards 9.30pm, all of us are in varying states of happy fog. Lizzie loudly announces to the room in general:

"It's no good. Can't do without a fag break any longer. This will only be my third today."

With a defiant glare of her emerald green eyes in my direction, she deftly prises a single cigarette from the packet and attempts to rise from the wooden chair. Eventually, she manages, swaying ever so slightly left, right, left, to wrap a coat around her shoulders and exit the cabin. Emma on the other hand has been afflicted in her boozy haze with an attack of hiccups and Caroline is, yet again, recumbent on the sofa, eyelids heavy.

Barely five minutes passes before Lizzie bursts back in through the door proclaiming.

"You'll never guess who's in the cabin next door..." But without pausing to draw breath, she answers herself: "It's those bloody lunatics on motorbikes from this morning. Quick. Look through the window."

We all rush to pull back the token curtains on the small rectangular window in the far corner of the room. Eager faces are pressed cheek to cheek, like fourteen-year-old schoolgirls, snooping en masse at the neighbours. I am the first to voice a rhetorical question.

"Well, blow me down with a feather. Are they brave or just plain bonkers using the jacuzzi in mid-March?"

Squinting, four sets of pupils readjust to peer at the sparsely lit porch next door and we become hushed voyeurs, transfixed by the men lounging in the hot simmering water. Steam is rising in flumes towards the overhanging eaves of the roof, before being sucked off into the void of blackness encasing the cabin. The oldest of the bunch, at a guess about sixty years old, is leaning heavily on the frame of the French doors, half in, half out, his beer bulge hanging over his tight red underpants. I carefully unlatch the window catch and we bunch our heads even closer in order to hear the conversation.

"Those bloody Hooray Horseback Henriettas need to be sent packing back to their country estates. Who the hell do they think they are?" The senior gent waves his beer can in the general direction of his mates, then continues with his tirade. "Just coz they have the brass to waste six thousand pounds or more on their swanky, shit-propelled neddies."

A mop of wet raven hair flicks about above the muscle-bound shoulders of the youngest man in the jacuzzi as he interrupts with a slurred Irish attempt at coherence.

"Soooooo, Robert. Are you proposing to give them a written warning? Or perhaps you should get Jeremy to write to *The Times*? For God's sake. Stop moaning, man. They're long gone. Get your arse in here and boil your balls with us."

Closing the window abruptly, my tightened fist is matched by

Lizzie's peculiar prodding and lifting of her own chin with index fingers. A spray of spit flies out with her words.

"How dare they call us Hooray Horseback Henriettas!" My anger is twofold.

"How dare they assume I'm in the top tax bracket. My slaughterhouse-bound Rommel was destined to be a can of dog food if I hadn't agreed to take him on. He'd have been gobbled up in lumps, then squeezed along canine colons. Ugh! All he cost me was a few months of rest and rehab. A field of grass and several doses of worming paste was a small price to pay. Obnoxious pillocks."

Emma's conspiratorial whisper arrives as music to our ears:

"Fellow Musketeers, I have a plan... I believe revenge is best served cold, don't you think?" She tries to suppress her excitement but fails miserably while blurting out her scheme.

* * *

Hurriedly dragging on a motley selection of waterproof coats we bundle out of the cabin, giggling into the murk. The lid of the boot bin clatters to the ground amid cries from Lizzie and Caroline.

"Shuuuuuuush. Oops, we must be quieter."

Lizzie is firmly clutching the fluffy tail of Emma's onesie with both her hands. Caroline is stalking Inspector Clouseau-style, shoulders hunched, peaked cap jammed down almost to her nose as we round the end of the cabin. Submerged up to their chins, the four men have all closed their eyes and appear to be succumbing to sleep. Strains of 'Honky Tonk Woman' are strumming through the open French doors onto the veranda of cabin number two. Emma raises her arms on either side to halt the ragtag bunch just before the laurel bushes and mouths. "Battle cry, girls?"

In unison we utter a hushed, "Musketeers on a mission," and high-five each other.

I am struck by the hilarity of it all. *Grown women, what the hell.* I see the restrictive waistcoats of maturity, substance and motherhood rinse away in the murk and the rain, becoming puddles underfoot. Swinging my right leg in a large arc over the hedge, I totally misjudge the height in the dark and land with a low thud, flat on my backside. I start patting the ground in all directions, hissing, "Bollocks. I've dropped the Fairy Liquid." The palm of Emma's hand presses down across my lips.

"Shuuuuush, Jude. They still haven't spotted us."

Moments later I find myself crouched and leaning, as far forward as possible, through the railings on the far side of the veranda. Being the owner of the longest and skinniest arms, I have been unanimously delegated to carry out Emma's Plan. Arm outstretched, my chin is wedged hard against wood as I squeeze a slow stream of washing-up liquid gently into the water. Oblivious, the men continue their soaking slumber. All I can think is – *Breathe shallow, do not exhale.* I am so close to the Irish gypsy hunk's luscious dark curls that I can see the hairs just inside his nose wafting in and out, in time to his gentle snores. The tips of my fingers are pinching the squeezy bottle harder and harder. Not a murmur can be heard from the girls behind me as the soapy addition to the water begins to silently bubble. Then, without delay, our quietly squelching footfall returns us, four ridiculous Musketeers, to cabin number three.

Juvenile delight. It's contagious; it prickles from your fingers and up through your arms. It's naughty; it's fizzy; it happens when champagne is mixed with ice-cream and it swirls around in your mouth before being swallowed. We all feel it in the five to eight minutes that elapse before the Plan comes to fruition. An urgent male voice rings out: "What the fuck's happening?"

A frothy mass is cascading over the side of the jacuzzi as three of the men leap from the water and immediately line up in their underpants, bottoms to the glass of the French doors. The last, the athletic pale-skinned man hesitates a few seconds, places his hands securely on the rim, then swings a huge flurry of froth over the sill as he lands on the far side in the half-light. He steadies himself, strangely lopsided against the jacuzzi. A pang of guilt hits me. *Luc, his name is Luc. Was he injured under the weight of the bike this morning?*

Gypsy Boy pats his right hand in a jabbing motion against the wooden boards to his right, his gaze still fixed on the fairy tale scene. His searching fingers find and flick a light switch then become still. I am struck in that frozen flashbulb of a moment by the diversity of their outlines. Far left, the man with whom Caroline had her altercation, Jeremy. She said his name fitted his superior attitude perfectly. He is quite stocky, probably in his late fifties. He is the owner of a good head of lightly flecked brown hair but his barrel chest gives an illusion of shortness. His true height, though, is clearly several inches above that of Gypsy Boy alongside him, a candidate for Mr Universe in the muscle department. Soap suds begin sliding in lazy glops off his biceps and six pack, his loose cotton boxer shorts sucking wet against his thighs. And finally, on the right, the one called Robert – taller but also very unfit. His nakedness highlighting many upturned grooves of fleshy semicircles around his neck, man boobs and belly.

Everyone is watching the multicoloured bubbles with a quiet intensity. They can be seen popping dramatically as each one touches the hot bulb hanging in the low eaves immediately above the water. Mick belts out his own personal touch from a CD player propped on a chair, the slipperiness of the 'Harlem Shuffle' lyrics so resoundingly fitting!

In cabin number three, the hysterics are explosive. Doubled up in a heap on the floor, every few seconds a hiccup jolts regularly through Emma's body. Caroline's rigid expression is broken by a wailed,

"For Christ's sake, girls. Shut up. I'm going to wet myself," as she proceeds to cross and uncross her legs. Lizzie scrapes the back of her hand through a tear, wet on her cheek as we all high-five and I voice a unanimous joy.

"Wow. We nailed it, girls."

Chapter 5

The sunshine which beamed through the pale bedroom curtains had awoken Luc from his fitful lie-in. Screwing up his nose in distaste, he ran his stale beer tongue along the front of his teeth. He pulled on his jeans, T-shirt and jumper and decided not to disturb his slumbering roommate just yet. *Jesus, I haven't had a proper hangover for donkey's years. Keeping up with a pro like Isaac is seriously bad news. I should know better than to come away for a weekend with a publican.* He slipped out of the bedroom, assumed he was the only one up, but noticed that the kettle was already hot. Opening the doors to the veranda he waved a mug at Jeremy.

"Morning. Do you want a hand? Tea?"

With military precision Jeremy was clearing everything moveable from the veranda. His reply was prefaced by a wry smile.

"What a fiasco last night. Wish I could work out which of you buffoons sabotaged the jacuzzi. Though, actually it's not as bad as I expected now all the bubbles have disappeared. Thanks for the offer. This is a one-man job, can't leave this treacherous layer of slime."

He stepped off the veranda heading for a standpipe on the leeward side of the cabin. Mug of hot tea in hand, Luc grabbed his phone, slipped out of the cabin in search of a signal, somewhere, anywhere. He noted that none of the other Tinker's End residents

31

appeared to be about, especially in cabin number three, which was so close. Everyone seemed to have disappeared off into the forest for the day. He wandered around the buildings, paths and stables, irritability growing with each unsuccessful attempt to get any response from his phone. As he returned dejected to the cabin, he caught a glimpse of Jeremy, back towards him, intent on hosing the wooden floorboards.

Bzzz... bzzz... bzzz... bzzz. In one long motion, Jeremy dropped the hose. His mobile was humming on the table. He swivelled on his right heel and lurched for it.

"Hello. Hello."

Luc stopped mid-stride. Jeremy, unaware of his presence, stared at the screen then brought the phone up to his ear again.

"Hello. Can you hear me?" He stepped off the veranda, two geese waddling in his path briefly, and strode a couple of metres to the paddock railings.

"Is that better? Yes, I can hear you OK." He cast a sudden glance at the cabin behind him, pressing the phone tight to his cheek. Luc edged a little further along the side of the building.

"Why are you phoning? You know I'm away till Monday." A few moments passed.

"Look, we've had this conversation before and I haven't changed my mind." His stare, fixated on the ground, intensified and a deep groove appeared between his brows.

"I know how much it would mean to you, but I cannot do it to the boys. I cannot destroy who we are as a family." Jeremy lifted his boot, twisted his ankle to one side. An impatience crept into his next reply.

"OK, OK. You may think three years is a long time to mourn, but I'm not ready, doubt that I ever will be. The kind of relationship you want is too big a statement. You must accept that it's finished." Jeremy's nose wrinkled as he brushed his boot against some long grass.

"Don't force me to bar your number. What, what did you say? I can't hear you."

He moved sideways a couple of feet, peered at the screen again, then waited a few moments. Eventually, he stuffed the phone in his pocket, shook his shoulders as if to remove an imaginary fly, scraped the sole of his boot about several more times, then carefully coiled the hosepipe in loops over the tap.

By the time Jeremy stepped back into the cabin, Luc had locked himself in the toilet. He felt the need to ruminate; he dropped the pan lid and sat down. *Jeremy, what a dark horse! Been in a relationship. Kept it under his hat well yesterday. Wonder if Robert knows?*

After ten minutes or so, Luc decided he was composed enough to come out. He found Jeremy in the kitchen–diner digging around in a rucksack. In quick succession, an OS map, a marker pen and a pair of glasses were placed on the table then Jeremy sat down. Map spread out in full, he started drawing blue lines along a route of lanes and by-roads. When Robert padded in, Jeremy continued peering at all the tiny dots and dashes.

"I'm bringing the map with us today. No more relying on the navigation system inside Luc's head – it's clearly flawed!"

And with that, he headed straight for the bedrooms. Thud, thud, thud... There was no reaction from the booze-weary occupant to the sound of Jeremy's fist on the door, but he waited for three seconds anyway. Impatient, he returned to the bedroom door with a large wooden spoon from the kitchenette. He entered Isaac's room, picked up the waste bin and battered the spoon against it incessantly. Isaac, eyes tight shut, shifted his head very carefully onto the other stubbly cheek.

"Bog off, Jeremy."

Undeterred, Jeremy continued, "Come on, Isaac. Rain's gone and it's a perfect morning. Eggs and bacon ready at 1100 hours, motorbikes away at 1200 hours. Let's make the best of our time here."

True to his professionalism, Jeremy had the four men pushing their bikes across the livery yard towards the main drive at 1205 hours. The Petersons had never before accepted a booking for bikers and it had taken all Jeremy's wile, eloquence and diplomatic skills to persuade them that motorbikes would not cause absolute mayhem with the equestrian residents. Safety must be paramount so, as promised, the four men dutifully walked their bikes 200 metres up the main drive before daring to start any engines, well away from the stables.

* * *

Perched on the edge of the sofa back, Luc continued to peer intently at the screen on his mobile. The tiny connection indicator kept flickering. The time, he noted, was already 6.45pm.

"Did any of you lot find a spot with a signal this morning? Its thirty-six hours since I checked any of my emails."

Robert volunteered an answer.

"Yep. Go all the way out behind the Dutch barn almost into the first paddock. There's a spot in the middle of the electric-fenced walkway."

Once he reached the spot which Robert had recommended, the bright evening sun, low on the horizon, forced Luc to squint at the screen. He couldn't quite read the lettering and was completely engrossed in his own world. His thoughts were 'online' and distracted. It was two days since he'd last checked in to the Elite.com website.

He thought, *You know that's too long, Luc. Frances seems really keen. Hope she's left a phone number for me. I wonder if she saw the last three photos I added. Cannot believe how seriously fit I look in that bare-chested shot on the Honda.*

A polite female voice from behind jolted him from his quandary. He turned to watch the petite woman, roughly in her mid-thirties, hovering ten feet away with her large pony. She appeared agitated when she spoke.

"Excuse me, but can you shift over a little please? You're right in the middle of the walkway." She kept biting her bottom lip as she pressed one hand hard into the shoulder of her mount. Her exhaustion was obvious to hear in the tetchiness and slight squeak in her voice. "Four and a half hours I've been riding today and he still hasn't slowed down."

The chestnut cyclone started to whizz around in tight circles, causing her to spin on the spot, occasionally jamming her boot into the ground in a valiant attempt to gain some purchase. Her other hand was grasping the lead rope very short up under the pony's head. Luc grinned, and didn't temper his sarcastic reply.

"Looks to me as though someone is running you in circles! No problem, I shall get out of your way."

Rocket's coiled energy, the excitement of strange surroundings and a new rather tentative handler suddenly got the better of him and he barged against Emma's shoulder, followed by a lunge towards the yard. Luc was upon the loose rope within seconds, his grip stopping Rocket in his tracks before he had any chance to pick up speed.

"Gotcha. You're not going anywhere."

Five minutes later, Emma's pale face gradually relaxed into gratitude as she leant over the stable door.

"I cannot thank you enough for catching that rope so quickly.

Sorry… err… I don't even know your name." He noticed her sudden sheepish need to study her fingernails, the hesitancy in her demeanour. A well-recognised thought surfaced. *Bring it on, I shall never tire of having this effect on women.*

"Oh, yes. I'm Luc and you?"

At barely 5'3" high, Emma had to stand on her tiptoes in order to shake Luc's outstretched hand. "Emma Crawford. Very pleased to meet you." Her head tipped quizzically to one side as she continued, "Um, are you in cabin number two, by any chance?" He nodded but couldn't fathom the mirth which brimmed over in Emma's eyes.

"Did you and your friends enjoy your jacuzzi yesterday evening? You appeared to have a rather bubbly time?" Luc felt his cheek muscles contract. He couldn't decide if she was mocking him or being plain nosy. Ignoring her question, he stepped back, raising an arm in a vague wave.

"Glad to have been of service. Must be off now. The lads are cooking steak. Enjoy your holiday. Bye."

Luc's left shoulder dipped on every other step as his receding body marched away. He sensed her stare boring into his back and adjusted his stride a little shorter. It had been easy to hide his limp when he had one hand on Rocket's neck, but now it required concentration and the wince, which Emma could not see, told its own tale.

* * *

Luc hoicked up the leg of his tracksuit then began scratching the stub of his index finger deliciously along the edge of the scar tissue halfway down his calf muscle. Itchy, so damn itchy. The malevolent thoughts which whirred around inside his head were getting louder. *I don't lose. Jeremy should have sussed this about me.*

I don't lose games like this. He's in civvies now and if he barks just one more order at me today, I'll deck him fair and square. It's been a constant, 'Luc, you're at the back today. Luc have you got the maps? Luc, you and Isaac can lock up the bikes while Robert and I grab the shower.'

Luc had already set his jaw by the time he entered the living area – it was a conscious decision. He was also pleased when Robert looked him up and down and clearly noted the temperature of his mood. However, Robert's attempt to diffuse the tricky atmosphere did not please him – the screwed-up face, supposedly in a gesture of concern, and the way Robert rested a hand on his shoulder and enquired,

"How is your leg holding up?"

Luc turned on him, colour flushing in a rush starting at his Adam's apple and heading quickly up through the stubble on his chin. He spat out his reply.

"Take your hand off me. I'm fine," before he brushed the offending hand swiftly off his shoulder. Jeremy twisted his head around to better observe his companions.

"All right, Luc, it's been a long day and we are all hungry. So, cheer up, man." But the venom in Luc's answer caused Jeremy to take a reflex step backwards:

"*You patronising, jumped-up bastard.* Who the hell do you think you are?"

Jeremy rolled his eyes and raised his brows in a calculated mock sneer, driving Luc even closer to full-blown anger.

"Jerry, just because you live at The Hall *and* you graduated from Sandhurst doesn't mean you can effing well pretend to own all the rest of us!"

The one thing Jeremy couldn't prevent when he became either nervous or riled was the twitch of his right eye. The greater the tension, the shorter the time between each pinch of his top cheek muscle finishing with a momentary closing of the far corner of the eye. He took an exaggerated deep breath to stall for two seconds before he replied with very slow upper-class articulation:

"Do not call me, Jerry. I was christened Jeremy and that is my name. Understood?"

Moving forward, hands firmly on his hips, elbows in batwings, Luc was within two strides of Jeremy when a hefty rapping on the cabin door stopped him in mid-stride. A clear sing-song voice called from the far side of the door.

"Hellooooo. Anyone iiiiin?"

Luc had to stop himself envisaging the satisfying crunch he would have felt as his own knuckles found the flesh and bone of Jeremy's smug face. *Shame really. Oh well, never mind. At least now I know exactly how to get Jeremy seriously wound up... simply call him Jerry!*

Bouncing in, red wine held aloft, Luc watched the four women immediately succeed on three counts:

(1) Raising the decibel levels with incessant female chatter;(2) Overpowering the heavy testosterone-laden air with wafts of shampoo-scented fringes and, what he could only guess was saddle soap;(3) Fortuitously, stopping him within milliseconds of letting fly with his right fist.

This timely, face-saving entrance quickly sent Jeremy to find a corkscrew, while Luc sank gratefully into a corner chair to appease his ruffled hackles. After the initial round of complicated handshaking and name-swapping had finished, he was left alone for a surprisingly long time. Unobtrusively, he studied the ensuing melee – a peculiar mix of disjointed exploratory conversations between two groups of complete strangers. All of them, unprepared in any way for the sudden social interaction, were wearing a mix of very functional clothing. Luc decided that it was incredibly refreshing, the lack of coquettish eyelashes or killer heels swivelling on the end of bare ankles. Instead, stripy woollen socks and grubby trainers.

Robert appeared to offer his phone number and throw out his 'impress all' voice in Lizzie's direction. *Technically, she is both striking and tall; a bit retro somehow even in a pair of jeans, but she also knows it. That look she gave me, when we shook hands though. Scary!* Luc's attention then moved to Caroline, just as he overheard Isaac enthusiastically enquire, "So, has your husband always been in the City?"

Luc's reflex conclusion was immediate. *Married and definitely not my type.*

When he looked across at Jeremy and Judith standing side by side near the sink, they appeared to be having a pleasant discussion. He was struck by the understated sense of calm which surrounded her, almost an aura. She turned, as if suddenly pricked by his scrutiny. He nonchalantly grabbed his beer bottle, tilted it against his lips, slurped down the last dregs. But within minutes, she skirted around the coffee table, bringing a full bitter. She accompanied her gift with a direct question.

"Interesting phrase, 'Hooray Horse Henriettas'."

"Thank you, kind lass." He took the bottle, grinned mischievously when he spoke again. "Robert should get the credit for that remark though. Unusually eloquent for him."

He noticed, *There is a provocative shine to the gentle way her eyes have widened.*

Luc paused briefly, using the time to try to muster a suitably witty opening line. He missed the moment and suddenly Lizzie was hovering at Judith's side, giving apologies for whisking her friend away. Apparently intent on, 'being in a fit state to get a full day's riding in tomorrow,' the gaggle of women suddenly departed the cabin as predictably boisterous as when they had arrived.

Chapter 6

Judith

There are a total of twenty-one Royal Doulton plates, seven jugs, fourteen cups and matching saucers, a twelve-inch carving dish and sundry vegetable serving dishes, all squeezed into my mother's tiny kitchen/diner area. As I open the door which links the 'granny' annex to my own house, I am already projecting my voice.

"Mother, I'm home."

"No need to shout, dear. I'm right here," Mother croaks as she creeps out from behind the door.

A teacup in one hand, she steps forward gingerly. The tea towel in her other hand drops to the floor as she instantly goes to clutch the edge of the sink to steady herself. I know better than to reach out or to offer to support the tottering body, I have been rebuked so many times in the past. Instead I simply offer:

"Would you like me to put all the crockery back on the shelves for you, Mother?"

My mother, Adele, is eighty-two years young, but the physical frailties of her body have recently been chipping away at the very core of her internal spirit. Her ritual of washing and drying all her precious Royal Doulton has become more and more frequent as her memory confuses the passing of weeks and days. What began as a monthly session to rid the china of any dust, slowly moved to weekly until now, when it has become an almost daily ritual. Her next sentence is one that I hear possibly two or three times a week:"Yes, please, dear. Thank you, I don't know where all the dirt comes from in such a small space."

"Mother. Did you eat the fishcakes and peas I left out for your lunch?"

Her soft blue-grey eyes light up with glee and she waves the teacup up and down dramatically in the general direction of the microwave to emphasise her point. "Yes, dear. Thank you, dear. But how do I stop that microwave thingy beeping at me all the time? It won't stop. I had to switch it off at the wall just to make it be quiet."

Stepping towards the offending kitchen appliance, I swallow a giggle.

"Oh, don't worry, Mother. It will always beep at you once the cooking time has finished. All you have to do is open the door and take the food out, then it will desist. Did you follow the times I left you OK?"

"Of course, of course, I can read instructions! I'm not senile just yet. The fishcakes tasted rather good, actually."

"I'm pleased to hear it, Mother. Now make sure you don't fall asleep in the chair again tonight. Shall I help you upstairs now and you could watch TV in bed rather than downstairs? Only Lizzie is coming over to see me so I shall be busy until probably eleven-ish."

"No, no, dear. *Please* stop fussing and thank Lizzie for my pot of daffies, will you?"

"Will do. Just about got thirty minutes for a quick sax practice. Let Lizzie in if I don't hear the door, please." Without hesitation Mother reaches towards the fridge-freezer.

"Lovely that you are playing regularly again, dear. Shall I get a cheesecake out for you? Lizzie might like some too."

Obedient to my own ritual, I walk up twelve stairs and then pause, always at the same spot. Halfway up, halfway down. Fifteenth-century stairs in my twentieth-century life. Can't help myself, the tactile need to run fingertips over polished oak, to marvel at the craftsmanship – spindle bannisters sweeping in a regal curve towards the landing. A creak here, a socked foot there, I pad along the Tudor corridor past two bedroom doors and a chaise longue. Next, the adjoining door to Mother's end of the house, complete with her neatly positioned slippers. As I enter my office, Branston jumps from the chair, ginger cat hairs floating out behind him.

"Saxophone practice first, cheesecake afterwards," a quote branded by Mother into my psyche at the malleable age of ten. A ritual impossible for me to shrug off. The cheesecake was meant to be the reward, but on one particular occasion I used youthful guile, persuading her to let me eat first, play afterwards. Big mistake – digestive biscuit mixed with saliva is a troublesome blockage when blown into a narrow brass tube! As a child, I thought practice was a dirty word. As an adult, my appetite is rarely sated. I unzip the case, extricate the saxophone, gather my lips around the mouthpiece... and blow.

* * *

Standing in front of the bedroom mirror, I peer critically at my own reflection, mentally ticking off a list of attributes and failings: medium, almost-tall height and reasonably slender, though tending towards a swimmer's shoulders – these developed over a lifetime of lifting straw bales, daily mucking out or pushing and shoving unyielding horse-box ramps and trailer hitches into position.

I wish I could have included simple facts about 'what I am', rather than 'who I am' on my profile page. I remember how wrong-footed I felt when I filled in the profile section on the First Glance website, but it certainly forced me to take a long, probing look at myself. 'Drearily two-dimensional' was the phrase which kept repeating on a loop in my head – work, home, ride, work, home, ride. Only a month ago, Lizzie became seriously disgusted with my petulant outlook. After several glasses of wine one evening, she sat me down and forced me to pick four of my best photos. Then pressed save. The CV-style description of my aspirations in the man department proved bloody impossible for me to pinpoint. How the hell, at fifty-seven years old, can you be expected to encapsulate your priorities in less than roughly fifty words and without sounding either self-opinionated, sarcastic, woolly-headed or just plain nutty?

Squaring up my posture, bending one knee slightly and dropping my chin into a coquettish pose, the woman in the mirror speaks back to me as she mouths the heading to my online persona. 'Eternal Optimist.' Yes, eternal optimist. The brunette in the reflexion sports the trappings of a smile, but it doesn't reach up to touch the corners of her forgettable hazel eyes. A subcutaneous layer of sadness lurks, unwelcome and uninvited, on her shoulders. She speaks:

"Again, Judith, again. With more conviction."

I am jolted into the present by a high-pitched, "Are you there, Jude? Shall I come up?" followed by the muffled thud of Lizzie's rapidly approaching footfall. She always takes the stairs two at a time, her boundless energy being the part I love the most about her. We've been thrown together in the last six months to spending more and more free time in each other's company, as the majority of our friends are still in that secure kingdom named 'coupledom', while the adhesive mortar in our bond is horses.

* * *

Leaning into the roaring flames, Lizzie is perching on the low leather-topped stool, her palms stretched forward and rotating slowly as we ruminate on our lives. One of my wellies is propped against the wall of the fireplace, a couple of feet from the burning logs. As I go to turn it upside down, Lizzie cannot stop a jocular sarcastic barb.

"Why on earth are you attempting to melt your boots, Jude?" Without hesitation, I wield an accurately aimed cushion at her legs.

A little exasperated, I answer,

"Because the end of a bloody nail went straight through the bottom and I had to walk some incredibly wet grassland today. Sod's law, it was my first farm on the list this morning. My foot was sopping for the rest of the day. It's all right for you in your lovely warm consulting rooms with a receptionist to make on-tap coffee and appointments. At this time of year, I truly regret my choice of career. Agronomy – I imagined it would be so idyllic being in the fresh air *all* the time. Had this rosy picture of myself walking for miles every day under blue skies; looking for the signs of germination in tiny grains of wheat; working out why the sugar beet in one corner of a field has grown at half the speed of all the other plants; helping to feed the British masses! No one warned me about my knee joints wearing out, or the numbing cold, or the rain, or what a solitary profession it is."

Lizzie looks up at me, grins. "Have you finished. Got it off your chest?"

I grimace back. "Sorry, just tell me to shut up. Unfortunately, I had to make an irritating choice this week between buying a replacement pair of boots for myself or getting Rommel shod on time. I rest my case."

Sparks erupt in a noisy firecracker effect from the hearth sending me to frantically grab for the brass brush.

"Damn pine. Wish he would deliver decent English wood. Threadbare this rug may be, but it will have to last a bit longer."

"Do you regret keeping this place?"

"If I'm brutally honest, yes... but no. In even quantities. Can you really see me in a new-build? Patrick was prepared to settle for an ongoing allowance when we divorced but a clean break was the right choice. And Mother. If I hadn't stayed here, her options would have been horribly limited. An old people's home! No way."

I notice that, uncharacteristically, Lizzie's purple nail varnish has chipped in several places. Her grubby jeans are scrunched at the ankles into thick red-and-white-striped welly socks. Her often spikey hair seems to have taken on a new style all of its own, managing to swirl up high in a wind tunnel effect off one side of her face.

"Sorry, I didn't change after doing Tarquin this evening, Jude."

Lifting her right arm, she buries her nose in her sweatshirt sleeve and screws up her face. "Phew, I reek of horse. Would you mind if I light up indoors? It's freezing outside."

As she lowers her arm heavily again, I notice the sunken circles of tiredness around her eyes. A plume of smoke is billowing silently around the lower edge of the oak fire plinth, spiralling to the upper reaches of the room. I gesture towards the ceiling.

"Yes, feel free. There is so much sodding backdraft from this fire when it's not drawing properly, we may as well be in the San Francisco smog basin. Tough week was it, Lizzie?"

"And then some. On the plus side, though, you do realise that we are saving each other at least £90 an hour in counselling fees each time we meet?"

Halfway into swallowing a gulp of Rioja, the splutter I withhold sends a teaspoon of wine the wrong way up my throat into my nose.

"Bloody hell, Lizzie. Is that how much your clients pay for just an hour on the shrink's sofa?"

Lizzie turns her boyish profile and astute green eyes in my direction and her lips screw into a thin line. "Yes, but I don't get anywhere near as much for the NHS clients. If I was to be more ruthless, I would scrap all my NHS work and stick solely to private patients." Leaning into the eaves of the fireplace, Lizzie deftly flicks ash into the leaping flames. My voice has risen unnecessarily as the ache in my bladder reaches fever pitch.

"Why don't you try hypnotherapy to stop your smoking, Lizzie? There must be someone in your practice who can do it? Oh, excuse me. Gotta go for a wee." I rise gingerly and head for the downstairs loo.

Strategically wiggling my tight jeans over my thighs in order to prevent a urinary accident, my attention is caught by the cracks in the grout between the floor tiles. The glorious relief of emptying my bladder is overshadowed by the thought – *Yet another house repair I cannot afford*. I turn the hot tap into the 'off' position and yell across the hall in the direction of the sitting room.

"I nearly forgot to ask. Did you get around to meeting The Lone Ranger?"

There is no reply. I screw the tap harder to the left but the drip persists. I give up and return to the comfort of Lizzie and beams. As I enter Lizzie scowls.

"Well, he was a flipping waste of time."

"Come on, give me the gory details. Let's swap seats. You lay back on the sofa and let Dr Judith listen to your woes."

Lizzie dutifully obliges, fluffs up a cushion to support her neck and continues. "He had everything, on paper, that I want. Good-looking, at least in his photos. Divorced, no teenagers underfoot, fantastic sense of humour, had me in stitches several times on the phone last week."

I had come to accept Lizzie's occasional tendency towards drama queen tales as a complement to the fact she clearly felt she could trust me to keep shtum. The weighty responsibility of soothing the woes of weird, often psychotic, people to rebuild their minds had rendered her own survival mode into a default of mocking humour. Curious, I probe a little deeper.

"Did you meet at your usual haunt? What on earth was wrong with him, Lizzie?"

She pauses briefly before replying. "Yes, of course. The 'Duck & Dog'. I should probably swap venues a bit but it's so convenient. Anyway, it gives me the chance to sit in my car at the back of the car park. Then I get roughly thirty seconds to really give a man the once-over when he has no idea I'm watching."

Feeling a little impatient, I raise my tone. "And?"

"Well, a bright red S-reg Impreza came haring in, stopped, reversed, manoeuvred. Shot forward into the spare space, gravel projectile everywhere."

I am all ears. "What on earth is wrong with a flash car? Surely you're not going to hold that against a man? It means he must be successful."

Exasperated, Lizzie spreads her palms, tilting them upwards. "But he was wearing *white* trainers *and* a gold chain around his neck!"

"Eeek! So what was he like as a person?"

Folding her arms across her chest in classic defensive fashion, her answer surprises me. "I'm ashamed to say I didn't even get out of the car. He disappeared into the pub so I drove off without meeting him. I know it was a spineless thing to do. But I didn't see the point in wasting his time and my precious money when I already knew he wouldn't be right for me." Unabated she finishes: "And before you chastise me, Jude, I rang him the moment I was a mile up the road to make an excuse. So, don't look at me like that."

I remove my stony face and ask: "You'll be back trawling the Dancing in the Moonlight website again, I imagine?"

Lizzie downs a couple of swigs then grins. "I may ring the changes, actually. Thinking of trying Plenty of Fish."

I raise my glass defiantly into the smoky haze above my head and try to speak.

"A toast. To plenty more…" but a cough explodes in red spray over Lizzie's head,

"… fish in the sea."

Lizzie stretches her glass tentatively in my direction. "Hear, hear. Fish in the sea."

Interlude

Lizzie lifted one cheek of her buttocks a few inches off the cold stone step and began rubbing it vigorously with her gloved hand. She'd been here, outside her office, looking out over the car park since 6.40pm. She was worried that if she waited inside for the computer man to arrive, he'd get the wrong building and go home again. A hesitant voice startled her attempt at reviving circulation. She stood up to greet the small wisp of a man who seemed to have materialised from nowhere. His smart pressed trousers, she noticed, were barely visible beneath an old-fashioned buff-coloured mac.

"You must be Stanley from System Tech. Hello."

"Sincere apologies, Miss Everett. Or would you prefer I call you by your first name? My last job turned out to be particularly complicated, but from your description, I'm sure we shall be able to sort out your little problem in a jiffy."

She wasn't in the mood to stomach his ingratiating manner. Her urge for a cigarette had been growing exponentially all afternoon. She was also too cold to feel the need for niceties so she was quickly on her feet and showing Stanley into the building. They climbed the stairs to the first floor and Stanley sat down in front of the offending PC.

Lizzie proceeded to jiggle the mouse about a few times on the desk. "See, absolutely nothing. As I said, completely frozen."

"What is the desktop password, Miss Everett?"

"Our sports physiotherapist has this consulting room so I'm afraid I don't have the password. Apparently, it crashed when he was in the middle of using it. I have his mobile for you to phone if you need to speak to him."

Lizzie turned to leave. "I'll be downstairs in the furthest room all the way along at the end of the corridor when you finish."

Lizzie scooted her office chair a little closer to her desk, then reached into the second drawer down. Pulling up her jumper sleeve, she pressed a nicotine patch firmly onto her upper arm. Her eyes flitted several times between the laptop case leaning against the desk and straight ahead, her office monitor, all blank, dead. Her laptop beckoned, time to jazz up her profile.

CLICK	**Website:**	Dancinginthemoonlight.com
CLICK	**Sign In:**	Sunbeam
CLICK	**Edit Profile:**	
	Headline:	"Life is for Living"
	City/Location:	Bury St Edmunds
	Age:	52 years
	Hair Colour:	Blonde
	Status:	Divorced
	Profession:	I Have One
	Height:	5' 10"
	Body Type:	Slim
	Children:	No
	Religion:	Agnostic

About Me: Happy, adventurous and upfront. That's me. There are so many places I would love to visit, but I would prefer to go with a tall, intelligent, independent-minded man.

My spare time is quite busy looking after my horse, so I
am hoping to find someone who also enjoys country events.
Contemporary art is also high on my list of interests.

Anyone pulling a trailer-load of baggage need not apply.
Life is too short!

Happy with her changes, Lizzie made a quick recce to the door,
checking the corridor was empty. She touched in the number,
wedging the handheld set between the crook of her shoulder
blade and her ear. Her swivel chair moved a little left, right, left,
right, in time to the waving of her leg in the air.

Judith picked up. "Hiya, Lizzie. What's cooking?"

"Been rephrasing my online blurb and adding a new picture.
Have you had any exciting replies yet?"

"I did send a few messages to a chap called Tudor Type. He
was really interesting – on paper."

"Did you phone him? Remember, it's always best to speak in
person early on. You'll know within minutes whether you want to
even carry on the conversation."

"OK, OK. Hold your horses a minute. Let me finish.
Vincent. His name was Vincent and I should have known
straight away that anyone with that name would be far too
earnest. He dresses up in Tudor clothes to do re-enactments at
medieval festivals *and* he's a twitcher. Travels all the way across
the world to sit and watch birds in Tasmania!"

Lizzie spluttered into the receiver. "No. Possibly not the best
match for you. But don't give up. It's a cert that you're going to
have to talk to a few frogs before finding a prince."

She heard Judith as she inhaled slowly then exhaled, clearly
gathering the resolve to be firm.

"I'm not like you, Lizzie. Internet dating is too much like a marathon for me. It's almost a part-time job constantly checking for and sending messages. No, if I'm meant to meet someone then fate will sort it out. Got to go now. My dinner is boiling over."

* * *

By the time the sound of Lizzie's footfall had faded away down the stairs, Stanley had already rebooted the computer. He'd clicked 'Yes' when asked, 'Would you like to restore the previous page?' On viewing the webpage which presented itself so out of the blue before him, Stanley's immediate reaction would normally have been to exit. He had seen every connotation of weird in his professional career but this was a first, and his curiosity won. His fingers hesitated over the mouse. His eyebrows formed a low V-shape. He focused a little more closely on the content – row upon row of women's faces. He folded back the cuff on his sleeve, noted the time, threw a swift glance over his shoulder at the door.

The web address at the top of the page read E Harmony.com. He wiggled his nose, inhaled noisily, then hit the 'Search' button at the top. A new supermarket selection of faces popped up. He began scrolling. A few moments passed; the cursor hovered briefly over a pseudonym just as each fleeting aspect of his thoughts became mirrored in body language. A coy, understated face and he smiled shyly. A hard Lara Croft 'I *am* beautiful' face and his eyes went blank. A face with a cleavage attached and he jumped back, visibly startled.

Occasionally he paused to double-click on a picture then scroll down to the 'Personal Statement'. He checked his watch again and impatiently jiggled the mouse on its pad. The cursor was soon hovering over the 'Search' button again when Stanley spotted a row of other tabs listed on the left. He began enthusiastically filling in details:

Age:	50 to 60 years
Height:	4'8" to 5'4"
Location:	Within 50 miles.

He was just about to press 'Search' for one final pitch when he heard Lizzie's distant voice calling.

"Will you be much longer? Perhaps you could come back tomorrow?"

The reddening of Stanley's cheeks was as telltale as his frantic clicking of the mouse and a shouted,

"All done. Got it running again OK. Just closing the PC down now."

Chapter 7

As Luc pushed open the heavy door to the Gardener's Arms, it banged against someone on the other side. Luc stuck his head around the door, a little surprised to see a clutch of three hikers plus Robert all squeezed into the confined porch. Robert's eighteen-stone frame appeared to be wedged against the backpack of a tall, slender, fresh-faced blonde woman in her late twenties. The two strangers tried in vain to manoeuvre around each other in the tiny space and Robert's back pressed for a brief moment into her bust. Robert turned to face her, the zip on his coat snagging on her chunky sweater. Luc, half out, half in, decided to be helpful.

"You two look a bit entangled."

The woman's friends had already moved on through the door into the bar, but Robert seemed to seize the chance to linger five seconds too long. His presumptuous comment caught both Luc and the entrapped damsel off guard.

"My sincere apologies. However, I am more than happy to remain crushed into a small space with such a beautiful woman as yourself."

Luc watched as Robert made no attempt to step sideways, instead half-heartedly picking at the strand of wool straining on the offending zip fastening. As the wool finally escaped, Robert looked up, lust written in his pupils. The woman visibly recoiled a few more inches as her features hardened and, accompanied by a heavy Swedish accent, she slammed the thick heel of her walking boot down hard. A dull thud confirmed it had hit the target – Robert's foot.

"My mother always warned me not to talk to large English beasts."

Giving him no time to muster a retort, her hand flicked the metal catch and she jerked the solid inner door open, unexpectedly bashing his knee in the process.

Luc stifled a cough. Robert spat out a belated, "Scandinavian bitch," before squaring up his shoulders again.

The two men entered the busy pub, strolling up to the bar. Jeremy's corduroy-clad legs were hanging neatly over the seat of *his* stool in *his* spot at the lounge bar. Luc had often observed him resting his back against the wall, sipping his wine, always red. He could sometimes be seen unobtrusively scanning the clientele or staring through to the other bar. As they approached, Jeremy was already trying to catch Isaac's attention, using his iconic open-palmed royal half-wave, swiftly followed by a minor lift of his chin – the cue for another round.

"What'll it be, Robert? I'm getting a bottle of Merlot."

Friday evenings at the Gardener's Arms: what had started as a chance encounter between the four men only six months ago had now settled into a regular excuse to meet up and check out who was riding that weekend. Jeremy, Robert and Luc were already swapping plans when Isaac picked his way towards their table, carefully balancing two Adnams and another bottle of wine on a tray. The early-bird rush of locals stopping in for a quickie, before heading home for their dinner, had subsided.

Isaac placed the drinks on the table and sat down next to Luc. He proceeded to place two fingers lovingly through the handle of the pint glass, brought it up to eye level, studied the amber liquid, its rising gases and the depth of its head, before putting it to his lips. His mouth widened akin to a basking whale taking in plankton and his Adam's apple bobbed up and down in jerks as he gulped. All three of his companions waited and watched silently. A particularly male phenomenon, this reverent appreciation of quenching thirst with a beer.

The short sleeves on Isaac's white T-shirt strained over impressive biceps as he casually wiped the back of his hand across a remnant of froth around his mouth, before he caught Luc off guard with a playful thump to his arm.

"It must be four weeks now since Thetford Forest. Has your exhaust pipe stopped spitting out sand yet, Luc?"

Seated a little back from everyone else in order to accommodate his giraffe-like legs, Luc had to stretch in order to pick up his pint glass from the table.

"Bike's fine. My skid lid has a whacking great gouge in it, though. Must have hit a stone."

Grinning, Isaac kicked into one of his favourite sports. "So, when are you going to stop pratting around on that Honda two-stroke? It wouldn't pull the skin off a rice pudding."

A scowl walked across Luc's face followed by a telltale tiny dimpling of his chin.

"Sod off, Isaac."

Undeterred, Isaac chipped in again. "You should've bought a man's bike."

"Ha, ha. Very funny. Anyway, unlike dear Robert here, I don't need the horsepower of a Sherman tank to propel my body around the countryside."

Luc turned to face the eldest of his companions. "By the way, Robert, talking of Keeper's End, did I overhear you persuading that woman called... um, what was it? Oh yes, Lizzie, to give you her phone number?"

Robert absentmindedly tapped a beer mat against the table before giving his considered reply. "Luc Stockdale, it took me forty-five minutes of my best lines to get it out of her. Give me one good reason why I should divulge that hard-won information to you?"

Luc snapped back in mild irritation. "Oh, come on. Robert. You're a happily married man. Are you honestly telling me that you are going to make use of that number?"

The sound of a feedback whine cut dead the comfortable hum of a country pub on a Friday evening. Robert pulled a grimace. It was Open Mic Night and a skinny forty-something woman had been persuaded by her companion to have a go. She began speaking rather than singing an excruciatingly tepid version of Madonna's 'Holiday'.

Jeremy returned a pained glance in Robert's direction.

"Ugh. For goodness' sake. See if you can persuade Luc to take over the microphone, will you?"

Luc grabbed his empty glass and waved it gently, firstly at Robert then Jeremy.

"If you want me to rescue your sonic senses, it'll cost you!"

As Robert stood up to take the glass, he pushed gently at Luc's ribs adding, "OK, OK. Just hurry it up and stop that woman's racket, will you? Quickly."

Luc ambled over, gave the wannabe singer one of his special winning smiles and she handed over the microphone without a second's hesitation. Luc needed no accompaniment, his voice clear and on the button. He began, without aplomb, a Supertramp classic and gradually heads began to turn in his direction, cutlery became still and all chatter ceased.

The verses flowed. Luc's voice was comparable to Sting rather than Rodger Hodgson and the moment he finished, a flurry of appreciative pub-goers all clapped and cheered. The applause and back-slapping quickly subsided and he was about to make his way to the bar, when the blonde Swede quietly sidled up to him, her perfect teeth flashing, all glassy-eyed with adoration. He politely exchanged niceties, all the while very aware of Robert's sideways scrutiny. When the Swede made the mistake of allowing her hair to fall briefly across his hand as she whispered,

"I'm just going to get my mobile. Back in a moment," he decided he would make a quick escape towards the other men. As Luc came within earshot, Robert turned a gratuitous grin on Jeremy and boomed,

"You could do with learning a few pulling tips from Luc."

An elderly couple, tucking into roast beef and trimmings, stopped chewing. A trickle of gravy oozed unnoticed at the corner of the gentleman's mouth as he swivelled his head in eager anticipation of a morsel of village gossip. Jeremy's shoulders began curling in on him like an autumn leaf which has fallen, crisp and dry, to the ground. The telltale tiny muscles on his right cheekbone began to contract once, twice... three times.

Luc looked across at Robert, felt the muscles between his own shoulder blades mirror Jeremy's angst. He scowled at Robert before speaking.

"Quite the reverse. He has class and women will flutter – butterflies to nectar – in his company." Then he winked at Jeremy.

And there they were on cue, two butterflies, Lizzie and Judith, falling in through the door. Jeremy appeared to resurrect his debonair self, getting in a round of drinks. Isaac disappeared to pull pints again and Luc felt the loss of his social wingman. Initially, he was happy to jolly along with the topics that clearly turned on two parish councillors. Robert and Jeremy in full flow, holding court with two women. Luc had to admire Lizzie's unphased determination to shun any advances from Robert. Any question or quip he directed at her was met with an arctic look. Luc withheld his tap of charm, so well-practised. He nodded in all the right places, allowed the topics of 'self-employed versus zero hours contracts' and 'loss of decision-making processes to Brussels' to come and go. It gave him a chance to sip his beer and study her properly. *What would I liken her to? A mountain lion or possibly even a panther, methinks, toned to perfection. The understated but poised way in which she stands. Judith, a strong, no-nonsense name. It suits her.*

"So, Luc. Do you live in this village or are you a town dweller?" Judith asked.

"I'm very close. Live at the end of the lane, up from this pub." *A buttercream skin, no freckles.*

"Do you have any special hobbies, passions, other than motorbikes of course?"

"Whenever I'm not working, I'm renovating an old cottage so I struggle to find any spare time. But in winter, I sing a bit for a band." *Rather distinctive, even glamorous. That Marilyn Monroe mole on her cheekbone.*

"Oh, I am impressed. I play the sax, though Mother has often accused me of creating a sound that resembles a massacre in a corrugated-iron shed!"

Jeremy shifted forward, gently touched Judith's elbow before interrupting.

"Going back to the subject of footpaths. I would really like to get my facts straight."

A brief silence fell as he topped up her wine glass and continued, "We've got a parish meeting tomorrow. Where do we stand in law? Does the farmer have to spray off the line of the footpath across a field of wheat or not?"

Luc swivelled his bar stool on one leg so he was facing Jeremy.

"Why would Judith know the answer to that question?"

"Because she is an agronomist. Haven't you been paying attention for the past twenty minutes, Luc?"

The wooden legs on the stool clunked as Luc's weight brought them down on the floor. His breezy, relaxed tone evaporated.

"So, Judith, you know about ecosystems and wildlife, right? And are you responsible for deciding what sprays are used on farmland? Because I have a bone to pick with you."

Judith's attention appeared to ricochet for a few split seconds between Jeremy and Luc. Waiting so intently for her answer, Luc suppressed an intense urge to gloat when he clearly won the flipping of the coin she made in her mind. Her two-word response matched her gaze, measured out slowly.

"Yes, why?"

"Since moving here, I have become more and more angry at the dire decline of many species of wildlife in our countryside. Tell me, why do farmers continue to sterilise whole swathes of cropped land when they could save time, effort and expense by going organic? My cottage is surrounded on two sides by cereal crops and there is a lovely three-metre margin on the edge of the field which is left uncultivated." Luc took in a breath.

Judith jumped into the pause. "It's called set-aside."

"OK, I do know the correct term… But if land can be left fallow around the edges for birds, bees and insects to populate, why the hell does the cropped area have to be totally devoid of all life? Why can't all farmed land be organic? When I walk around the fields to the north and west of my house, they are wastelands like some horribly manicured lawn at a cricket ground. Not a blade of wheat out of place. Not a single crawling, buzzing, moving living thing within. Along the hedgerow and set-aside, it's a totally different story."

61

Judith let out a resigned kind of sigh. "There are a multitude of answers to your question, Luc, but I shall try. Firstly, a farm is a business. If it doesn't make a profit or at least wipe its face, then it will go to the wall, just like any other business. That is why farmers have to be paid to leave all those lovely headlands free of crops. Secondly, why do you think the price of a loaf of bread is so ridiculously low? Answer, because the price of wheat is low. In fact, the price of wheat, and grain in general, is pretty much the same as it was five years ago. But farmers have had to swallow increases in the price of both fertiliser and sprays in that time, not to mention labour, and it has gone straight out of their profit margin."

"You mean, they can't have a new Range Rover every autumn! You still haven't told me why sprays are used on most land?" Luc picked a little at a callous on his knuckle, looked up to see her pinch the stem of her wine glass even tighter.

"I was getting there, let me finish. If all farms were organic, or even just not using sprays, the amount of grain harvested per acre would gradually drop. Year on year, if blackgrass is left unchecked, it will throttle the chances of a good grain yield. Aphids can—"

Luc held up his palm. "Exactly what is an aphid? Is it a beetle, a bug? What?"

He thought, *Never seen a frown as deadly as that before!*

"It's very similar to a greenfly but it's black and it gathers in clusters on the plant. Sucks out all the goodness. But when it does that, it also infects the plant in a way that leaves it sort of sickly and slow to grow. As I was saying… it's a fact that if an organic farm is surrounded by land where sprays are still used, it doesn't tend to have any major problems with either pests or fungus. The farms around it create a buffer zone that keeps it healthy and safe. On the other hand, where there are several organic farms close together, fungi can sweep through the whole lot, field to field, farm to farm – crops plagued by brown rust, yellow rust, mildew, etc. So, in short, you are looking at a rich person's pipe dream for the whole country to be part of a rose-tinted kitchen garden effect. The checkout girl at Tesco and your average London bus driver will never pay through the nose for their pasta, biscuits and cakes. Fact."

Wish she wouldn't push her hair back behind her ears like that. It's so lush, she should let it fall loose.

"Well, all the same. Can't stand the smell that comes off that sprayer when it circles around my cottage with its enormous booms out."

Despite what appeared to be her best effort, with a distinct throat-clearing and readjustment to her pitch, Luc noticed that Judith's voice had gradually been creeping higher. He felt a strange delight in goading her, seeing her fists grasp together in a wringing action. Her rather sharp final comment made even Jeremy turn around to listen.

"You are not necessarily smelling pesticides, Luc. A lot of farms spread liquid seaweed fertiliser with a sprayer. Don't be so prejudiced. Tens of thousands of farmers cannot afford a Range Rover. And a rich farmer is not automatically either an indiscriminate profiteer or bad at farming. People need to put food on the table." With that, she abruptly half turned her back towards Luc and moved a little closer to Jeremy.

He was damned if he would let her get away with such a haughty attitude. He raised his chin a little in time with his eyebrows, addressing his reply at both of them.

"You and Jeremy are clearly cast in the same mould; I'm sure you'll get on like a house on fire."

Why, oh why, does she wear those glasses? She keeps pushing them up the bridge of her nose. They need binning!

＊ ＊ ＊

Luc always chose to walk the quarter-mile up the dim footpath from the Gardener's Arms to his humble cottage rather than faffing around and driving the short distance. His habit of pausing to take six deep lungfuls of air on leaving the pub had become a personal salute to having survived active service; no matter how cold or inclement the weather, he felt the need to inhale these precious breaths of life.

As he marched purposefully up the dirt track, his limp was pronounced and he reached down to his right knee, using his finger to press and prod through the thick denim. *You're a fool, Stockdale. It's not tough to postpone appointments with the hospital. Phone them tomorrow.* Straightening up again, he spotted two little owls. They burst from the bushes, calling as they reached the field beyond, their round bodies carried by short, sharp wing movements silhouetted between misty grass and a charcoal sky.

He fumbled in the dim light but as he tried to insert his key into the front door, he heard a distant sound – *pom-pom, pom-pom, pom-pom.* He hurried past a metal toolkit and planks of skirting board. Catching the tip of his shoe on a plaster-covered bucket, he lurched against the wall, recovered his balance and rushed out of the hall. He reached for his mobile, vibrating frantically on the kitchen worktop. Slightly breathless, he still managed to compose his dulcet voice.

"Hellooooo, foxy, feisty, Frances. Good to hear from you."

There was a pause as he listened to the reply. He moved to rest his two elbows on the worktop, spoke softly into the mobile pressed to his ear, "I wondered if you would like to come here for our next date. It's hard to get to know each other properly if there is always a table between us." The fingers on his left hand began to gently stroke up and down on the inside of his right wrist. "Excellent. I shall cook. But do you mind if we eat off our knees in front of the fire? I can show you my work-in-progress, rebuilding my cottage."

Another thirty seconds ticked by and a mischievous twinkle wetted his irises.

"No, please don't wear a skirt, Frances. This is only our third date and I don't want to be tempted into testing your virtue too soon. Besides, you will have to pick your way around all the detritus. In fact, I may even ask you to walk the plank upstairs. Two rooms no longer have any ceilings or proper floors."

Luc pulled a tatty calendar out from behind the fruit bowl and finalised the how, where and when details before hanging up. Rooting around in a cluttered table drawer, he selected a red biro and wrote '7pm Frances' in the space beside Friday. He then quietly raised his palms heavenward.

"This is a one-off, but thank you, God, Mohammed, Allah, whoever you are up there."

His right fist parted the air with a skyward bound punch.

"Yesssss. Foxy, feisty Frances is coming to play."

Chapter 8

Judith

Shoulders hunched over the laptop screen in my office, Lizzie's fingers continue to scroll deftly between open windows. I had called her in desperation a few days earlier and wailed down the phone. "I just don't know what to say to a blank screen with a random man on the other end who, for all I know, could simultaneously be picking his nose while he types in incredibly eloquent ripostes."

The heat burning from my ears and rising in a furnace out through my scalp suddenly becomes too much. I fling open the office window, allowing a breeze laden with the scent of crushed grass cuttings to waft in. "Damn hot flushes. You're so lucky they haven't hit you yet."

Lizzie ignores my tirade and continues squinting at the variety of photos. I peel off my sweatshirt and move my back closer to the window, waving my arms, elbows bent in a flying motion to create more draft. Gleefully, I continue:

"You are over fifty now. So, menopause mania may hit you any time soon."

Lizzie beckons me to her side.

"How about this one? He looks quite handsome, lives within thirty miles. *And* he's ticked agriculture and fishing, plus the usual default dining out, rock bands, etc."

Resting a hand on Lizzie's shoulder, my interest has at last been piqued.

"Ooh yes, he is quite dishy. And I love his pseudonym – 'Four Footprints in the Sand Not Two'. Can you bring up his description? I need to know whether he can string a sentence together."

Reading through the profile of 'Four Footprints in the Sand Not Two', a flicker of anticipation is stirring in my stomach. Perhaps online dating isn't so stupid? After all, if I am looking to find the perfect horse then I study advertisements in magazines and online. I decide what my parameters are, i.e. height, breeding, temperament, previous schooling and competitive experience plus location. There is no point in finding your perfect mount if it's 400 miles away in the Outer Hebrides! Therefore, common sense dictates that the same rules will apply to finding my perfect man. It's simply a question of height, education, sense of humour, upbringing, weight, looks, hobbies and interests, fitness and, last but not least, children. Jeepers creepers, what a list. Is it any wonder that I still struggle to take that first lurching step towards actually contacting a man? Only last weekend Mother screeched at me, "You're going to have to compromise. There is no such person as Superman!" Wrenched back to the present by the noxious fumes blowing up to my face from the cigarette clipped between Lizzie's two fingers, my focus rejoins the screen. Lizzie adds another proviso. "One more thing to check."

Irritably, I attempt to look her in the eye. "For goodness sake. *What?* I need fewer criteria, not more!"

"His height. You're not nearly as tall as me but you wouldn't want to be looking down on a man the moment you wear heels. You need someone a minimum of 5'10"."

Scrolling again to the front page, my reaction on reading the height detail is immediate.

"*Bollocks* – he's only 5'7" when he stands on his bloody tiptoes. Why didn't we notice before? Bring up that photo with the large fish. There, second from the right. I swear it probably weighs more than him! *It's not fair.* Just when I was starting to get excited."

Lizzie's shoulders begin to tremble.

"Small man, big fish syndrome. Classic text-book stuff. Haven't you noticed yet just how many men include a photo of themselves with either a big fish, big shiny car or a big shiny monument in a far-flung city. They can't help themselves – instinctive hunter-gatherer portrayal. We spent half a term studying image perception in our first year at uni. It's fascinating stuff."

Lizzie suddenly swivels around in her chair.

"I nearly forgot to tell you. Guess who bloody well phoned me with an invitation for us to go to a motocross competition?"

Screwing up her nose and exaggerating a grimace, she pauses for effect before continuing:

"Only that older chap, Robert, that we met at Thetford Forest. He said the invitation is to all of us. I'm convinced he's got the wrong idea about me, he's sodding well married, for goodness' sake." Stifling a yawn, Lizzie stubs out her butt in a small saucer.

A guilty prick punctures my own self-indulgence.

"Oh sorry. I've been so engrossed in my own dating constipation. You haven't told me for weeks what you've been up to…"

Lizzie's reply is mouthed through an unexpectedly grave plastic expression.

"I've just had a seriously awful experience. Not even sure I want to talk about it."

The angst sitting on Lizzie's shoulders is palpable. A beam of low evening sunshine flicks long fingers of shadow across the surface of the desk.

"What on earth has happened? It's not that many weeks since I last saw you. Let's wander down to the paddock, get some fresh air. You'll feel better if you spill the beans."

Stepping silently out of the office, there is no leaping or frolicking from Lizzie while descending the stairs. Lifting the cast-iron latch, I swing the front door wide to let her pass. She still hasn't uttered a word. A cacophony of birdsong hits us as we crunch along the path skirting the side of the house, past my favourite flowerbeds, ochre and custard daffodils in profusion. Lizzie stops briefly; Branston is sauntering after us, his insistent *meow... meow... meow* is successful. She scoops him up into her folded arms and we stroll on another eighty yards or so. The gravel path leads us through the pear trees en route to the paddocks, where I stop to rest my elbows on the wooden rails. The blossom is floating in fits and starts on the breeze, creating a wedding carpet of white and pink on the grass. I wait patiently.

Lizzie begins. "Do you consider me to be a good judge of character?"

This is clearly a seriously loaded question and the floundering of my thoughts makes me hesitant to reply. I decide something innocuous to be the best bet.

"Of course you are. Especially as you've been trained to deal with the inner workings of anyone and everyone's minds. Why do you ask?"

Branston has started purring while lolling in Lizzie's arms, his back legs stretching out in a feline equivalent of ecstasy as each stroke of her free hand runs the length of his spine. She continues tentatively.

"It all began three weeks ago. I'd already exchanged several online messages with a chap called Peter and we progressed to chatting on the phone. It was amazing. Even though his profile was not at all informative, it turned out he was a proper country boy. A mechanical engineer/project manager by profession from a family with a freight haulage business, and he's very well travelled. He said he'd been married once and then got stuck in a long-term relationship which just didn't work well. He was such a bubbly, fun guy and we had so much in common, even that he's trying to quit smoking. I did my usual double-entendre pratting around and he let slip that he really wanted to find someone a little unusual. Apparently, he's always been considered the black sheep of the family. I was convinced he would be right up my street."

Pausing, she lifts Branston onto her shoulder, burying her nose in the softness of his fur.

"Anyway, I sent Peter a text message saying, 'Happy Easter, Black Sheep. I hope you have a lovely Easter Sunday with your family flock. I am so looking forward to meeting you properly when we get past the Bank Holiday.' It was a simple message as we had already agreed on the phone that we would meet very soon."

In the middle of the paddock, my two boys lift their heads skywards startled by the *kak, kak, kak* in the far treeline from a wary pheasant. I stick my foot onto the middle rail of the fence and heave myself up by my arms, parking my bottom on the top rail. I pretend to be studying the horses. Branston is squirming on Lizzie's shoulder, threatening to slide head first off the far side. She takes a sharp breath.

"I didn't think anything of it. Just got on with my day until about an hour after I'd sent the text." Lizzie's voice has become a whisper but she continues, "My mobile rang. It was Peter's number, so of course I answered it."

Lizzie's face begins contorting, her mouth suddenly so wide, I get a bird's eye view of multiple fillings.

"Well, this irate, rude, 'Only Way Is Essex' woman starts screaming at me on the other end of the phone. '*Who the hell are you? What the f * * * are you doing phoning my Peter?* Why are you sending him a text message? When did you last see him?' I was completely silent for the first few moments as the penny dropped."

Tipping backwards in wobbly shock I have to frantically hook my toes around the middle rail again to rebalance myself before blurting out, "What on earth did you say?"

"Well, this woman would barely let me get a word in edgeways. But I did manage to say, 'No, I haven't even met Peter yet'. She kept saying, 'Why have you got his number? How do you know him?' Eventually, I had to scream back at her. '*For goodness sake just shut up for a single moment* and I'll explain. One: I've never met Peter. Two: I got his details from an internet dating website. And three: I had absolutely no way of knowing he already has a... what are you? Partner? Wife?'" Clearly warming to letting her story out, Lizzie's cheeks are now stoked with heat. "Then this woman came piling in again with, '*I'm his f * * *ing partner, what do you think I am?* We've been living together for over two years!' She then started quizzing me properly with, 'What's the name of the website where you met? Has he got photos on the website? Do you know how long he's been on there?' I had to try to bloody well persuade her that... one: *no*, I've never slept with him because I've never actually seen him. And two: he told me his daughter helped him put together the photos."

By now Branston's body language is turning a tad rigid under Lizzie's rough and over-zealous stroking. He jumps from her clutches, landing in the rough grass.

"You'll never guess what? This bloody woman then started threatening me. In her toughest Essex drawl, she said, '*I've* got a girlfriend in the Essex Police Department. And I now have *your* phone number. And if you ever contact my Peter again, I'll get the police to check out your address and come and knock on *your* door. *Get it?*'"

Sliding my derrière off the fence and planting my feet on terra firma, I am out of my depth as to how to console Lizzie, so I simply respond:

"Oh gosh, what did you say?"

"I told her in no uncertain terms that, after discovering his true situation, I clearly have no intention whatsoever of speaking to him again. She finished with a couple more threats preceded by the F-word yet again and we hung up."

Stepping forward into Lizzie's personal space, I wrap my right arm firmly around her waist and turn her towards the house. I can sense the worst of the rage is beginning to ebb but she spits out a final venomous:

"Never mind Peter referring to himself, with pride, as a black sheep. He's just a rogue bloody sheep as far as I'm concerned!"

We meander arm in arm under the pear trees and her words start to catch in mini hiccups of hurt. "I didn't see it coming and I'm supposed to be a psychotherapy expert! I felt so incredibly guilty for over twenty-four hours and yet I didn't do anything wrong. I'd absolutely no way of knowing he was attached! Why, oh why, is it always the wrong type of man who chases after me?" I tweak a gentle squeeze of consolation with my fingertips.

"We are all human and fallible – even you. Don't beat yourself up over this."

By the time we reach the front of the house, Lizzie has wiped the tears off her cheeks. Mother's 'Visitor Radar' has brought her out to meet us. She reaches forward to press her own hands tight around Lizzie's.

"How is life treating my Most Favourite Person In The World After My Daughter?"

Lizzie, never one to ponder on the macabre for too long, leans in to give Mother a peck on each cheek. Her reply is crisp, though rather loud for my Mother's specific benefit.

"Good evening, Mrs M. Yes, I'm managing well. It's good to see you out and about."

Lizzie has an ability to make chameleon-like changes to her emotional output. I envy her. Without warning, she spreads the fingers on both her hands wide, quite a manly movement, then rakes them through her hair. A laborious action as if she is running a thick comb through her thoughts, getting rid of all the knots. As she finishes, her hair stands sentinel, punk-like, and the whole style of her demeanour changes with this simple movement. She rests her palms gently on Mother's shoulders, studies her, composed once more.

"You would be the perfect person to tell me something. What does 'Que sera sera' mean? There's a bloke online with that pseudonym. These dot, dot, dot intellectual types. Why can't they speak plain English?"

Mother smiles.

"It means exactly as the song says. 'Whatever will be, will be.' You are possibly too young to remember it." She cannot contain herself, throws a conspiratorial wink in my direction, then continues, "We have a little tradition in the McBride family. We have our very own uplifting ditty. I'm sure you will pick up the tune once you hear it. It goes like this…"

I step towards Mother, my arms moving into ballroom-dancing position, one hand carefully on my mother's waist, the other meeting the outstretched fingers of her right hand. I return the wink.

"I'll be Daddy this time. Off we go."

The rose repeat pattern in Mother's dress twirls in tiny circles as we begin a well-practised waltz. No lacquered wooden ballroom floor for us, instead the shingle driveway. We float through the one-two-three, one-two-three, one-two-three rhythm, the stiffness of geriatric years melting from Mother's bones and our voices shouting our own ridiculousness at the vacant outdoors. Lizzie quickly joins in with each repeat of the, 'C'est comme ci, comme ca', goes quiet for the next two lines of McBride lyrics.

'My aunt found a flea, ea, ea.
It sat on her knee, ee, ee.
C'est comme ci, comme ca.'

By the time Mother and I belt out our final verse, Lizzie is wiping her fingers through laughter tears and wet mascara.

'If I could find a crystal ball
I'd ask the gypsy if she can see
Has he got brothers? Is it a plague?
Or shall I just set him free?
C'est comme ci, comme ca. My aunt found a flea, ea, ea.
It sat on her knee, ee, ee. C'est comme ci, comme ca.'

Lizzie breaks into spontaneous clapping as Mother and I take a gracious bow to her applause. I feel a need to explain.

"I promise we are not completely barking, Lizzie. Mummy and Daddy always used to sing the McBride 'C'est comme ci, comme ca', and dance around the living room whenever life dealt them a low blow. It worked every time to cheer us all up. Come on, you try it now."

And with that, I grab Lizzie's waist and Mother's shoulder and the three of us flounce about in the lengthening shadows.

'C'est comme ci, comme ca. My aunt found a flea, ea, ea
It sat on her knee, ee, ee. C'est comme ci, comme ca.'

* * *

Later, peering up at the carvings neatly spaced along the inner panel on my four-poster bed, I shift into my comfortable crossways position. I have frequently considered moving the modern double bed from the spare room into here, thus facilitating enough space for my feet and a decent night's sleep – heaven. But this bed gives me such an innate sense of history. My forebears have been cocooned in its timbers before me, rattled and romped to implant their seeds of fertility then screamed and laboured to spew forth new generations of flesh and blood. For me to think ill of them for their lack of foresight in the stature department would be decidedly churlish, and besides, I feel the need to be a part of its story.

The bedroom curtain billows slightly; stars are pricking in and out. A giant sparkler has been waved across the sky. My thoughts wander back to Lizzie's departure a couple of hours ago. My bright, resilient, beautiful friend conned, duped, sucked in. What are my chances if I set sail on the open seas? Will I be casting off into a storm of inclement half-truths and broken souls all buffeted by the vagaries of search parameters on age, height and location? Or will I arrive, sails stretched by a fair wind, in a Caribbean harbour of romance, certainty and happiness? It does happen, you know it does, Jude. What about Celine who runs the music shop? Second date in, met 'the one' and she tells me they're getting married in August. Or the seriously serious chap at the library in Bury who divulged his success in finding Miss Right via an online app for chess buffs! Have I got to be in it to win it? Or would I rather spectate, feet firmly planted on shore?

Interlude

Stanley continued trundling his trolley along aisle number ten. He knew his shopping list was complete, but force of habit walked him all the way up aisle eleven and down aisle twelve – just in case. Being a Sunday, he knew that Iris should be on till number fifteen, so his walk quickened in anticipation of reaching the checkouts. A young male supervisor with a Tesco shirt proffered an outstretched arm as Stanley approached.

"Excuse me, sir, this till is opening. Would you like to come this way?" Stanley's eyes flicked briefly from till to till.

"No, thank you. I'm happy here." And he slotted in behind two customers in Iris's queue. He always tried to shop on either a Sunday or a Wednesday, between 8am and 4pm, because those were Iris's shifts. By the time the stoop-shouldered mother in front of him had begun unloading her shopping onto the conveyor belt, her two children were becoming fractious. Stanley suspected that the younger one might be five years old and, accordingly, his expression was one of wary disgust. Both feet on the bottom rung of the trolley, the child bounced it back and forth and his elbow eventually jabbed into Stanley's leg. Stanley grabbed at the elbow, a reflex reaction accompanied by a flicking of his comb-over, just as the mother finished transferring items. She promptly snatched at her son's sweatshirt, pulled him close into her stomach.

"Come 'ere. Stop bouncing." A lioness suddenly protecting her cub, she stood up straight. A bad smell appeared to have passed her way when she added, "Creep."

Iris beamed her plum-cheeked smile at Stanley the moment he moved up to the till. He reached forward to remove the plastic divider from the conveyor. Iris gently leant forward to pat the cuff of his coat momentarily.

"Don't worry about them. If you hadn't stopped that little bugger swinging off the trolley, I would have. He'd soon have yelled if it'd toppled over."

She began carefully swiping items through the zapper and Stanley began packing.

1 x 2kg bag – Rabbit Nuggets

1 x 150g packet – Loose Leaf Earl Grey Tea

"How many years have you worked here, Iris?"

She stopped, mid-swipe, shook her thick perm about a bit.

"Ooh, that'll age me. Since way before I saw you coming in through these doors, and that must be at least fourteen years."

1 x one-pint carton – Full Fat Milk

2 x packets – Bourbon Biscuits

"Still on your own, Stanley? Found yourself a nice lady friend yet?"

Stanley lifted his shoulders, let them drop again.

"Not easy, I'm quite choosey."

2 x packets – Jacobs Cream Crackers

1 x 400 g – Wrapped Stilton

"Well, if I wasn't a happily married woman, I'd snap you up right sharp, I would."

1 x ½ wrapped cucumber

1 x paperback novel

Iris swiped the final item, turning it over in her hand.

"*You Before Me* – you've chosen a good one. Jojo Moyes always makes me cry. Bit of a softy, are you, Stanley?"

He hurried to stuff the book into the plastic bag, paying without comment. He eventually mustered a tiny wrinkling of his lips with a glance in Iris's direction.

"Sometimes. See you next week. Bye."

Chapter 9

The moment Frances stepped over the threshold into Luc's cottage, he felt his limbs go strangely light and he became acutely aware of each subtle nuance of colour in her skin. She flung both arms around his neck and planted her lush, welcoming lips on his before she got any further than the hall! In a trice he gave her 'The Tour', and her adventurous spirit meant that she was the one who insisted they clamber up onto the scaffolding at the back of the cottage.

The early evening temperature dropped fast but she seemed as beguiled as he was by the sky, the dying sun, the peace. He stood with her, his chest intimate with the contours of her back, his arms warming her waist. Eventually, just as the sun was finally being snuffed out, a 'tu-wit, tu-woo' sound made both of them turn their heads towards the wood. Luc unwound the strap of his binoculars from the scaffolding rail, peering off into the trees on their right.

"That will be a male Tawny. Every type of owl has a distinctive call." He continued his determined scanning, then stopped and excitedly pointed with one hand while still peering intently. His enthusiasm was infectious when he pressed Frances to take the binoculars.

"If you look halfway along the fence, you'll spot him."

The 'tu-wit, tu-woo' rang out again, clear as crystal in the still atmosphere. Luc noted the hushed reverence in Frances's voice when she answered,

"Got it, got it. He's so handsome with light and dark bars and streaks. The type of pattern and colours you'd see in a tweed jacket at some old-fashioned London gentlemen's club. Oh, he's off, taken flight, what a shame." Frances lowered the binoculars and Luc saw a new dewy-eyed softness in her face.

"I never truly believed that an owl actually goes 'tu-wit, tu-woo'. I always thought it was a sort of Disney version of an owl's call. I'm staggered to find it's real."

Luc replied. "Oh, it's real. What is even more Disney-sentimental, though, is the fact that the sound you hear is actually from two male owls. It's a territory signal – one owl says 'tu-wit', then another replies with 'tu-woo'. A sort of polite owl translation of 'Piss-off, this is my patch'."

After climbing down from the scaffolding, they toasted themselves, huddling close to the open fire. The aroma of slow-cooked boeuf bourguignon sent her into verbal ecstasies as she entered the kitchen, and the quiet lust in her mischievous eyes kept his head spinning all evening. He enjoyed comparing notes on cash-strapped students who only ever phone home when they need more money, usually to stock up their fridges. She seemed to have a knack for pressing his laughter button and, wow, she was so instinctively tactile.

* * *

In the first few days after her visit, he kept listing in his head all the possible reasons for her sudden lack of contact:

1. It had scared the shit out of her, the moment he had broached *the* conversation.
2. She'd had a car accident or some other major calamity.

3. She wasn't single at all and the moment the relationship looked to be getting physical, she had bottled it.
4. She had lost her phone and had no record of his number

But the reconciliation in his personal Book of Reasons refused to add up or balance. It remained 'out', missing £1.86 at the bottom of the page – a doubt, a shred of anger, a slice of rejection. *Why?*

* * *

Luc slammed the front door hard behind him. He was acutely aware that he had only a shaky hold on his emotions. Unnerved, he thought, *Shame a person cannot simply swallow an indigestion tablet to quell a need to regurgitate a Foxy Frances!* He took a few hurried strides, stopped, then unclenched his teeth. One breath, hold for two, three, then exhale. Second breath and his lips puckered. Third breath in and he coughed. Fourth breath and he realised that a slightly sweet but noxious taste was hitting the back of his throat. It must have arrived on the moisture-ridden breeze from around the corner of the cottage. *Chemicals; there must be another way to keep pests at bay. Or is it fertiliser? Have I become a prejudiced Nimby? Is the price of this tranquillity simply an occasional misty distaste on my tonsils that I should learn to swallow without complaint?*

Save for the squelch of his boots on the muddy drive, silence coated Luc's walk to the Gardeners Arms, the dull atmosphere matching his mood perfectly. Initially, he'd thought her visit had gone so well. Only last night, knackered from a tough day pulling down old plaster, he had fallen asleep on the sofa watching *Wallander*. As he awoke, he was transported by the remnants of her Angel perfume still lingering on the cushion. *Damn her, how many times had he called and texted?* Whatever her reason, he couldn't get over the fact that she'd left him dangling and fretting for two whole weeks before eventually sending a cursory text.

'Ever so sorry, Luc. But this simply wouldn't have worked. All the best – Frances.'

Avoiding the main entrance to the Gardener's Arms, Luc let himself straight into Isaac's garage through the side door. Isaac, sitting on a bench under the sole strip light, immediately clocked the rigidity of Luc's stance and knew his friend well enough to keep quiet. Instead, he reached for his glass of Amino Energy and gulped down the sweet liquid.

Luc flung all his outer clothing to the floor. The damp walk had rendered the laces on his walking boots singularly uncooperative and he had to wrestle with them, stony faced, for several minutes before he pulled on first a pair of leggings, secondly a dry pair of trainers. Last but not least, he strapped on his kidney belt then unfolded a ground mat from his bag. Not a word was uttered as the two men dropped into a familiar routine.

First – stretching exercises. Isaac lay on the floor, contorting himself into strange shapes with a resistance band, Luc preferring to elongate his limbs while standing. Still no word had passed their lips. Second – Isaac reversed himself deftly onto the Ab Crunch Board and began slowly pushing backwards and forwards while Luc hopped up onto the cycling machine and threw himself with venom into pedalling. He marvelled as the stiffness in his quadriceps began to dissipate but after only ten minutes his duff leg was already feeling tender so he cursed out loud, "Poxy bloody thing," and readjusted the pad around his calf. More comfortable, he straightened up into a standing position on the pedals. Tension flowed and evaporated as heat from the surface of hot skin, seeping out through cleansed pores, revelling in the motion of his pumping thighs, unbinding the hurt.

Strands of Isaac's thick brown locks were now sticking to his forehead. A drip of sweat slid past his cheek to his top lip and he stretched his tongue out to lick off the surplus water. His sixth sense told him the time was now right to speak.

"Are you using the squat rack next?"

Between breaths Luc answered, "No."

"It's been frenetic in the pub these past few weeks. Dare I ask if you've had any interesting dates lately because I've got a burn hole in my curiosity."

Luc ignored the question and climbed off the cycling machine. He picked up his towel and mopped his face and neck then moved to position himself over the mat again with a firm grip on the Ab Wheel. Isaac moved to stand under the weight bar of the squat rack as Luc hissed back at him:

"Remember Frances? I brought her into the pub for a drink about a month ago." Isaac's blank expression prompted Luc to continue, "You commented on her incredibly long legs. She drank gin and tonic, insisted on Hendricks." He waited as Isaac nodded then adjusted the bar to the correct height.

"Well, *she* blew me out completely. I didn't see it coming. Bloody redhead. I've always wanted to have a redheaded girlfriend. Dropped me like a hot coal the moment I told her. I'm not a sodding cripple, for Christ's sake. I'm still a fully functioning *man*." Luc straightened his arms and lengthened his torso forward slowly into the wheel then back again.

The note of inquisitive cheerfulness was gone when Isaac replied.

"Not all women are duff ones. I wouldn't swop Fiona for even, oh I don't know, say Katy Price if she walked naked into my bar."

The sinew on Luc's biceps stretched and heaved. He disliked

the fact that Isaac was stretching their unspoken protocol to 'keep your nose out of another man's business'. But he saw the depth of concern in Isaac, the seriousness of his face, the way he'd become completely stationary. When Isaac spoke again, it was not at the floor, his hands or the wall, instead he spoke straight at him.

"You've just been unlucky, mate. Perhaps internet dating is not the best place to meet a genuine woman. How about that Lizzie woman from Thetford Forest? Robert keeps going on about her. She is really lovely and horsey girls are never fazed by anything. It's all well and good putting yourself out there, but I sometimes think you're simply bungee jumping with your genitals, mate. I couldn't do it."

Neck muscles taught, Luc's flying spit appeared to emphasise his suppressed bile.

"Just make sure you never let her slip through your fingers – Fiona, that is. Foolish. I was an arrogant, blind fool to let Juliet go last spring. Made this ridiculous assumption that our lives would stick together, like bricks and mortar, just because we'd stuck our pound notes together in a house! Seven years. Why didn't I realise she simply had the 'seven-year itch'? Why didn't I chase after her, win her back?"

They fell silent again and dropped into their own physical battle zone. Luc eventually placed the Ab Wheel to one side. Always mindful of how precious Isaac could be about any damage to his gym kit, Luc rolled out a weight bar, slid a fifteen-kilo weight deftly onto each end and lay down on his back. Isaac duly moved to lower the weight bar over Luc's chest. Luc's arms began heaving the weight bar methodically up and down.

He found himself scrutinising the peculiar patterns of fly shit stuck in clusters to the strip light above. It was consoling that he could shut out all other conscious thought if he totally focused on something visual. Ten minutes elapsed before the pain in his biceps became too acute. Isaac instinctively knew how long to wait before straddling above his friend again and lifting the weights away.

An ear-grating squeak of the door hinge announced that the companionable solitude for Isaac and Luc was to be broken. Clad in full leathers, Jeremy and his son stepped into the garage. Luc found himself wishing, yet again, that he had a son. His two daughters were the apple of his eye, but though he had tried every trick in the book from six years old onwards to encourage them to be tomboys, their hearts had never really been swayed by a desire for speed or the joys of cleaning Silkolene grease out from under fingernails. Besides, he reminded himself just how proud he had felt posing for photos on the steps of Canterbury Cathedral, his eldest in her mortarboard and graduation robe. Louise had inherited her mother's stunning looks. Thankfully, the genes for his own decidedly Roman nose had skipped past both girls.

Jeremy hovered near the door, waiting for the sharp clunking of weights to cease.

"Isaac are you finished?" Then he turned and added as an afterthought, "Hello, Luc. Do you fancy going for a burn-up for an hour with Isaac, Mathew and me? The cloud is clearing and the roads are almost dry again. It's not that often Mathew is up from London. The more the merrier."

Luc couldn't help himself. "No thanks." Then a momentary pause before throwing his voice loudly across the void of the room.

"*Jerry* – you know what my thoughts are on the lunacy of 80–100mph on open roads!" *Will he or won't he be goaded? Come on Jerry, retaliate. Show just a tiny bit of ire. It would make my day.* Three pairs of eyes peered in Jeremy's direction. He quickly brought his hand up purportedly to scratch a spot just under his right eye, his index finger successfully hiding the reflex twitch of his eyelid. His chuckle sounded dry and forced.

"Come on, Lucas Stockdale. My treat. Fry-up at Maxine's Café then straight home again."

Isaac suddenly slapped a chilled water bottle into Luc's chest. The ribbed plastic grooves pressed hard into Luc's T-shirt and he swallowed his own stream of sarcastic thoughts, not allowing them to spew out through his lips. Isaacs's 'no arguments' stare held him completely still and silent. Luc felt the air in the room wait, hanging. Jeremy headed for the door and barked over his shoulder.

"Your loss, Lucas."

Luc knew he couldn't allow a distant childhood memory to become a petty name-throwing weapon in Jeremy's hands. Luc's mother had only ever called any of her children by their full Christian names if they had committed some heinous crime within the Stockdale household. Her pet gripe, with a rabble of four to manage, was swathes of smelly socks and half-worn underpants littering the bedroom floor. He could never refrain from smirking at the vivid memory of her Yorkshire drawl.

"Lucas Stockdale…" or "Margaret-Ann Stockdale…" or "Harold James Stockdale…" – "I wasn't put on this earth to spend all my waking hours as a laundry woman! You'll feel the leather of your father's belt on your lazy backside if you don't pick up those clothes in the next two minutes." This was often yelled from an open upstairs window to Luc's favourite spot perched in the fork of the Victoria plum tree in the front garden. His attention would then return to studiously searching for any dark purple fruit with a tiny brown pockmark on its skin. He would press his two thumbs together on each side of the hole till the tiny beige larva popped out. Then he would savour the glorious sweetness as each morsel of fruit slipped down his throat. On so many occasions his mother's sharp rebuke would bring him scuttling from the tree, the bark scoring a few fine, red weals on his bare calves before his feet hit the ground. His mother frequently had to resort to a frugal high tea of sardines on toast served with a hearty smattering of, "We are thankful, oh Lord, for what we are about to receive." Consequently, he had always felt loved and secure, but would always associate the words 'Lucas Stockdale' as being followed by the stinging wallops of hard hand on young skin!

From his vantage point in that special tree, he would look up and survey the giant looming swathes of the Hebden Moor Hills. With the arrival of each winter, the dying bracken created a brown, slightly over-baked crusty loaf effect and in summer the clouds cast dark, dancing waves of shadow over the rolling verdant panorama. Whenever he could catch the fickle northern sunshine, he would lie, cat-like, stretched along the thickest branch and daydream of all the wild, exciting places just out of sight. He imagined, over and over again, baking-hot Sahara dunes or black waves of angry sea, or vast impenetrable forests. Anything more challenging than the course in life his father had taken.

He could pinpoint to the second his own pivotal moment of sea change. He had been sixteen years old and soon to finish school. The whole family were stuck in their bloody predictable family rut, glued to the TV, the three lanky lads, elbow to elbow, thigh to thigh, squashed onto the sagging sofa; Margaret was hogging the comfiest spot on the bean bag; his mother was in her special high-backed chair sewing patches on a motley selection of clothing. Following adverts for Prudential Life Assurance and shots of a pinny-clad, glamorous housewife proclaiming in a singsong trill: "For hands that do dishes can be soft as your face – with mild green Fairy Liquid", an enormous Sea King helicopter had burst onto the screen. The old Phillips set had vibrated with a deep incessant strumming as a clean-shaven serviceman deftly made a complicated sequence of hand signals with a round, white table-tennis-bat-sized baton.

Maggie had screeched:

"For Christ's sake, Luc, you've got the remote. Turn this racket down. It's hurting my ears." Luc remembered being transfixed, watching the ground crew on the ship expertly guiding the three tonnes of airborne steel to land on a two-metre yellow circle on the deck. That evening, still sacrosanct in Luc's memory, his father had bellowed, "Of course you're not going to join the army. Why the hell would you want to do that? These bloody adverts on TV are designed to suck in young lads like you." His father's cheeks had been blotchy with anger, but Luc had ploughed on regardless.

"The army says I can *Be the Best* and that's what I want, Dad, more than anything else." Luc could still picture his father jumping up from his chair to get closer to his rebellious eldest son. "You do realise you could come back in a wooden box. Or worse still, with no legs?" Tightening his rough grip on Luc's wrist he had poked his nose to within inches of Luc's blanched cheeks. A move which previously had always cowed Luc into acquiescence now had the reverse effect and only served to diminish his father's power.

"I don't care how long it takes. They train you up and it doesn't cost anything if I start at the bottom. I've already sent off for the forms." Luc remembered embracing his own transition from protected youth to adulthood.

Interlude

Lizzie slumped into the reclining chair in her conservatory and for a few uncluttered seconds drank in the warm sunshine, then reached for her laptop and placed it across her thighs. She immediately signed into her own profile before clicking the, 'refresh search' icon.

CLICK	**Website:**	Dancing in the Moonlight
CLICK	**Search Criteria:**	Woman Seeking Man
	Search Results:	**0–15 of 129 results**
CLICK		On photo of selected man

Lizzie's words of glee were heard only by the large beetle which she flicked off the coffee table before she pointed at the screen. "Now *you*, look interesting."

Hook Line:	Young Free & Single
City/Location:	Cambridge
Age:	52 years
Height:	6' 2"
Weight:	Average
Eye Colour:	Blue
Hair Colour:	Brown
My Dislikes:	Aubergines

About Me: I love life, walking on the beach, squashing up on the sofa, cooking for friends, travelling to far-flung cities, tinkering with my trucks. Not fun alone. Are you the one to join me?

He ticked *all* the right boxes so Lizzie had met him in person the following weekend. He didn't flinch or comment when she walked across the car park in her "Let's test if you are shockable" purple tights with the yellow flowers and lime fruit pattern. They were teamed with her short dark purple skirt and cashmere cardigan and a pair of tan brogues. Her regular venue – The Dog & Duck.

He was polite, smelt good, but was a tiny bit on the portly side (not to worry, she could fix that). He spoke reasonably well, a non-placeable sharpness to his diction. He owned his own landscape gardening and maintenance company with several staff. He told funny stories about a dyslexic employee felling the left-hand horse chestnut tree in a client's garden instead of the right-hand ash tree. It was only a mere eighty years old! *C'est la vie.* He insisted on paying for lunch – no arguments allowed. Three hours had vanished.

* * *

Lizzie couldn't wait; the moment she got home she flung her handbag down in the hall and flipped open her mobile.

"Come on, pick up. Please, Jude."

"Hiya, Lizzie. What's cooking?"

"I've found him, Jude. *At last*, I think I've found him. He's absolutely perfect."

Chapter 10

Judith

Mirror, mirror on the wall, who is the fairest of them all? For a few moments, I stand still to scrutinise my glad rags – my rarely worn vivid aquamarine dress, hugging every contour from bustline to upper knee. *Not so bad at all, Judith, you've brushed up quite well.*

I have never before thought of myself as a 'selfish woman', but I am beginning to understand how easy it is to slide into a one-track groove. To become a self-centred, self-gratifying, intolerant person. I would run over hot coals for my mother, fight off a tiger with my bare hands if it threatened my precious son, Ollie, however the bulk of my waking hours are about me and me alone. Yes, my work is essential, but otherwise I ride any time I choose, wear whatever I like, laugh, drink and play with whoever pleases me. Do I want to remain single or not? I looked it up in my thesaurus and some of the alternative words for single are:

- Free (*tick*);
- Unattached (*a collar and lead were never my thing. Tried it once – no, no, no. Kept getting the lead knotted around my knees*);
- On the shelf (*I am most definitely not a can of beans, waiting to be purchased!*);
- A spinster (*an archaic throwback to prudish, church-going matrons*);

- Spouseless (*tick*).

Having disembarked from a matrimonial state into, what should be, nirvana, why am I so restless? Instead, a lurking realisation has seeped insidiously through my bones – being a single woman in your fifties is bloody hard work and on occasions lonely.

Then the glossy Table Talk pamphlet plopped onto my doormat a couple of weeks ago and it promised everything I hoped for. On the front page, a glowing couple laughing back at me heartily through immaculate flossed teeth, glittering stars spiralling in flumes around their dinner jacket and chintz-clad bodies. The words read:

TABLE TALK
"Strictly Singles"
Norfolk and Suffolk
July 2015 – March 2016

Inside, each page detailed a different enticing evening dinner dance or 'Refined Singles Sunday Lunch' gathering – to draw the lost, the lonely and the hopeful as bees to summer nectar. Pictures of a silver-fox gent gazing lovingly into the eyes of a wide-eyed Goldie Hawn lookalike. Or the chiselled profile of a woman who immediately floods my thoughts with Neapolitan ice cream – her chocolate hair has a pageboy curve around her vanilla cream skin and strawberry highlighted cheekbones. Her gold droplet earrings reflect a sparkle equal to the promises the brochure dangles before my hungry eyes. Her hands are cupped around a glass of wine, the warm familiarity of alcohol no doubt a crutch to many a prospective attendee.

The date, the time, the age range, are all displayed in brightly coloured fonts and boxes or embellished with neat fuchsia hearts. I had wondered obliquely, *Should I consider the Mixed Age Group as my appropriate peers?* Flicking on, I began to feel a tingling of hope. The choice was wonderous:

- Champagne Dinner Dance, OR
- a Singles Drinks Party in the City, OR
- a Singles Hot Tub Party (definitely not quite up for that just yet), OR
- a Three-Day Break to include New Year celebrations and walking in the Cumbrian hills.

Initially, my heart had gone cold at the prospect of driving alone and far afield to either Norwich or Ipswich, to arrive unescorted at a corporate hotel. After much soul-searching and diary-checking, I had settled on booking a space at the "Timeless Love Singles Dinner Dance" only a stone's throw away in Bury St Edmunds at a beautiful timber-framed hotel and pub. I decided it was a pretty good bargain to fork out only £46.50 for a three-course meal plus wine and music, with the added comfort of knowing I would be only twenty minutes from base camp. If I felt uncomfortable, then I could just slink home straight after the meal. The dress code was very specific, "Jacket & tie for the gents, long or short dress for the ladies."

Padding carefully in my stockinged feet to the wardrobe, I unzip the plastic cover on my precious ivory Karen Millen coat then lay it reverently on the bed. The thin layer of fine dust sitting across the top of the cover threatens to besmirch the immaculate cloth as I gingerly manage to extricate it. This coat a poignant symbol – the last purchase Patrick and I ever made together, amid the flurry of a decadent last-ditch shopping trip – a token nod to a marriage in its death throes. Never worn since its original purchase – madness, absolute madness and a timely reminder of my non-existent social life. Sliding my bare arms into the sleeves and neatly buttoning up the coat, I grasp the collar with my freshly varnished fingers and vow to find any and every reason to enjoy its sumptuous folds more often. Doris Day's rich, creamy voice glides into my thoughts. It is what I hear when I begin to sing, not the cobbled acoustics of my own voice.

"C'est comme ci, comme ca."

I click the bedroom door shut and head along the hall.

"My aunt found a flea, ea, ea."

Turning forty-five degrees sideways, I place my slippery soles tentatively on each oak step, one hand grasping the bannister just in case.

"It sat on her knee, ee, ee."

Branston brushes past my leg when I open the front door to leave.

"C'est comme ci, comme ca. My aunt found a flea."

* * *

Teetering over the slightly uneven brick floor in the entrance lobby at the Anchor Hotel, I pray I can make it through the evening without a high-heel incident of any description. The small of my back has been forced into a curve, my buttocks have magically shrunk a whole dress size and my shoulders no longer droop. *I swear that a heel-wearing driving test should be compulsory at my age, I am so damn out of practice!*

As promised in the membership bumph, the Table Talk evening begins with, 'Your welcoming host will be there on your arrival.' A table has been set out just inside the bar area and

Catherine swiftly introduces herself with a cheery smile amid immaculate black curls.

"Good evening, lovely to meet you. What is your name please?" The little toe on my right foot is starting to burn. *Mental note to self – buy shoes half a size bigger in future.* Catherine is peering patiently at her clipboard.

"Yes, my name. Sorry. Judith McBride." She duly ticks me off her list and her warm demeanour sets me at ease.

"Oh, I'm delighted you could come this evening. Judith, you are on table five. I'd like you to meet Sarah. She has been to several of our events before. She can show you the ropes."

On cue, a beaming brunette in a flowing, off-the-shoulder, thoroughly tasteful number steps forward and waves me on in the general direction of the throng. The bar area is packed with men and women of all shapes and sizes and, joy of all joys, absolutely everyone is smartly dressed. *No sleazy trainer-clad oiks in here.* Sarah slides through a narrow gap between a tall, gaunt chap sporting a silver-grey goatee and a roly-poly, freshly scrubbed farmer. Though I have no proof as to the latter assumption, there is a tell-tale weathered skin look which always betrays a man or woman with a hard, alfresco occupation. *The underside of the tips of his fingers all cracked and still ever so slightly grubby.* Sarah turns from the bar to catch my attention and asks, "What would you like to drink? We all buy our own tipple before dinner then there will be wine provided at the table."

Sarah duly passes me my G&T but is quickly distracted by another guest seeking her attention and I am suddenly alone in a room full of total strangers. *Help!* My subconscious screams are followed swiftly by: *Stop being such a wimp – everyone is paddling in the same stream.* Many, many pairs of male and female eyes are sussing me out, none in the least bit salaciously

– some simply quizzically, some brazenly, some surreptitiously. The hum of excitement, coupled in equal dollops with a roomful of unfamiliar people, batters at the well-practised social safety net I've been hiding under for years. Yet the very fact of our 'unknownness' to each other feels strangely comforting, as if all the lonely, outcast mustangs from a wild prairie have been thrown together in a corral. In the casual turn of a profile, friendships and attractions, likes and dislikes flash through thoughts and chit-chat.

Deciding I will feel safer with my back to a wall, I steer my wobble-prone Louboutins towards the less populated fireplace. I sidle into an empty space and my eyes are drawn to the inert man on my right (I shall call him Fireplace Man). His soft green/beige tweed jacket is helping his general attempts at camouflage. I pin him at probably his late-thirties, early-forties. Pallid complexion, stick-insect thin, he appears to have a fascination with everyone's footwear. Clearly much more out of his comfort zone than me, I proffer a cheery,

"Hello, I've never been to one of these dinners before. Is this your first too?"

His eyes appear to want to apologise for his very existence. They flicker momentarily up to meet mine before his shoulders curl forward slightly and his focus returns to the melee of shoes. He musters a faint, "Yes, it is."

I plough on undeterred, "Did you have to travel far?"

Twisting his fingers around and around his glass, I realise my mistake was to assume he would prefer to talk to someone (anyone)! My heart goes out to him, to be this shy…

His reply is forestalled by Sarah.

"Everyone is to make their way through to dinner now – this way." And she gently takes his arm.

* * *

As I go to sit down at table number five, the large, cuddly chap to my left introduces himself as Steven, and the rather glamorous lady pulling out the chair to his left offers her hand across the table in my direction. Her black sparkly evening dress is complemented by the classy engraved silver bracelets on both her wrists, but despite her plummy accent, nerves have clearly taken hold in a big way. She clutches my hand as though I am a long-lost friend and gabbles,

"Hello, I'm Victoria. I've never done this before. It's all very strange isn't it?"

Then placing a feline palm on Steven's shoulder, they make flirtatious studies of each other's eyelashes. I get the nuanced message immediately – as far as Victoria is concerned, *this* man is already *her* property! Laughing a tad too heartily, she continues, "Steven and I have already been chatting at the bar. I'm *so* pleased we are sitting next to each other."

As I reach behind me to pull the chair closer then bend to sit down, Steven's grey-blue eyes drop from my face in a slow sweeping rove. Oblivious, Victoria digs in:

"Are you a sportswoman, Judith? Steven and I have discovered we are both shooting enthusiasts."

Grabbing the opportunity to be just a little wicked, I reply:

"I grew up surrounded by a country sports family, and equestrian pursuits have taken up all my leisure time." I lift my left arm in a straight line above Steven's head and, bending my right arm into a hook close to my chest, I then pull an imaginary trigger.

"Boom! But, I've never had any inclination to blast pheasants up the bottom even though my father would have been chuffed to bits."

Victoria's claret lips part in a delicious half-smile and she leans across the table purportedly to be closer to me but, conveniently, her neat cleavage has moved into Steven's direct sightline.

"Oh wonderful, how wonderful. I've never been brave enough to ride." She then swivels her shoulders away from me and unceremoniously I am removed from their intimate conversation.

On my right, an immaculately manicured male hand reaches for the name card neatly placed above my dessert spoon and fork and the owner of said hand politely observes,

"Ah, Judith. An unusual name. Are you also an unusual person?"

I fiddle about pressing the toe of one shoe into the heel of the other and prise my sodding shoes off – *Relief, blessed relief. Now I can wrest my thoughts from pressure points and concentrate.* Phillip proves to be a thoroughly nice man. A semi-retired agricultural machinery salesman, attentive, chatty, tennis player. It's clear that Catherine has gone to quite a lot of trouble to make sure that the dinner partners on either side of me for the first course are both in my age range and have the same background – I am impressed. Once the starters have been heartily consumed Catherine and Sarah move between tables chivvying the gents to relocate to the next table.

Phillip appears to genuinely mean it when he places his long fingers over my hand and whispers, "I really wish I could sit next to you all evening. I've never met anyone as interesting and attractive as you before at one of these dinners. You will take the second dance with me, won't you?"

After writing my name in spidery letters next to the number '2' on the back of his place setting, we are interrupted by a hearty guffaw in my left ear. Steven snatches my card up and scrawls his name next to the number '1'. Victoria appears to have disappeared to powder her nose so, cockily raising one eyebrow, he completely ignores the fact that Phillip is hovering.

"We must make sure we stick to the correct format, Judith. I believe mine is the first dance?"

I cannot resist a sarcastic "If you say so" in reply.

The evening marches on – a whirlwind of intense conversation goes around and around and around again. An LP stuck on repeat: 'Hello, lovely to meet you. Ah, yes and your name is? Do you work? Oh really, what an interesting job – helping to keep this country's economic deficit down. Have you been to a Table Talk dinner before? Do you live locally? Have you got any children? Ooh, that gives you an excuse to visit South America, lucky you.'

And so on and so forth. Most suitors sit down beside me desperate to impress. One (more seasoned Table Talk chap) comes with an inattentive nonchalance which smacks of hubris. On the other side of my table, two bingo-wing belles grow bored with the painful silence of Fireplace Man, who is parked between them for dessert. They engage in a raucous sharing of holiday mishaps and comedy stories of ex-husbands while intent on consuming their fill of hospitality drink. Their coiffed manes are bunching close together; he stares, invisible, over the top.

Dessert finished, plates cleared away by the efficient waiters and waitresses, the DJ has switched on his flashing neon lights. They are circling in bright yellow, lime and electric blue across the shiny wooden floor then climbing in an arc up the white wall and returning again like fireflies in flight. The volume is slowly ramping up until 'Dancing in the Moonlight' is in full flow: a slow number clearly chosen to leave no room for even the most shimmy-shy people to excuse themselves. The seasoned veterans in our midst have already pinpointed their relevant partners written beside the number-one slot and are escorting them onto the floor. Steven appears at my elbow; an acrid hint of smoke assaults my nostrils as he bends to take my hand.

"Follow me, Judith. This way."

To my utter shock, Steven has rhythm! His clammy palm grips mine and he does a very creditable cha-cha-cha. His merry eyes encourage an attempt at civility from me and by the end of the dance I have discovered that, despite his filibuster best efforts, it's all a big ruse. He isn't, as a never-married fifty-year-old, the 'Man About Town' he likes to pretend. Free liquor has loosened his tongue and his only real objective in whisking me onto the dance floor is to establish:

"Do you think Victoria likes me? It's so hard to tell. She has been laughing a lot with me, but I'm just not sure. She said she would like to go on the organised day out to Newmarket Races. Do you think that's a good sign?"

The collar of his white shirt is restricting the folds of flesh under his chin and the proximity of his affable smile is just a tad too close for comfort, but his right arm is firmly around the back of my waist, pressing our chests together. The Toploader lyrics continue their serenade.

"Yes, of course it's a positive sign. And yes, you two seem to be having a great time together. Go for it, Steven. Nothing ventured, nothing gained."

Another four smoochy numbers later, and the partner listed on my dance card beside number six is nowhere in sight. I crumple, relieved onto my chair. Absent-mindedly, I roll a tall glass in my hands, the iced water helping to chill my hot palms, and I lapse into people-watching. Michael Jackson's upbeat 'Wanna Be Startin' Somethin'' is packing the dancefloor. A strange sense of social liberation has been flushing through my mind in sporadic bursts all evening. This amorphous collection of single human beings all thrown together with a communal aim – to find a companion, an amour, a friend, a listening ear, a passionate affair, a confidante, a collaborator. Someone, anyone, before we stare shocked and bemused into the face of our own sell-by dates. I hadn't anticipated such a total mishmash of diverse beings.

Males and females all swivelling their hips or bopping their bop in time to the music. Over-confident, under-confident, hard-working, chatty, educated, retired, cocky, polite, and that's just the men with their designer stubble, speculative searching, eye-to-eye contact, or under-arm sweat patches. Ties and jackets kept on in order to hide sweaty shirt patches or to cover up beer bellies hanging over excessively tight belts holding up trousers!

The women: a stunningly pretty Malaysian woman in a scarlet cocktail dress is being delicately handled by a bespectacled forty-something chap in clean-cut Gant trousers. What looks suspiciously like a dry-cleaning label is flicking about from under the hem at the back of his fetching waistcoat. A galloping granny's lithe hips are swinging with far more energy than many twenty years her junior, her beau intermittently brushing his cheek against her bobbing grey curls, pure joy etched unmasked on every groove of his expression.

Smiles, smiles, smiles, best foot forward intent on a good time whatever. Hands on backs, hands on hands, hands on rumps. The jiving bodies carry on through number after number. Amazing – Fireplace Man is still here! He has continued his chameleon ability to morph into any background. He is leaning against an upright oak pillar, his only prop a large beer glass. Occasionally he raises his hand to run a finger inside his shirt collar. He continues to watch, but there is nothing in the least bit questionable in his demeanour. All he wants is to simply be here, in the room, amongst all these people.

Eyes resigned, eyes excited, eyes unsure – all searching. An intoxicating mirage hangs in the air. *A communal rolling and smoking of a joint of hope.* Phillip materialises and I am happy to slip barefoot into the throng. We attempt a conversation by shouting at each other's earlobes, then give in unreservedly to bopping but I make my excuses after twenty minutes and disappear to the loo. *Pleasant though he is, I really don't want to lead him up the garden path.* Time has flown, exhaustion hits me and home beckons. I slide away to sit on a chair and I am fumbling around on the carpet for my shoes when Steven slumps down beside me.

"Judith, do you know where Victoria is? I can't find her."

Straightening up, my head comes up with a resounding clunk on the underside of the table.

"Bugger, that hurt. Can you see my shoes Steven?"

"Would you mind going to check for me, see if she's in the Ladies? Ple-e-e-ease, Judith."

The pleading tone to his voice is completely unexpected so I decide I must be kind to him. "I saw her leaving when I went to the loo about twenty minutes ago."

Steven's dejected face stares back at me. "But she didn't say goodbye, Judith. Why did she just leave without a word? What did I do wrong?"

We are now sitting facing each other, chair to chair, so I gently place my hands on his knees (so peculiar to feel the need to reach out and comfort this man when only a few sparse hours ago, we were complete strangers).

"I don't think you did anything wrong, Steven. She said she had a splitting headache. I'm sure she didn't mean to be rude."

He raises his angst-ridden eyes to meet mine. "But I didn't even get her phone number. I won't be able to contact her."

This bear of a man has been brought to his knees in the puff of a realisation – he might never see her again. *Hope is an incredibly fickle mistress.*

Interlude

Judith picked up her phone.

"Hiya, Lizzie. What's cooking? Good weekend with Perfect Man?"

"Stop taking the piss, Jude. If I didn't know better, I'd think you were jealous. We stayed in a quaint B & B near Kelmarsh. It was his choice of destination. It's brilliant to be with a man who actually chooses to go to country events. I've never been to a Game Fair before, it was such great fun. He even tricked me into trying on a pair of Fairfax & Favour loafers and sneaked behind my back to pay for them before I had a chance to protest. He's so generous."

"Thank goodness for that. At last, you're looking *up* a man's hairy nose rather than down your own. How tall is he?"

"Tall enough for him to make sure the B & B had a bed with no footboard on it!"

"How is it going in the bedroom department?"

"Not bad, not bad at all. All moving parts are functioning."

"Woo-woo. Do I take it you'll be running him up the A1 to your parents' next?"

"Aah, not just yet."

"Cluck, cluck, cluck, cluck. CHICKEN!"

Chapter 11

Judith

Summer has arrived overnight as if a divine hand flicked the barometer one click further around the dial of seasons. All three of us are sporting sunglasses, the May heat having already kicked in by the time of our departure at 11.30am. A Girls Day Out – Lizzie, Emma and I, chattering with gay abandon as the VW Golf hurtles along the narrow back lanes. I am already regretting my flippant, "Oh. I'll be fine in the back, it's only a thirty-minute journey." Until today I've only ever been in a vehicle with Emma when a trailer is dictating our speed. How can a woman so tentative and lacking confidence on a horse be this same gung-ho, gear-crunching Emma? An aspiring Lewis Hamilton behind a steering wheel. I shift my bottom, re-park it in the middle of the back seat, fix my vision on the road straight ahead.

"Emma, your idea of how to drive a car is akin to treating it like a go-kart!"

We veer around another bend and I am struggling to stay upright. I dare to unclench my whitening knuckles from where they are digging into the seat and stretch sideways to press the button. The window whirs down and a blast of pollen-ridden air swirls in. The pungent oilseed rape scent hits my nostrils, translating a message straight to my stomach.

"Emma. *Please* can you slow down a little. Otherwise in the next five minutes the footwell of your car will have a close encounter with the ingredients of my breakfast menu! We don't have to get to the motocross track for a deadline. There will be racing all day."

Scarily, Emma turns her head, eyes no longer 'front', in order to fling a comment towards the passenger seat.

"So glad your spontaneous idea worked for all of us today, Lizzie. Shame Caroline couldn't join us though. We're one Musketeer down. That Robert chap who we met at Thetford Forest, is he an organiser for Moto GP, or is it just that the competition is run on his land?"

Lizzie pushes a stray lock of ex-fringe behind her right ear. Since the winter, she has grown out her normal boyish, short crop. I prefer the new soft look.

"He definitely owns it. In fact, he couldn't stop harping on when he rang me to boast about his entrepreneurial success and how he started out with only the shirt on his back etcetera, etcetera, and how he has built up his business. Apparently, he now has three major car dealerships and land earmarked for development on the outskirts of Barton."

Emma's chortle is followed by a nasal Liverpudlian riposte. "Bit self-opinionated, is he, pet?"

Lizzie, her hands on both hips despite the confines of the car seat, replies with unusual vehemence. "Yes, but I can cope with that. However, you two must promise me faithfully that you will *not* leave me alone with him. I know he was inebriated when we met him in that cabin but it was still no excuse for the seriously lecherous way he kept staring at me."

To my relief, I manage to keep the contents of my stomach in their rightful place for the final mile till the Golf bumps and bounces through the rutted entrance into Blaxhall Racetrack. A rotund youth in faded navy jeans beckons us into his lane with a wave of his yellow plastic bucket. He leans in through Lizzie's open window.

"Ten pounds each, ladies, please."

Lizzie clearly does not appreciate finding herself in such close proximity to his shaving rash chin and stuffs the passes, which she is holding in her hand, unceremoniously into his face. Not normally prone to any kind of condescension, she suddenly acquires a rather la-de-da voice.

"We are here by invitation, young man. Robert Hunnable is expecting us. Do you know where we might find him?"

The steward stands upright again, screws up his nose and attempts to sniff in the snot about to drip from one nostril before declaring in a slow Norfolk drawl: "Ah, Robert. He'll be busy with the ma-a-a-arshals checking the track, I imagine. You just drive over there to the right with everyone else. We don't have any VIP parkin' 'ere."

Emma is edging the VW forward but Lizzie cannot resist the chance to announce loudly and to the world in general: "Ugh! Disgusting. Didn't his mother ever teach him to use a tissue."

I frantically prod Emma's shoulder and point into the distance. "Put your foot on it, Emma. *Quick* – before Lizzie gets us into trouble." My head hits the roof with a resounding thud as Emma duly puts her pedal to the metal across the uneven grass. Once we're parked, I extricate myself gingerly onto terra firma.

Emma cheerfully pipes up, "Did Robert say if they have a hospitality tent here? There is always a marquee for guests at Newmarket Races or Point to Points. Do you think we might get a free drink and some nibbles?"

Lizzie proceeds to readjust her Hermès scarf so that it drapes fetchingly over the shoulders of her pure white blouse then fiddles about tying it in a neat knot at the front. Her scarlet lipstick matches perfectly with the red splashes of colour in the pattern on the silk and the 'starlet on a day out look' is finished off with a fashionably large pair of Ray-Bans. She ignores Emma's question. She has spied the stream of very ordinary people in their very everyday clothes walking in threes and fours towards the track about 300 metres away.

"I knew it – I've overdressed. I should have worn my bloody jodhpur boots and a T-shirt."

Always the optimist, Emma isn't going to allow any misconceptions on Lizzie's side to spoil her day. "What on earth did you expect at a motocross track? Champagne and strawberries?"

Lizzie carefully cups her manicured thumb and index finger around the rim of her glasses, graciously sliding them an inch lower. She peers down over the rims imperiously at the parting in Emma's hair.

"I suspect we shall probably be lucky to be offered a mug of tea and a wedge of pork pie, darling."

Emma reaches out to clutch Lizzie's hand in her own and looks up puppy-eyed at her ever-so-elegant friend. "Aaaggh. Never mind, pet."

And so, the tone for our day is set. We begin to stroll past rows of large vans in solid blues, greens or black. Not your average little white delivery van but the big square, fit-your-whole-family-plus-a-few-refugees-in-it kind of van. We cross a crushed line of grass, indented with the patterns of tyre track. Intermittently, a rider on his bike chunters quietly past on his way up through a copse of trees. I follow Lizzie and Emma as we pick our way through a line of snazzy white campervans interspersed with yet more open-sided vans, many of them cleverly adapted to house row upon row of spanners, wrenches, oil containers and spare parts. Some have awnings either alongside or fitted to their roofs under which, waiting redundant for the time being, stand motorbikes.

The distant revving of engines is coming closer and having navigated a fenced-off arena, we climb the slight incline towards the source of all the racket – a row of six to seven-foot-high billboards. The backdrop to the start point. The classic names associated with motocross display their sponsorship status in huge clear letters: Yamaha, Foxwood, GH Motorcycles, Steve Lumley. Above these a couple of sail-like hoardings reach up into the sky, billowing in the gentle breeze. Beneath them the fidgety line of approximately thirty to forty revving motorbikes stretches away into the distance.

We are all mesmerised by this unfamiliar scene, remaining strangely mute. We simply stop side by side, resting our elbows on a gate. Lizzie keeps one eye on the action, while drawing in air through a cigarette and simultaneously flicking her lighter. She sucks in a mouthful of smoke and exhales before throwing out a rhetorical question:

"What a riveting line-up of obscure propulsion. Whoever designed a motorbike and thought it was a good idea? Sometimes I truly cannot fathom the human psyche. Why is it so exciting to sit an inherently squashable human body atop a sophisticated metal carcass of whizzing parts, then cushion it from the unforgiving solidity of the ground with chunks of revolving rubber?"

A man identified as 'crew' by the lettering on his bright blue waistcoat begins walking briskly across the track away from all the watching spectators. The sighting of his large green flag starts an immediate flurry of extra activity from assorted riders. Their feet still planted firmly on either side of their bikes, some begin shaking their arms in the air or waggling their necks and shoulders. Helmet straps are being frantically double-checked while collars and clothing receive a last-minute fiddle. A cloud of noxious smoke billows in swirling puffs around a rider whose bike is being revved till it gives out a high-pitched whine in stationery protest. Others are clutching their throttles, the rattle and growl of pent-up engines pulsing in unison with each screw backwards or forwards of a wrist action.

Lizzie chips in again,

"This reminds me of a hungry group of pigs grunting in expectation of food."

My chin is resting on my forearms. I do not turn my head when I speak quietly. "No, no, Lizzie. I have an overriding feeling of witnessing a slightly irritable collection of bees."

Suddenly, thirty-six heads point as one, straight ahead. Despite the increase in decibels from a polite buzzing to a heart-stopping roar, the concentrated tension has become palpable. Two feet in front of each throbbing bike, a low square of metal protrudes into the air – seventy-two honed eyes spot, somewhere off in the distance, a signal. All the metal gates slam down. An incredibly angry hornets' nest of sound hits our ears as all that horsepower rips away down the track. The aroma of burnt two-stroke is left behind in the vacuum. Three seconds later, I feel an elbow in my ribs as Lizzie nods her head over her left shoulder.

"Oops. Not everyone got out the starting gate successfully."

Our eyes fall on one poor sod, whose bike has managed a mere fifteen metres before unhelpfully stalling. We are watching the disconsolate rider pushing his bike towards the exit when a dulcet male voice speaks from behind and within inches of Lizzie's right ear.

"Hello, ladies." Lizzie takes a quick step to her right. The owner of the voice continues, "So sorry I haven't managed to catch up with you till now. Are you enjoying the action?"

I watch Lizzie react on the hoof giving Robert no time for any cheek-to-cheek air-kissing nonsense. She deftly switches her glowing cigarette from one set of forefingers to the other and proffers her empty hand to be shaken. A tight smile twitches briefly at the corners of her mouth.

"Good morning, Robert. It's so kind of you to treat us to such an exciting spectacle. Yes, we are loving it."

Robert's chin remains still but his eyeballs descend from Lizzie's pretty high cheekbones in a sweep to her feet and up again. He proceeds to direct his words solely at her.

"I'm afraid I shall be a tad busy today, ladies. The joys of running the competition and all that. Jeremy will be joining us in a minute or two and he can walk you around the track and entertain you for a while on my behalf, if that's OK?"

I am not normally a touchy-feely sort of person, but I am struck by an urgent need to protect Lizzie. Walking forward two strides, I grasp Robert's fist gently in my own – the feel of his fingers brings a picture of sausages to mind. I grin kindly into his face and try to expel the sausages. He is forced, through social propriety, to turn his attention in my direction. I blurt out:

"I must admit it would be great to fire questions at someone who knows what's what. Could you perhaps point us in the direction of the loos first, though?" I purse my lips and airily add, "Girls and their bladders," before hooking my arm in a sisterly fashion through Lizzie's and marching her off in search of the facilities.

The toilets are only twenty metres away, discreetly positioned behind a narrow bank of tall bushes. My ruse to rescue Lizzie was a lie; instead of joining her in the short queue I wait quietly, happy to people-watch. Moments later, I notice Jeremy heading with his two Labradors up the slope and Robert meanders up to meet them. The bushes are in full leaf and the two men seem unaware of my close proximity because Robert greets Jeremy in his usual intemperate voice.

"Oh good, Jeremy, you're here, perfect timing. Before the ladies get back, I've got a suggestion."

I can see Robert's exaggerated wink just before he moves a little closer to Jeremy. He continues to speak as though the wide-open spaces of the motocross venue might actually have an innate interest in their conversation.

"Lizzie has brought Judith and her other friend Emma with her. You could do a lot worse than casting your line in the direction of Judith, the brunette. She's just your sort."

Jeremy's authoritative answer appears to squash any further debate.

"I shall not dignify that comment with a reply." Then he looks sideways briefly, placing his hand for a split second on Robert's jacket as if he's changed his mind. All my concentration suddenly pitches in one direction. Will I be able to hear what Jeremy says? It's muffled but I get an overwhelming sense of pride when he speaks.

"Sensitivity and discretion, Robert. Sensitivity and discretion."

Promptly followed by the thought, *That sounds suspiciously like a well-worn quote from one of his council meetings!*

When I stroll up to the two men, I see a lightness immediately flood across Jeremy's face. *But why am I emitting a light-hearted waft of laughter at the simple formality of saying 'Hello'? Get a grip Jude, get a grip.* Lizzie and Emma are soon in our midst and Robert lumbers off to fulfil his supervisory duties. I find myself ticking an 'I approve' box in my head as I observe Jeremy's Armani jeans, loafers and crisp, pale green shirt. His unfashionable but very neat sideburns are frosted with grey and his demeanour gives him a very distinguished air of assurance without any hint of arrogance. Ever so politely, he guides our trio off towards the main part of the track. I comment as we pass two parked ambulances and a fluorescent paramedic's car.

"I imagine motocross is as dangerous as eventing and point-to-point racing? Have you ever competed, Jeremy?"

The same race is still in progress and we enter a concrete underpass in order to get to the middle of the track. The droning of engines above our heads means he doesn't reply until we come back into the hot rays again.

"No, I haven't. It's definitely a young man's sport. You need a surprising amount of stamina to be able to travel this fast handling 222 pounds of heavy bike for twenty to thirty minutes *and* with the intensity of concentration."

The undulating ground lends itself to easy spectator viewing with thirty-foot mounds and naturally sandy soil. We climb to the top of a small hillock and are surrounded by motorbikes hurtling in ones and twos on all sides. Emma pulls a camera from her pocket and exclaims,

"Wow, this is incredible."

She focuses the zoom on two bikes within spitting distance of each other, capturing them as they soar up over the hump below. They stay airborne for about three seconds, the riders lifting their bottoms up off their seats and taking the concussion of landing expertly through the bend in their knees. Bike after bike flies through the air within metres of each other. We have to stand bunched up on the small space between lumpy grass tussocks and my bare arm is pressing against Jeremy's shoulder. I take off my sunglasses and fold them into my shoulder bag. My technical curiosity is kicking in.

"I grew up with two motorbike-besotted brothers. They didn't do anything as daring as this. Tell me, does it matter whether they land on the front or the back wheel doing these huge jumps?"

Jeremy turns to answer me but instead pauses as if speechless, he is looking right into me, almost as if he is counting the different layers of colour around my irises. Mother has always reassured me that they are subtle rather than stunning hues – a base of hazel, flecked with hints of green and black. He opens his mouth. *Is he or isn't he going to speak?* I wonder. "I've been in a dad's race at a club meeting so I did learn a few techniques. For example, if you open the throttle while the bike is in the air, then it brings the back wheel down first. Conversely, you can brake while you are in the air and this tips the bike forward."

Oh, sweaty bra, to run my fingers along the strapline. If only! Inelegant blush creeping, it must be spreading in pink meringue blotches up my neck by now? Bet it's reached my chin?

Lizzie butts in with another question.

"There's a man standing on the edge of the track over there holding a yellow flag. What does that mean?"

Relief, thank you, Lizzie. Just in time.

Jeremy wrenches his one-to-one gaze away in order to reply.

"That's to tell the riders there's an incident ahead and they must slow down. If he was actually waving the flag about, that would be much more urgent – a body in the middle of the track."

Lizzie slips her glasses down her nose a little, all the better to fix Jeremy's attention.

"Horsepower. Why do we crave pure horsepower? You must get irresponsible thrill-seekers on motorbikes who rush out and buy a fast bit of impressive kit only to get deposited head first into the nearest tree? Probably within fifty minutes of flinging their leg over it!"

I notice a teeny tiny flinch of the skin above Jeremy's cheek as he clears his throat a little and replies, his voice flat: "Of course, it can happen with any of these off-road bikes, though there are strict rules and testing procedures for anyone who goes on a public highway."

The flinch pips in again, once, twice. I see Lizzie stifle a smirk; I warn her with a thunder frown, just in case. She's got the message and sidles off a little to the right, repositioning her sunglasses. *This is a cruel streak in her I haven't seen before.* The reactionary vehemence in my reply pops out before I have a chance to adjust it.

"Stones in glass houses, Lizzie! What about all the numpty parents who rush out and spend a fortune on a ready-made, whizzy pony for their precious, precocious Arabella? She's probably only been riding for six months and the first show they attend, she does a somersault over its head at the second show jump. Or the moneyed suit who decides he quite fancies poncing about on a horse so he can feel like he's part of the Country Set. Only to get kicked in the face because his mobile phone lets off the sound of a police siren when he's trying to pull a tail bandage off."

Jeremy clears his throat as if calling his attendant audience to heel.

"You're both absolutely right, ladies, because we get exactly the same problems with bikers. Too much, too little. Be it money, engine size, common sense or experience. Human beings are the problem, *not* what they ride."

He raises an overly wide smile and turns to make a wave, taking in the clusters of onlookers spread out below us.

"Look, ladies. There is every manner of person and price tag here. Take your pick – working class, middle class, upper middle class." He gives me a playful elbow jab in my side. "No royalty though. We don't really stretch to royalty here." And he is clearly pleased with himself – tricky moment handled.

We watch intently for another fifteen minutes as the bikes snake up and down, in and out through a serpentine course of loops and hills. Below us, down the steep slopes of the bank, a mixed selection of families and couples are sauntering about enjoying the spectacle or chatting in small groups. Several children, four- or five-year-olds, are riding tiny plastic two-wheel mini-bikes, their chubby legs walking them along, no pedals necessary. I bend down to rub the ears of Jeremy's chocolate Lab. The hot, canned meat breath is panted into my nostrils, Chester's tongue lolling to one side in a vain attempt to lower his temperature.

Jeremy looks sideways; he appears to read my thoughts and pre-empts any comment I might make by suggesting, "Shall we move on down to the corner over there, ladies? I want to grab some water for the dogs."

Thirst quenched, the two Labs promptly sprawl in the shadows of an elm abutting the track on the first hairpin of the course. Another race begins with a cacophonous drone from the distant start gates, each rider fighting for an optimum position coming into that testing bend, looking for the whole shot. The riders are spread out across the full width of the track. We three women cannot help but gasp and marvel at the bloody-minded determination needed to hurtle through rusty, brown dirt – competitor to within inches of competitor, shoulder to within inches of shoulder, foot pedal to within inches of exhausts, front tyres to within inches of rear tyres. The bravest gain precious ground, then hog the inside line but have to drop off the throttle, some preferring to keep the speed and use the extra space of taking the wider line.

I notice Lizzie carefully remove her sunglasses again before looking Jeremy unashamedly full in the eye.

"I can see that some of the riders stand up as they come out of the corner. Is that so they don't batter their nuts to bits on all those horrible bumps?"

I dare not allow myself the luxury of getting angry for fear of flattening Lizzie with a death stare. *Why is she so determined to embarrass him?* is all I can think. Jeremy's reply seems to feature very rounded vowels and deliberate spacing between each word and he completely ignores her stab at coarse humour.

"I wouldn't know but... all those uneven spots are called 'breaking bumps'."

A loop-the-loop of thoughts keeps somersaulting inside my mind. A joy in Jeremy's courteous attitude and style in clothes; his respect and kindness; a need to jump to his defence; an irritability with Lizzie's stoking. *Or is it that underneath I am also feeling a little vexed at Jeremy's lack of fire, his almost submissive, turn-the-other-cheek way?*

Emma, one knee bent in a crouching position, has stuck the zoom lens of her camera through the rails of the barrier to catch a wheel-height shot. Jeremy reaches down to tap her shoulder.

"You'll get a roosting if..." A motorbike travelling within a foot of the outer perimeter throws out its wake of grubby soil in a fan, hitting Emma full force – she topples backwards, landing flat on her backside as Lizzie helpfully catches the earthbound camera. An icing of red-brown sand is delicately sprinkled over her ginger crown and duck-egg-blue T-shirt. A few seconds too late, Jeremy's voice trails off, "... you're not careful."

Emma, clearly feeling rather ridiculous in front of Jeremy's parent-to-child expression, blurts out through marginally polite but decidedly grit-splattered teeth,

"What the hell is roosting?"

"Well, Emma, as you have just experienced, in all its glory – it is spinning mud in someone's face."

Lizzie fluffs her fingers gently through Emma's hair then hands back the camera.

"What a great expression, Jeremy. I shall pass that word on to Caroline. She's always complaining that it happens to her out riding."

Lizzie steps back as if ready to leave, cocking a sly wink at Emma.

"Jeremy, it's been very kind of you to show us the ropes, so to speak, but we wouldn't want to keep you from your biker friends any longer. We are in need of a cup of tea. Perhaps we might bump into you a bit later?"

With that she drags us away in an escape towards the nearest burger van and we purchase hot beverages. Once we've parked our bottoms on the ground in the shade of a particularly large Ford transit van, we begin gazing out towards the transient scene. Lizzie is the first one to break the impasse, which is hovering unsaid between her and me.

"Sometimes I wish I knew less, rather than more, about the workings of homo sapiens' grey matter." She pats my leg and continues thoughtfully, "I'm sorry, Judith, but Jeremy does err towards being rather frigid company, don't you think?"

I know that the compact, vocally humorous but telepathically caring bond between our happy band of female Musketeers does not lend itself well to an interloper for the day in the form of any man. I also know that it is very out of character for Lizzie to be so intolerant, that her job frequently saps her to the core, leaving her with no patience for any sense of time-wasting on free days. It is a discussion we've had many times but right now I have a sense of sick injustice which is wrapping one arm across my midriff and digging my fingers into loose flesh. I dare not answer her. Luckily, Emma comes to the rescue.

"Today has been a Builders Tea Day, girls, not a Fizz Day. But I'm ever so glad we came." She grips the paper tab and pulls the teabag on its string up the rim of her plastic cup, then begins wringing out every last drop of thick brown flavour into the milky depths. We are all transfixed by her simple movements so she raises her drink for a toast.

"Bottoms up, girls."

Across from our vantage point, we watch a strapping lad in his late teens (number 87) as he rolls his Suzuki up to his waiting mum and turns off the engine. He lifts it expertly so that the engine is balanced on the flat upper surface of a metal stand and the back wheel is touching the ground. While son begins peeling off helmet and gloves, his mum sets to with a pressure hose. Mud and grime fall away to reveal shiny blue and yellow stripes and arrows, the letters 'Suzuki' emblazoned in white across the side. After ten minutes, not a spec of filth is left. Son then walks forward and sticks out his long padded boots for the same treatment.

To our right, two leggy lads lounge in fold-out canvas chairs. They remind me of a picture hanging in my hall. Patrick and I brought it back from a safari holiday. Two cheetahs, near maturity, languidly feline on the branches of a baobab tree, their limbs propped at obscure angles. The muscles on these two lads don't fit the size of their knees and shoulder blades and their heads have not yet grown to fit their ears. Whenever they speak their Adam's apples jump about in immature necks. Their convivial conversation is intermittently broken by gulps from water bottles. Quietly working under an awning close by, their dad is completely engrossed in spraying oil on cogs and any other exposed parts of the engine. The number 461 on this bike is barely readable beneath a coating of grimy sand. The mat under the bike promotes its sponsor, 'Honda', in bright red. Any spare inch of metal has a

'Honda' or 'Lings' or 'Castrol' sticker. This is clearly very much a family sport, which necessitates the attendance of the family dog, too. Pretty much every other family appears to have said dog, tied by a long string and winding itself in ever-shortening circles.

Tea has broken the spell of discontent and we have settled into a well-worn groove of ridiculous comments and disjointed observations. Thinking out loud, Lizzie pipes up.

"I don't know what you two think, girls, but today has convinced me that men need their heads seeing to. This lot are absolute lunatics to race around a track so damn fast, hurling chunks of metal around corners and jumping ten or twelve feet in the air. Do you think they take their brains out and leave them at the start gate?" I make no comment but simply raise one eyebrow skyward. Lizzie is clearly on a roll.

"I know, I know. I ride a thoroughbred over immovable cross-country fences, but those riders out there on the track today get so incredibly aggressive. I'm sure it's because society is so horribly devoid of danger for men. All their hunter-gatherer instincts have absolutely nowhere to go. You're very quiet, Judith!"

Lizzie knows that when I'm on good form, I pride myself on off-the-wall ideas. She's goading me into one right now, challenging me, her forehead rippling slightly in anticipation. I take my time.

"Here's a revolutionary idea for you, girls. Perhaps we should start a brand-new chain of supermarkets. Instead of blandly tromping down aisle after aisle once a week to throw the sustenance we need into a trolley, how about if we set up a Catch Your Dinner shopping experience?" Warming to my theme, I raise my index finger.

"One – if you want to take home a fish, you have to catch it with your bare hands from a tank of water." I add a second finger to the first.

"Two – if you want to bag a rabbit, you have to bring your own dog to the field out the back of the supermarket where there is a greyhound-type track set up. Each customer can take it in turns to race their dog out of the traps after a fluffy mock rabbit. If your dog doesn't catch the ball of fluff, then you go home and eat carrots."

The remnants of Emma's last dregs of tea suddenly spray projectile across Lizzie's Persil-white blouse. Emma tenses, sucking in air in anticipation of a scolding, but Lizzie simply takes another long, slow drag on her Marlboro before raising three of her own fingers.

"Wow, that's a brilliant idea, Jude. It's my turn now. I've got number three sorted. The whole supermarket shopping area has hens running around loose. They are all sorts of different breeds, but it costs you twice as much at the till if you catch a slow breed of bird than it does if you catch a fast one."

The hysterics are starting to kick in. Lizzie is frantically scrunching her fag butt into the earth with her heel. She takes a breath and clutches her stomach with both hands before adding, "Black Rocks – they are the flightiest. A customer only has to pay a fiver for a Black Rock but a waddling Moran would be really easy to catch. So, what do we think? Ten pounds for them?"

Emma's eyes are popping with mirth and she is desperate to chip in too.

"Imagine all those plump eight- to twelve-year-olds skidding around the aisles with their urban dads yelling 'Catch it, catch it, that one over there'. Diving at a White Sussex, missing it completely when it flutters up just out of reach, and clonking headfirst into the bottom shelf. It's *so* hard to catch a hen in an open space with your bare hands!"

She wipes a finger hurriedly down her cheek to remove a sliding trickle of tears. Her high-pitched, girly trill rings out.

"Wait, wait – *this is the answer to the obesity problem.* Everyone will have to run or swim or crawl to catch their dinner. We've found the answer."

All three of us are now oblivious to our surroundings, slapping at each other's arms. A familiar baritone voice arrives from behind an awning and momentarily ahead of its source. Robert's substantial frame saunters up.

"The answer to what, Emma? I am dying to know what answer is so wonderfully hilarious to three grown women."

Interlude

Beep, beep. Beep, beep. Beep, beep.

"Good afternoon. Hunnable Motors."

"Hello, Robert. Lizzie Everett speaking. How are you?"

"All the better for talking to you, ma darlin'. Sorry I couldn't say goodbye properly on Saturday. I'm always being dragged off to sort out some last-minute panic."

"That's why I'm phoning you now. Judith, Emma and I all wanted to thank you so much for inviting us to the motocross. We thoroughly enjoyed it. Would you please thank Jeremy, too, we didn't manage to bump into him before we left."

"I will. He's very knowledgeable about motorbikes of all kinds. Was he with you for long?"

"Yes, he was very helpful but I think he struggled a bit with supervising three women at once. I do hope he wasn't offended? I'm not at all sure that he took to our jocularity very well. He's quite old-school, isn't he?"

"Good way to describe him. But you lot are probably a right handful en masse. In fact, *you* alone are a rather delicious *two* handfuls!" The air on the end of the phone had to wait for several seconds before being parted again.

"Anyway, Lizzie, what I would say is: don't misjudge Jeremy because of his public-school exterior. He's one of the kindest, most generous men I know. After his wife became terminally ill with cancer, he realised how few hospices there were around this area.

He gave away a seriously valuable plot of land on the outskirts of Bury St Edmunds *and* set up a trust to fund the building work."

Lizzie hadn't expected vehement loyalty in Robert and it wrong-footed her.

"My apologies. It was rude of me to pass comment when I don't really know Jeremy at all. Anyway, thank you both again. We really appreciated the chance to see such an exciting spectacle. Bye."

"Bye, Lizzie. Keep in touch."

Chapter 12

Judith

The worms of doubt and indecision are careering around in my stomach. They've been doing it for over an hour already – I have thoroughly well-evacuated bowels! Mother's 'Mother Radar' spotted my second visit (in quick succession) to the downstairs loo and the consequence is that she has followed me up the stairs. She corners me in my bedroom and begins quizzing me unashamedly for twenty minutes as I try in vain to make a simple choice on trousers. Her barrage consists of:

"What did you say his surname is? I'll ring Susanna, she lives near Barton. She's sure to know something about this Jeremy, especially if he's lived in the area for some time." A couple of tiny grey moths flutter out from behind the coats as I slide the hangers along the rail. I mutter at the inanimate collection of skirts.

"Clearly there are far too many lepidopterous insects lurking in my life right this minute!"

Mother immediately chips in.

"Pardon. What did you just say under your breath? I'm not completely deaf, remember."

Pointing a finger at my temple, I proudly start to repeat a tiny section of the encyclopaedic details which were part and parcel of my agronomy degree.

"Moths, butterflies, skippers and…" with a pause for effect "… certain mothers, are all lepidopterous insects that, in their adult state, have four membranous wings more or less covered with small scales." Her momentary offence evaporates instantly, and she sinks, chuckling, into a comfortable spectator position in the chair.

"Very impressive, darling. Now get on and apply your mind to the task in hand."

Indecision; my head is in a mire of indecision and nerves. *Shall I wear my best Armani slim-cut blue jeans with a classic white shirt and a belt – a casual but crisp look? Then I can put my blue blazer with the half-sleeves on top; that should create a good impression. Jeremy doesn't strike me as the kind of man to ever buy anything less than 'quality'. Or shall I go for something a bit more classical which is probably more Jeremy's taste ie. my tartan mid-thigh fitted skirt but with the fluffy, lightweight, loose cream jumper? Is it best to look truly feminine on a first date or is it more important for me to feel completely comfortable?*

"Going back to your first question, Mother. I haven't a clue what his surname is and *please* don't start asking all your friends about him. It would be embarrassing."

Shifting her buttocks to one side so I can lay the jeans across the arm of the Chesterfield, she continues unabated.

"It's really important that you have some notion of what his history is, dear! Do you have any idea whether he's been married more than once? Or if he has a *properly* successful business?" She raises her white eyebrows and giggles in anticipation of her own punchline. "Men are very good at bigging-up their prowess and assets, my darling girl. Both financial and physical."

Swallowing my shock, I reply with glee, "Mother, at your age you shouldn't be discussing such a subject as men's physical assets.

Now let me concentrate on getting ready or I shall end up being late!"

The moths settle on the inside surface of the wardrobe door. I press my thumb and forefinger down quickly, first on one, then the second. Their bodies disintegrate into puffs of light grey powder. *Perhaps there is no moisture in a moth's body?* A gentle blow and the smudgy remnants of their dust is gone.

"Mother, all I really want to know on this first date is whether or not we *get on*, all right? Do we have the same interests? Is he fun to be with? I must admit he does appear to be a tad too serious for my liking, but who knows, he may just be shy." A third moth zigzags erratically across the room. Mother lurches from her chair and claps her wizened hands together with a satisfying thwack.

"You are incredibly lithe when it suits you, Mother. Did you know that it's not the moth stage of the life cycle which is the culprit for munching on clothes, it's actually the larvae? They convert the keratin of wool and other natural fibres into their own food source."

Right, no more procrastinating – Armani jeans and white shirt it is.

* * *

I am immensely relieved Jeremy was of the same mind as me – to stay well away from home territory for either of us and meet at an anonymous hotel/pub mid-distance. Strolling through the entrance lobby, I spy the public bar in the distance. *Four years of singledom and my sense of propriety is still jarred by the act of walking into a public space like this, completely unescorted. I suspect I shall never either like or accustom myself to it. But hey ho, self-pity is an ugly bedfellow, Judith, so get over it.*

My eyes take a few moments to focus between the dimness of the low-ceilinged bar area and the warm sunlight streaming in via the huge bay windows. A smattering of mid-week customers are dotted about at the selection of small tables and on comfy leather sofas cleverly positioned to maximise the tranquil view across the water meadows. Unsure whether to march up and confidently order a drink or whether to find a quiet corner in which to hide, I hesitate and shift from left to right foot several times. I then sense a tentative touch to my elbow.

"Hello, Judith. What would you like to drink?"

I turn to face Jeremy and he catches me completely off guard by planting a delicate kiss first on one, then the other cheek. *Ooh, he has a rather distinguished silver sheen to the front edges of the hairline. The smattering of grey runs down to his neat, unpretentious sideburns – it really suits him. Dutch courage, I need some Dutch courage.*

"A dry white wine would be lovely, thank you." Heady particles of Polo aftershave are seeping deliciously to the top of my nose. Jeremy steers us to a reasonably secluded table and reaches to pull out a chair for me.

"Would you like to sit facing the view, Judith. Or will the sun be too bright in your eyes?"

I should be delighted that he has such immaculate manners. Instead, I am already fighting the urge to be generally naughty. He bends to neatly slide the chair under my bottom and I spy a tiny constriction of the muscles under his right eye. Five seconds later and the outer half of his eyebrow flicks in unison all the way to the far corner of his eye. So – *No, I must behave myself.*

We both begin tentatively dipping our toes into our respective histories, work and general family lives. There are no ungainly or over-invasive faux pas and he is a gentleman to the core, but *his voice has the intonation of someone who has memorised his own CV for public presentation only.* We swap anecdotes on the horrors of both private and state education, quickly progressing to discover that we both have a son currently working in South America, his as a student medic and mine, Ollie, as a linguist for Oxfam. With pride, he pulls out a tatty black-and-white photo from his wallet. I quickly interrupt his flow.

"Hold on a sec. Just get my reading glasses." The glasses case squeaks as I open it, then to my dismay I spot the vivid red masking tape inexpertly wound around the edge of one arm and across the top corner of the frame. I quickly clunk the case shut again. "Truly embarrassing, but I broke them yesterday. They're not really presentable enough to put on."

"Don't be silly. We can do it together." I look up, startled by his comment, as he swiftly places a pair of gold-rimmed specs on his own nose and adds, "Go on, your turn."

I can feel their lopsidedness, but manage a mock movie-star pout from below the lenses and, without warning, Jeremy's eyes light up. He shapes his thumbs and both forefingers into 'O's.

"Miss Moneypenny. I like."

"You are too kind, sir. Bag lady might be a more fitting description." *Genuine compliment or piss take? Not sure yet.*

Our attention returns to the photo. Jeremy's profile has softened and he volunteers:

"Of course, they've both grown a lot since this was taken. Hamish is twenty-seven now and Peter is thirty."

I study the photo with genuine interest. Wedged shoulder to shoulder and propping their bottoms against a Kawasaki motorbike, the jubilant faces of his two teenage sons are laughing into the camera. However, I can feel my impatience champing at the bit – *I want to know what really matters to this man. How can I delve beneath the façade without causing offence? At no stage today has he mentioned his wife. What happened to the mother of his children? He must have been married.* But gut instinct stops me from pressing him on the subject. I can feel an enormous thought bubble of intrusive questions floating immediately above my own head. *Stop it, Judith, there is no rush. Rome wasn't built in a day – slow down.*

By the time our starters arrive, the lightness of alcohol has already begun meandering osmotically up from my empty stomach through into my veins. I attempt to spear a prawn from amongst the slippery cocktail dressing, but errant bits of shredded lettuce persist in shooting over the edge of the round glass. Hoping Jeremy hasn't noticed I look up to find his soulful eyes registering every single move I make. *Most disconcerting.* I jabber:

"Prawn cocktail, my favourite."

"You appear to have some rebellious greens on your plate. Perhaps you should attack them with the fork. It's simply not possible to eat delicately from a glass designed for whisky, rather than food." A creeping warmth is ascending my neck. *Change the subject, Judith.*

"You mentioned rebellion. I imagine you are a Cameron fan. Am I right?" Jeremy's demeanour stiffens. For a moment he considers his reply.

"I am convinced that the political and economic contours of this country will change irrevocably if Brexit goes ahead."

Oh, he went to public school. That's a surprise! I can picture him standing on the raised stage in a village hall speaking to the assembled voters. Note to self: *Don't smirk, and wrong move, Judith – find something lighter but still intelligent as a subject matter.*

Between mouthfuls of pâté, it quickly becomes clear that Jeremy's antipathy is towards the subject of politics rather than

130

me. I glance out to a large pond. A young woman in her twenties is squatting beside a pushchair and pointing at a swan circling regally, the Persil sheen of its feathers glinting off the water. The man (presumably the father) is helping to break off chunks of crust and is handing them to a young boy to fling wildly in the direction of some mallards.

The tricky subject of the Government of the Day is dropped and Jeremy deftly steers us onto a new topic, an expertise he has perfected.

"I was standing in the queue in the bakery only a few days ago. No one ever says either 'excuse me' or 'sorry' to a stranger anymore. They just push past you regardless. I was brought up with my father's voice booming in my ears. Manners maketh man."

By this point in our date I have been emboldened by a second (large) glass of Pinot Grigio, while waiting expectantly for the main course to arrive.

"I agree totally. Speaking of manners, my Grumpy Old Woman pet hate is the use of the F word everywhere and by everybody. Some of the younger generation appear to have absolutely no adjectives or adverbs in their vocabulary."

As if on cue, the young family are settling themselves at the table next to ours. All of them, bar the five-year-old lad, have sat down quietly. Suddenly, the steely voice of the mother becomes much more insistent.

"Jason, I told you to sit down." There is a two-second pause before she continues:

"I'm going to count to three, Jason. Are you listening to me? *One.*" The little tyke has defiantly turned his back to his mother, so her voice climbs up a note, "*Two.*" He kicks a chair leg with his tiny trainer-clad foot and his mother's gritted whisper goes up one more note for the crucial number. "*Three.*"

Both Jeremy and I are glancing sideways and have given up even pretending to be listening to each other. The mother stoops on one bent knee and forcibly turns her son's shoulders till he is eye to eye and shouts,

"I told you to fucking well sit down."

Five seconds of total hush lands without preamble amongst the surrounding diners, then everyone feels guilty for staring, and the low hum of conversation resumes. The little chap's top lip starts trembling ever so slightly and, cowed, he hops up onto the chair, folds his hands neatly on his lap and stares at the floor. Without warning, Jeremy swivels his legs sideways and directs a question very calmly at the mother.

"Excuse me. I'm sorry to interrupt but my own boys, when they were little, were always fidgety in restaurants. May I show your son a magic trick?" Shocked and wrong-footed, she darts a hesitant peek at her man.

"Um, well. OK."

To my astonishment Jeremy then pulls a liquorice allsort from his pocket, and two sets of young minds become a rapt audience. Firstly, he carefully places his thumb and forefinger on the edges of the stripy sweet. Secondly, he quickly closes both his fists, turns them backwards and forwards several times. Finally, he asks the boy to choose which hand might hold the sugary reward. The mesmerised little face falls when he picks the wrong hand, but lights up again with eagerness to please when Jeremy quietly explains:

"Now, young man, if you can manage to eat your lunch nicely with your mummy and daddy like a grown-up boy – and I know you are a much more grown-up boy than your baby sister here – then I shall give you three sweets each when you finish." Jeremy then reaches forward to take the boys fingers in his own.

"We are shaking hands on this, so that means we have a deal – yes?"

Our main course arrives. The gravelly smell of charred steak assaults my internal squeamishness and I fail to stop my nose puckering ever so slightly till Jeremy comments helpfully, "Is there something wrong with your fish pie?"

I hesitate momentarily. A second glass of red wine to the better and Jeremy's coat of reserve has at last begun to unravel before my eyes. "No, no, not at all. It's absolutely perfect. I apologise, but occasionally the smell or sight of freshly cooked meat catches me off guard."

A look of anguish appears on his face until I lean in a little closer and press a reassuring gentle touch from my fingers onto the back of his hand and continue: "I am a pescatarian. I have been most of my adult life."

At this point I find myself regaling him with the reason for my abstinence from all foods meaty.

"To cut a long story short, when I was probably about thirteen years old, I had a rather unpleasant surprise one day when I walked into a friend's outhouse. She was my bestest friend and we spent a lot of time knocking about together. Well, her father used to shoot occasionally and he would hang the birds up in brace in the outhouse." Attentive to the core, Jeremy is on familiar territory.

"It's important for you to know that I only ever shoot clays. No stomach for killing these days. Active service does that to you…"

"What about the Labs?" I ask.

"Don't actually need Bruno and Chester for any sporting purposes. But yes, I am guilty of coming from an archetypical hunting, shooting, fishing family, so I can picture the scene well. Go on." Pressing himself backwards against the chair and criss-crossing his arms in front of his chest, he smirks at me. "No doubt there were small drops of blood congealing under each bird and the trauma of this carnage put you off meat for life?"

He is mocking – how dare he. On the other hand, I like him the better for it. I feign outrage in my tone, but my heart is singing.

"May I continue my story? … I rushed into the outhouse on my own to wash my wellies. It was late afternoon so the light was fading, I didn't look up at all as I was concentrating on getting the mud off. Unfortunately, as I turned to leave, my coat brushed against one of the birds and several small white bits landed on the wet concrete." An involuntary shiver runs up my spine and Jeremy notices, comes in closer, leans his elbows on the table, quietly cupping his chin in his upturned palms; he waits attentively.

"And ugh, when I poked one of the pheasants, the skin around the gunshot wound began to squirm with maggots. I was only about a foot away. The pheasant's beady eyes and its feathers were all completely still, but there was this rolling and heaving movement going on all around the broken flesh. It absolutely freaked me out. Mainly because it was so close to my head and I couldn't bear the thought that some of the maggots could have landed in my hair!"

He hasn't stirred; he keeps watching me. *Rich, dark brown, Aberdeen Angus eyes. Incredibly soulful.* Eventually he speaks.

"I am surprised. A resilient, outdoorsy woman like yourself: actually, it's one of the reasons I find you so attractive. There is a refreshing purposefulness in the way most equestrian women walk. They appear to have no need for provocative sashaying in their movement or to add any contrived buttock swinging."

Why is his voice trailing off? Why is he studying a spoon, clinking it against the cup? He isn't truly in this room with me anymore. Is someone walking across the horizon of his mind? He doesn't look up when he speaks.

"In fact, your walk reminds me so much of Esme. My late wife."

Late wife. Deceased, pushing up the daisies, she is no more of this world. How not to stomp through the flower bed of his heart? Gently does it, Jude. Find the stepping stones.

"Can I have the sweets now?"

A boyishly hopeful trill from the next table demands Jeremy's immediate attention and the moment is lost. Jeremy quickly joins the young family. He peers down at the bouncing bundle of blonde hair while trying, with great aplomb, to establish whether his criteria have been met:

1. Has the little boy eaten all his lunch?
2. Has he been polite to his mother and father throughout?

He then magically produces six sweets for the siblings to share and ceremoniously shakes the hand of the little boy. The happy chappie skips joyously after his parents and a mildly smug look of satisfaction accompanies Jeremy's quiet return to his seat opposite me. Feeling much bolder, I lean in and rest my elbows on the table between the melee of glasses, plates and condiments then fix him with (what I pray is) an inviting look. I beckon him closer.

"Well done, Jeremy. You made that little boy's day. Are you as good with women?"

* * *

The key slides into the ignition – the radio softly whirrs into life. George Harrison's melodic, male harmonies arrive:

Car engine fires up: *Got the thought of you in my sights*

Depress clutch, into gear:	*Will I need cash to impress?*
Hand brake off. Turn volume up:	*Right... wrong. Right for me?*
Look over left shoulder. Yeah – brass:	*Have I got the time, priceless time?*
Reverse – volume up, disco level:	*Am I too impatient? Keen to be wild?*
Inch forward:	*Can I do it this time?*
Peer around edge of hotel:	*Of course, it's for real.*
Traffic, traffic.	*Clear, I think it's clear. Damn it,*
	the hotel sticks out onto the bend.

WHOOOOOSH!

Motorbike: *Bloody hell, that was close!*

Interlude

Judith's number flashed up, so Lizzie answered the call and without preamble, Judith dived straight in with the bittersweet invitation:

"You mentioned a couple of weeks ago that Tarquin could do with some fast work, that he needs to be fitter. I was meant to be going to a meet on Sunday with Caroline but she's backed out. In fact she's lending me her horsebox to drive there, coz she's feeling so guilty. I wondered if you would like to join me instead? We can lord it up with five-star travel arrangements and en suite facilities."

Lizzie's mobile clattered onto the kitchen tiles. It gave her an unintended distraction for a few seconds, time to find the right words to reply.

"That's very kind, but you know I have an intrinsic dislike of moneyed privilege *and* my principles are definitely in the anti-hunting camp. It would be hypocritical of me to go."

"Honestly. You're actually being a hypocrite by not going! You've never been out with us before. So how can you make a judgement on something of which you have no first-hand knowledge?" Lizzie prised open the cigarette packet, stuck a Marlboro Light into the corner of her mouth and listened. "The bloodhound pack is totally different to your usual 'Hunting' fraternity. It's not expensive. In fact, it's a darn sight cheaper than your average football fan spends on a match at Leicester City. And yes, there are one or two upper-middle-class types. Truthfully, though, the bulk of the followers are very ordinary Sam Smiths or Helen the hairdresser."

The cigarette bobbed up and down when Lizzie mumbled,

"You'll be telling me next that the butcher, the baker and the candlestick maker all ride horses with your pack. Am I right?"

"OK, OK. Ha, ha, ha. Point taken. But seriously, you know we don't chase fluffy animals of any description. Not a fox, or a hare, or any magnificent stags. We chase human runners, for goodness' sake. People who take it in turns to run, then rest, then run again. People who love the thrill of trying to outwit and outrun a pack of hounds across the countryside. What's wrong with that? The only molestation that happens is a slobbery dose of canine licking when they finish each run." Lizzie took another leisurely drag.

"So, I won't have to yell 'What-ho', or curtsy to any assembled dukes before we set off?"

"Only if you desperately feel the need. Be serious."

"OK. Granted. You shot me down in flames with that explanation. And you've certainly given me succour for my moral conscience."

"Stop talking like a lawyer. You're not in a courtroom giving your professional assessment on someone's mental issues. Is that a 'yes', or a 'no'?"

Lizzie stubbed the butt into the wetness of the sink.

"Thank you. And yes, I shall look forward to it."

"Excellent. I'll pick you and Tarquin up at 10am sharp. No one stands on ceremony with the bloodhounds so you don't have to plait Tarquin's mane. Oh, and some riders wear a body protector over their jackets. Please, just promise me you'll do one thing."

"What's that?"

Judith's four-second pause gave Lizzie a moment to feel her pulse already quickening slightly, to acknowledge that the daredevil in her hankered after a new challenge. The reply she heard was also unexpectedly firm.

"Shelve your preconceptions for the day, will you, please? Just leave them behind in the stable. These are good people."

"No problem. I promise. Scouts honour."

Chapter 13

Lizzie wedged the toe of her leather riding boot firmly onto the metal step of the horsebox and heaved herself up to the passenger seat. Judith, clad in full hunting regalia bar her riding hat and jacket, cut an enviably attractive image. Lizzie watched her as she proceeded to fiddle about with the steering column lock. She noted Judith's unfettered mahogany locks cascading over the shoulders of her puffer jacket; the attractive tilt of her chin as she concentrated on deftly twisting the ignition key; the assured way she had swung herself up into the cab; her delighted grin as the DAF engine purred into action.

"How the hell did you persuade Caroline to allow us the use of her precious Hilton on Wheels?"

Judith shifted in her seat and adjusted the wing mirror.

"There were numerous advantages to growing up being treated by my dad as an equal to my brothers and one of them was being expected to drive the lorries. Haulage is a cut-throat business and, if the workload was heavy, Dad would sometimes send me off with an HGV to Doncaster or Newmarket to pick up a load of sales horses. Same as riding a bike, you never forget the rules for driving a lorry. Caroline's box is big, but technically it's not HGV. So here we are, lucky girls for the day."

Judith was too busy concentrating on edging the box out

onto the main road to chatter. Tarquin's feet clattered and banged dramatically as they turned sharp right. Judith threw a reassuring comment across the cab.

"He'll soon get the hang of travelling herringbone. He'll start leaning on his bottom for the corners." Lizzie began fiddling with the stereo knob on the dashboard and made a conscious decision to kick the ass of her own jealousy squarely into the bushes for a day. After all, how often would she get the chance to travel in such style?

"I'm going to have a snoop in the back while you're driving?"

Lizzie squeezed herself through the archway between the cab and the living area then quickly had to clutch at the worktop to balance herself.

"Goodness gracious. Is this mock slate on the kitchen tops? It's good enough to put in my own house, never mind in a horsebox!" She couldn't quite hear the reply over the hum of the engine noise because she was already peering around the door of the shower cubicle. She mouthed, 'Nice, very nice.'

The journey proved joyously uneventful and forty minutes later they pulled into a surprisingly unostentatious, typical East Anglian red-brick farmyard. A meandering line of assorted four-wheel drives, trailers and a tatty blue Bedford TK were crawling their way through a narrow gap between open-sided Dutch barns. Judith fired an urgent instruction at Lizzie.

"Shit, this is tight. Am I clear of the barn eaves?"

Lizzie stretched her head and shoulders through the open window. Her elevated position in such close proximity to the milling cattle below meant that her nostrils were suddenly hit by a pungent cloud of bovine excrement and silage steam.

"You're OK. Keep going." Then, as an afterthought, "I'm beginning to think there may perhaps be some advantages to my meagre old Land Rover Defender and Richardson trailer compared to a monster like this!"

They navigated the box safely through to a six-acre field at the back and lined up neatly just as the side ramp was being dropped on a huge Mercedes 6 horsebox. On the far side of the wooden partition, Judith spied several erect black and tan sterns waving erratically.

"We'll have to get a shift on and tack up quickly. Hounds are already here."

Judith stretched across the cab, nudging Lizzie in the ribs. "That's Stephanie standing on the ramp. She is one of our regular runners. She will be waiting to go in with the hounds. It's what's called 'Laying On', to make sure they recognise the right scent."

"Does a runner always go alone?" Lizzie asked, rather incredulous.

"Mostly, yes. Except if there is a new runner learning the ropes, then they go off as a pair. Right, no more chattering, into the back of the box."

* * *

First Run

The Quarry

Luc had always known he was good with dogs, but he'd only ever had to contend with one or two, never three or more simultaneously, and certainly not a pack. Isaac's reactionary words when he told him the plan were keeping him stoked. "Nothing ventured, nothing gained. Go for it, mate. We both know you can run so what the hell does it matter if you have a prosthetic leg? It won't make any difference to a bunch of dogs!"

That fateful day, years ago, it had taken only seconds for the daydreaming driver who sideswiped his motorbike to become his nemesis. The surgeons had managed to save a good six inches of bone and calf below his knee so, compared to many amputees, he knew he was extremely lucky. They had cast the prosthesis to the individual shape of his own leg and he had a moulded foot, so that ordinary shoes were quite easy to wear. The mechanics of the whole process had been strangely fascinating. Inside the mould was a carbon-fibre strip which could bend with his movements. Isaac was the one who'd persuaded him to venture outdoors again, stretch his limits, but was this going to be too far and too fast? He'd put an old spare leg in the Landy just in case.

Kitted out in loose trousers, a light sweatshirt and trainers, Luc was directed by a helpful follower to the right horsebox. He hesitated at the bottom of the ramp.

"Excuse me. Are you Mrs Caruthers?"

The slender woman at the top of the ramp turned to face him. She was of medium height with rich cocoa skin colour and dark, wide-set eyes. Her thick, contoured eyebrows added to his impression that she must have Indian ancestry.

"You must be Luc. Really appreciate you volunteering to try this. Oh, I'm Stephanie but call me Steph." And she held out her hand. He climbed the steep ramp very carefully, noticing the smallness of her hand when he shook it.

"Pleased to meet you. I gather you've been doing this for years. Did the secretary fill you in on my limitations?" The weight of two pairs of sturdy front legs was making the wooden partition bow out. Stephanie thrust her long brown ponytail to one side, stretched up on her toes then yelled into the dim interior.

"Duncan, Dodger get down... *now*. Honestly, it won't be a problem at all. We can choose the pace, especially for the first run. We just need to leave in good time."

The moment the two hounds dropped down, she flicked back a metal clip and grabbed Luc's arm. She hauled him through the tight gap into the throng of heaving bloodhound flesh. One hound managed to jump up in the crowded space, expertly placing its paws on each of Luc's hip bones for purchase, then dragged a warm, wet tongue across his chin. Stephanie's uncompromising voice demanded.

"Dodger. Will you get down. Death by slobber with this lot." She paused to fondle the nearest pair of ears then addressed her contained audience in a soft, liquid tone. "Boys and girls, meet Luc."

Several blunt claws on the end of giant canine feet were catching at the skin above his right ankle. Stephanie chuckled at the site of his rigid torso, arms held high above his head.

"Come in a bit further, Luc. You must mingle with all of them, even the ones at the back. Handle them a bit. It's really important that they all get a chance to sniff you."

The weather-beaten features of the Master appeared above the partition.

"Stephanie. Are you two ready to get going?" His ingrained laughter lines deepened and there was a mischievous tweak to his lilt when he spoke again. He'd clocked the tense inverted crescent shape of Luc's lips.

"Enjoy yourself, Luc. I can guarantee, by the time you finish the third run, you'll be telling me it's given you a bigger kick than puffing on any wacky baccy."

Five minutes later, the two runners were being bounced along in the back of a pickup truck to the start of the first run, half a mile up a dirt track. Once deposited on the brow of a hill, they set off at a leisurely jog heading north around the perimeter of a barley crop. Luc noticed that Steph had become rather quiet, but he put it down to her concentrating on the task in hand. He considered, with no need for boastful pride, that he was bloody fit. He'd done a few practice runs with Isaac recently and extra gym workouts, so he found it easy to settle into a rhythm alongside his female mentor, legs pumping, breathing measured. They skirted around the outer edges of several fields of winter wheat, sticking to the grass on the twenty-foot wide headlands. There was an unseasonable chilly breeze. The ground underfoot was soft in places, but that gave him the confidence to spend less time worrying about ruts or tripping.

They had only been running for approximately fifteen minutes when he was perplexed to notice heavy beads of sweat dripping from Steph's forehead. He had assumed she would be so much fitter! They entered some thick woodland with a broad track meandering away ahead when, between erratic panting, Steph suddenly broke the silence.

"I'm going to stop quickly and water the weeds. My stomach is playing up and I really don't feel too great." Luc could feel his blood pressure do a whoopsie and barely recognised his own voice making an involuntary girlish plea:

"Surely we haven't got time?"

Her ashen face glared back at him.

"Damn it. I've got to go. Right now." She rapidly stomped off, snapping sticks underfoot and threw a final comment over her shoulder. "Don't worry, I haven't heard hounds yet."

Forty seconds later, she reappeared.

"Right, that's better. Now let's crack on." And with that she picked up the pace into the labyrinth of trees.

"At the next fork, I want you to go left. I'll go right. Splits the pack, keeps everyone on their toes. See you at the far side."

Luc revelled in allowing his naturally long strides to eat up the ground. He noticed the fresh green buds bursting out of elm and sycamore; a haze of bluebells came and went. Feeling cocky, he even straddled a three-foot high hunt jump strategically placed on the final boundary to the wood, his feet briefly thrusting off to land on the far side. Steph was resting against some rails.

"Beat you."

She set off in a straight line, peering left and right to the far hedges then, between pants, hurled yet another instruction.

"Can't see any walkers. Remember, we must run straight across the line of the footpath in the middle of this field. Don't want hounds getting distracted by another human scent."

The sticky clods of soil hitching a ride on Luc's trainers were splattering his trouser legs. Steph's profile was weirdly pale with a few clusters of pink blotches creeping out above her collar.

"OK, Luc. We'll hook left here quickly away from the hedge. That's it, keep going, keep going. *Further.*"

Another 200 metres on, Steph did a sudden about-turn, creating a small loop and, still at full pace, retraced her steps. Luc was starting to feel like a child running along in Steph's wake while she barked at him, his machismo a little battered. Within seconds he caught up and found she was rubbing her sleeves firmly in and out of a low hedge. Inhaling, she ordered.

"Quickly. Do the same as me. Want to make sure they come back after the false trail we've laid and jump here. Hounds can get over this one because it's not too high and there's a rail in the middle."

Then she was off again, squeezing her way through a clump of thinner branches in the hedge line to the grass field on the other

146

side. She raised her flattened hand to shield her eyes and squinted into the distance.

"Where are the sheep? You're taller, can you see them?" Luc wobbled himself up onto a thick felled trunk before replying.

"Yep. They're all bunched up together in the farthest corner." Then he cupped his hand to his ear and exclaimed,

"I think I can hear hounds."

Every few seconds, way off in the distance, they heard a bark from just one hound followed by silence, followed by several hounds giving tongue, followed by silence for another ten seconds.

The two runners were soon past the field of sheep and spotted a waiting pickup truck to mark the finish point. They had slowed to a brisk walk for the final 500 metres and Luc left unvoiced a sense of anticlimax that it had been so easy. A tiny, ancient lady hopped out of the cab, hunched over with a permanent bend in her back. She grabbed two buckets and handed one each to Luc and Steph. They waited patiently for several more minutes, their own breath calming. A burst of baying broke out immediately before a dozen black and tan bodies flew towards them over the final hedge.

"There, Luc. Did you hear that? They raised their voice at the hedge we marked."

The rest of the pack appeared in threes and fours over the brush, their ears flying skyward as they leapt off the top rail. Luc copied Steph and flung handfuls of chopped liver and dried biscuits in a sphere around himself. Mouths open, tongues lolling, the pack started snuffling about, searching for their tasty reward in the tufty grass. Steph crooned praises.

"Hiya, Romeo. Well done, Daphne. Hurry up, Duncan… last again."

* * *

First Run

The Field

Lizzie decided she would always remember this day as a flashing series of magical revolving snapshots vividly seared into her memory bank. It went as follows:

Judith – glamorous as ever in black jacket, hair corralled into a straining hairnet and black velvet bow.

The stirrup cup – a choice of ginger wine or port, handed around in polystyrene cups by two jolly ladies. Tarquin was unable to stand still for more than a few seconds, knocking sausage rolls flying as the aforementioned jolly lady passed them up to Lizzie's gloved hand.

The field – Lizzie had anticipated the rising of her own hackles if there was a plethora of Hooray Henrys, but instead the refreshing mix of followers included an extremely round Humpty Dumpty middle-aged farmer chatting heartily with a very dapper gent; several fifty-something women like herself on their favourite and only Riding Club mount; a couple of nubile young ladies complete with full make-up, prancing around on their shiny thoroughbreds; three teenage girls in their uniform of tweed jackets and Pony Club ties; sundry other unmemorable riders: and last but not least an extremely hairy 14.2 pony ridden by a character of an old boy celebrating his seventieth birthday. The only gratingly upper-crust monotone she detected came from a father of twin twelve-year-old boys called, unsurprisingly, Barnaby and Rufus – their father regularly throwing these names out to hang important in the air above the assembled riders.

Judith quickly reminded Lizzie, "You promised to behave, remember…" when Lizzie expressed an urge to yell, 'Barn Roof!' each time the twins came past her.

The Master addressed them all, welcoming any newcomers and pointing out how very lucky they were to be hunting over land which was never otherwise open to the public. His serious expression demanded that we heed his plea to respect the farmer's land. Then with his free hand he gallantly lifted his hat and doffed it in our direction.

"Enjoy your day, ladies and gentlemen."

Hounds followed the Master out through the farmyard and were immediately held in check by the confines of the narrow lane. Occasionally, a particularly keen hound would make a run for it along the verge to get ahead. The Master briskly dropped the long, coiled loops of leather whip to dangle beside his leg then raised his arm swiftly. An impressive thwack rang out as the whip whooshed through bare air and he yelled,

"Romance, Renee. Hold up." Then with more urgency, "Romance, Renee. *Will you hold up.*" The mavericks in question cast a look behind, caught guilty of disobedience, then duly dropped back.

Lizzie's knees had turned to jelly. She didn't consider herself to be a sissy rider but she suddenly regretted her reckless decision to risk life and limb. Judith grabbed Lizzie's arm, then pointed in the direction of an official-looking rider at the head of the procession.

"Pay attention. This is important. That's the Field Master on the right and, as his name suggests, he is in charge of the field. That's us. Always follow any instructions he gives you without question."

The horse in front had a thick red ribbon tied at the top of its tail. It fly-bucked dramatically, its shod hooves missing Rommel's nose by inches. Judith swiftly grabbed at the reins and shortened up Rommel's trot before suggesting to the offending rider,

"Red ribbon. You should be at the back."

The two large ports Lizzie had swigged in quick succession were sloshing around in her empty stomach as the clattering throng suddenly hooked right through an open gateway. She vaguely registered a final instruction yelled by Judith.

"However strong Tarquin gets, for God's sake don't ever ride in front of the Master."

And they were off.

A baying stream of black and tan ran ahead, everyone lurching into a fast canter. Caught off guard, her reins far too long, Lizzie had allowed Tarquin to leap twenty feet ahead of Judith and Rommel. But within minutes Judith had worked her way forward past several riders to reassure her friend and ride side by side.

"Don't panic, Lizzie. He'll settle down. Ram your left fist into the base of his mane and use it as an anchor."

That first run for Lizzie flew by and she really couldn't remember much about it. Except that, true to Judith's expertise, she'd got the hang of controlling Tarquin. In the blink of an eye, the field reached the first stopping point. Sod the orange squash. She tugged her gloves off with her teeth and lit up.

* * *

The Quarry

Luc was feeling really quite good. Apparently, the couple doing the second run had already set off and this was his chance to relax and soak up the sense of ambient camaraderie. He gulped down a quantity of elderflower cordial. Everyone seemed happy, enjoying a breather at the end of the first run, so he filled his cup up again and began to saunter over towards a group of riders when... wallop – something hit him from behind and he lurched, knees first, onto the ground. The bay horse in question was already ten feet past him as he recovered himself enough to stand upright again.

The rider pulled her horse around to face him spluttering,

"I am SO sorry."

Luc, still gathering his faculties together, looked up into his assailant's face.

"Lizzie?"

Her horse appeared to be dancing on hot coals so her answer came out rather disjointed.

"Luc, what are you doing here?"

He had to throw a reply at her back as her horse headed away from him.

"I'm running."

Her second apology was frail.

"I really am sorry. Perhaps see you later?"

Luc decided that he'd be much safer if he stood in the middle of all the people and dogs; let someone else get bowled over on the periphery! He watched as a group of vehicles pulled up and parked at higgledy-piggledy angles on the track before disgorging sundry foot followers. Odd, he thought, he'd always assumed that hunting only ever involved those who could ride a horse – a sport for toffs, an anathema to your average man on the street. Yet he was quickly cracking jokes with a plumber and a loud, fleshy Lancashire lass who ran a cleaning business. Her two Springer Spaniels, eyes glistening, tails fidgeting, kept weaving their leads in knots through her legs. Occasionally, the farm labourer, standing a little apart from their chattering group, would uncross his arms and let out the baler twine attached to his terrier. Then he would chip in and grunt an observation – a succinct, 'Runnin' well today,' or 'Scents risin',' – before crossing his arms across his grubby coat again.

The pack was quietly being held together in a group by two hunt staff on horseback. They cut an impressive sight, rich-red hunting jackets, polished black riding boots, white stocks folded in loops and held in place with gold stock pins in the shape of a hunting whip. The crooked but absolutely delightful old biddy was helping them. Luc found her highly amusing – at full height, she would have been no more than 5' 2" and she was swamped by blue overalls plus a pair of green wellies reaching up over her knees. If a hound tried to break away from the pack, she barred its exit with raised arms, a stern growl and a 'get on back,' and they always heeded her.

Then Stephanie dropped her bombshell – she'd beckoned him over to have a chat with the Master. She rested her palm on the neck of the Master's horse as if to steady herself.

"Ever so sorry, chaps, but I feel really unwell. I can't possibly do the third run. You'll have to manage on your own, Luc." And, despite her queasy stomach, she valiantly travelled in the back of the pickup with him, blurting out reminders and directions till he was deposited alone at the agreed start for the third run.

* * *

Third Run

The Quarry

He checked his watch, found a dryish spot in the lee of the hedge and leant back against a post. He shivered then began pummelling his calf muscle; the last thing he needed was cramp. He kept running through the list of dos and don'ts in his mind – wait till hounds are close, don't set off too soon, scent is vital. He looked at his watch again – a quarter to three, they could be here anytime soon. He stood up. He cupped his hands to his ears; could that be them or was it just a trick of the wind? Absent-mindedly he raised his hand to his mouth and began chewing a nail. Another five minutes passed; his teeth accidentally nipped too hard.

"Bugger." He walked a few paces forward, unzipped his fly and marvelled at just how far piss will go when the wind is behind it!

Then he heard them.

He gulped in a lungful of air and set off up the narrow bridle path. He settled into his cross-country runner mode, but this was different. He knew he had a twenty-minute start while the field stopped for their second rest break, but there wasn't another soul in site. No Steph. No pacemaker.

The valley opened up as he came out of the bridle path. He turned left, skirted the edges of three fields, scuffed his feet about a bit on the nearside of the ditch, slid on his bottom going down and rubbed his arms on the upside. He headed for the jump over to the right. He registered that his chest was already rasping in and out and forced himself to cut the pace a tiny bit. Despite the extra layer of sock, he could feel a tender spot growing on his stump. Steph's words popped up again: "The first time you run alone, no matter how tough you think you are, you'll struggle not to panic."Now he had a quandary. Both the Master and Steph had said the longer route to the finish was up through a little copse, creating a loop, but that if he felt bold and brave it would give the followers a great ride to have to cross the river. So, which way? He decided, *To hell with it,* and braced his legs for running down the hill towards the river. *Think, think, think.* What else was he supposed to do? Had he forgotten any tricks? The grass was damp, the gradient was steep, he slipped, banging down hard on his backside. *Oops, better stop for a few moments, catch my breath.*

Perhaps I should do a mini triangle shape with the run, coming back to this point again? Yep, I could do that. And off he ran again.

Then he heard them.

Down the valley. *How far away?* He realised he'd been too damn cocky. He headed for the lowest edge of the field. The bank dropped away gradually, the imprints of cattle's feet trodden in patches. It was bare of grass and his trainers sucked a little into the soggy sand. He stopped. Thankfully the water was perfectly clear, he could see the darker round edges and shapes of the stones. He fretted – *what if I lose my leg here? But there's no time to paddle in timidly.* He put his good leg in first, braced himself. The current was gentle and the water only came up about a foot. The muscle-seizing coldness was what surprised him. The water dragged at his legs, so he lifted each step high, wading the eighteen-feet to the far side. As he scrambled out, soaked to his knees, all he could think was, *Wet stump sock, just get on with it, man.*

The baying was so much closer. *They must be coming down the hill.* Heart thumping, he scuttled into the oilseed rape crop, cutting off the corner, his brain belatedly telling him he'd just committed a crime. Still running, he panted an angry

"Fuck it", knowing he should have run on the boundary. He registered that the valley had become weirdly quiet, only an occasional solitary bark rang out. *What's happened? Just keep running, Luc.*

He was now only one short field away from the finish when a cacophonous *Hound of the Baskervilles* baying rang out the full length of the valley. Still running, Luc dared to swivel his head; he saw that four or five hounds were within 100 metres. The fear in his temples pumping, he hurtled to the waiting Isuzu and the haven of Ancient Woman and her blue overalls. Blowing hard, he positioned himself behind the tiny dot of a woman, hurriedly reaching his hand around her to grab a fistful of raw meat. He glanced down at the pure white crown of her hair. *She barely comes up to the height of my heart!* A grown man shielding from the approaching wave of black and tan flesh. He knew it was ridiculous, utterly ridiculous, but he felt miraculously safe in the knowledge that she could control them.

* * *

The Third Run

The Field

The cumulative effect of two runs meant that by the second break Tarquin was a wired mass of thoroughbred confusion. He had slowly wound himself up like a ratchet, more and more and more. The moment the pace had slowed from a canter or gallop down to a trot, he would throw all his might into heaving the reins straight through Lizzie's fingers with a leaping plunge of his head high in the air, then down to the ground. His neck, clipped only the week before in anticipation of this special day out, was dripping with soapy sweat. The moment the field had caught hounds and stopped, Lizzie flung herself out of the saddle onto terra firma, ran up her stirrups and began walking Tarquin in leisurely circles a little away from the throng. The tendons in her wrists were screaming in protest. Judith strolled up to join Lizzie, Rommel's reins neatly slung up over her right shoulder. Despite his impressive 16.3 hands of grey-coated meat and muscle, he was plodding along, a picture of manners, calmly to heel behind Judith. Bloodhounding was a regular event for him and it showed.

"Here, Lizzie. I brought one for you." Lizzie grabbed at the cup of orange liquid in Judith's hand. She attempted to slurp the contents, but Tarquin pushed his head impatiently into her back, knocking sticky juice down her brand-new polka dot stock tie. Lizzie turned on her steed, pushed to her limits, her voice decidedly angry:

"Tarquin, will you sodding well stand still. I can't even light up when you're like this."

Judith handed her friend a chocolate brownie and the two women continued to stand a little apart from the field. Judith put Rommel between herself and the east wind filtering its way through a copse of beeches. Even the hounds, hot only fifteen minutes earlier, had edged towards the shelter of the bushes and long grass at the foot of the trees. No longer ripe for the run, energies partly sated, they were lounging quietly in a group within twenty feet of the Master. Occasionally, a follower or one of the helpers would potter up to run a casual hand over the silky crown of a black head and stare mesmerised into the dark pools of those soulful eyes. Still mounted, everyone else was chattering or wolfing down cake. A cheery burst of "Happy birthday to you. Happy birthday to you" broke out as a collection of riders raised their cups in the air and others backslapped the septuagenarian.

Tarquin eventually became stationary, one hip dropped and his left pastern bent in order to rest a weary leg. Judith rummaged around in the depths of her inside jacket pocket and retrieved her special hip flask – the very first present her (once, but no longer) dearly beloved Patrick had given her. He'd gone to the trouble of having her initials engraved in the silver in flowery italics. She held it out to Lizzie.

"Time for some sloe gin."

Refreshed at last, Lizzie chirpily observed, "Now I know why you suggested I should buy a sensible cob. Not a dot, dot, dot thoroughbred. If I remember correctly, your exact words were, 'Choose a horse for comfort and durability, Lizzie, not flashiness and speed.' And right now, I wish I'd listened to you."

Judith began gathering up her reins.

"Never mind. Most of the time Tarquin suits you so well. You're not the kind of woman to pootle about on a horse that steers around corners like a Land Rover. You're a '2.4-litre whizz round the lanes' kind of gal." She touched Rommel's shoulder and he sidestepped closer to the wooden fence. Hanging onto the pommel of the saddle Judith reversed up the rails then flung over her jodhpur-clad leg, landing expertly in position.

"Come on, mount up. You'll be fine. He's settled down again. This next bit of country will sort out the men from the boys. And it's stunningly beautiful scenery."

Mounted and ready for the off again, Lizzie found, sure enough, that Tarquin was less fractious. At last she had the chance to actually take in the atmosphere. The field were still milling around in one corner of the huge grass meadow. Alongside the adjoining field was a twenty-metre strip of headland. Normally topped once a year by farmers, this land had instead been left to grow cover for wildlife and birds. Lizzie became aware that the hairy bay pony and its birthday-boy rider had sidled up. The old gent's jacket was sun-faded from decades of wear and Lizzie noticed a couple of small chunks of dried mud still clinging to the underside of the pony's badly brushed mane. So, she was surprised to hear him address her in such a quietly sophisticated manner, the voice belying the rather tatty exterior of both man and his mount.

"May I introduce myself. I'm Percy. Are you acquainted with hunting or just new to our pack?"

Tarquin began snuzzling his lips in small circles on the crest of the pony's neck and, by default, the closeness of the two equines soon squashed Lizzie's boot hard against Percy's knee. He carefully removed his glove and reached over to shake Lizzie's hand. Lizzie felt her cheeks warming.

"Lovely to meet you, Percy. My apologies if my horse is being a bit too familiar, but this is the calmest he has been all day." Percy waved an arm in the general direction of hounds, noses skirting inches above the ground.

"Did you know that a bloodhound can follow the faintest scent trails quite undetectable by any other dog?" Lizzie felt she could at last voice a burning but probably stupid question at this kindly man. She hadn't dared ask Jude.

"Please tell me – why are they called bloodhounds? It creates such a grotesque image."

Percy visibly puffed out his chest a little and cleared his throat in order to reply.

"The name bloodhound is thought to have originated in the same way as a thoroughbred is called a blood horse, thereby a thoroughbred hound. Or put simply – a hound from bloodlines and *not* a bloodthirsty hound!"

"Ah, thank you. Now I understand."

"The breed was originally imported by William the Conqueror possibly from stock of the Flemish monastery of St Hubert."

"Goodness, you really know your stuff, Percy."

They watched the Master circling his horse at the walk and letting out an intermittent "Yoo, yoo, yoo" call. Then all hell broke loose. The tall grasses and half-dead maize stalks swayed and rustled sixty metres away and... whoosh... ten roe deer flashed in a bunch, fleeing as one. Bloodhounds are not sight animals and, uncannily, there was a good twenty-second pause before two hounds spotted the bobbing white tails heading away towards the skyline. A couple of barks rang out followed by an urgent "Dibble… *no*," from one of the whippers-in. He kicked his horse from a standing halt in hot pursuit, clods of earth flying, and within seconds all that could be heard was a diminishing "Dibble… I said *no*."

The two hounds got no more than 300 metres before the whipper-in managed to arrest them in their tracks. He quickly positioned the hulk of his stunning grey steed ready to bar any escape and the brown outlines of the receding deer merged into the horizon. Then the pack picked up the runner's scent and…

They were off.

Tarquin stuck like glue to his new friend, the hairy pony, as they bowled along. He began adjusting and finally slowing his canter, giving Lizzie a chance to marvel at the pack streaming across the fields. You couldn't call them fast – they lolloped and barked, ears flying up and down, up and down, but the effect on her senses was primal, real, heart-punching.

Hot on the heels of the Master, the twin boys were the first to tackle a big hedge, the tabletop rumps of their matching coloured cobs jumping as a pair. Rider after rider flew at the obstacle, bar a few who scuttled off to one side to hop over a ditch. The flashy ex-racehorse waited till the very last second, then in that penultimate stride, rammed on the brakes, launching his Poser Babe rider in the flip of a cartwheel straight over his shoulder.

Out hunting, there is no hanging about whining. No time to dab tentatively at falling tears. Poser Babe was on her feet within seconds, limping as she hustled her horse out of the way, brown branch stripes patterning her jacket, a testament to her fall. No time for hesitation, Lizzie stuck with Percy and the shaggy pony, riding one horse's length behind the resolute pair. The blackthorn obstacle loomed higher than the pony's shoulders as Percy's energetic kicking and growls of "Go on boy, go on" propelled the pair up and over. Four pairs of hooves bit deep into the grassy landing and Lizzie could just make out the words which Percy threw out against the wind.

"No corpses at this one."

They galloped on amid frantic swerves to left or right at a screeched call of

"Ware rabbit hole." Her mental translation 'beware' too slow as a gaping one-foot-wide hole in the ground flashed under Tarquin's belly. After ten minutes, the pack ground to a halt on the side of a steep hill and began snuffling about. Judith parked Rommel alongside her friend.

"Told you this would be a good run."

Then they were off again.

Down the hill, stumbling through a muddle of loose undergrowth, no chance to bottle it, Tarquin was sandwiched between Percy's pony and Rommel, heading straight for the river. Lizzie spotted Jude steal a worried glance in her direction, heard her flung instruction, "Remember to breathe, Lizzie. Breathe."

Lizzie's words – "You know he isn't good with water" – disappeared into the air as unlike his veteran friends, Tarquin leapt rather than trotted into the Stour. Lizzie flailed wildly to regain a dropped rein while still miraculously managing to remain on board.

Judith giggled and yelled,

"Impressive. Pippa Funnel is in our midst!"

The horses waded; the water churned. They were out the other side and off again. The icy water had soaked in uneven blotches through Lizzie's jodhpurs and knickers; the seams under her knees were already chafing but she didn't give a damn. Inhibitions buried, all fear thoroughly rousted, all worldly cares scorched away, she rode like the rest of them, alive, excited, hungry at that final hedge and flew. Free, so joyously free.

* * *

Twenty-five black-and-tan heads were leaning over long, low plastic troughs. Panting and slurping, panting some more, here and there one would shake violently, sending flumes of slobber and water sideways. A few had flopped down only to change their minds and rise to quench their thirst a little more or roll in the grass, legs akimbo. Judith and Lizzie were walking side by side cooling their horses. A whipper-in was making his way past and calling to all and sundry.

"Did anyone notice a stray hound slink off on the last run? We're missing one."

Dejected at all the "No" replies, he wandered off.

The two women enthusiastically thanked the Master and headed on foot down the lane towards the farm. Necks stretched tired and low, Tarquin and Rommel were striding quietly behind their owners. The ring of their hooves on tarmac was barely audible over Lizzie's high-pitched babbling. The highlights, the lowlights, Lizzie kept bombarding her friend with a large dose of verbal diarrhoea and neither of them really looked, until the last few yards, at the woman marching towards them. There was a steady click, click, click as her walking stick dug into the road and she strained to brace herself against the forward propulsion of a bloodhound. Hair tousled, she was wearing walking boots and a thick jumper and appeared 'normal to the eye' in every way. That is, until they got closer. Lizzie had a quick sideways glance at Judith, but said nothing. The woman came closer. Lizzie's focus confirmed what her mind couldn't quite process...

the short constraint with which the hound was being led was a white bra!

The two women halted their horses, keeping them to one side in the narrow lane, and Lizzie smiled openly when she voiced her barely disguised incredulity.

"Is that really what I think it is around his neck?" Bra Lady stopped, the elastic of one shoulder strap clenched tight in her fingers, the second straining into folds of black skin and hair. Totally matter-of-factly, she replied.

"Yep, that's right. I didn't have anything else I could use and he wouldn't stick with me otherwise. Needs must and all that."

Lizzie jammed her tongue into her cheek and waited till Bra Lady was out of earshot. Pent-up laughter brewing, she turned to Judith and exploded with,

"Wow. That has to be the daftest sight I've ever seen."

They continued up the lane, slowly getting closer to a solitary figure walking ahead of them. Lizzie recognised the height, the build and the clothing of Luc, but with each metre that their faster walk closed in on his, her concern grew. He was limping badly, an incredibly bedraggled and wet-to-the-knees sight. She found herself racking her brain, trying to remember if she had ever actually watched him walk? No. She realised that on the two previous occasions that they'd met, he'd been pretty much stationary at the cabin or the pub. As they came up behind him, Luc stopped, moved over to give them space. They halted their horses, stood face to face. Lizzie moved to get closer and the quake in her voice was genuine:

"Goodness, Luc. Did Tarquin injure you? Have you twisted your knee or something?" She reached out to touch his arm but he raised one hand palm first at her, held it for a few symbolic moments, then rested it back on his hip.

"I'd feel happier if you don't get any closer with your wild beast, thank you, Lizzie."

Her lips and nose folded in towards each other.

"Can't even offer to give you a lift, so sorry. Oh, and everyone has been saying how brilliant that last run was. Sincerely hope I haven't scared you away from doing it again? Must have been incredibly hard for you to keep on to the finish when you are clearly in pain. I am seriously impressed."

Luc visibly rallied himself a little, unrounding his shoulders.

"Honestly, this…" he pointed at his leg, "… is nothing to do with earlier. And no, I admit I'm pretty exhausted but it's been the best adrenalin rush I've had in years. Fantastic experience and I'm sure I shall be back."

Lizzie found herself sneaking a quick backward glance at Luc as they walked away. Her internal radar was beeping and she thought that, perhaps, she rather liked a military man. No predisposition towards flashiness, no drama queen tendencies, just resilience and intelligence. By the time they reached the next gateway she had made a decision. She halted Tarquin and hailed Luc as he came closer.

* * *

The shrill whistle of the kettle demanded that Lizzie turn off the gas. In hindsight it felt to her as if it announced an ugly shift in Judith's whole persona. Before its piercing noise, Judith had been her best ebullient self. Busy stacking tack in the locker on the side of the horsebox, offering the horses water, locating the teabags. But then she had disappeared into the back of the box eager to hang up the hay nets and by the time she re-entered the living space, a black van with 'Stockdale Carpentry' emblazoned on its

163

sides was squeezing into the narrow space by the ramp. Once Luc had hauled himself carefully into the box, Lizzie became hostess; after all she had been the one to press the hospitality:

"Come and sit down, Luc, you deserve a rest."

She gently pushed Judith's arm away from the fridge, waved a teaspoon in the direction of the empty space next to Luc.

"You're driving us home. I'll make the tea." Judith gave her a strange sideways look of rebellion and ignored the implied order.

Mug in hand, Lizzie knew she was on a mission. She sat down thigh to thigh beside Luc, leant back into the soft cushions, turned on her interviewing voice. She wanted to know, what kind of man is Luc? She smiled, he reciprocated, the questions flowed. Cleverly intertwined between observations, exclamations and a joke here and there, she watched and listened. All the while, very aware that Judith's veil had descended, that her friend's attempts at appearing civil were short, verging on belligerent replies. *Why is it that Jude only ever reveals the exciting colours in her character to very close friends and family? Plonk her on a horse or in the driver's seat of a twenty-five-foot lorry and she shines with panache and confidence. Where has that Judith gone?*

The journey home proved unexpectedly quiet, considering their joyous mood prior to Luc's entrance. Judith's focus remained unusually fixed on the road ahead, and the quizzical inflection of tone when she did eventually speak was not lost on Lizzie.

"You seem to get on especially well with Luc." Lizzie dug the nails of one hand into her other wrist, replied as calmly as she could manage. She avoided looking across at her friend:

"Oh it's just banter. Thought I should be friendly after bashing into him with Tarquin. He's a little above my preferred age range in case that's what you are wondering?"

"How's Perfect Man, are you seeing him this week?" Lizzie suddenly turned towards the side window and pointed at a bird gliding above the hedge.

"Ooh look, a buzzard." She brought her hand up to cover her cheek, continued staring out of the window long after they'd passed the bird. She wished her blush would subside.

Chapter 14

Judith

The trouble with owning a horse is that, unlike a cat or dog, you cannot house them within the comfort of your own home. Slamming the back door (*note to self – really must get it fixed before the hinges shear from the frame*), I step resolutely into the persistent drizzle. *No one will see me and I don't give a fudge how unsexy my hat is.* I flip the earflaps down and pick up a jog through the dim haze for the few hundred yards heading to the stables. Britain in May – the heavy, bulbous, slate-coloured clouds have cast a looming weight over the landscape. Thor, God of thunder, is starting to make his presence known. He is brewing up a severe case of indigestion – his grumbling stomach a distant, audible entity.

I hate getting back this late to sort out my boys and it's so damn dark this evening. The methodical daily routine, so familiar to me, kicks in – I swing both stable doors wide and flick on the internal lights. The rays from the windows and doorway cast pathways across the yard and out to the paddock beyond. *It's bloody cold out here for early summer. Why are my calf muscles aching so badly today? Must be from trudging across all those clay fields at Holland Place. I swear there was close to a kilo of soil on each of my wellies every time I lifted my foot. Typical, it was that particular farm today, when the land is sodden – all 400 acres to walk in one afternoon! Never mind, Jude, get a shift on then you can run a seriously hot bath.*

I grab the stuffed hay nets, one in each arm, from the open-sided hay store. I lift the first above the dustbin-sized plastic container and ever so gradually start to submerge it in the cold water. *I wonder how many hundreds (probably thousands) of hay nets I have soaked in this way over the years?*

My peripheral vision momentarily registers a flicker of lightning zigzag across the sky. *Oh, hurry up, Jude, for goodness sake.* I crouch over the narrow bin and press down hard, straining to force the overly large second net where it really doesn't want to go. I should know better – the dispersed water suddenly whooshes up the side and pours out, water falling predictably straight into my left welly. *Oh bollocks.* One dry foot, one seriously wet, I pull the collar of my wax coat up to stop the damp seeping in any further than my chilled neck, and hurry to the gate. *Where have Rommel and Nugget got to? I bet they're sheltering under the trees with this storm brewing. Little buggers – why the hell is it that when you most want them to be waiting patiently to come in, they piss off as far away as possible?* I climb onto the second rung of the gate and balance my body forward so I can cup my hands around my mouth and yell.

"*Come on, boys. R-o-o-o-o-mmel. N-u-u-gget. Come o-o-o-n boys.*"

I have no idea why lengthening the 'O' when I shout works for calling the horses from a distance. Must be something to do with that particular sound projecting well in an open space. *But tonight, it isn't!* So I jump down, unlatch the bolt, swing the gate wide open and walk back to the feed room.

'Ping Ping – missed call'. *Ooh, it's from Jeremy and he's phoned me so soon after seeing him only yesterday. Yippee.* I know that I must not appear too keen; I decide to wait an hour or so till I've finished putting the horses to bed. *Perhaps if I switch the radio on to full volume? Music is a higher pitched sound and the horses may hear it. Any cue is better than none.* The prospect of resorting to a torch and trudging around the field in the relentless murk is not appealing. I decide, *Radio 4 is no good. I need something more upbeat to wing its way to the nether regions of the field.*

The numbers on the upper surface of my seriously tatty Phillips radio are obscured by a thick layer of dust and general grime. Drips have been making their way in a trickle from my sleeves to my fingers. I use them to smudge the glass clear then twist the dial to Smooth FM. Volume up, I unplug the radio from the wall and place it in the doorway. Michael Jackson blares back in my face. Disco – a perfect panacea at the end of a tough day. I swivel around to wrest the lids off feed bins. Rhythm, beat, rhythm, beat. 'Wanna Be Startin' Somethin'' demands that I move to the groove and, in time to the drum, the floppy feed buckets thwack to the floor. *Am I on the cusp of a personal revolution here? Should I break the mould, let rip with the vocals? Mother's out of earshot. So, damn it – deep breath in, Jude, and... go.*

In my world, the voice that pitches to the rafters of the feed-room roof is Beyoncé's or Annie Lennox's, and I intersperse the song, the beat, the pure joy of the rhythm with flamboyant arm and leg moves.

I twirl to dump the handfuls of chopped dried grass. *One, two, three.*

I am a hot, lithe twenty-year old clad in figure-hugging, glittering Lycra. *Woo, woo.*

I am gyrating my hips beside Michael Jackson. *Yeah, yeah.*

I am banging two large, wooden mixing spoons hard against the tin bins. *Yeah, yeah.*

Heel, toe, heel, toe – moonwalk (not easy in Hunters). *Rhythm, beat, rhythm, beat.*

Then silence… *Oh, peanuts, why has the radio stopped?*

A small female voice, which I recognise so well, cuts immediately into the void.

"Goodness, darling. You seem incredibly cheerful despite this gruesome weather."

Mother is nonchalantly resting a shoulder against the door frame. An expression of delighted amusement on her angelic face is framed by a chequered head scarf, tied very firmly under her chin and topped off with a broad-brimmed wax hat. *Very much 'The Queen at Balmoral'. All she needs is a few corgis at her heels and the look would be complete!* However, the thick coat swamping her from the neck all the way down to her knees dispels any regal impression.

"Mother, that's not fair. Have you been watching me all this time?"

She pushes her hands deeper into her pockets.

"No, not really. I've only been here a minute or so. You were enjoying the music so much I didn't want to spoil your moment. I haven't seen you this carefree for such a long time. Has anything in particular happened?"

Mother knows me far too well. At times, living in such close proximity to her can leave me feeling constantly scrutinised and accountable, but it also means we are scarily telepathic and there is no point in me being anything less than truthful.

"Yes, it has… well, at least I think it has. I didn't tell you: yesterday I left work early and met Jeremy to take his dogs for a long walk. We went along the old railway line. It's lovely out of the wind down there."

Mother's eyebrows appear to make a dash for her hairline.

"A second date with Jeremy. It must have gone well for you to be so happy. Yes?"

I am a little reticent about giving her too much information just yet. I dare not tempt fate or presume that kismet is playing for my team. My hesitation gives her a reason to probe even more.

"Oh, and it was so lovely and sunny yesterday, darling. Very romantic. Tell me, has he kissed you yet?" I am struggling to stop the upward inflection in her question from grating against the personal privacy settings in my head and, besides, I have also clocked her footwear.

"Mother. Why on earth are you wearing your slippers to come down to the stables? Your ankles are all wet!" Briefly she glances down but is not put off the scent in the least and continues like a terrier down a rabbit hole.

"Well, did he or didn't he kiss you?" I bite my lip but Mother continues unabated:

"Oh, for goodness' sake. You are old enough and wise enough now to know that women always have to take charge in a relationship."

Mother's words prompt a flash visual reminder of Jeremy and me saying goodbye at the end of our walk. We'd been so wonderfully relaxed and chatty strolling together, his two chocolate Labradors bouncing in and out of the undergrowth, tails in permanent wag mode. We'd had quite a heated discussion on politics and any differences in our ideologies seemed to draw us closer, as we recognised in each other a thinking, literate, functioning adult and rejoiced in the friendly sparring. So much so, that for a mile or so towards the end, we had even held hands. However, the convivial atmosphere had suddenly evaporated as we arrived back at the cars. Jeremy became unnecessarily busy loading his grubby dogs into his Discovery. Neither of us could quite work out the correct "form" our parting should take. Jeremy had rather formally gone to open my car door for me, but I couldn't just let myself leave without knowing what it would feel like. Our bodies were within inches as I bent in order to squeeze past him into the driver's seat. But the urge to know was ricocheting around off the squash-court walls inside my forehead. Surely, he must want to know by now, too? No preamble, no gazing into each other's eyes with pent-up expectation, no caressing each other's cheeks, no soppy words of love. Instead I had stood upright again and, clutching his coat sleeves in each of my hands, had pulled him up tight to my own chest, then planted a real smacker of a kiss firmly on his unprepared lips.

"Thank you *so* much, Jeremy. This has been a lovely afternoon treat for me."

His neck had flushed red in a way that I assumed only ever afflicted women so I had quickly brushed past the embarrassment and slid into my car. *Brazen; had I been plain brazen? Had I completely mucked it up?* He had quickly recovered his composure and leaned in to make eye contact.

"Yes, Judith. I've really enjoyed your company, too. I'll ring you in a few days and we can arrange for you to come to my house."

Mother has, by now, folded her arms across her chest while waiting patiently for my reply. This time I cannot contain the sharpness in my tone.

"But I did, Mother. I... kissed *him*."

The metallic clatter of shod hooves on concrete spontaneously distracts us both from a tricky moment and I grasp the chance to avoid a full-on confrontation. Firmly and swiftly, I guide her out of the doorway as a vivid streak of lightning illuminates the landscape.

"All right, boys, not so fast. Steady, steady."

Rommel and Nugget would normally slow right down on getting close to the yard and, with regimental daily repetition, I have trained them to walk quietly and sensibly into their respective stables. Not tonight. A few seconds pause is followed by an almighty clap of thunder. Both horses suddenly veer away from the monster in the skies and lurch with pent-up power for the safe familiarity of their straw beds. In his haste, Nugget catches the left side of his rib cage as he trots through the doorway at the wrong angle. I wince on his behalf then rush forward to bang the door shut. Galvanised into action, Mother, bless her, is doing the same for Rommel.

Then the deluge arrives.

Interlude

Judith

Brr, brr. Brr, brr. Brr, brr. Brr, brr.

Lizzie's recorded, light voice speaks politely into my left ear. "Sorry I missed your call. I am probably with my horse. Please leave a message."

"Still in the shower, Lizzie? Thought I'd catch you early. I'm coming around now; in a dash, got to get to Bury by nine this morning. I shall leave that loose-ringed snaffle bit you wanted on the doorstep."

As I press the red phone picture with my thumb, I am already reaching for the car keys with my other hand.

It is beginning to drizzle when I navigate the Shogun between the hedges into Lizzie's drive. My necessity for speed means I leave the engine running. I lurch out of the front seat. Keeping my head low, I flip up my hood, study the three steps to the front door, gauging the slipperiness of the stone. Time and motion; getting to work fast is my sole priority of thought. A gust of wind sideswipes rain across my face so I wrap the plastic bag a little neater around the bit and place it by the door. Then for some bizarre reason, as I carefully place my rubbery soles on the steps again, I happen to look up and over the bonnet of the Shogun. To be 'stopped in your tracks' is a worn-out cliché of a description, but it fits – for my world grinds to a sudden, involuntary halt. There, with its bumper barely visible at the side of Lizzie's house is a black van.

In the few seconds it takes me to pull back the cuff on my coat and peer at my watch, a fast pumping sensation has started in my chest. I try hard not to scuff the gravel with my wellies as I approach the van, getting close enough to recognise the 'Stockdale Carpentry' lettering. My furtive glance in the direction of the back door feels as though it matches the furtive clamp I want to inflict immediately on my wild imaginings. As I slam the car door shut, hurriedly slipping the gearstick into first, I can already feel a sequence of flying words passing like deadly bullets through my head – Lizzie... 8.30am... Why Luc, when Perfect Man seems so perfect? Deceit, Lizzie...? No, not her... but?

The weight of soil which sticks relentlessly to my boots all day becomes an almost welcome distraction. Each time I return to the Shogun, ready to drive on to the next gateway or farmyard, I find a spot to sit; a low wall or a damp bank. The necessity to scrape the mud with a stick from between each groove in the sole of my boots becomes all-consuming. It takes me away from the heaviness. By early evening, even the trill of a skylark as I bring Rommel and Nugget in from the field for their feed is unusually sharp and irritating to my ears.

At 6.30pm my mobile screen is flashing. The words 'Lizzie mobile' are clear to see. The 'Ding, dong. Ding, dong. Ding, dong' persists. I press the red 'Decline' space.

At 9pm my mobile screen declares, 'Two missed calls', and I cannot escape the thickening layer of disbelief on my tongue, which has insidiously congealed into anger.

* * *

By 8.30am the next day, I know that I am ready to face the flashing words 'Lizzie mobile'. Stoked, I press the 'Accept' space. Lizzie's chatter is immediate.

"Where on earth have you been? I was getting worried."

Three words is all I can manage to say. "Long day, yesterday."

I have an overwhelming sensation that my bile is about to be regurgitated, together with my breakfast, straight into the phone. I can picture lumps of it, all mixed in with flakes of muesli oats and watery yoghurt. Oblivious, Lizzie quickly fills the pause.

"That snaffle you dropped off is brilliant, Jude. I schooled him in it for over an hour yesterday and he barely threw his head up to resist at all." Lizzie's jumble of words lasts long enough for me to realise that the sour flavour in my throat has morphed into dryness. It is so bad that I know I shall struggle to reply. When she launches into her next sentence, I am already reaching for the glass of water on the counter.

"I didn't hear you ring the bell yesterday morning. How early were you?"

An eruption of tension has swept across my abdomen, my stomach muscles have contracted. I cannot quash my thoughts. *Benefit of the doubt. Reasonable explanation, there cannot be one, Lizzie?* The gulp of water I swallow is tepid but it helps me to breathe, then hold the flat coldness in each syllable of my verbal sword.

"Early enough to notice that you had a visitor." Lizzie's reply has a quick note of consternation to it.

"What visitor?"

In the world inhabited by Lizzie and me, the term 'visitor' is code for an overnight liaison. There is no risk of her misunderstanding my meaning. She is simply stalling, I am convinced of it.

175

"Luc, of course… your Stockdale Carpentry visitor! Who else, *that* early on a work morning?" The initial sound which Lizzie makes is similar to the alarm call of a woodland mammal – clear, mid-pitch. I can picture her suddenly alert stance, her blonde hair vertical, an animal caricature in *Spitting Image* form. She belts out a screech of a reply:

"Oh, don't be ridiculous, Jude." It is loud and not what I am anticipating. My reactive movement of the mobile away from my ear is sudden. My knuckles hit the cupboard hard. Then she starts laughing.

I cannot fathom it. I cannot bear it, her flippancy. She must listen. I interrupt her merriment.

"Come on, admit it. You've been attracted to Luc from the start. It just didn't register with me because I was too busy trying to fathom Jeremy. You said, in the lorry a couple of weeks ago, that Luc's not in your age range but hell, admit it, you were fluttering your eyelashes at him so hard they came close to flicking into his lap!"

The silent seconds meander. I have time to notice a reddening circle of skin on a couple of my knuckles. I wait… Lizzie eventually begins. She exudes a stream of compassion down the phone and my shoulders gradually relax into a sag.

"You are a numpty. I thought you realised. I was interrogating Luc because I think he could be *so* good for you. *Not* me!"

"But… you know Jeremy is more my type."

"Is he though? You deserve someone who is less uptight, more rambunctious, more alive, for goodness' sake!"

"Lizzie, stop it. You're describing exactly the template for your ideal partner, not mine and besides, you've changed the subject! I still want to know… *why* was Luc's van outside your house?"

"S-i-i-imples… I've asked him to replace the units in my kitchen. He came over yesterday to measure up."

"Oops, sorry," is all I can manage to reply, because a painful arrow stabs true and straight in through the front of my conscience. It exits, covered in blood-smeared tendrils of guilt. *Damn you, Judith McBride, for ever doubting her.*

Chapter 15

Luc popped the lid off the Lynx deodorant, reached in under his open shirt front and sprayed liberally under each armpit. A swift glance at his watch set him hurriedly doing up alternate buttons on his shirt. *I doubt she will notice. No time for perfection, Luc. Just get yourself out there on time.*

The public loos in the Swan pub; not an ideal place to have to change but he'd had to drive straight from work, so needs must. The part-disgorged contents of his ancient toilet bag were strewn around the washbasins and he had to fumble around before finding a comb and holding it under the cold tap. He quickly ran the comb through his short-cropped fair hair till, several passes later, he hoped the worst of the dust had been removed. Finally, he stood back a few feet to view his handiwork in the mirror.

When Madeleine had first sent him a 'Meet Me' message, he had been about to click the 'Hide' icon but had persuaded himself to take one last peek at anyone on the Elite.com website who may be interesting – just in case. Isaac's words a few weeks ago had taken root in fertile soil and he had convinced himself that all this preoccupation with finding the love of his life online was a fruitless quest. Madeleine's profile photo had unexpectedly swayed his resolve. There she was, a vivacious brunette laughing back at the camera in full ski kit. Slender, bright-eyed and full of life. *One last time*, he had thought, *One last crack at kicking destiny through the goalpost.*

He settled himself in the corner at the far end of the public bar so he had a vantage point from which to study everyone as they entered through the door. It appeared to be quiz night – a large whiteboard was propped against the wall and a motley selection of people were clattering the door open and shut, arriving in a steady stream. A group of women in their sixties pushed through to greet other team members at a table including: a dapper Henley-on-Thames couple in his and hers navy blue blazers, her crisp white hair permed meringue-like; a nondescript woman in her late forties swathed from head to foot in a black blouse and flowing heavy skirt which merged into loose-fitting leather boots, the folds in the black clothes struggling to conceal her spreading waistline beneath; four girls in their late teens, under-skirted, over-lipsticked and loud. Teasing aromas of steak pie and chargrilled chicken permeated the room and Luc's stomach gurgled in protest.

Where the hell has Madeleine got to? Luc double-checked his watch again. Twenty minutes late. *Is she going to be a 'no show'?* A niggling irritation popped into his mind that he may have been a fool. He had never before broken his golden rule of travelling more than fifty miles to meet a date. He raised his glass up to his mouth ready to take a long swig then realised that the aforementioned, less than noticeable Woman in Black had eased in beside him. She made a point of looking him full in the eye before speaking directly to him:

"Excuse me, are you Luc by any chance?"

Oh shit, please tell me this isn't her – surely not? Up close, Luc was able to see that the Baltic-blue eyes staring intently into his own were one and the same as the woman in the skiing photo. For

179

a few split seconds he imagined denying his own name. He could be a George, Thomas, or Mathew, anyone except Luc Stockdale. Instead he spluttered,

"Oh, so sorry... Madeleine isn't it? I didn't recognise you."

He could detect the brief silence his words provoked, gathered his wits up from around his own feet then formally offered his hand out ready to be shaken. His palm barely touched hers; perhaps a second before he whisked it away as though snapped by an electric shock. Madeleine's nonplussed expression said it all. Her confusion. His rudeness. *But what the hell did she expect? Advertising herself as one image on her profile, when in reality...* Luc turned to lean over the bar and beckoned in order to get the landlady's attention. He chastised himself. *Don't be a bastard, Luc.*

"May I get you a drink, Madeleine? You've probably had a long day. Just like me."

Two pints of Southwold Bitter later and Luc's abrasive thoughts were well diluted. He found himself quite captivated by her deliciously long lashes. Surprisingly, for a brunette with quite a sallow skin, she had vivid blue eyes and her make-up was, he thought, probably the best he had seen on any woman. A waiter glided past balancing a sizzling plate of steak and chips on his forearm. The aroma made Luc's decision easy.

"Shall we stay to eat, Madeleine? We both have a good hour's drive to get home."

He caught a hint of triumph in her answer.

"You certainly know how to sweep a girl off her feet with romantic persuasion, Luc." She bit her bottom lip provocatively and giggled.

"I suspect your hunger pangs are driving your gallantry. Am I right?" she followed up with a cheeky wink.

Luc had assumed within seconds of clapping eyes on Madeleine that, if he were to stay, he would have a rather pointless evening. He couldn't have been more wrong. She hooked his attention from the moment they sat down to eat. Her casual remark seemed so innocent.

"I imagine if you have been meeting online partners for over a year now, Luc, you must have had some odd or rather unusual experiences?" Luc wasn't able to control the colour rise in his cheeks and Madeleine caught his hesitation and ran with it.

"I'm itching to know – come on. Is it as tough for men as it is for women?" And with this she put on a proper bottom lip pout and fluttered her long, long lashes Kate Bush style.

"Bloody hell, Madeleine. You said you are an editor by profession, but I'm beginning to think you may actually be a reporter! Give me one good reason why I should divulge *any* of my experiences?" She ran her red nails casually through her fringe. Her whole face lit up.

"OK, OK. I'll go first. Do women put up ridiculous photos? Because I have seen some absolute stonkers amongst the men. I'll give you some examples: a sideways profile shot – couldn't see the expression in his face at all. Left me wondering whether there was something terribly wrong with the other side of his face. No other pictures on his profile to look at; *or*, quite a lot of men take a photo of themselves, in the mirror with their mobile; don't they have a friend who could take it for them? It immediately gives an impression of Billy No Mates – sad, very sad; *or*, a photo of the head of the driver in a car, the window is down and his hand is resting on the mirror. Why?"

Their dinner arrived and they both tucked into forkfuls of food, too hungry to bother with any conversation. Luc stole a sidelong glance at Madeleine while she wasn't looking. She was devouring her steak and ale pie as if it were a last supper before her crucifixion. Eventually she took up her previous topic.

"*Or*, and there are quite a lot of these – man lounging on a deckchair with a bare chest and/or bare legs." Madeleine then lifted her chair away from the table another foot, leaned backwards, tipping it on two legs, shoved her feet out in front and spread her legs apart in a pose so common to men.

"Then the shot is taken looking straight up the shorts with their crotch displayed for all to see!"

Luc coughed his part-swallowed mouthful of beer across the table, a small smattering of which flecked onto Madeleine's blouse. She neatly shuffled her chair back under the dining table. Luc grinned at her.

"You could be a stand-up comedian. You remind me of Jennifer Saunders." He suddenly realised that he was revelling in an uninhibited freedom of speech with Madeleine that he would normally only ever enjoy with his best mates.

"Right, seeing as you've had a good man-bashing session" he jibed, "it's my turn now… You'd be shocked at how often women put up a profile picture of themselves in a skin-tight glittery cocktail dress while they teeter on their highest heels."

Luc demonstrated his next point by splaying his upturned palms into a pudding bowl shape and contorting his face into a pop-eyed leer.

"And their buttocks are *always* staring back at you, saying 'Grab me, grab me.' *Or*, a profile photo of two pugs in matching jackets for a woman whose online pseudonym is 'Sophiepug' – why would I want to waste time contacting someone who is a complete visual non-entity? I could understand her thinking if she had written an interesting description of who she was or her hobbies and likes, but she didn't bother. *Or*, a lot of women, particularly if they are still in their forties, put up what could be a lovely close-up picture of themselves if only they didn't either pout or do a celebrity sucking in of their cheeks that simply cries 'Take me, take me!' A picture of a woman hiking up the side of a mountain or walking along a beach says so much more to me about who she is. Your skiing mugshot really tweaked my interest."

Madeleine mirthfully replied,

"Well, you've answered your own question. Think about it. *I've* just described to you how men who find themselves single and on the pull in their fifties and sixties want to portray themselves as sexy, fit and masculine. *You* have just given examples of all the single women out there who want to portray themselves as *exactly* the same – sexy, fit and feminine!" She brought her hand down with a gentle but definitive thwack on the tabletop.

"I rest my case. Both men and women have exactly the same hang-ups and aspirations."

Luc pursed his lips and shifted his head from left to right and back again – venturing slowly, "Possibly, possibly not. I still think we have very different priorities."

Madeleine crooked her flashy scarlet fingernail once, twice and a third time till he leant in close for her to whisper,

"Tell me. What is one of the first things you as a man notice when you meet a woman, other than either her hair, her figure or her eyes?"

Without a heartbeat of hesitation, Luc replied, "That's easy, her hands. Or more specifically her nails."

"There you are. I have to admit that when I arrived here this evening and you were ordering drinks, the first thing I registered about you was the state of your calloused fingers. That led me to dig deeper and, once I had established that you are a carpenter by profession, I was happy to accept all the cracks and ingrained grime in your hands as being manly."

Their coffee arrived. Luc breathed in the rich Arabica steam before taking a sip but also dropped a sly look at his own battered thumb wrapped around the cup.

Madeleine picked up her thread of thought again.

"Some women, on the other hand, would find the slender, clean fingers of a musician much more appealing. For both men and women one of the best ways to get a 'handle' on who you are as a person is to study your hands."

The steady timbre in Luc's voice reflected his new-found respect for the woman sitting opposite him.

"I'm curious to know. What sort of things do get a woman's back up?"

Madeleine had been lazily caressing the contours of her wine glass but couldn't contain a gusty laugh at his question.

"Oh, that's easy, especially if you mean first impressions online. *The* most cringeworthy first chat-up message I ever received was – 'Hello, Nutkin, you can squirrel away my nuts anytime!'"

Luc let out a proper guffaw. "I can tell you that my pet peeve is the number of people who put, 'Fill in later' in the 'Description of Yourself' section. Although it's even worse when they can't spell and the meaning of their words comes out all wrong. One woman wrote – 'Looking for someone to forfile me.' Derrrr. Fulfil, fulfil, fulfil. I was left with an image of trying to forcibly stuff her into a filing cabinet!"

Hesitant to interrupt and unobserved by either of them, the pole-thin waitress had been standing just behind Luc's shoulder for a couple of minutes. Luc sensed rather than saw her hovering and realised she must have been eavesdropping. He tipped his head to acknowledge her presence and added a surreptitious wink.

The embarrassed girl blushed copiously and promptly stuttered, "Your bill," as she placed it on the table.

Alone again, the brief interruption had calmed the two diners. Madeleine was the first to speak again.

"Forgetting all the downsides to internet dating, Luc, I have to say that I've met one or two really lovely people in the past couple of years. I certainly don't regret having at least tried."

He nodded.

"I have to agree with you on that one. Sod's law is, though, that the wittiest women I find always live too far away. I'm trying to remember the best line I've read in the 'About Me' box. Hmm, yes, it went like this. 'Essentially you must have legs, arms and a pulse. I also require goosebumps caused by a quirky soulmate companion who enjoys a good ramble and inappropriate laughter.'"

It had been a long day and Luc could feel a weightiness in his eyelids. He couldn't ignore any longer the fact that in the past thirty minutes Madeleine had gone from accidentally brushing her arm against his, to regularly clasping his arm or wrist in order to accentuate a point, and now she was leaning in, in a quite pronounced message against his side. *Major problem. How the hell do I let her down gently? Had an absolutely brilliant evening. Just do not fancy her. Must think of something plausible.*

The waitress returned and smiled politely as they both counted out notes. Luc waited until she had moved away to another table. He found himself gently placing a couple of fingers on Madeleine's sleeve.

"I have to say that I have genuinely loved your company this evening."

He saw her cheeks tighten. She retrieved her arm, flicked back her hair defiantly, then rather sharply interrupted him by saying,

"Yes. Ditto on my part too. But I do normally have a very busy schedule. In fact, I'm often away working for two weeks at a time. It probably isn't practical for me to arrange to see you again."

Gracious – she got in first. Consider yourself rebuffed, Luc.

Pride intact, she wilted in closer to him again. He touched shoulder to shoulder. "I agree. It's always best to be perfectly frank. No point in leading anyone up the garden path."

He was pleased to see a mischievous twitch of her nose as she retorted flippantly, "From now on I shall always remember you as Frank. Not Mark or Albert or Phillip or Reginald, not even a Luc. But instead, a scrumptious, tall, interesting one-night date I had with Frank."

Luc escorted Madeleine to her car and courteously opened the door for her to slide in. "You know, you really are very witty, Madeleine, and some of your stories are such clever observations of people. You're moving in publishing circles. Why not write an article about internet dating? I'm sure it would go down a storm."

* * *

His house – it was so late to see him return, so very dark, so horribly chilled, so dead and worst of all so incredibly empty. Whisky, whisky, whisky. His crutch, his solace, his friend. It would ease the pain, it would numb wounds, it would force sleep on his fractured thoughts, his raw heart, his bare life. Where had he put that bottle?

Hot, so furiously hot, he was vaguely aware that he was thrashing around. A boxing match in his bed – round two, ding, ding. Sweat, the vapour from his armpits was seeping out from under the cover. He ran his fingers across his chest; the hairs felt damp. He stretched out his right leg, he needed to cool his feet, he must get them out from under the duvet, but he knew the sheet was tucked in down the side. Was he conscious, was he asleep? *Why* wouldn't his foot reach the side of the bed. *Where* was the edge? Then he remembered before sliding back into the darkness, that bottomless black.

Black coffee. He wasn't sure – was he asleep, was he awake?

His memory of her, his recurring dream always began with black coffee. Seven years with his Juliet and he'd never learned to share her love of that bitter coffee. The throaty bubbling of the percolator as it scalded the beans. He would pour the dark liquid into Juliet's special mug, raise it to his nostrils and inhale the steam. The smell always promised so much, the harshness left his tastebuds cowed. Black, she always insisted on black coffee first thing in the morning – nothing more, nothing less. Danish roots.

Thirsty, so thirsty, too tired.

Singing, he was singing the words to the Dire Straits song when he put her mug down on the bedside table. His song to her. Their song, 'Romeo & Juliet'. *But* she was asleep, motionless. He dropped his dressing gown to the floor, sat on the bed, unclipped the belt holding his prosthetic leg in place, lobbed the damn thing away, away from him. It wasn't part of him. He found its ricocheting thud off the wall a strangely satisfying salve. He didn't need it when he was with his Juliet.

Lying face down, her angel arms framing wanton hair, spread across the pillow. Erotic, the back of her neck so incredibly downy, he ran his fingers along the hairline, touched his lips to her spine. She stirred, sleepy. His palm fitted perfectly into the groove of her hip bone, the other settled on her shoulder. He flipped her over. He felt his voice singing, he knew he was singing. Memory or dream, he would always sing to his Juliet. And he had that night, just as he knew he was now, here in this lonely bed.

She stretched one arm up above her head, hooked two fingers through the slatted headboard, closed her eyes. He grabbed her other wrist, pushed it high out to her side and *crash*...

Slow motion. Both dreams and memories love slow motion. He flung his body headlong to save the mug; black liquid splattered.

In slow motion the coffee cup rolled under the bed.

In slow motion arms flailed, they screeched.

In slow motion he clung to her, they landed in a heap. His laughter was alive within him, her skin was alive beneath him.

Wedged in the confines of the narrow space, Luc bore down on her with his full weight. Deliberately crushing and exerting what power he possessed. Her swollen lips bore testament to her arousal. The violet-flavoured creaminess of her neck lingered on his tongue as she arched into their rhythm.

Afterwards, they lay exhausted. He remembered being vaguely aware that his thigh was suffering an indent from a suitcase handle. He watched a final drip of coffee descend lazily down the wall and inhaled the sweet, earthy scent of spent passion. Then he sang to her the final lines. A song of Juliet and love. A song that made her cry, because their timing turned out all wrong.

He awoke thirsty. So incredibly thirsty – for her, for love.

Chapter 16

Judith

'Barton House', the tasteful plaque tells me. At last I have been invited by Jeremy to his home for a late afternoon tour of his personal domain. The daunting wrought-iron gates are unmissable, hinged on substantial stone gateposts. The effect is verging on Gothic and, as promised, they are already open. I find myself driving at a snail's pace, my arms moulded around the steering wheel as I lean forward to gawk. The drive curves its way past a small copse of ancient beech trees and eventually opens out in a sweeping circle before a beautiful Georgian house. The interior of the Shogun, with its tatty seat covers, containers of assorted grain samples and bits of spare tack, is thrown into stark contrast the moment I park it in this auspicious setting.

I rap once, twice, and again with the enormous brass door knocker. Its hard thudding breaks the peace of the warm afternoon. I wait for what may be perhaps a minute but feels so very much longer. Excitement and curiosity are vying for pole position as I begin a second round of rapping on the door. Will this be the pivotal date? *Lizzie knows I'm here, but I'm glad I didn't tell Mother. Shame about the lack of flower beds, he could do with some roses or well-placed variegated bushes to set off such an impressive frontage as this.*

The sound of barking dogs comes closer and closer, till eventually the door swings open releasing a barrage of boisterous canine bodies, wagging tails and Jeremy's welcoming smile. Pushing themselves between us, the dogs make sure any formalities are forgotten and I bend to fondle Chester's silky ears.

"Excellent timing, Judith. Come in, come in. Let's go through to the kitchen and I'll pour you a Rioja."

Jeremy beckons me forward and walks ahead into the hall, dogs' claws clicking on flagstones as they trot along behind him. I fail miserably to disguise my awe. I gesture with an outstretched hand towards a ubiquitous collection of oil paintings lining the walls down the long hall and up the stairs.

"Goodness gracious, Jeremy, what a wonderful collection of portraits. Are they all relations?" Jeremy allows his leisurely gaze to meander over the nearest canvasses, a hint of pride pacing up the speed of his reply.

"Yes. There is a long line of first-born sons with the name Jeremy Albright. But a couple of my forebears were apparently rogues of the first order." I move in closer to squint at the neat nameplate under a portrait and am about to make a suitably felicitous observation but Jeremy continues: "Before we get bogged down with my family skeletons, I would love to show you around outside."

Jeremy marches me from the hall through the kitchen at a brisk pace. I am rapidly learning that this man never ever strolls anywhere – left, right, left, right is clearly his set style, straight out to the spacious courtyard at the back of the house. Pointing towards an immaculately restored group of timber wattle and daub buildings, his face lights up.

"These cart lodges over here are thought to have been part of a Tudor coaching house, which would have been the original dwelling in the sixteenth century."

I find myself running along like a spaniel puppy across the concrete in his wake. *If he stops and turns around to speak to me at the far side, should I plonk my bottom on the ground to sit and longingly prick my spaniel ears to await his next instruction? Oops, no. Behave, Judith. This is an informative tour!*

Jeremy rummages around in his trouser pockets and pulls out a weighty set of assorted keys.

"Would you like to see my boys?" He looks at me expectantly. I refrain from saying out loud that I think he is mad; however, my rapidly changing facial expressions must be exposing my confusion. Eventually he lets out an embarrassed cough and adds, "My collection of motorbikes. I refer to them as 'my boys'." He screws up his nose.

"I know. A little silly really."

I give his arm a quick squeeze with my hand and giggle.

"Don't apologise. I love as much silliness in life as possible. I would love to see 'your boys'," and I push past him through the open door. Regimentally parked, noses to the wall along both sides of the interior, is an incredible assortment of motorbikes. I wander up to the nearest and run my fingers over the taut leather seat.

"I'm impressed. How many bikes do you have?"

He smiles shyly.

"I know – it's decadent. But there are twelve in here and I have another Triumph arriving in a few days."

We begin to move haltingly up the row of glistening machines, Jeremy eloquently spouting forth a fascinating flow of information and anecdotes about each individual bike. Deep creases appear in the corners of his mouth as his joy at talking about 'his boys' increases. The weighty yoke of responsibility and steadfast correctness which he perpetually carries around vanishes.

In one ear and straight out the other side, he bombards me with details such as: 'This Harley Davidson'... and 'this Triumph'... and 'this Enfield'. The makes and models fall effortlessly from his mouth in a stream of words clearly as precious to him as liquid gold.

I think back to our previous meeting. *Perhaps it's time for a little cunning to become part of my repertoire – I think a smidgen of visual stimulation might be necessary. See if I can kick-start Jeremy's machismo.* Choosing my moment strategically, I wait till Jeremy is standing at the exhaust end of the Triumph... before swinging my right leg expertly up over its seat and leaning forward to clutch the handlebars. Precociously aware that this is giving Jeremy a front row view of what my ex-husband always referred to as my best asset, I wriggle my buttocks into a comfortable position.

"Goodness, it's such a long time since I sat on a motorbike." *Stay cool, Jude.* I still avoid turning around to check Jeremy's reaction.

"My two brothers used to career around with their off-road bikes when we were in our teens so I sometimes tagged along."

Jeremy casually moves up to my side and I turn to sit upright and lock focus with those deep Aberdeen Angus eyes. *Bloody hell.* I feel my heart skip one of those much written about poetic but agonisingly elusive beats. *This is it. NOW. He's going to kiss me...* Out of the blue, a troubled flicker of a frown appears and he takes a tiny half-step backwards while also reaching out to touch my elbow, to placate.

"Let's go inside. A glass of wine beckons."

Except that, as we cross the yard, Jeremy decides he must replenish the dog's water. He waves me ahead, tells me to go inside and pour the wine. I oblige, and it takes me several minutes, as per his instructions, to find the necessary corkscrew and glasses.

Through the kitchen window, I can see him using a short hose to top up what looks like an old metal pig trough near the fence. I wait and watch. Rather than peering down at the trough as it fills, Jeremy is staring off across the field towards the woodland. *Odd, surely that trough must be full – perhaps I should go outside again?*

Not wanting to creep up on him from behind, I get to within several feet when I stop. A gentle cascade of water has begun oozing over the edge of the trough, pooling under Jeremy's feet. He seems oblivious. *Why can I feel a no-go zone around him?* He looks down at the hosepipe clutched tight in his fist. I can see that a trickle of water has begun seeping past his wrist. *That water must be cold, his shirt and jumper must be wet. Why doesn't he let go? His fist is clutching it so tight.* I sneak backwards quickly, before clumping forward again in a noisy, purposeful way towards the tap on the wall.

"I'll switch it off for you."

Jeremy remains still, transfixed. When I reach his side, I have to gently peel off each one of his chilled fingers from the pipe. It drops to the ground and I instinctively squeeze my warm hand into his as a replacement and leave it there. Finally, my stare follows his. I too spot the four hinds and a stag. Their heads are down; they are grazing in the field. At last, he speaks.

"Esme's favourite – roe deer. I wish so much that she could be here, right now. Her fingers were warm in my palm, just as yours are now. I can picture her when she went to sit by the copse on that day. She still had a full head of hair. She said all she wanted was some quiet time. I wrapped my arm around her waist just in case, guided her across the uneven ground. We walked shoulder to shoulder and I opened the fold-out chair for her, left her sitting and waiting patiently for the deer. She did a sketch in pencil, nothing elaborate, but the shapes and lines of the doe and her fawn were exquisite." I place my other hand over his. We still stare towards the front.

"Her Rive Gauche perfume, it kept snagging at the back of my throat because it no longer masked the sickly hue of chemo embedded in her pores. Rive Gauche; once upon a time it was hers, it was ours, but it became a trigger for me. The faintest whisper of its hue and I would rush away, pale, to retch over the nearest washbasin."

We head, silent, back into the house and while Jeremy busies himself in the kitchen, my sense of discretion sends me to wander into the hall. I feel unnerved, but strangely honoured to have witnessed the unmasking of Jeremy's inner sanctum. *A distraction, that's what we need. I can truly feel his pain, but mawkish sentimentality can also be addictive. Can I bring him up again?*

I notice that the wall, from the dado rail up to the cavernous heights of the ceiling, is covered in a green flocked wallpaper. I place the palm of my hand flush against its surface and became childishly captivated by the texture changes between the smooth finish of the flat paper to the protruding velvet. Completely engrossed, I begin running my fingers along the intricate repeating pattern. Jeremy speaks from behind me.

"I don't recommend that you keep caressing that wallpaper much longer, Judith. Did you know it has arsenic in it?" Startled, I pull my palm away.

"Goodness gracious – really?" Jeremy is carefully balancing two glasses of red wine and an ornate silver dish of cheese straws on an equally ornate silver tray.

"The green pigment in that flocking was developed from a compound of copper arsenite. It brightened the colour in the wallpaper but the dust particles in the factories caused some terrible health problems."

This man is so damn frustrating but fascinating at the same time.

"So what time period was this then? Clearly well before anyone had thought of coupling up the onerous words of health and safety?"

"We Brits were very slow to get our act together because of the huge profits the factory owners made. By 1874 they were producing 32 million rolls of wallpaper, but arsenic was used in all sorts of products – artificial flowers which women wore in their hair, toys, cosmetics and last but not least most homes used it for killing rats and mice."

Jeremy's hands are still occupied with holding the tray, but the slightest hint of his twitch is now flicking across one cheek. I pull a face at him.

"You bugger. You're winding me up, aren't you? I can tell."

A few wisps of hair flick onto his forehead as he emphasises his reply.

"No, I promise it's all completely true. But I did fib in the sense that the paper on these walls was replaced about fifteen years ago. So, no more tincture of arsenic present."

Chester and Bruno patter in, sticking close as always to their owner's heels and we all head along the hall. Jeremy pauses in a doorway. "Is it OK if we sip our drinks in the snug? The drawing room is too formal and roomy for just the two of us."

I am rapidly learning that any and every aspect of Jeremy's life is tidy and organised. His snug has all the usual trappings that you would expect. A squishy two-seater sofa with a suitably dog-friendly cover, a man-sized TV screen across one corner, a pair of well-worn slippers peeping out from under a dark leather chair. Unexpectedly, what immediately hits my visual consciousness on entering the room is the contents of five shelves on the far wall. Lined up in a kaleidoscope of colours is a hoard of motorbike helmets. On the top three shelves are hues of black, dark red and midnight blue with black-and-white stripes over the top or glossy, unadulterated, solid white. The lower two shelves contain what I recognise as off-road and motocross headgear in much more flashy red, black and white stripes or solid fluorescent greens and yellows, some with a brand logo. Jeremy spots the focus of my attention. He swallows a gulp of Rioja before moving his fingers along the edge of a shelf.

"I have lots of motorcycle helmets. Sixteen currently. Some get used on a daily basis. Others just sit around waiting to be aired again when I have another bike that matches them." *Feign surprise, Judith. What the hell do I say? Do all motorbike riding men go to these lengths with their accessories?*

"Well, it's a wonderful selection of colours."

Clearly encouraged by my comment, Jeremy continues, "Helmets are to me as handbags and shoes are to a woman."

Why do I feel the tiniest bit uncomfortable about that comment? Change the subject.

"My favourite snack – cheese straws. May I?" And I manage to fill fifteen valuable thinking seconds with suitably appreciative *mmm* eating noises before speaking again.

"Men and motorbikes. They fit together as solidly as women and horses, don't you think?" Jeremy brushes a crumb of cheese straw from my cheek. His expression is almost paternal. He moves away again.

"How do you mean?"

I reach for the pile of *Motorbiker* magazines lying in a heap on the low coffee table, pick one up to use as a momentary prop and begin flicking. The pages show groups of bearded, leather-clad men in threes and fours on the open highway – each rider clutching nose-height handlebars as they speed towards the horizon. Or close-ups of immaculate steel engines and chrome exhaust pipes, not a speck of engine oil in sight. Jeremy must have said my name twice before I look up. I am trying to compare the huge variation in bodies, engine sizes, suitability for the job of all the different types of bikes and the wine helps make sure my mouth goes into gear well before my brain.

"Do men think of themselves as a particular brand, shape or make of motorbike in the same way as women identify themselves as a particular breed or type of horse? In other words, what bike would you describe yourself as?"

I watch the light bulb mirrored in Jeremy's face as it comes on in his mind and he warms to my slightly ludicrous thought processes. He gently takes the magazine from me, our shoulders rubbing together, his aftershave hanging in the air space between us. He finds a page with a Triumph Bonneville on it and prods enthusiastically at the photo.

"This is me."

"Excellent. How about some of your other friends who are very different shapes, sizes and characters compared to you?"

"Not so easy. Isaac would be a Suzuki – fit and quite powerful. Luc is possibly a Honda – quite slender and incredibly quick with a 450cc engine. But Robert would be the slowest, rather lumbering. He's probably a Harley."

My mind is now humming with images of an open road in Midwest America, the sun low on the horizon, the vacuum of the speeding bikers causing a wake of rustling and swaying in the corn close to the tarmac. I'm clutching Jeremy tight around the waist, my nose buried deep into the back of his shoulder. *Stop daydreaming, Judith.*

"So, if you were doing a road trip, say across one of the big continents, how would you choose a bike? Would it be for speed? Power? Comfort? I'm curious what your priorities would be?" I slump down onto the sofa, tucking my legs up under and lounging back, then pat the empty space. Jeremy sits down fitting himself efficiently into the small gap.

"That depends entirely on all sorts of factors; what terrain you are likely to encounter; is it flat or very steep? Are the roads tarmac or dirt country tracks as for example in Asia or India? Are you transporting camping gear with you? Will you be able to get spare parts? The list is endless."

"Sounds like exactly the same horsepower dilemma as me and my girlfriends have!"

* * *

Perhaps if I count cobwebs, that might work as a distraction. Up in the top corner. A silky network of fine threads hidden in my four-poster. One, two, three. That one stretches right across. Cobwebs, a sticky spider's web of doubt criss-crossing my mind. Yes, he had drawn me close by the front door, a preamble to my departure, but his kiss had no depth to it, no passion, no meaning. A friend-to-friend kiss given in consolation. A duty, no more.

Cobwebs of doubt forestalling sleep. *Sheep; go back to sheep. Jumping a wall? A hedge? A gate? No. Singing sheep. That's much better.*

Chapter 17

Sometimes, if Luc felt that the sweaty armpit of life was getting too much, he would clamber up the ladder onto the scaffolding. Hanging onto a thermos mug in one hand while ascending the ladder and getting his duff foot in exactly the right place on each rung had taken a while to perfect. He'd got the hang of it in the end.

He carried his mug to the farthest end of the boards – his favourite spot. At this end of the cottage, he could observe the flight paths and habits of all the wildlife as it entered or exited the wood. On a still day, sound travelled easily. He'd heard all sorts of conversations as walkers followed the footpath along the edge of the wood and across the footbridge. At the front end of the cottage, he could use his binoculars to see down the slope as far as the pub. People in, people out, people snatching an illicit smoke in the beer garden before their spouse came out with the drinks. People feeding burgers to someone else's dogs when the owner has gone for a leak. People kissing, people falling out. He'd seen an awful lot in the couple of months he'd been fitting the tiles.

He unwrapped the strap from around his neck and brought the binoculars up to his eyes. He wondered, *Will they be out yet?* He twiddled the focus and began a slow sweep along the tree line, zooming in a little closer on the burnt-out shell of an oak tree.

He could just make out the camouflaged contours of the barn owl, motionless. *There you are, you beauty. Hunting early tonight.* His binoculars: top of the range. Silly he knew to have spent so much when kitchen units should have taken priority, but he didn't regret his choice. Not now, when he could see, so clearly, the heart-shaped ring of amber feathers framing the bird's face – see him swivel his head away and back, scanning the low covering of wheat, see the blink of his lids.

The bird, startled, took off hurriedly. Luc trained the binoculars along the path. *What spooked you – a fox, a walker?* Sure enough, a male figure was striding out at a brisk pace, followed closely by a chocolate Labrador. Luc sat down on the two breezeblocks behind him, steadied his forearms on the lower scaffold pole, then fiddled with the focus again. *Exercising your pooch, are you, Jeremy?*

Jeremy's marching footfall reverberated, thud, thud, thud, along the sodden planks of the narrow bridge. Chester hurtled past his right leg in blind 'chase' mode, his sights set on the iridescent flash of green plumage he'd spotted retreating into the foliage. The dog launched himself into the stream with reckless zeal, his instincts to flush up birds overriding any sense of self-preservation. A stagnant wave of mud and chilly water doused Jeremy's trousers. Luc smiled a little then continued watching, transfixed.

Jeremy strode a little further along the bridge then turned his head suddenly, appearing to stare back towards the village. Luc froze. *Oops, has he spotted me? Nah, my coat is roughly the same colour as the house.* He readjusted the lens again. Luc's concentration was broken by a more urgent mixture of barking and squawking. The poor unsuspecting duck had been sent frantically skyward and Luc saw Jeremy follow the flight of the bird with a look of what appeared to be envy.

Perhaps I also envy that duck, the sensation of flight. To engage every muscle in your entire body, sinew, wings, eyes, beak. To follow with absolute abandonment the need to flee. I'm with you, Jeremy, on this one. Then Luc felt, rather than saw, or imagined he saw, the first twitch. Jeremy appeared to ignore it, continued concentrating on the mallard. Luc tilted the binoculars up a little, hearing all the flapping and quacking. The duck escaped violently upwards, free. It cleared the hedge, a gust of wind blowing it sideways, frantic extra wing strokes correcting its urgent course.

Luc lowered his view again to the man, that face as immobile as the body. Except for, *I saw it, Jeremy, your twitch. So, what on earth is bothering you? You're out on an idyllic walk with your dog. There is absolutely no one else to stress you. What could possibly be wrong in your world – a personal revolution? Something volcanic must be churning up your innards. Where's the third twitch, Jeremy? Come on, there is always a third one, mate.*

Jeremy did not disappoint his spy. He brought up the flat of his hand and slapped it hard across his right eye once, twice. No third twitch arrived and the angst which had been contorting his face seemed to dissipate. He rolled his shoulders around as if to unstiffen his neck. Luc widened out his view. Jeremy was now watching carefree Chester revelling amongst the reeds, ears flying when, without any preamble whatsoever, he lifted his arms into aeroplane stance and... leapt. The force of his bombing weight, backside first, hit the murky water in an incredibly dramatic whoosh. Chester was stunned briefly into stillness and appeared ready to flee but Luc was more interested in the man. *He's army through and through. What the hell is he trying to shock himself out of? I've been there, the services does that to a man. The rough terrain training, the sub-zero nights under canvas, the wading in a river with a full kitbag on your back. What are you trying to feel, Jeremy?*

How many countless streams have you been forced to wade in or cross? I know what it's like. The freezing sharpness as water seeps in and around first the layers of your coat, then jumper and trousers, quickly reaching your skin, your balls and around the nape of your neck.

Thinking this a joyous, unexpected game, Chester jumped on top of his master and began licking his face and yelping with delight. *The purity of that cold and wetness will have migrated into your bones in a minute, Jeremy. Oh, he's lifted up his arm to push off the dog. I'll bet a rush of water has travelled from his elbow to his armpit, foreign yet strangely exciting.*

Jeremy attempted to rise but the sheer suction effect of the mud meant he fell back, recumbent again. His second effort succeeded and he rose, silt and leaves dropping. Chester joined in, bouncing and splashing around in giddy circles. Once up the bank, Jeremy flung his wellies one at a time high in the air. They came crashing down to earth. His socks quickly followed suit and he started to race headlong over the meadow on the far side of the stream. *So intense, isn't it? That sensation of running through grass with bare feet, calf muscles thrusting, lungs filling deep – intoxicating.*

Jeremy had managed to propel himself to the top of the meadow, but by now he appeared totally lost for a shred more impetus. He collapsed in a wet, dog-entwined heap on the ground. He lay staring upwards. Luc watched as the dog shifted his chin into the crook of Jeremy's shoulder. Fingers began caressing the comfort of damp canine ears. *Ugh, canned dog breath. Must be huffing up your nostrils. Doesn't that bother you, Jeremy?*

Luc refocused the binoculars again. Stretched across Jeremy's torso, the dog seemed to be bobbing up and down in time to the short fits and starts of Jeremy's ribcage. *Is he laughing?*

It arrived on the light wind – Luc hadn't even realised he was listening so hard, but it was there, distant, clear – guttural laughter. Followed by a bellow at the sky.

"Fuck the lot of you."

Interlude

Judith

Brr, brr. Brr, brr. Brr, brr. Brr, brr. Brr, brr. Brr, brr. Brr, brr. Brr, brr. Brr, brr. Brr, brr.

Twenty-four hours pass.

Brr, brr. Brr, brr. Brr, brr. Brr, brr. Brr, brr.

I cannot help it, a paltry distraction – studying my own fingers strumming on the counter in time with the ring tone.

Brr, brr. Brr, brr. Brr, brr.

"Damn it. Pick up, Jeremy. Where are you?" The curt answering service voice requests that I leave a message: I oblige.

"Judith here. Please can you phone me when you get a spare minute. Thanks."

Twelve hours pass.

Ding dong. Ding dong.

I pounce on my mobile. "Hello, Jeremy. Where've you been hiding?"

"Apologies, I've been rather busy."

"I'm so glad you're OK."

"Judith, I wanted…"

His voice is faltering. He sounds powerless to do anything about it. So unlike him. I dare not stop to draw breath between sentences.

"I was starting to worry something horrible had happened and I wanted to reciprocate for the other evening. May I cook dinner for you on Saturday? The forecast is perfect for us to go for a romantic stroll beforehand and Mother would love to meet you."

"Um… well. The problem is, Judith…"

I press a finger into the bridge of my nose, push my glasses up higher. *Why has my world stopped? Why am I suddenly dreading his reply? Can I smell a rat?* I know that I'm not a natural observer of human beings, I prefer horses. I can interpret the pitch and urgency of Rommel's whinny and comprehend what he needs in that very moment. I can anticipate from the direction or twitching of an ear if his next movement will be a soft nuzzle, a bruising nip or the sight of his rump receding up the field. *Why can I see a beacon flashing up ahead? It's large and horribly red. Have I read Jeremy completely wrong? Is he seeing someone else?*

"I'm ever so sorry, Judith. But this just isn't going to work."

"I don't understand, Jeremy. Don't be vague. Tell me the truth. Why do you think that?" On the other end of the phone, I hear a sound somewhere between a sob and a laugh; it prompts me to spit out my next words.

"No more evasion. I had a stomach full of that with my ex."

"It's not *you*, I promise. It's me. I'm only trying to be civilised about this."

The hard edge of the mobile is hurting my ear. I keep it there.

"Civilised. But that's the problem, Jeremy. Isn't truth the first casualty of a civilised society, an ongoing need at all costs to avoid offence?" His impassioned reply throws me off kilter. A desperation has crept in.

"It really isn't your fault, Judith. I promise. You deserve to be with someone very special."

"Fine. Goodbye then."

* * *

Stinging – a sudden realisation that my eyeballs are stinging. Why does mascara mixed with tears hurt so? Countless times over the years I've fled headlong to this stable sanctuary, to my four-legged rock, my mute, uncensoring friend. I flick the switch on the wall and Alanis Morrissette begins amplifying my pain. A close friend in the radio unveiling all my fears. An avalanche of questions begin streaming in my head, to match the lyrics so grotesque yet apt.

No way is life helping me out. How did this sneak up on me when I thought everything was going so right – wrong! *What did I do wrong? I tried so hard, but it's all blown up in my face.* I cling to that neck, feel a hungry need to inhale *eau de equus. It is ironic. Hoped I'd met the man of my dreams.*

The softness of Rommel's coat against my face allows me to let go of the handrail on Mount Emotion. To free-fall, rolling over and over; to somersault from a quiet weep into heavy sobs; to acknowledge the shock of how rich and decadent the flow of tears feels; to remember my ex-husband's words, his label pinning me as 'tough to the point of sentimental frigidity'. Have I shown enough warmth to Jeremy? Is it me? Is it him? The lyrics pound on, taunting the indiscriminate hounding of my own conscience.

Sneaking up on me – the woman whose favourite smell is horse, the woman with equestrian hands and muscles of steel. No pretty frills or perfumed silky hair. No, no, her wish instead – good hay and a new pair of wellies. Is she, am I, simply 'not good enough'? Between sobs I hiccup a sharp intake of breath. Dust and stray horse hairs invade the back of my throat. I cough. I curse. A delicate muzzle swings around to flip over my dangling fringe. The song aches out its final words but I cannot bear to speak my own.

I thought everything was going so right, but now it's all gone wrong.

Chapter 18

Judith

I made the mistake of building a castle in the air, but no more pipedreams. I'm back on the bus to reality. My life is on repeat. A near exact repeat of July 2014, which was a repeat of June 2014, which was a repeat of May 2014. Here I am in July 2015, which is a near exact repeat of June 2015, which is a repeat of May 2015.

I think back to April, so near yet it seems so very long ago. Jeremy delivered a new, opening score of a blockbuster in my life, but then insisted for who knows what reason on taking it back. Now I'm stuck again with the tattered little 45rpm single that is my life. It comes complete with its own special scratch which keeps sending it back to the beginning. The record plays as follows:

(A)   Dress. Check water trough. Check Mother is up. Check emails. Check the day's schedule. Drive, walk, check crops, drive, walk, check crops, drive home. Sit at my desk, write up my reports and recommendations. Check Mother has eaten. Check horses. Poo-pick the field, a pet hate of mine, second only to cleaning windows. The former a daily necessity, the latter achieved grudgingly no more than twice in any twelve-month period (much to Mother's chagrin).

Apologies, I digress. Check emails. Check the fridge. To bed. Sleep. Friday evenings Lizzie usually rings. Her work is hectic, her house is chaotic, her horse is lame, but she's not too worried because: Perfect Man is taking her for a day trip on a launch up the Orwell Estuary. Perfect Man brings her expensive chocolates. Perfect Man enables her to wear heels without fear of being likened to a giraffe. Perfect Man has been to the homestead, met her parents and cracked jokes with her brother. Perfect Man occasionally nods off on her sofa curled up with the cat. Perfect man has planted his feet firmly under Lizzie's table. Perfect Man is filling her life and I am truly pleased for her.

I really must start referring to him by his actual, christened name. Otherwise I shall fall into the trap of introducing him at a dinner party. He will be holding a beer glass in one hand then reach out to shake my mother's tentative grasp when I shall glibly announce, 'Mother, this is Lizzie's Perfect Man.' Ding Dong – stupid Judith. 'Mother, I'd like you to meet Lizzie's friend, Jack Stevenson.'

On Saturdays – my weekend differs in that Rommel lifts my day for a few distracting hours. We share inconsequential pottering up bramble-infested byways and sweaty speed taking in big sky, East Anglian landscapes. On our return to the yard he performs his special party trick, a haphazard drenching from the hosepipe which he grips between his teeth.

On Sundays – I usually Skype for a whole hour with Ollie. It hits me hard, that thump-in-the-stomach knowledge – I've done too good a job. He simply doesn't need either of his parents in his bountiful life anymore. My urchin of a bumptious boy is suddenly twenty-six years old. He leans into the laptop screen, proud as punch and enquires,

"What do you think, Mother? Does it suit me?"

Then he rubs his thumb and forefinger absent-mindedly through a neat, dense brown carpet of beard covering his chin. It brings to mind the colour and consistency of my bristle doormat. I actually run the tip of my forefinger in a couple of tiny circles on the screen in a ridiculous need to be able to touch him. To reach through the tens of thousands of miles and join him.

"Ooh, yes. It makes you look so mature, Ollie. You could do with a kitchen scissors session on that overgrown mop though."

He gives a thumbs-up sign. "I wish."

"Remember how you always struggled to stay still on that tall stool I used to make you sit on in the old porch? Your chubby little legs used to dangle a good foot off the floor."

"The image that stuck in my mind, Mum, was all those clumps of severed hair drifting onto the flagstones. I was convinced you were hacking off bits of my body and that I could hear it screaming as it fell!"

"You never told me. Silly boy. I still have the tea towel I used as a bib on you, tied in a little knot behind your head. What I'd give to be able to do a No. 37 cut on you now."

"Don't get soppy, Mum, I'll definitely come home for Christmas this year and I'll probably look like a wild bushman. You can cut it then. Enough about me, you haven't told me what you've been up to. You should stop devoting all your spare time and money on that horse. Find a nice man to spoil you."

I reach across the table to shift a pad to one side, busy my hands unnecessarily stacking three fertiliser catalogues. In that distant room Ollie sits up a little in his chair, points his index finger straight at me.

"You're hiding something. Come on, tell. I'd be *so* excited if you've met someone."

"Well… I have… and I haven't." I scrape my fingers roughly around the skin on my jaw; pull at a solitary overgrown hair missed in the last pluck; hold back a pressure hose of sadness behind my eyeballs. My mini train crash with Jeremy shall remain out of any press releases I give. Ollie continues to wait patiently.

"Lizzie has persuaded me to dabble a bit with internet dating, but I decided to hide my profile a couple of months ago. It doesn't really suit my nature, advertising myself." Ollie's head jerks backwards, hitting the wall, and I cannot help but laugh at his reaction.

"Wow, I'm shocked, Mum. You of all people! I hope you've picked a respectable website though?"

"Don't fret, Lizzie is my guru." Ollie leans forward and his voice drops, becomes quiet.

"Watch out for the sleazeballs, Mum. There will be some out there. You will be quite a catch for someone, especially as you have a decent house."

I chuckle.

"Great. My only son considers that I will be a worthy catch, not for my beauty, brains or wit. Only for my assets!"

"Sorry, Mum. You know what I mean, I don't want you to get hurt or fleeced. Please be careful, really careful." He pauses for a moment. "It just seems surreal how our roles have reversed. I remember the little lectures you used to give me about not getting legless, or swapping girlfriends, or rolling in at breakfast time on a workday. Should I be saying it to you?" He leaves no time for me to gather together a suitable quip, but suddenly slaps his hand against his thigh and his face breaks into an enormous smile. He shouts at the screen.

"Be brave, Mum, reactivate your profile. Have some fun, let your hair down. Go on!"

* * *

Monday morning – Repeat (A).

The hawthorn hedges green. The roses bloom. End of May into June comes and goes.

Monday morning – Repeat (A)

The sun scorches. The birds chirrup. End of June into July comes and goes.

* * *

One afternoon I stick my head around Mother's kitchen door.

"Anything extra to add to the shopping list? I'm off now. The best-before bargains should be on the reduced section."

Mother turns from the sink. I have seen her studying me recently, perhaps conscious of the new lines around my eyes, the way my mouth seems set these days into a thin line of acceptance. Her countenance morphs into That Look. The one I've seen so many times in the past. That Look… reserved by all mothers of small children. Needed when a wan cherubic face at the school gate whispers, "Mummy, I feel sick." Needed when my cantankerous yeti of a Shetland pony called Brutus decided to get down and roll on the ground. I was seven at the time. Trotting along merrily we'd been, my short legs flapping, a thick lump of ebony mane held tight through my fist when, hey presto, bang, Brutus had buckled his knees, dropped his rump and rolled onto his side, rubbing his neck backwards and forwards in the grass to alleviate an itch. Mother had rushed up so concerned, my spindly leg having been pinned briefly beneath his squirming ribs.

That Look and roughly half a century, later nothing has really changed between a mother and her daughter.

"Judith, you've been looking really peaky lately. Have you been taking your iron and multi-vitamins?"

"Yes, I have. And don't start again on the lack of red meat in my diet. I'm not in the mood."

She opens her mouth to object then catches me off guard, steps closer, pulls me into a tight, camomile-scented hug. A prickling behind my eyes. No, I mustn't cry. I was born to be a survivor, that's what Daddy always drummed into me. He'd say with puffed-up pride, "My little girl is a survivor, she's tough." Resting my chin on her bony shoulder, I make a stoic decision not to burden her with my woes. My growing fear of the void, the one where nothing is known or certain anymore. My fear of the tiny crevices pointing vertically towards my lips and prone to collecting traces of chocolate ice cream. I have no fear of survival, I know I am perfectly capable of that. My fear is of travelling the road alone. Telepathy steps in and Mother's whispered words brush past my ear.

"Why don't you pop along to one of those… err, what were they called…err. 'Under the Table dinners'? Tell me, was there a lot of fumbled thigh grasping in addition to conversation, darling?" The warmth of her shoulder trembles against my cheekbone. I cannot see her face. She dares to mock my self-pity and I know I love her the more for it.

"For goodness' sake, Mother. It's Table Talk and, yes, I shall. That's a good idea."

A few fairy strands of octogenarian hair tickle my nose. I pull away sharply to sneeze, jolting her in the process. A bubblegum object spins across the tiles and very quickly we find ourselves grovelling around on our knees giggling like a couple of schoolgirls. Eventually, by utilising a carving fork and a pastry knife, we manage to extricate her hearing aid, together with a smattering of crumbs and dust, sticky from down the side of the cooker.

* * *

TABLE TALK

SINGLES BISTRO DINNER
THE STEAK HOUSE
LANGTON
SUFFOLK – THURSDAY 5TH AUGUST 2015

Dress Code: Smart Casual   **Reception:** 7.30pm
Dinner: 8pm   **Carriages:** At your leisure

- Join us this evening for a tasty three-course classic meal at this renowned family-run restaurant.
- Could romance be in the air at this delightful venue overlooking the river? You may meet your kindred spirit. Be there or you will never know.
- Limited places available for this intimate evening. Make sure you book now.
- Men circulate to the right with each course.

MENU
Delicious three-course dinner includes wine.

Satnavs, I hate satnavs. Ollie's birthday present to me last Christmas. Excellent idea, but why the sodding hell has it brought me down this one-track C road? This is such a rush on a weekday after work. I stop in the middle of nowhere, resort frantically to thumbing through my good old tatty 2000 version of the *AA Road Atlas of Britain*. Langton – back the way we came – reversing skills imminent!

Sure enough I have arrived late. The venue – a copy of the copious other unwanted pubs littering our quaint English countryside. It has been zhuzhed up, the exterior a fresh Farrow & Ball 'Mouse's Back' hue with a crisp, white 'The Steak House' board. *Hopefully, the chef has a proactive respect for his pescatarian customers and knows that nut roasts are no longer de riguer.* 'Welcome drinks' kicked off at 7.30pm. *No chance to collect composure or smooth my windstrewn mane. I suspect I could pass for a scarecrow this evening.*

Fireplace Man is sitting at the table beside the entrance door. *Smart move on Catherine's part, she has clearly given him a job to do, bolster his self-esteem.* Clipboard in one hand, I watch as his other hand pulls gently at his tie, perhaps to alleviate the slightly pink line of chafing skin visible above the collar. He has spied me bumbling in his direction. One arm half out of my jacket sleeve, I jam my glasses back up my nose; my handbag slides unhelpfully to the floor. *A female version of Mr Bean, is that my part to play this evening?* Fireplace Man turns a worried sideways look towards the bar. He is flipping a shiny, blue ballpoint pen round and round through his first and second fingers. It clatters as it hits the chair, giving him an excuse not to have to look directly at me as I reach the table.

An enveloping cloud of Angel perfume arrives with our hostess Catherine as she strides up beside me.

"Just in time, Judith. So pleased you could join us this evening. Everyone else has gone through."

Fireplace Man retrieves the pen and carefully adds a stilted tick to the piece of paper then rises to follow us. I wasn't sure what to expect of this evening but it rolls out as, in essence, twenty or so unattached hopefuls congregate to paddle about in a little food, wine and companionship. There are faces I recognise from the Black Tie Dinner Dance night and that comforts me a lot. A large dining room has been booked to hold the Table Talk soiree. Very much London bistro effect, the walls are bedecked with a contemporary selection of fat fish pictures. Each one made with hundreds of brightly coloured sequins in lime green, cobalt blue or metallic grey glued into position and shimmering. Catherine ushers me to the empty seat on a table for six.

The starters on plates of slate are placed carefully in front of us. We all introduce ourselves. Opposite, to my right, is bob-haircut Angela. Beside me sits an accountant. I shall call him Abacus Man. I quickly establish via all the usual politenesses the following:

He is sixty years old. He plays golf several times a week.

He has four grown-up children and paid for all of them to go through university.

He has Tony Benn's eyebrows. They meet, windswept, in the middle. They remind me of those trees you see clinging perilously to the edge of a Cumbrian crag, endlessly buffeted to grow lopsided facing one way.

He is very specific, doesn't want to have to live with a woman, she must own her own house and remain completely independent. Fingers burnt and all that.

I am struggling to concentrate, already zoning out.

"I consider myself to be a particularly clean man" – this said with a deadpan expression and no hint of irony. We are but fledgling aquiantances; does he think that I will be impressed? I manage to hide a coughed laugh; tart lemon juice coats my throat and shreds of part-masticated whitebait batter inelegantly ends up in my napkin.

I splutter, "Apologies. Do continue."

Then a revelation – he admits that he is a Newby. That this is his first ever dating experience and without warning, my perception of him does an infuriating volte face.

Judgemental is the description that comes to mind, Judith. You have no right whatsoever to judge him. He has no idea how to do this, how to put himself on the line, how to set out his stall. What gives you the right to criticise his honesty? He is clearly a good man. I don my teacher hat, regale him with my pearls of wisdom on why face-to-face meetings like these are so civilised compared to the vagaries of internet dating. He seems impressed and I wish him luck in his quest. Someone, somewhere, will snap up his company, but not me.

Catherine stands behind his chair and announces clearly, "Gentlemen. Will you all please move to the right."

Chairs are grated, warm smiles reproduce in bunches, a couple of guests mutter, not keen to abandon a spark of attraction already lit, several jackets are shed. The next man arrives complete with his glass of water. I shall call him Aqua Man. The waitress delivers the main courses. I quickly establish via all the usual politenesses the following:

He is forty years old but he is attracted to women who are more mature!

He has no ties, never been married, doesn't want children – the irresponsible masses have created a burgeoning world population already. The baked rainbow trout beneath my fork stares back at me. *I hate this bit.* I stick my knife into the cavity of its skull and remove it to a sideplate. I reach for my glass, take a distracting swig. *This Chardonnay is too floral.*

Aqua Man has a wicked sense of humour. He has an English mother and an Indian father and they believed a good education vital.

"Judith, you are so lithe and your son is how old?"

Guilty, I am guilty. Have I ever been flattered by a younger man before? No. Perhaps it's my own fault; I've always assumed I should choose someone at least four years older than myself. Everyone else is chattering, topping up glasses, discussing the immigration problem. There is a busy vibe to the evening. Stomachs are filling. Spices. Aqua Man's skin is infused with cayenne, curry powder and turmeric and he whispers husky words into my ear.

"My temperature is rising." He then intimates that he wants to spend most of the rest of his life on a retreat in India studying the Koran, but only with a like-minded female spirit. *Bat it back, Judith. Return the serve.*

"I'm sure she's out there waiting for you to find her. Of course I'm only here to make up the numbers really. A bit of a favour for Catherine when someone dropped out at the last minute." *I swear the black button eye of the salmon on the wall is staring at me. It knows. Liar, liar, your pants are on fire.*

Out of the corner of my eye I spy Fireplace Man hovering, oozing a kind of visual angst. His top lip lifts, together with his eyebrows, but there is no sound. His feet are shuffling ever so slightly. A few quiet words escape.

"Could you please... everyone." He casts a beseeching glance towards Catherine who is seated close by. She gestures her open palms upwards and mouths a silent, "Bit louder."

Wonder of all wonders. I can see he is actually getting a tiny bit angry.

He jams his hands hard into his pockets and shouts, "Will all the men please move to the right now," then jumps back a couple of inches, shocked in the same way as a puppy when its very first accidental bark pops out. A few heads swivel in his direction. The male occupants of the room rise in dribs and drabs, collecting their glasses. Shirt-tails are re-stuffed into straining leather belts and a new suitor parks his bottom beside me.

Brief platitudes follow, but Anonymous Man is clearly very chummy with the lovely lady to his right. Opposite me now sits a tiny man, no more than 5'3". I am struck by the thought that he could play the part of a corpse in a coffin, his skin is so pallid. He has a Brylcreemed comb-over and the bone structure of a pubescent youth. He offers his hand to me over the top of the water jug and the stainless steel salt cellar.

"May I instroduce myself? I'm Stanley." I have to rise out of my chair slightly in order the reach his hand. It's clammy and cold all at the same time. Fish skin springs to mind. *Oops, must try to expel fish from my thoughts – seems to be popping up rather too regularly this evening.*

"Hello, Stanley, My name is Judith. Are you new to these dinners or an old hand?"

The expression on the face of Angela to Stanley's left would suggest that she has swallowed half a lemon, and yet her mouth is empty. She rolls her eyes skyward while tilting her head in Stanley's direction. A specific message aimed at me. *Oh dear.* For want of anyone else to speak to, I put my best foot forward and engage Stanley's attention. It's a struggle. I have to prise information out of him, one uncomplicated question at a time. I slowly get the hang of pressing the right buttons but his replies are frustratingly monosyllabic. We tuck into rhubarb mousse topped with ginger crumbs. I glean the following:

He is fifty-four years old. He lives alone in a secluded cottage amongst woodland. He has never married, giving me a quizzically amused smile with his retort.

"Me? Children. No. Children are aliens to me. Irritating little things." His eyes shrink to slits in a rock-face, laser intense. *I wouldn't want to put a child in the same room with him anyway.* There is a fuzzy thin line of blackish hair running just above his lip, can't call it a moustache, nearer to the downy hair on a woman's legs – I doubt he has to shave more than once a week. He lights up when I ask about his hobbies.

"I play a little in church. The organ. There are very few people nowadays who can play the organ."

I can picture him perched on the edge of the organ stool in order for the tips of his soft-soled shoes to reach the pedals. Passionate, it's sure to be the only subject that 'lights his fire' – his spindly fingers no doubt pound the keys, tendons in wrists bulging, his chin jutting forward, elbows bending and straightening to create depth or lightness in a chord. As he reaches the crescendo of the piece I'll wager that his comb-over breaks free, flopping with aplomb onto the bridge of his nose. An awkward silence arrives.

"Excuse me, Stanley. Can you point me in the direction of the ladies, please? Women and their bladders."

The ladies' loos are in sharp contrast to the dining room decor. Marilyn Monroe wallpaper in every direction, precocious lips, skirts swirling, ornate grooved silver mirrors. There are five of us crushed in at the same time, female body functions working to a similar clock. Angela has to wait to use my washbasin; she touches my arm, addressing me between squirts of Bromley & Fisher handwash. Her lemon face has reappeared.

"Judith, how are you getting on with Stanley?" *Why do I feel that this is a loaded question?*

"Not too bad actually. He's a computer geek by profession so not easy to find common ground. But, hey ho, I'm still enjoying the evening."

Her back turned to me, she continues our conversation speaking directly to my reflection but the assembled toilet goers are merely feigning disinterest.

"Well, be careful. I've sat next to him before. I remember that when I left to walk across the car park, he was hovering in the shadows; offered to open my car door. He still makes my skin crawl. He's creepy. Plain creepy." I catch her stare eye to eye via the mirror and hold it. My retort escapes with more vehemence than I anticipate.

"Not my impression at all. I think you are mistaken."

* * *

The car radio is blaring, keeping me conscious, driving me home. I shout words at the dark sky, the empty road in the headlights. "Owner of a lonely heart." I keep wrestling with my own demons throughout most of the journey home, the hedges crowding in on the cluttered ramblings in my head. A virus of doubt pulses through my veins. *Should I, shouldn't I, unhide my profile? I've heard tales of brilliantly matched people – one date and... bang. I've heard that it happens sometimes. That could be me, no endless round of multitudinous failed liaisons. A strategy. Do I have a strategy? Make a list, Jude. As soon as you get home. Then you can implement it tomorrow. Without fail.*

Fifty minutes later, and the front door clunks shut behind me. Branston's valiant attempts to trip me up as I cross the hall fail. The fridge and its contents beckon. A cheesecake tastes best when you cut a slice big enough to satisfy the urge, yet small enough to avoid seeming vulgar. A quality cheesecase (more specifically, a Latham's strawberry one) is a must, no insipid or flavourless junk, as is a dessert fork with which to eat it. To gulp it down would be a travesty. So I allow myself this indulgence, this savouring of tiny mouthfuls of decadence at one o'clock in the morning because, *I am determined to stop hiding behind the skirt of my own cowardice.*

Interlude

Luc slumped onto the kitchen chair, flipped open his laptop, rolled his loose trousers up till they sat neatly above his knees. He craved any breath of cool air to his naked legs. He tapped the thermometer propped against the dead Foxy Frances houseplant – twenty-nine degrees. The plastering could wait. Phsst, pop – the can of Becks froze itself to several fingers on his right hand, a numb, burning cold.

CLICK **Search Criteria:** Man Seeking Woman
Search Results: 0–15 of 174
Age Range: 48–55 years

Rows of prospective faces smiled, scowled or pouted back at him. Blondes, brunettes, a bobble-hatted woman and, thankfully, no redheads at all. He'd made a vow to himself never to risk a redhead again. Blue eyes, huge saucer espresso eyes, shy bespectacled eyes, hungry eyes, sad eyes. They are women seeking men, women seeking women or transgenders. Every shape, size and flavour you could wish for.

Do I want a woman with an earring in her nose at fifty-years-old? No, thank you. Why am I on here, yet again? Is there a hook line worth my effort? Perhaps?

'The world is your lobster'

A possibility. Genuinely happy? Or...

'Back again'

I know the feeling. Or...

'I'm gust me'

Spelling, spelling, spelling. Absolutely not. Or...

'I'm free'

She's been on here as long as me – nooooo...

'Looking for Miss Right not Miss Right Now'

Is she perchance insinuating that men only want one thing?

'Carpe Diem'

Two of those. Intellectuals – haven't got the energy.

'This Goldfish Bowl Is Empty"

Clearly the same as your life darling!

DOUBLE CLICK/Individual Profiles/Details:

Ethnicity: Caucasian
Star Sign: Gemini
Intent: Looking for a relationship
Dislikes: Dried fruit & smelly dogs

Luc limped to the sink, drenched a tea towel under the running cold tap, draped it across the back of his neck. Sat down again. *Who should I choose?*

Personality:

'A poet'	*or,*
'a beach bum'	*or,*
'a traveller'	*or,*
'a fashionista'	*or,*
'a homebody'?	

The tea towel was already warm; he folded it twice, pressed it flat then dragged it in a sweeping motion across the dusty screen. Squinting in a little closer, he occasionally muttered a comment. *Ok, girls, let's have a look at your—*

Conversation Starter:

'Whatever'	*Go back to school.*
'Coffee somewhere nice'	*or,*
'A glass of wine'	*or,*
'Lunch, somewhere we can both feel comfortable'	*or,*
'A place we can chat'	*or,*
'Tea and a sticky bun'	

For f***'s sake. This lot are about as wild as a walk of snails! I want a chick with a sense of adventure.

'I am intelligent, witty, easy-going and mildly self-deluded.'

Better.

'Coffee up a gum tree – bring a twinkle to my eye.'

Ten out of ten. Shall I send her a message?

| CLICK | **Children:** | Four |
| CLICK | **Pets:** | Eight Yorkshire Terriers and a Siamese cat. |

A house-full of hormones and hair. Nooooo.

Photograph

Photos, go back to the photos.

Sitting on sofas. Hugging Labradors. Astride bicycles. Grinning proudly beside graduate offspring. Caught on camera by friends, by family, by themselves in their car, at a wedding reception, standing atop a Himalayan mountain or just plain serious, staring Madame Tussaud's waxen-faced at the lens.

'Life begins at the end of your comfort zone.' *Ooh, I like the look of her.*

* * *

Tap.Tap… Startled, Luc looked for the source of the sound. Couldn't immediately pinpoint it. He lent down, frantically unrolled his trouser legs before swivelling on his seat to squint at the farthest window. Tap, tap… Tap, tap. Knuckle on glass, the kitchen pane. A white UPS Parcels insignia filled his eyeline by the back door. In the foreground, a shaven dome of a head above a wide bulbous nose, a hand flattened horizontal to allow the owner to peer inwards.

Eleven years on and he knew it shouldn't matter to him anymore who saw his leg (or more to the point, lack thereof). Pride

226

and his prosthesis. On the one hand, he hated the dependence it represented – his disability. Take it away and he had to hop or balance wobblily. Or lean. Or shuffle incongruously dragging his bottom along the floor. On the other hand, it heralded his independence, gave him wings to do everything that mattered – walk, drive a car, stand up to a saw bench, ride his Honda.

Juliet had been the only one to allow him to forget himself. Everyone else up to that point would insist on commenting or observing or congratulating him on "How well you've done today, Luc, considering," or "It'll take two men to get that bed up the stairs, leave it till Jamie gets home," or "Your limp is much worse, Luc. Are you using the right pads?" Being patronised, the condescension, the fussing (particularly by the fairer sex): he hated it, he'd borne three agonising years of it. Then Juliet fluttered into his life. She demanded that he take the oars along the Cam on their daytrip to Cambridge. She expected him to accompany her on a ten-mile bike ride. To her, he was whole. With her he had pranced around in his underpants crooning love songs. Lifted her onto the table, ran his fingers up the inside of her thighs. If he tripped, she would leave him to find his own feet or foot, whichever the case may be. She would often cock a sly raising of her eyebrows followed by: "Sort yourself out, boy. Come on. Chop chop." To the rest of the world he wanted his leg hidden and totally unavailable for either opinion or concern. He limped to the door yelling at the vacant face still squashed against the window.

"All right, all right. I'm coming. Hold on."

Chapter 19

The postman waited till the last ten metres then slammed on the brakes of his requisite red Royal Mail van and, unsurprisingly, the tyres lost a brief battle with the gritty surface. Stanley heard the sound, a distant ricochet splattering, a mixture of sand and stones peppering the mesh fence. He recognised it well, a recent addition and a highly irritating phenomenon in his world.

As Stanley appeared through his front door, the wicket gate swung back on the fence with a firm crack. He hadn't been quite quick enough today. It was an unspoken contest which he and Petru had been playing out for the past three weeks whereby whoever got to the gate first, won. If Petru got there before Stanley, he would rush through, head down simultaneously peering at the clutch of letters in his grubby hand and walking fast, thus creating an illusion that his day was incredibly busy and stressful. Today, they played out the scenario yet again.

The two men met halfway along the flagstone path and Petru having triumphed gave Stanley the reason to chide in a hissed whisper,

"My gate does not appreciate brute force."

Petru's gloating grin was wasted on the top of Stanley's comb-over.

"Post, sir. Sorry, sir. What you say?"

He knew Petru was faking ignorance. He'd known since overhearing him having a perfectly coherent, loud conversation on his mobile phone while sitting in his van. That was one of the few times when Stanley had beaten Petru to the gate. It meant he could bar Petru's entrance and accept the post from the safety of *his* side of the gate and remain on *his* territory. He was now acutely aware that the gentle creaking of the gate back and forth, back and forth was matched by a small grinding of his own molars. Stanley steadfastly refused to look up into the shaggy-dog face of his cocky protagonist. Instead he addressed the Royal Mail logo embossed on Petru's shirt pocket.

"Is this your last day? Will the new postman be starting on Monday?" For three seconds the two men had hold of each end of the brown A4 envelope. Stanley made a quick tug, taking possession. Petru chuckled nonchalantly.

"Yes, sir. New man here Monday," and waved over his shoulder as he left.

"Have nice day, sir," then slammed the gate behind him.

Stanley stood motionless, mid-path, pursed his lips, turned the envelope over several times, looked up at the gate, his brow furrowed, his focus following the van's dust cloud as it billowed into the distance on the slightly raised track. A few seconds passed till a gentle movement amongst the lower leaves of a Japonica bush preceded the appearance of Stanley's primary companion in his secluded forest idyll – a large, grey buck rabbit.

"Well, Thumper, we must make sure we remedy two problems before Monday, mustn't we? Firstly, the new postman needs to know we are here. And secondly we don't want him stepping past the gate." The rabbit loped out onto the lawn, stopped a couple of feet away, sat back and began to rigorously scratch behind its left ear. Stanley put his hands on his hips and peered in earnest at the rabbit.

"Feeling soporific yet or will you help me pick the best colour to spruce up the nameplate?"

Heading inside, Stanley deposited the post on the bureau in the hall and collected a single skeleton key dangling from the row of tiny hooks in his under-the-stairs cupboard. Whilst still inside the cupboard, he sat down on a low, ancient milking stool placed neatly in the middle of the tiny floor space. He changed his loafers for a tatty pair of short work boots. He disliked their heaviness on the end of his delicate feet and, key in hand, clumped his way awkwardly out through the back door. A rancid whiff caught at his nasal passages as he navigated past the stack of black bin bags piled high against the brick wall and the yard gate. His foot slipped briefly on a patch of slime oozing from a split bag.

He was beginning to question his own decision to build such a high wall so close to the house. Mother would have hated it, which is why he'd had to wait till she passed away to have it erected. One of her favourite pastimes had been supporting her ageing limbs against the kitchen sink and gazing, sometimes for twenty minutes or more, out to the silver birches, watching at dusk for badgers grubbing around or muntjac nibbling the sweeter more luxuriant grasses close to the house. *But*, he thought, *this is my house now and I don't want any hikers, bikers or any other stray forest people nosing in* at my *windows.* The worst offenders he remembered, a group of five hippies who'd taken up residence in the clearing. They had appeared out of nowhere four summers ago and parked a large decrepit Ford van and a small off-white camper van without a single 'by your leave' or 'do you mind?' request to himself! They developed a habit of appearing once a day often scaring the living daylights out of Mummy. A head of crazy dreadlocks would pop up unannounced at the kitchen window asking, always politely (he had to concede that much) to fill their plastic containers with water. The round blue kind which follow many caravaners like a pet on a lead. Stanley had always made a point of standing to watch as the blonde girl with the edelweiss plaits tugged and bumped one of the rolling containers over the rough tussocks. He had felt the need to double-check, to be certain they were gone again. On those balmy summer evenings, he quickly learned to anticipate their lighting of the campfire, a precursor to wafts of barbecued sausage and marijuana floating in the breeze and he would hurriedly shut all the back windows. In short, the wall had been a necessary addition.

He eyed the dormant heap of bags as he pushed the high wooden gate a little wider. The loud creak brought Thumper skipping around the end of the house in search of his food benefactor.

"No, it's not time to come in yet, little fella."

Stanley made his way across the short stretch of patchy grass and carefully undid the hefty padlock on the door of his large shed. He scrutinised the chaos. Propped higgledy-piggledy around and on top of a broken Mountfield ride-on mower was a rake, a couple of plastic buckets, a stone birdbath with a chunk missing from the base. Other items were strewn ad hoc on several shelves running the full length of the shed. He began rummaging in a tea chest stacked full of paint pots then stood back to ponder the problem for a moment. He could feel the damp cotton of his shirt sticking to his underarms. How best to tackle this problem task, he wondered?

He was proud to be his mother's son, always switched lights off if he wasn't in the room, collected barrow-loads of dry branches for the fire, only ever ran the bath half full of water, no more. He liked to think he made clever use of Economy 7 energy with any of his own physical efforts, so he began repopulating the cans of paint from the tea chest onto the shelves. Thumper's quest for culinary nibbles had brought him to the threshold of the doorway where he hesitated, nose twitching, muscles bunched in anticipation of flight. Stanley, aware of his presence, needed a sounding board.

"Olive Green. That was one of Mummy's favourites, but it's dried hard." And he placed it in the corner on the floor.

"Granite Stone. That might be nice." He rolled the can around, squinted at the writing on the metal tin.

"Oh, no good. This one is emulsion. Or how about Cobalt Blue?"

Fifteen minutes later and pleased with his efforts, Stanley scooped up the rabbit, holding him close to his chest, felt the fur slide velvety under his palm in a long, luxurious stroking motion from the base of Thumper's ears all the way to his tail. Never, ever rough leporine fur up the wrong way. He'd made that mistake once, just once, and received a painful, deep scratch in response as Thumper leapt from his grasp and landed with an upturned splat on the ground to then scuttle off in a huff. So now, Stanley returned the bundle of living warmth carefully to the ground.

"OK, Cornflower Yellow it is. No arguments"

* * *

Stanley carried a dining-room chair out past the garden gate and plonked it on the track facing the cottage. He sat down to view his handiwork, brought his cup up close to paper-thin lips and savoured the distinctive tang of Earl Grey as the hot liquid slid over his tongue. First, he'd sanded the old wooden sign and applied undercoat. He'd pottered back inside to answer some client emails. The paint dried quickly in the sunshine, so he had repeated the process through a first coat, then returned to his computer to deal with an 'urgent Trojan virus issue' with Barnley Electronics Ltd. Plonkers – why did they keep making the same mistake and installing new hardware but forgetting to call him out to check the malware?

To complete his DIY efforts, he'd painstakingly enhanced the words 'Rose Cottage' with a shiny black gloss paint, then finally he'd dug out two old bits of malleable wire from the shed. With delight he eyed his refurbished wooden sign hanging neatly on the gate. The sun had spent the afternoon travelling slowly around to the south; now it was casting leaf-shaped shadows across the thatch. Stanley's cheeks stretched into a serene open smile. He liked the Cornflower Yellow – in fact the freshly painted sign made the front door look shabby. Should he change that to match, get rid of the Olive Green? He sipped delicately from the china cup.

He addressed the world in general, but his home in particular, and raised his teacup in a toast.

"The new postman will have no excuse for delivering to the wrong address. Clear for all to see now. This is Rose Cottage."

He savoured the last remnants of tea then turned the china cup upside down on the saucer. A simple but effective trick he'd learnt to prevent the precious cup wobbling off the saucer. Seared into his memory, it was, his mother's wrath when she saw the shattered pieces strewn over the flagstones. Once teacup and chair had been returned to their rightful homes, he placed a thick chain over and through the wicket gate. He ambled off into his humble abode, a contented man.

* * *

A quarter circle of orange sun descended silently behind the pines. A faint breeze brushed forest limbs. Nothing else stirred until a—'Thwack, thwack, thwack, thwack' sound echoed across the clearing – no response.

'Thwack, thwack, thwack, thwack' – no response.

'Thwack, thwack, thwack, thwack.'

Stanley, crouched on his haunches behind Rose Cottage, was wielding a chopped-off piece of square fence post in a four-beat pattern against a paving stone underfoot. He raised his calling instrument six inches, ready to beat again when, at last, Thumper bunny-hopped idly out of the rough grasses under the hedge. Stanley stood up, took a few hurried steps and positioned himself just inside the backyard. The rabbit skidded to a halt close to his heels. Gate safely shut, Stanley bent down again, his face lighting up as the rabbit took cubes of cucumber from his outstretched fingers.

"Time for bed, Thumper."

Interlude

Judith

Reactivated, my profile that is. It's official, I am out there again, displayed on the department store shelf in the section marked 'Singles'. I've added an extra photo to the website. It was taken by a professional photographer for an article in a farming magazine. I love it. I'm carefree, relaxed and it shows; walking in a crop of sugar beet complete with my mud-weighted wellies. I've also made a decision – from now on I refuse to squeeze myself into a 'standard woman of fifty' image box which has been decided by modern society. Instead, I must celebrate my foibles and cast off the cross of conformity I've been lugging around on my shoulders. My nail varnish can solidify in its bottle for all I care.

Now go forth, Boudicca, drive your chariot fearlessly into battle against the marauding legionaries. Watch the flames of womanhood trail out behind you and be proud. This dream continues playing throughout my turbulent night's sleep; a sporadic *Hunger Games* video in my imagination. The folds of my heavy velvet cape are billowing and the potency of two magnificent horses surging forward is intoxicating. Except that, at some point in the early hours of my restless indigestion, it becomes a parody. No longer armed with a glistening sword, I'm fighting the ocean of baying male warriors streaming towards my chariot, with…

slices of apple! Even worse, in order to cut the apple, I have to drop the reins and lose all control of the horses! Is it the fact that I ate too much Stilton and a Royal Gala just before bedtime or is it nervous excitement that's creating these vivid pictures? Have I taken off the handbrake on my life? Is that how I should view my first meeting with an internet date tomorrow morning – taking off the handbrake?

* * *

Phillip, I decide, unnerves me right from the start. Comprehensively unsettles my decorum. Our first date, a coffee and cake. Initially, I am not in the least bit impressed – he arrives thirty minutes late. Yes, he phones to apologise but his shirt collar is threadbare (clean, ironed, but fraying nonetheless); his shoes, I note, could have done with acquainting themselves with polish, but at least they are not trainers. He is sporting designer stubble, quite a chunky chap. He rushes in with a complicated excuse about a tenant's broken-down washing machine and my instantaneous sensory reaction is to the wafts of oil aroma coming off his trousers. I am already the 'wrong way out', imagining a myriad of other things I could be doing with my morning.

We amble through the chit-chat and I decide it's probably a good plan if I implement my standard cocktail party conversation and tactics. Things are going quite well I feel, that is, until I come out with the most ridiculously pompous sentence I think I have ever uttered in my whole life. Phillip asks me something perfectly friendly, a sort of conversation opener about Facebook and Twitter and the merits thereof. My uncensored reply pops out, as incongruous as the sound of air being released from a deflating balloon.

"Friendship involves reciprocity and empathy to which social media does not lend itself."

That sentence is promptly branded into my memory as *the* most up-my-own-derrière collection of words I have ever uttered. Phillip looks me up and down from my turquoise sandals to the sunglasses stuck on the top of my head. He tut-tuts, inclines his head with a wry twist of his mouth.

"Get that quote from *The Times*, did you? Rod Liddle?"

I notice that he never blinks when he is watching me. *A Russell Crowe scrutiny. Be advised he knows exactly where the delicate woman in you hides, Jude.* From now on, I sense that I will get away with jack shit.

Skip a beat – it happens when I hesitate in the foyer at this first meeting, unsure what the protocol is for saying goodbye. Phillip rests his hand on my bare arm, comes closer as if to kiss my cheek. Unexpectedly, he tightens his grip and his other arm goes around my waist, he pulls me closer and makes the tiniest almost conspiratorial compression of my midriff.

"Just wanted to know what it would feel like – to give you a squeeze."

Skip, that's when my heart skips a beat, just before I think, *Personal space, he's invading my safety zone. Help, I've gone rigid.* Mouth into gear, not brain, I know I sound an incy bit indignant.

"You caught me off guard. I don't like surprises."

I notice the pores down the side of his nose oozing the merest hint of sweat. I cannot pull away; his hand is still firmly embedded in my waist flesh. He whispers a deep, quiet promise straight into my ear.

"Oh, I shall always surprise you, Judith." Then he is away again, six steps off, grinning, a half-wave, a "Shall I phone you sometime?" Chirrups, "Would love to see you again," and he is gone, out the door.

My insurgent heart continues to skip and settle, skip and settle. It matches the inconsistent muddle of thoughts lurching around in my headspace.

Chapter 20

Lizzie marched from her car towards the square Georgian-fronted building, heard the slap, slap as the soles of her sandalled feet took the steps three at a time. She stopped for a moment to run her fingers lovingly along each edge of the brass plaque. Inscribed in bold lettering are the words 'Granville Therapy Practitioners'.

She pondered for a moment, remembering the determination she'd had to muster to bring her business idea to fruition. She had been the instigator, the driving force. A catalyst between a chiropractor, a hypnotherapist, a dietician, a physiotherapist and herself, a psychotherapist. She stared at the lettering making a wish for luck because, within weeks, she would be adding acupuncture to the spectrum of therapies all housed under this one roof. This, she felt was her very personal legacy, her baby. She'd never hankered after nappy-filling sprogs. Instead, her mission, her dream – to quell the angst in confused teenagers, to un-train the habitual handwashers of this world permanently enslaved to an obsessive-compulsive disorder, to teach broken adults how to have an actual conversation rather than simply shouting at their children. Her speciality, and by far the scariest of all, to coach anorexic minds into understanding that food is not be feared or reviled.

She was late, she knew she was late, but she pressed her fingertips once more to the nameplate. Her own tiny obsessive-compulsive routine prior to entering. Today marked an anniversary – these doors had opened eight years ago to the day. It had been a culmination of an endless stream of form filling: Medical Council Fit To Practice forms, DBS forms, Licence To Hold Medicines forms, Public Liability Insurance forms, Employer Liability forms, Fire Safety and Emergency Exit Procedure details, Health & Safety at Work procedures and last but not least, Sub-Letting agreements.

The moment Lizzie was inside the door, Magic Margaret's wholesome smile greeted her. Dependable Margaret, given the prefix 'magic' within months of her arrival. Her bounteous bosom often the receptor of homely hugs when teenage tantrums turned into tears and flight. Her reception desk positioned immediately opposite the front door, she was a master at distracting a fleeing patient as they stomped or scuttled up the long hall. Some fled in anger, some fled in truculent frustration: 'You don't understand, you cannot possibly understand what it's like. I've tried so hard,' yelled over a shoulder at a hovering parent. Some would flee, thinking that if they melded into the hall walls, they might slither out the door surreptitiously.

Magic Margaret could always be counted upon to distract or coax a ten-year-old as he paused within a foot of the door to tap the handle three times, turn three small circles then tap the handle again three times. Magic Margaret would always pick the perfect split second to intervene or distract. Sometimes a simple throat clearing did the trick, but more often an even simpler: "Juice, umm, Nathan, isn't it?" And she would waddle from behind her desk clutching a small carton of apple juice. "My hands can't grip this silly plastic screwcap, top, thingy. Nathan, your hands are just the right size to do it for me." She would press the carton into the palm of the Nathan or Joe or Louisa while her arm was magically guiding them gently to one of the funky reception chairs lined up either side of her desk. She always kept a box of Man-Size Kleenex tissues between the pen holder and the appointments diary. And the professionals had all come to respect her talent so that by the time they had walked the 35–40ft from their consulting room in search of said Nathan, Joe or Louisa, they would find the child secure in her seated presence, a Kleenex mopping a cheek, or strolling along the corridor holding her hand. Safe, diffused, acquiescent. It made no difference how big, small, smelly, truculent or hysterical the patient was, Magic Margaret could handle them.

The reception area, warm in the full-on afternoon sunshine, hit Lizzie with an accompanying noxious lily-haze. She addressed the wearer of the starched mid-blue pinafore dress and white blouse. She always felt that Margaret would have fitted right into an episode of *Call The Midwife*.

"Good afternoon, Margaret. Is all quiet on the Western Front today?"

Margaret glowered at Lizzie from behind her NHS prescription glasses. She was a consummate professional and didn't always agree with Lizzie name-tagging in the workplace. Even if it was only ever out of earshot of any clients.

"Yes, Dr Everett. Your first appointment is the Morgan family. I've put them in waiting room No 2 just in case."

The building, originally a house, Lizzie had loved from the moment she stepped through the front door. It was deceptive in that it still appeared residential from the road and boasted an unnecessarily wide hall and staircase, but the previous owner, a veterinary surgeon, had relocated out of town, leaving a legacy perfect for Lizzie's grand scheme – a flat-roofed extension at the back boasting four consulting rooms, plus a locked dispensary/

storeroom and two economical but functional waiting rooms. Lizzie cocked a mischievous tweak of her eyebrows at Margaret.

"Ah yes, the Morgan family. Any breakages yet?"

* * *

"Where has the day gone, Margaret?" Lizzie began unbuttoning her white work blouse; her other hand whooshed open the bottom drawer of the filing cabinet. Margaret was busy pouring a glass of water carefully into the vase of lilies on the windowsill.

"Isn't it time you were off home, Margaret? It's Friday. Leave that, I'll lock up. Off you go now."

She wanted Margaret away, off the premises, not in a position to judge her. Despite being Margaret's employer and professional superior, the woman had a knack with one chilling look, one miniscule jut of the chin, of making her feel small, silly, even childish. Stripping down to her bra, Lizzie pulled a crumpled magenta T-shirt from the drawer. Unfortunately, her head and arms were all halfway through the holes when the doorbell rang. A warm rush of circulation went to her cheeks and she muttered a hurried

"Sorry, Margaret. Can you get that? It should be Emma and Judith. I'd better not answer half-dressed, just in case."

Margaret peeked through a four-inch gap, then swung wide the heavy wooden door.

"Good evening, ladies. Dr Everett is part-dressed but do come in anyway. She appears to have abandoned any sense of decorum lately."

Margaret then swung her handbag strap up onto her shoulder, hoicked her left double-E-cup breast up with her palm and repositioned the strap into the groove underneath. Lizzie visualised a speech bubble above her own head which read, 'Stones

242

in glass houses.' Margaret flounced through the open door casting a belated "Remember to use the mug mats under your glasses. We don't want any more red wine marks on the white oak surfaces, do we, Dr Everett?"

Emma ceremoniously clunked the mortice lock into place. As one, Judith and Emma opened their mouths and a mocking repeat ensued.

"We don't want any more red wine marks on the white oak surfaces, do we, Dr Everett?" and burst out laughing.

"OK, OK, you two, pack it in. This practice would fall apart without Magic Margaret."

They meandered arm in arm chuckling down the corridor. But without warning, Judith halted and dramatically flapped her hands from side to side as she spoke.

"It's no good. I've got to tell you both. I've taken the plunge, at last."

Nonplussed, Lizzie turned to stare at Judith. Emma was also looking blank-faced at their friend. Judith bunched her fingers into fist shapes and grinned at them.

"I've been on an internet date! *Two*, actually." Judith reached forward to pat her palms on Emma's bare shoulders before adding quickly.

"*No*, not two different men. I mean I've seen the same man twice. Ninny."

A gabble of questions came thick and fast amongst a flurry of waving arms, thumbs-up signs and flicked back hair before Judith could speak at all.

"OK, one at a time. His name is Phillip. Our first date was weird, I wasn't at all sure about him, but the second was great. We had a lovely wander around Framlingham Castle, got incredibly wet though. It poured."

Quite suddenly, Lizzie realised that her thoughts had turned to full-blown irritation and she interrupted Judith, her words tumbling.

"*You* didn't text to let me know you were meeting. I've told you before, it doesn't matter how last-minute it is or whether you're in a rush. You must let someone know where you are going."

Judith's whole stance wilted.

"I'm sorry I didn't text you. Mother was my 'phone an escape' contact instead. Letting her in on my dates with Phillip has distracted her from incessantly trying to dissect my failure with Jeremy! And I didn't want you to expect too much, didn't know if the scaredy-cat in me would win. Am I forgiven?"

Lizzie suddenly flung her arms around her best friend, hugged her close.

"Of course." When she released Judith from her embrace, she stood back a little, saw a very new radiance and vitality and felt a wave of joy envelop her.

"I am so pleased for you. This requires a celebration. Now, come on, let's find the wine glasses."

Lizzie's consulting room. She'd pulled rank over her co-workers all those years ago and nabbed the room with a double-aspect view of the paved patio and brimming terracotta plant pots. She gestured her girlfriends to enter.

"Make yourselves comfortable, girls. Back in a tick with the glasses. I've had to hide them out of Margaret's sight otherwise she is prone to taking them home, ostensibly to make sure they get washed properly, then, oh dear whoops, she forgets to return them! I swear she's hoping I shall resort to slurping good quality Pinot Grigio from a mug decorated with the words 'The Voices In My Stethoscope Made Me Do It'."

She headed back up the corridor spinning a set of keys around her index finger. A joiner had been in only the day before to fit a new lock and Lizzie found herself jiggling and fighting with the key. In an attempt to lift the whole door a centimetre or two higher, she impatiently resorted to wrenching the handle several times. The key eventually gave with a click and she lurched over the threshold. Unfortunately, her kitten heels did not go well with the freshly mopped floor and... splat! Down she went. She heard Emma's distant voice chime:

"Lizzie, what are you doing? Do you need a hand?" Followed by the pitter, patter and click, click of two sets of shoes. They found her compos mentis and relatively unscathed, sitting, shoulders hunched, on the sparkling clean lino. Lizzie smelt the intensely sharp pong of citrus Flash and contorted her face into a Wallace and Gromit grimace. She raised a palm to her throbbing skull as a wave of queasiness swept over her. Judith and Emma quickly hooked an arm under each of her elbows and helped her to her feet, but by the time her cotton skirt touched the vinyl of the dispensary chair she had realised that the worst of her pain was actually internal.

Judith started to carefully part the layers of compacted hair before softly announcing,

"You'll live, Lizzie. Probably have a corker of a lump. Have you got any witch hazel?"

Lizzie knew she was peering into a precipice of remorse, but she also knew that her throbbing cranium was merely a tap. She'd hit the tap hard and the pressure of water was building behind her eyes. She rubbed quickly at a couple of sliding tears. Judith's face, so close, morphed in fluid succession from concern to alarm.

"It isn't that bad. Truly, Lizzie. What's the matter? Not like you to cry over a little bump on the head. You're a fighter."

Lizzie sucked in a breath of courage, then blurted out her own news.

"I'm not crying over my head. I'm crying with despair. I finished with Jack."

Emma and Judith took the set of keys from Lizzie and opened the cupboard labelled 'First Aid'. They gathered up two wine glasses from behind a box of cotton swabs, boiled the kettle and escorted her back to the comfort of her consulting room. Designed to put patients at ease within a professional setting, Lizzie had picked warm, stone-coloured paint for the walls and a practical mid-blue for the carpet. A three-seater sofa, soft but also businesslike in a slate-grey material, encouraged a sense of informality. It was offset by upbeat canvas artwork on the long wall, a series of three conjoined works in swirling bright Smartie colours. To one side, a more upright high-backed chair suggested it would often be moved to place the occupant immediately opposite Lizzie and her desk.

The three women lined up side by side on the sofa, well away from Lizzie's desk. No risk of wine stains on white oak – they had concurred! Lizzie's lower legs were folded up under her bottom, both hands were clasped around a mug of coffee. Her mascara had been smudged and squished up and out across her temples, her lipstick was no more. Her two friends were swinging between shades of commiseration, consternation and anger.

Emma, sitting in the middle and quaffing unlimited Pinot Grigio, proclaimed,

"What the hell did you do that for? For Christ's sake, Lizzie! You are absolutely nuts. You'll never find anyone else as nice as Jack." Being the friend who best understood Lizzie, Judith was the one to voice the truth.

"Perfect Man, but that's the problem, isn't it? He may have

been perfect but he wasn't really man enough for you. You don't need a puppy who runs around looking adoringly into your eyes. You need a character. An outdoorsy, hot-to-trot, professional man. A cross between Daniel Craig and Bear Grylls should fit the bill. Jack ticked so many boxes for you, but you would have ended up poking your high heels in his chest." She gave Lizzie's knee a token pat. "It wouldn't have been a pretty sight!"

Lizzie's craving for a nicotine hit had become unbearable; caffeine was a poor substitute. She reached across Emma's lap, snatched up her handbag, rummaged a little, extricated one of the deadly tubes of tobacco, then casually flung the bag back. Emma stroked the wine-red eel skin, brought it up hard to her nostrils and inhaled a lungful of leathery heaven before fixing Lizzie with her 'I'm trying to be tough' eyes. Then she shrugged her freckled shoulders and dug in for another guilt swipe.

"Are we keeping the earrings by chance?"

Lizzie's index and second finger were firmly gripping the cigarette, her lips were ready, her head tipped at an angle. She didn't inhale, transfixed for a moment by a daddy-long-legs bobbing erratically as it tried in vain to land on the upper edge of the lampshade.

Her voice cracked as she said,

"There was an inevitability about our relationship that was gaining momentum. However hard I've tried to walk away from that fact, I couldn't. I hated it – all his unspoken assumptions. Not for me." She sucked in a shot from the smouldering tobacco, relished the sense of serenity it brought. Emma continued to view Lizzie with an air of disbelief; she resumed her inquisition. A child with a complicated new puzzle, still unable to fathom the workings of Lizzie's mind.

"I get the feeling you are only really attracted to rogues,

Lizzie. It's gonna come around and bite you in the backside one day. Good luck, is all I can say."

A lack of speech pervaded the room. An alien condition in their female world and Lizzie knew they all felt its discomfort. She was relieved when Judith, sitting pig-in-the-middle between them, was first to break the impasse. Judith addressed the far wall, which had become of great interest to all present.

"If there is one thing I abhor, it is an atmosphere, and I am sitting in the middle of a pregnant pause right now. Such a ludicrous description for what is, in essence, simply an awkward silence. I've often thought – 'sarcastic response pending' – might be a more accurate description so I looked it up once, in a thesaurus, back in high school before including it in an essay. The explanation was simple – apparently it is the amount of time it takes for you to look at a woman and wonder whether she's pregnant or just plain fat!" She stood up, gained higher ground, a bit of authority. "Pregnant pause. Not allowed girls."

Lizzie took a long draw, puckered her lips and puffed out four perfect O shapes. Judith addressed the Cherokee smoke signals hovering above Lizzie's forehead.

"Do you know what I do whenever I'm down, girls?"

Emma flashed her attention at Judith, a friendly lifeline.

"What? Go on. Knowing you, Jude, it'll be terribly practical." And warming to the theme, she jumped back in again before Judith could speak. "I'll bet it's… ooh, let me think. You mix a cheesecake. Or you spread manure on your roses or…"

Lizzie huffed away the lurking remnants of smoke, the tiniest glint of humour swelling her irises. She butted in,

"I know, I know – you collect bugs from a ten-acre wheat field in plastic containers then sit at the kitchen table sorting them into different species and counting them for two hours!"

Judith grabbed the strap of Lizzie's rudely expensive handbag and swung it playfully at her friend's shoulder.

"Stop taking the piss out of me. It's a much simpler remedy than that. Doesn't cost a dime, doesn't require any energy or equipment or any other person for that matter, other than yourself." Judith's voice had risen in anticipation of her punchline. She stood up straight, spreadeagling her arms for dramatic effect. "I sing."

Lizzie shot Emma a brief sideways glance, unsure whether Judith was in earnest or winding them up. Judith took this as a cue to enlarge on her answer.

"Whenever I'm feeling truly down, Lizzie, I always pick myself up by singing. It works a treat."

Judith tugged her two friends to their feet and began conducting. They were a motley trio but Lizzie felt they did their best. She enjoyed Judith's barely disguised pained reactions to the haphazard but hearty racket which ensued. Using a ruler as her baton, Judith made exaggerated downward whooshes of her arm in an attempt to keep a uniform beat going. Emma, however, simply shouted the words as they belted out 'You Got a Friend in Me'. Lizzie suspected her own version was more of an off-key wail. Two verses were all Judith could stand before she sat sideways on Lizzie's knee and ordered,

"Group hug."

Woman-to-woman contact: it demands truth, it demands a frankness too easily brushed aside when at a safe, physical distance. Lizzie used the moment to her advantage.

"Now, Judith. The truth. What is your gut feeling about this Phillip chap?" Judith hesitated, shifted a little on Lizzie's knee and looked sideways at her.

"He's a bad boy. Don't get me wrong, I don't mean dishonest or into anything unsavoury or illegal, but he is a b-a-a-a-d boy."

Emma began gently bouncing on the sofa, crossed fingers on both her hands.

"Are you seeing him again?"

"Probably."

Chapter 21

Judith

Ding, dong. Ding, dong. Ding, dong.

"Hiyah, Lizzie. What's cooking?"

We slot immediately into a well-worn groove – the click, click of the cigarette lighter on Lizzie's end of the phone lasts six seconds, followed by another six seconds as she both inhales and then exhales her first puff. Each action forestalls any dialogue and I have learned to indulge her. Eventually she speaks.

"Actually, I'm ringing to ask what's going on in your world, not the other way around. I was so bogged down with my own romantic quagmire at the practice a couple of weeks ago, I barely registered that you've met this Phillip chap twice already."

"Well, I was glad you didn't press for a full debriefing. It would have been difficult with Emma there. I'd rather full disclosure is kept to only you and me." I stand up and begin padding along the landing, speaking in a hushed tone.

"Hold on a sec, will you? Only be a mo." I gently reach to click the upstairs adjoining door shut. Back in my office I settle myself into the folds of my swivel chair, rest my chin into my palm and cup the receiver close. I am firmly stuck on the horns of a dilemma – should I or shouldn't I tell her? The three-second hesitation it is taking me to gather my reply immediately obviates any chance I have of staying schtum.

Lizzie pipes into my ear,

"Come o-o-o-o-on, Jude. Spill the beans. What have you been up to?"

I can picture Lizzie's 'I know you too well' scrutiny through those searching irises, emerald flecked with black. She constantly grumbles about her short, nondescript eyelashes, but when she sticks on falsies and eyeliner for special occasions her eyes became absolutely mesmerising, in vivid bright contrast to her blonde, verging-on-white hair. I've witnessed men literally swoon, a kind of Medusa effect, unable to tear their gaze away.

Half an octave higher, Lizzie's pitch becomes more insistent.

"Jude? Are you still there?"

I know that what I have done could be construed as treading a very fine line between comedy and tragedy. I take a deep breath and decide to jump.

"Well, I saw Phillip again last Saturday."

Lizzie waits patiently.

"We met for a meal at the 'George and Dragon', the one near the water meadows.

Anyway, the car park there was full, so I ended up pulling into that tiny gravelled area with lots of low-hanging trees just off to the side of the hotel. Do you know where I mean? Everyone starts their walks from there, along the railway line."

Lizzie butts in, her words coming fast.

"That must be date number three or four isn't it? Excellent." Her tone morphs to efficient again. "Right... Cut to the chase. Stop prattling on about the parking."

"I know, I know, but it's relevant. I promise. Anyway, you know I don't normally drink more than a couple of glasses of

252

wine, but I let my guard down and sort of forgot. Phillip isn't my type at all, I get the feeling he comes from the wrong side of the tracks but the electric energy he exudes is intoxicating and he's so damned persuasive. It was getting pretty dark when we came out and he insisted on walking me to my car." I choke up a little before whispering into the earpiece, "It felt so good, Lizzie. Why does holding hands to walk even a few hundred yards make me melt?"

"Because you're a woman. There's nothing wrong with that. And you've been plodding along in a tactile desert for far too long now. Any skin-to-skin touch will feel especially poignant. Go on."

I hear a leisurely draw on the fag Lizzie must be balancing between fingers, her chin tipped slightly sideways in order to smoke and keep the earpiece close simultaneously.

"Jude, please tell me you're not leading up to saying that he hurt you?"

I feel my mouth stretch into a giant O, the kind clowns wear as their eyebrows rise into a half-moon shape to mimic horror or gleeful surprise. I screech back,

"No, absolutely not. Pleeeeease – he was brilliant. In fact, far too brilliant. It was dark and my Audi was sort of around the corner out of sight under the trees and," I pause, "well, one thing led to another." I hear a sharp gasp on the other end of the phone.

"Judith. You didn't, did you?"

A smidgen of me is beginning to revel in this unfamiliar territory – me surprising Lizzie! In the past our friendship has always been peppered with the boot firmly being on the other foot. I linger for another moment and decide to stretch the words apart, elongating them for dramatic effect.

"Yes, we reclined the seats in my car. He had incredibly salty

253

balls, but that was fine." Lizzie's immediate coughing fit on the other end of the phone is interspersed with a screech.

"Bit of seasoning added flavour, did it?"

An unfamiliar sense of smugness is wrapping its arms around me. Liberating, so joyously liberating to be the naughty girl.

"In fact, I ended up with my feet wedged against the ceiling to get a better purchase."

Lizzie splutters one last time. I can picture the droplets of spittle now covering the mouthpiece. She is gathering her reaction.

"*What?* You let him use his gear lever in your car. Broke your four-year famine with an auto bonkathon! Bloody hell, Jude. Never in a million years would I have expected that. You're a dark horse, aren't you?"

"Let's not get too carried away with crudity because I'm pretty sure I shan't see him again. I'd be far too embarrassed to look him in the eye." Another long, slow drag on her cigarette.

"I'm guilty in the past of telling you to abandon your inhibitions but not all sense of coherent reasoning! Way to go, girl. Way to go."

* * *

I come off the phone confused. I make my way downstairs – eighth step down, I shimmy to the left and place sock feet gingerly on highly slippery oak to one side of the carpet. Mother is miraculously able to hear the eerie creak from boards numbers nine to eleven if the hall door is ajar. I need to think. I need to ruminate. Pudding bowl of chocolate cheesecake and Carte D'Or ice cream in hand, I tiptoe back to my office, the one place she understands not to invade. My swivel chair beckons.

It's 7.30pm and a hairdryer breeze is ruffling the loose papers on my desk. The office has the best view in the house. Though quite small, its window draws my vision linearly down the short gravel drive between two enormous horse chestnut trees either side then on to the rolling Constable hills. If I lean all the way across the desk and stick my head out a few inches, I can just see Rommel and Nugget off to the right. Recovering from the exhausting heat, they are both out for the count. Rommel's enormous grey mountain of a stomach is forced exaggeratedly high by his recumbent position. Horses are prone to appearing to be dead and it doesn't matter how old and wise one is, it still makes your heart skip a beat with worry.

Skip a beat. Such a simple but effective description and it's here again. A reminder of that first date with Phillip. Coffee and cake must have felt rather prosaic to him now I've witnessed his true colours!

As above.

Skip a beat with worry or fear.

Skip a beat with hope.

Skip a beat with shock.

Skip a beat in anticipation.

Skip a beat with excitement – is that what mine did last Saturday?

I jab the dessert spoon at a chunk of ice cream. 'Indulgent chocolate with dark chocolate pieces from Ecuador'. *Can't abide any kind of wishy-washy chocolate. In fact, that's true of my taste in men too. Perhaps that's why I succumbed to Phillip. He's an 84% cocoa kind of guy. Not your middle-of-the-road Cadbury's Milk Tray selection box. But a hardcore, 'slightly bitter in the first bite' block of rich taste. Though, I can only ever manage one row of pieces; more than that is too much.*

I begin rolling a part-melted blob in circles around the smooth enclaves of my mouth. It rests on a tooth a moment too long and a patch of enamel screams 'sensitive' at me. I swallow and snap back to the merits and demerits of men. *Perhaps that was Lizzie's problem with Perfect Man. He wasn't even a Cadbury's man. He was actually a smooth, swirly, shell-shaped, too-much-sugar-and-not-enough-cocoa kind of Belgian chocolate man. Very attractive when you open the box but far too sickly after a while.*

So, Judith, what the hell was Jeremy? Convinced yourself he was going to swing in through your window on a rope, dressed in a dinner jacket and say, "All because the lady loves Milk Tray." Got that wrong, didn't you, girl?

The swirls of uneaten ice cream cannot be left behind. I press my index finger into the centre of the bowl, twist it in a circle so the last delicious remnants can be consumed. *Jeremy. I thought I'd found friendship in Jeremy, coupled with taste and respectability, and I know I need that more than anything else. It will see me into my dotage. But there was a debilitating complexity to Jeremy. Does that mean I should completely forsake passion – am I not allowed to have both?*

Which is Phillip? Friendship, passion, neither, both. A quick fling? Something more? For Christ's sake, make up your mind, Judith. By default, have I become a whore, the currency being companionship?

"Judith? Are you there, dearie?" Mother's warm call sings in from along the corridor. I stand up, pop my head around the edge of the door.

"Be with you in a few minutes."

No. Even if Phillip rings – and I have no idea whether he will – I shall not be seeing him again. Sod it. Time is hunting me down, but I refuse to misread lust for anything more substantial.

Interlude

Stanley, a will o' the wisp performer, is caught by and totally immersed in the story of the music. The strains of his favourite piece, *Clair De Lune*, flowed. A physical reality, a creative current, he could feel it starting in his head and running through his shoulders. It pulsed down his fingers to the ivory keys. Written by Debussy for the organ, he rarely played it in church anymore. He felt the story it told was far too subtle and much better suited to a piano. He was oblivious to his surroundings; the cool, dim Beatrix Potter interior complete with repeat floral wallpaper. He had no need to turn the pages of music he knew by heart, and so he continued, hunched round and low. Initially, he caressed the keys with his fine-boned fingers but the delicate opening melody gradually built and progressed. The sleeves on his chequered woollen jumper stretched or compressed as they followed the movement of his arms and, in collusion with the piece, built in urgency. His hands splayed apart to pound out the crescendo of disparate notes.

He did not hear the intermittent whoosh, whoosh of air being released or the thud as a solid wicker basket hit the ground, or the shouted instructions between the three male occupants as they climbed out. Apart from an occasional click, clickety, click as Stanley's uncut nails broke the softness, the tune began winding its way down to its natural conclusion.

Bang, bang, bang. All peace shattered, he heard his front door being assaulted. Stanley unfurled his coiled fingers, waited another three seconds. Bang, bang, bang... Stanley slowly gripped each finger in turn on his left hand and proceeded to pull the knuckle out with a sharp tug, then he repeated the process on his right hand. He was very aware that his teeth had begun grinding.

Tap, tap, tap. The demand for attention via the window pane was now much more insistent so he straightened up and headed to the front door. He half opened it, blinked a couple of times.

"Sorry to disturb y'all." The owner of the American-drawl apology was backlit by the midday brightness but appeared to be male and wearing a thick coat. The voice, propelled from between a dark moustache and several folds of double chin, continued.

"Maa balloon. It's landed just behind yorre cute home. We need to get our back-up jeep to the right location to pick us up but we can't get a signal for our cell phone."

Stanley remained still and silent, a total lack of any facial expression being his default hallmark. He glanced at his watch.

"It would be wonderful if we could use yorre little old landline to make a phone call, please?"

The intimidating figure continued to loom in Stanley's porch, blotting out the light. Stanley narrowed his eyes, shifting his focus from the stranger's peaked cap to the track in the distance and back again. His isolated existence being very much one of choice, he never actively shunned human company but much preferred to seek it on his own terms. Consequently, he was feeling a strong urge to reply:

"The main road is one and a half miles that way. Nice walk on a beautiful evening like this." Instead, the hidden spectrum of unvoiced thoughts and reactions flickering behind Stanley's eyes caused the stranger to take a respectful step backwards.

"One call, that's all." Stanley swung the door a little wider. "Come in. This way."

The stranger grabbed Stanley's left hand in his own, squashing it with a steel grip, and smiled a cheekbone-to-cheekbone smile.

"Why, sir, the friendliness of you Brits is always so-o-o-o heart-warming. I'll only take five minutes of your time."

Inwardly cursing because he had forgotten to put the chain back on the front gate, Stanley pointed at the phone sitting on the hall bureau.

Chapter 22

Judith

Pit pat, pit pat, pit pat. I can hear Mother's feather-light feet approaching down the hall. I cease my laboured chopping as she enters my kitchen and await her predictable comment. She does not disappoint.

"Ah-hah. Your speciality, Judith. Freshly chopped carrot, coriander and cartilage."

Funny how one can come to both love and loathe certain repeating mannerisms or habits in one's nearest and dearest. She's been coming out with this one-liner since I was fifteen years old and added the tip of my index finger to the vegetable selection. I continue on to slicing a courgette. She addresses the back of my neck.

"I'm having one of my Slightly Befuddled days today, dear. Have you seen the insect repellent anywhere? It seems to have vanished and I must tackle the caterpillar invasion in my bathroom before they send in their second battalion."

Mid-chop, knife in hand, I slowly turn to face Mother and frown.

"Did I hear you correctly? A troop of caterpillars in your bathroom?" Mother's cheeks and neck are a pale flamingo pink above the thick fluffy collar of her dressing gown. Temperatures in the seventies and yet she still refuses to use the cool cotton wrap which I bought for her last birthday.

"Yes, dear. I was minding my own business in the bath and spotted one, halfway up the tiles and heading for the ceiling. How on earth it managed to grip, I cannot imagine." A lurking ache in my stomach reminds me just how hungry I feel.

"You can't call one bug an invasion, Mother. Just take a flat piece of card and a jam jar and you can pop it outside to live a full and useful life." The bubble above my head reads, "She's eighty-five, remain cool.""I've been doing that for the past four days, darling. Must have fiddled about carefully removing at least twenty, exactly as you suggest. Trundled them out one by one via the porch door; luckily this morning I spotted a stream of them tumbling out from the wall onto the flower bed below the bathroom window." She is rolling a thin, white postcard into a cylinder between her two palms.

"I'm just not sure exactly what they are because, since last winter and the sub-zero snap, one or two beetles have taken up residence in the cupboard under the washstand. So, are these caterpillars young cabbage whites? Or beetles or bees or some other nasty crawling pest? Should I be saving them or squashing them, dear?" I place the knife on the counter.

"OK, Mother. Show me one of these caterpillars. If that's what they are, then we can be happy in the knowledge that we are housing a future generation of butterflies or moths. But unfortunately, they could also be wasps."

We reach her bathroom and she picks up her story again.

"One caught me completely by surprise this morning. I got down on my hands and knees, thought they might be coming in by the pipe to the cistern." Her fingers are playing an imaginary piano of excitement. I cannot allow myself to be tetchy or impatient. Her animation is creating an unexpected glow deep in my chest.

I simply enquire,

"You're leading up to something, Mother. What happened next?"

"I had my head down the side of the loo for several minutes and when I looked over my shoulder to do a reverse crawl, one had crept up on me from behind, doing that weird kind of caterpillar humping motion. As I was already on the floor, I fixed it with my special stare." I accidentally nip a smidgen of cheek between my teeth in an effort not to laugh, struggling to meet her eyes. *Mirth. Keep it inside, Jude.*

"Oh, yes, Mother. Your Special Stare. The one you reserved for particularly heinous crimes when we were young. I remember it well. Haven't seen it for years. You must be mellowing in your old age." And on cue she does it. That laser 'pierce-a-hole-in-your-forehead' look while the tip of her tongue plays gently along her upper lip in acute concentration.

"You've put me off my story. Where was I? Oh yes. My Special Stare stopped it in its tracks. We eyeballed each other. Lots of teeny-weeny eyes in symmetrical pairs." She tucks her chin into her chest and deepens her voice.

"I told it face to face: beetle or bumble, you've been testing my patience for four days now. I've had enough of you lot. Pesky thing ignored me and started its caterpillar hump straight at me again! But I've misplaced the repellent."

My evening is clearly to remain devoid of dinner until I sort out Mother's conundrum. She yanks on the light cord then points towards the shower curtain.

"Let's see. Where did that last stalker get to?" I duly climb into the shower and quickly locate two of the guilty parties lurking in a groove. I carefully flick the wild beasts into my hand and peer a little closer.

"Thankfully, they've got too many eyes to be sawflies and enough legs to be sure they're caterpillars, so they won't mature into anything that stings. Mother, can you pass me that piece of card or whatever it was you were holding earlier."

We return to my kitchen, all marauding insects having been banished, when I notice that the card in my hand has printed lettering. I unfurl its stiff edges. My name is elegantly handwritten in ink at the top.

"What's this?"

"Oh sorry, darling. That's what I was bringing earlier. Someone must have popped it through the letterbox this afternoon. I opened the envelope by mistake."

Judith,

•••

GREAT WALMSLEY
VILLAGE HALL
HOG ROAST AND BAND NIGHT
16TH OCTOBER 2015, 7.30pm
Rock Your Socks Off With The Band DAMAGE
All Proceeds In Aid Of The "Village Hall Toilet Fund"

•••

I do hope all is well with you since we last met. This should be a really good night out and I immediately thought of you and your girlfriends. All in aid of a very good cause. Mention my name at the door and the tickets are on me. Hope to see you there?

Jeremy Albright

* * *

The track has been softened with a timely overnight dose of rain. A hint of a haze is still hovering over the fields. It is catching in droplets on the stray wisps of hair sticking to my cheeks and fringe. The faster the ride, the wetter both my fringe and Rommel's mane become. Up and out by 9am, no manic weekday van-drivers, no before-work joggers. Even the dog-walkers are tardy on Sundays, especially when autumn darkness has begun to creep away later and later. It is virtually impossible to be anything other than 'in the moment', and I am. We pick up a ground-eating canter around a couple of fields. The dreariness of the landscape and the woes of my single dichotomy have vanished as mile after mile flies along uninterrupted. Rommel's backside is power-housing to full capacity. The perfect mix of damp soil and a layer of springy headland grass underfoot means that his trot is on 'super-boost', bouncing me high out of the saddle. His neck is arched, and the symmetry of man and horse, often waxed of lyrically throughout history, is with me right now in this ride.

Eventually, we have to slow down. Rommel comes grudgingly back to a sensible walk, but as he clatters onto the tarmac, he jogs now and then, impatient with the sedate pace. This is the less-than-ideal, but necessary, B-road finish to our route.

Breakfast, when I get home – muesli and yoghurt with grapes? No, scrambled eggs.

A bright warm bank of sunlight breaks through the overhanging trees and the familiar aroma rising from Rommel's neck is sweaty, musty and welcome.

Only a mile, best if I trot again around the bend. Cheesecake? What flavour this evening? Lemon or shall I do that baked apple recipe I found? Steady, not so fast, Rommel, we've got to cool a little before we get home.

A distant whining growl is beginning to come closer. I cannot ignore it anymore.

Motorbikes. Several, by the sound of it.

I scan my surroundings, suddenly thrown into a horrible panic of visual information gathering. There is no verge on my left, a steep ditch is cluttered with brambles and too big to jump. I cannot see a gateway anywhere.

Should I leg it back to safety, the bridle path? No, there isn't enough time.

The ebb and flow of engine noise has arrived within ten seconds and the first motorbike comes flying around the blind bend straight at us. At a guess, a 50mph hell's mix of metal and cogs. The rider is crouched, low and streamlined, a black bullet in my world. The inside of my riding hat is the only recipient of my panic.

I have only one option. Keep trotting. I know that if I force Rommel to stand still and face the danger, he will immediately try to spin his whole body across the middle of the road and flee (ironically in the same direction as the very monster attacking him).

Stay calm, stay calm. Do not *relay your own panic. Look at the road ahead, not the bike, Jude. It's too narrow here. There is no escape.*

Vvvrrrmm. The first bike shoots past us before Rommel has time to really register. One, two, three seconds later the following bike is heading for us. I can see the black tips of equine ears flicking and Rommel's neck is rising higher.

Vvvrrrmm. I can hear more bikes, but I dare not move my hands off the reins to reassure.

One second – I cannot shift position in any way, dare not look anywhere except forward.

Two seconds – *Rommel is a big horse and if he swings around in an attempt to bolt, then we are certain to be splattered across the front of the next set of tyres.*

Three seconds – and… Vvvrrrmm.One second – *keep trotting. Don't flinch.* My lips are still, but the words are so very loud.

Two seconds – *I am sitting above an explosive device primed to detonate at any moment now. One weapon left at my disposal. Speak to him, Jude. Speak. Your best and most relaxing sing-song voice.* "Clever fella, Ro."

Three seconds. "Well done, boyo. Stay cool."

Vvvrrrmm. The fourth and final bike whines past us, leaving a vacuum of briefly displaced leaves in its wake.

The last half-mile of road seems endless, vast. I feel the urge to get off and walk (I never do that!), to find any way home except along the road. A thought keeps surfacing again and again. *They often ride in groups of ten or more. It's a Sunday, will there be more? Fear – I don't do fear. I don't do this shortness of breath, this hypersensitive listening.*

The moment we reach the safety of the drive, I dismount and stand for a moment, letting Rommel gorge himself on the long grass. My upper thighs are shaking as I move around him to run up the stirrups. The walk up the drive helps a little, but I am struggling to stop a vivid picture of a horse's skinned legs, a motorbike and limbs all mangled together. The image is appearing soundless in my mind's eye, again and again.

Why do I want to sit down? Normality, it helps. Untacking, rubbing a towel over Rommel's saddle-patch and legs, flinging a sweat rug over his rump, hanging a hay net up. My head has progressed to a blank numbness. *Pull yourself together, Jude. Go sort out the paddock.*

A pet hate of mine – moving the electric fence. Having to pull all the plastic stakes up, drag the whole kit and caboodle across the field to a fresh piece of grass, jam all the stakes back in again, re-tension all the tape and finally, refit the battery and its clips in all the right places. It's a bastard of a task, yet today it calms my jagged nerves. Stability returns to my wonky legs and the flashbacks are fading. As I stride along the line of the fence, an argument has kicked off in my personal honesty box. *Should I tell Mother?*

I pull out a strip of white nylon from my coat pocket. Stop mid-task. *On the other hand, it might be an idea for her to know where to scrape me off the road if I don't return home one day.* I tie the material in a little knot on the top strand of wire. March forward another ten feet, counting each stride, then stop again and pull out another strip, pink this time. Once it is also knotted around the wire, its spare ends dangling, I march on another ten feet and pull out a blue tassel. By the time I reach the end of the wire, I turn to admire my own handiwork – a line of pretty tassels all fluttering in the breeze. *No chance that the boys will run into that in a hurry! Perhaps best not to worry Mother with my near-death tale, though.*

I flick the switch on the electric fence box. *Is it ticking or is the battery flat? Only one way to find out. Am I feeling brave enough today?* Some obscure reasoning inside me is convinced that the longer the piece of grass I use, the less I will feel the shock, so I find a particularly elongated piece of grass then pinch it between my index finger and thumb. Standing as far from the wire as possible and holding only the very tip of the grass, I brace in anticipation of the jolt, but hover instead. *Just get on with it, Jude.*

The blade rests on the wire. *One, two, three, four...* Electric voltage instant, fleeting, surges from the grass into my fingers, up one arm and across my chest into the other arm. My hand has snapped back, recoiled in a stinging seizure. I shake it up and down a couple of times – a stupid attempt to flick off the pain. *Grr,* ow. *Brave – I think?*

Chapter 23

"Effing hell. Ow! That hurt"

Lizzie shouted to no one but herself, or so she thought. She continued turning the handlebars while also squeezing herself through the narrow garage side door. Her funny bone was throbbing. Unfortunately, too late she looked up to spy Tracey's robust Hyacinth Bucket figure making a resolute beeline in her direction. Tracey Bannister – occupant of No. 4 The Cart Lodge, her neighbour from two doors up. An incorrigible, well-intentioned busybody who abhors swearing under any circumstance, but especially in women. Tracey halted a few feet away, her brows beneath The Wig fixed in an arch of unvoiced condemnation.

"Good morning, Elizabeth. Perfect morning for a healthy constitutional." Lizzie propped her bike briefly against the wall and frantically rubbed her elbow.

"Good morning, Mrs Bannister." Lizzie knew from bitter experience not to utter anything other than a rushed platitude. It would be fatal to enquire, 'How are you?' Instead, she swung her leg over the bike, pushing off against the pedal and flinging a cheerful, "Have a lovely day" as she headed across the drive.

The row of four two-bedroom dwellings, Lizzie's being on the farthest end, were a smart conversion of an old cart lodge. She had to make a tough decision when she set up her own practice. It was a direct contest between keeping Tarquin and buying this up-to-spec, low-maintenance, terraced property or sell her horse and being able to afford a slightly more upmarket detached three-bedroom cottage. She hadn't really waivered for a moment even though (as the estate agent repeatedly pointed out), "You would enjoy absolute privacy in the cottage and so much more befitting of a professional woman like yourself." October leaves in parched rusts and browns were racing across the tarmac as she spent the ride to the stables trying to work out:

Do I really want to re-subscribe or not? – should I just give it all up?

I've had some great laughs. I've had some seriously romantic liaisons.

I've been chauffeured in a Range Rover up to London for the day.

I've squelched along the seashore pretending to the man at my side that, despite the howling gale, I'm still loving the date.

I couldn't begin to tot up how many Afternoon Cream Teas I've downed!

I've shared fish and chips with a hunk who had 'the child in his eyes', then thrown the uneaten chips into the long grass for his Weimaraner to search out. We shared the joke at the dog's expense, each time he made the mistake of grabbing one covered in vinegar. He had contorted his jowl and tongue, flicking out any last remnant of acidic potato. We laughed till I fell off the wall.

I've spoken to kind men, cautious men, crude men. I've corresponded with a pilot, a gardener, an electrician and countless property developers.

I've quaffed wine on a fishing boat followed by lovemaking on a blanket in the rocking bow. Since then any waft of fresh fish to my nostrils brings that happy memory bouncing back! And that's the point. I wouldn't wish to erase a single one of these memories either good or bad.

I've excused myself from several dates who would come under the banner of 'Sold as seen. No warranty applicable', but I am proud of the fact that I have always tried not to crush anyone's dignity.

The river to the right of the lane had veered off across the low meadows. Along the banks, soggy heads of thistle seeds were still valiantly clinging to their stems and blackberries promised a plump larder. Lizzie felt the familiar pull on her calf muscles; she stood up on the pedals to climb the short, sharp hill. Once over the brow she relaxed onto the saddle, allowing her mind to wander back to the day before.

His online profile was interesting. She had scrutinised it carefully before sending a message. She had become so incredibly stringent these days that rarely did anyone get past her initial filtering criteria of Age, Height, Smile, Geographic Location, Interests and basic written grammar.

Personality: Poet

Had pleased her.

Longest Relationship: Over 8 years

Was a must.

Do You Want Children: No

I should hope not. Too complicated at our age.

Within a week, she had skipped through all the messaging and a single one-to-one phone call, then with guarded optimism, organised a date. Costa Coffee in Haverhill – she should have listened to her instincts! The problem had been finding somewhere midway for both her and David. Neither of them knew the town at all so she'd left him to find a suitable venue. Costa in the centre was a sensible choice. But she'd got stuck in the one-way system, missed the car park sign, had to go around again, rushed breathless up the high street into the pedestrian-only centre until eventually she spotted the Costa Coffee.

She remembered thinking how drab it appeared. Normally Costa in any town was a cert for a buzzing, chatty atmosphere, but there was a motley selection of only three customers. A young, tattooed couple with a sleeping toddler in a pushchair and a solitary gentleman, his head bent over a paper. Despite her accumulated experience of meeting unknown people, it still unnerved her to have to walk into this unknown place in an unknown town far from her familiar haunts. She had walked back outside again, scanned up the street, down the street, but couldn't see anyone resembling David's profile picture. She remembered fiddling with her watch, debating whether to light up, decided. *Fag breath – not a great idea.* She wandered closer, trying to appear nonchalant, and double-checked the features of a grey-haired anorak man sitting alone on a bench. *Could this be him? Has he fibbed about his true age?*

The man caught her searching stare and returned a blank look. Lizzie had immediately dropped her scrutiny, carried on past, and back into the Costa. She checked her mobile – no messages or missed calls. She bought herself a cup of strong hot tea and positioned herself a couple of tables away from the front window where she could watch any new arrivals. She busied herself for a while cutting her piece of flapjack into tiny half-inch cubes, popping them in her mouth one by one, savouring the syrup and caffeine high as they began to course through her veins. Eventually she flipped open her mobile, rang David's number, it went straight to voicemail. Speaking in hushed tones she had left a voice message. "Hello, David. I do hope I got our meeting time correct. Are you on your way? Just let me know. I'm already here."Lizzie sipped her tea, studied the mini flock of jabbering starlings which had congregated in a tree overshadowing the bench. The old gent's chin was buried in his chest. A dead giveaway; he must have nodded off. She was sure that at any moment the starlings would take flight en masse and shower him with a splattering of poo. *Where the hell is this man? Perhaps he's had a puncture, but then he would have phoned to tell me. How long should I wait?*

She decided to risk leaving the table, thought it prudent to inspect for porridge oats between her teeth and headed towards the toilets. The swarthy man in grey flannels seated at the back of the café still had his back turned away from her; she couldn't really see his face. Bladder emptied, lipstick touched up, when she returned there was a new crisp, stripy shirt and jeans seated close to the toilet exit. *Is this him? Not sure. Not sure at all.* As she approached, the man looked up from his cappuccino and shortbread. *Oh, sod it. Hate indecision.*

Using her best mercurial voice, she asked,

"Excuse me, but are you David by any chance?"

The dead, pale blue eyes had taken a split second to look her up and down. He'd shrugged his shoulders nonchalantly before she was brushed off with a dismissive

"Nah, not me."

She did an about-face and started marching towards the dimly lit table at the back. Her resolve was simple. *If I'm going to make a prat of myself I may as well do it properly!*

Seeing her coming, gent number three in her quest was already smiling when she repeated what he'd already heard her say moments before.

"Excuse me, but are *you*, David?" Lizzie knew she had screwed her face up in a helpless maiden-in-distress fashion and despised herself for resorting to it, but nothing ventured, nothing gained. Gent number three answered with kindness.

"I can be David if you want." Mirth was etched in every crease of his face. Her hesitation left an opening again so he jumped in:

"I really would be very happy to be David."

Lizzie managed to release a wan smile.

"You're very kind, but that won't be necessary. Enjoy your day," and she'd spun on her heels.

The *ping ping* of her phone had stopped her in her tracks as she reached the car park. The text simply read. "Didn't think you were serious about meeting. You didn't reply to confirm. David." *No way. He got bloody cold feet. He could have rung me at any time if he wasn't sure.*

She'd spent the drive home convincing herself that it wasn't really a rejection, but it had hurt all the same.

An earthy smell of soil which shot up Lizzie's nostrils jolted her back to the present. She sometimes found at home, tucked up in bed, that she could send herself to sleep re-riding this route, she'd done it so many hundreds of times. She passed the village sign Upper Melling, automatically applied the brakes. *Slower, slower. East side speed bump caught me in the crotch last time – bruising painful for several days.* Originally, she hadn't expected to fit in to this quintessential English idyll. She knew she wasn't one for pretension or conformity, however, it had seemed only sensible to settle near the stables. The country ways had crept up on her; this was an area of neighbourhood watches and handbell ringing.

She threw a cheerful. "Hello. Your marrows are spectacular, Mr Williams," at the old boy outside Smithy Cottage as she whizzed by. In the full flush of summer his garden boasted tepees of beans and row upon row of purple sprouting broccoli, spinach and gooseberries. New potatoes covering every square foot of spare garden.

She veered to the right around pothole number one. Next on her left came the overgrown plot of wasteland: an acre earmarked for affordable houses years previously, still a patch of boggy ground, some prickly bushes and a colony of protected newts. She coasted down the main street past shops selling scented candles and enough antiques to furnish Downton, till she quickly reached the outskirts on the far side. Then finally, the house on the west side of the village, and the one which inwardly she always referred to as My House. She'd ruminated several times in the past month about booking an appointment to 'view', decided that it would be a pointless exercise to salivate over something so unobtainable. The unkempt hedge had been blown to lean perilously close to oncoming traffic; some of the outer rendering on eighteenth-century timbers had disintegrated leaving patches of ancient bricks exposed to the elements. A few battered apples were still hanging on to their branches, a neglected testament to long-lost fruitful owners.

West side speed bump passed, Lizzie turned left into the rough track signposted Melling Hall Liveries.

* * *

Two hours later and Lizzie knew she was trailing a mixed odour of fresh sweat and ammonia but didn't give a damn. Standing on the pedals, she expertly negotiated the uneven gravelly bits back up the Melling Hall track. Her thoughts did an irritating reversion. *Should I give it all up, retrieve what peace of mind there is to be had by becoming a spectator? Put my fate in the lap of the gods. Go with the flow. Allow kismet a kick?*

West side speed bump passed, she sped up to cycle past My House. She was ten metres further along the road when she slammed on the brakes; rubber on rubber emitted its squeaky protest and she jolted to a sudden halt. *My premium bond might come up.*

She started pushing her bike towards the entrance. She glanced over her shoulder in the direction of Melling. *No cars about.* She carefully propped her bike behind the hedge out of sight, did a double-check up and down the road, wrapped both her fists firmly around the post of the Carter Jonas 'For Sale' sign, and began pushing and pulling it backwards and forwards. The ground underfoot was surprisingly hard and the sign had been wacked in deep. Through clenched teeth Lizzie exclaimed,

"God helps..." and she thrust her biceps into pushing, "those who..." and she wrenched again towards her chest,

"help themselves..." and released her grip with a sudden "Ow, ow," as a shard of wood embedded itself in her index finger.

"Why let someone else snaffle My House?"

In the end, having picked out the offending splinter, she reversed up to the post and pulled the sleeves of her sweatshirt around her bare palms. She then put her hands behind her back and triumphantly heaved the uncooperative bastard out. The sound of an approaching car engine sent her scuttling between the hedge and the garage where she promptly flung the sign. Mission accomplished, she pushed her bike out onto the road again before setting sail through Upper Melling.

Self-pity, she felt, as she slowed for the east side speed bump.

An ugly emotion, she conceded as the countryside opened up again. *Judith would probably sing to pick herself up, but I'm hopeless.*

She registered the clusters of scarlet hawthorn berries, caught a pungent whiff of fox and cycled on.

Chapter 24

Judith

Ping, ping. Ping, ping.

I flip open my iPhone case, read the text: 'Sorry, Judith. We're on the drag. Max's cycling race ran late. Should get to the village hall by 8.15pm. xx Emma'.

The windows of my Audi hum and finish their descent with a series of four low clunks. A rush of autumn air brings in with it a mixed story of scents – damp, freshly turned soil, mown grass and sizzling pork crackling. A tractor in the adjacent field some eighty metres away is hauling its enormous plough laboriously up the gentle slope and despite its deep, straining revs, a collection of seagulls can be heard screeching and occasionally squabbling as they dive-bomb over juicy upturned worms.

I am regretting arriving on time, decide that I have no intention of braving a solitary entrance and settle back in my seat, a rare luxury to remain stationary. I watch a husband and wife team bustling to and fro around their Harry's Hogs catering van. Complete with requisite starched white apron and puce cheeks, the man keeps returning to baste the angry, scorching flesh. I wince and look away again.

A polite game of psychological chess is being played out for the few remaining parking spaces – it's mine, no I indicated first, no I was reversing before you. Pure driver body language – no actual words exchanged. Each car then disgorges a varied selection of Village Hop attendees: some with French sticks stuffed under their arms, others, large bowl of salad in hand, wobble along precarious in heels. Jolly chatter and instructions are spilling out of mouths.

"Neville, for God's sake don't drop that trifle," or "Hope they've got a decent beer in this time." It is clear that the locals are out in force to support the 'We Need New Toilets' campaign emblazoned on the public noticeboard. The posters are particularly eye-catching; the wording on each is surrounded by pictures of toilets in a medley of colours. I passed many of them in several villages en route, stuck to any and every telegraph pole, barn door or spare piece of inanimate fencing.

A distant growl of motorbike engines creeps up until an incessant vrmm, vrmm, vrmm, vrmm demands my attention. In they crawl, a latently menacing pack of growling, wild animals resplendent in black jackets, huge circular helmets and dark, dark sunglasses. Within the continuing stream of arrivals is an Injun bike, its strangely high handlebars tipping left and right, antennae-like, with each manoeuvre. Slowly, each rider lowers his throttle and chugs past to bump his or her way up the kerb and onto the short grass. They begin carefully lining up their throbbing Nortons and Enfields and one by one turning off their precious horsepower. Quiet descends again. I raise my wrist, check the time; an ache has settled into my lower back. *I love my work but just how many years is my body going to take the strain?* Painfully, I unfolded myself from the car, stretch my arms up, shake my shoulders, then prop my bottom against the bonnet and continue people-watching.

Another couple of bikes chug across the tarmac. I am hit by the importance of 'the gear' amongst the biking community. Not just the abundance of leather jackets and leggings, I can understand that: tanned cowhide being the best method of preventing a road from tortuously ripping the skin off your legs at 70mph. Many of the bikers are peeling off their outer layers like snakes shedding a protective skin and stripping down to their jeans. Within spitting distance, I cannot help but earwig in on bits of floating conversation. It seems to be a pre-requisite for 50% of the male riders to own the beard of a Schnauzer and a gruff baritone voice. One of these speaks to the assembled group.

"Any of you heard of this band? What are they called – Damage? Isaac swears they're good." A well-endowed forty-something woman with 'I Know I Ride Like a Girl, Try to Keep Up' across her boobs replies with a swish of her heavy red-wine locks.

"No moaning, Bill. It's all in a good cause. Go buy us a beer to drink outside, will ya?"

I decide that bikers are no different to riders: they love to announce to the whole world with logos and quotes exactly what their chosen passion is. The jumble of chat continues. T-shirt 'Four Wheels Move the Body, Two Wheels Move the Soul' and his beer belly grin at T-shirt 'Sons of Anarchy' and his grey ponytail and teases:

"When are you going to get rid of that postman's delivery bike?" A hefty backslap follows with the retort:

"One of the reasons I ride my bike is because I can spanner pretty much everything on it. No way could you do that with yours, mate!"

I sidle a little nearer the boot end of my car, keen to peek in the window of a world to which I am a complete stranger. An

278

almond-eyed blonde babe is attempting to squash her leggings into her rucksack. I am struck by the palpable sense of camaraderie which seems to pervade amidst the mixture of classes. A drawl of an American accent follows a true dude of a biker as he ambles towards the hall holding hands with his woman. She is beaming a buck-toothed smile. His sweatshirt proclaims 'If You Can Read This, The Bitch Fell Off.'

Two more Harleys arrive; they copy everyone else, parking up at the farthest side of the grass. A huddle of three blokes are taking the chance for a quick puff. One appears to be a coat-hanger for his biking kit, his stick-thin hips barely winning the battle to hold up the heaviness of his leathers. Even from a distance, I suspect he must be the newbie in the group – the only one clutching his helmet close to his thigh, a form of 'This is who I am' statement badge. I recognise it so well, this casual but staged look. Like dressage riders and show jumpers lounging around at shows in jodhpurs and long boots, their expensive pale blue cotton shirts cut to keep their arms cool, but *never* taking their boots off, whatever the temperature – for fear of relinquishing their identity.

I watch as the newbie tries to hang on to his beer, flick his cigarette lighter and keep his helmet wedged between his legs all at the same time. No way is he going to let his new status symbol leave his side. Between fags he pops his free arm around the shoulders of his young girlfriend and smiles a 'She's mine, all mine' smile. She is absent-mindedly jiggling a toddler on her left hip, the toddler's Babygro nightwear declaring: 'Can't wait to get my wheels'. I glance at my watch again and wonder whether to buy a drink and bring it outside. *Ping ping, ping ping, ping ping.* 'Be there in 5. xx Emma.'

* * *

The disco background music is in full swing when Jeremy strolls up to our table in a T-shirt with 'Krazy Horse' written in bold letters. His usual stiff-shirt persona appears to have evaporated and I struggle not to either gawk or laugh. Instead I politely stand up and introduce Max, Emma's partner of three years, but find that my concentration keeps returning to Jeremy. How could this possibly be? A T-shirt *and* a leather wrist strap... I cannot quite process the idea of a Jeremy alter ego. He touches my hand just before he speaks.

"So glad you could come. We really appreciate your support." He meets my eye contact and I can see the drift of his smile work its way through from hesitation to relief as he realises there is no animosity lurking in me. Max chips in with a question about the hall loo fund and before I have a chance to rewind the clock, or do any digging, Jeremy is whisked away to socialise elsewhere. Strange that only five months previously I held such high hopes.

We all sit down again. Our table, irritatingly, is way back from the stage so I allow myself to disappear into the background drone of an echoing hall, full of jolly people. Recently, Emma seems to be perpetually bouncing, a waggy-tailed enthusiasm for life, since she and Max have taken the plunge to start nest-building together. I feign a fascination with the pastry crust on my slice of quiche. *A gooseberry – who the hell came up with that expression. A bloody gooseberry!* From the corner of my eye, I spy the two of them putting each end of a long piece of pork crackling into their respective mouths, then crunching and chewing their way to the middle, bumping noses then tugging, teeth clenched to see who can nip through the skin first.

I jab at a chunk of potato salad, then progress to half-heartedly dipping a hard-boiled egg in mayonnaise and forcing myself to swallow. The flashing disco lights have been switched off and I am only vaguely aware that four band members are quietly fiddling about on the stage in the shadows. Their backs are hunched over various bits of drum kit and electric guitar leads. Suddenly, I feel a furious prodding in my bicep. Emma's golden curls invade my personal space, bobbing about, tickling my cheek as she points frantically at the stage.

"Look, look. Isn't that Luc? You know… the Luc we met at Thetford Forest?"

My attempt at a reply is drowned out by a sudden high-pitched feedback whistle from the microphone. Centre stage, the lead guitarist, back turned to the jabbering occupants of the hall, is strumming a chord here and there, carefully twisting the strings to a perfect pitch before nodding at the prune-skinned bass guitarist. I have a strong suspicion that the cumulative age of the band is probably a minimum of 220 years. They are all wearing rocker jeans and wide leather belts but have smartened up the look with matching black shirts. The four men exchange several thumbs up and cursory nods then three spotlights blaze into life. The opening riff, an Eric Clapton classic, begins winding its way silkily from Luc's lips through the microphone into the unoccupied spaces of the hall. The throaty laughter and scraping chairs do not check, the eyes of the audience do not rise any higher than the faces of their friends at each table. Luc is speaking rather than singing the words to one of my favourites, 'I Shot the Sheriff'.

Emma suddenly jabs her elbow hard into my right ribcage, cups her hands to whisper in my ear.

"Wow. He's a Honda 750cc – don't you think? Bet *he* could manage 0–60 in four seconds!"

I shrug my shoulders, mime back, "Possibly."

The evening starts to crank up before our eyes and in time to the volume of the music. Soon the floor is packed with a weird mixture of biker rally meets occupants of a rural English village. Add in Greene King beer, vocals, drums plus two guitars and a sound system then sit back to absorb the spectacle. I cannot stifle a chuckle at the short bare legs of a wide lady in a floral dress (her Sunday best no doubt) as, despite her ungainly beach sandals, she jives fit to bust. Next along, I spy a neat little man in a Rupert Bear pullover of zigzags in red and orange. His trousers are skimming the top of his ankles and his red socks appear to be doing a stick-insect hop in time to, 'Burn, baby burn, disco inferno. Burn, baby burn.'

Song after song ebbs and flows. An occasional beer makes its sticky addition to the hall floor. I pace myself – wine, water, wine, water. A wallflower, an observer, a non-participant, until the heel of a biker boot scrunches squarely onto the toe of my shoe. I let out a mini squeal then look up into a hedge of a beard. It mumbles an apology.

"Sorry, love. Dance floor's packed." I push my chair a little further back between the tables, and the guilty party resumes jigging his shoulders in time to the beat. The patch on his jeans resumes swaying in front of my nose again. 'Lock Up Your Daughters.'

I decide to succumb completely to the rock 'n' roll beat vibrating in waves from the enormous speakers. The rhythm is coming up through the soles of my shoes, and the heat in my thighs builds with every slap of my hands on my jeans. Knowing the singer, is making me wonder, making me want to dissect the act of singing, to admire Luc. It hits me, the shock of my own envy – to play that collection of fine-honed wood and strings, to possess such musical electricity, to lose all restraint, to seek out the microphone and throw the inner depths of your soul into it – an empowering instrument, a friend. To force the air through the throat in fits and starts over the tongue, past the incisors. To create a sense of palpable pain, or allure, or anger. In fact, anything and everything it means to be human. From nowhere Emma appears at my side. She wobbles briefly like a lamp accidentally nudged by a passing handbag, then sits on the next chair.

"Are you OK, Jude? Come o-o-o-o-on. Get up and dance with Max and me." A brief lull between songs makes conversation possible.

"Don't worry about me. I'm not a big dancer really," and I quickly shoo her away.

Luc begins announcing, "Next, is a song I wrote recently. This will be our debut public performance. It's a cross between a rock and a love song, and I'm expecting you all to let me know whether you like it. It's called 'Kick-Start'."

I move nearer to the stage and lean against the side wall, enjoying the chance to be alone within a crowd of people. Quiet descends as Luc's guitar intro catches everyone's attention and the first few lines feel personal, as though he is singing a private story to each individual person in the room.

"She threw sand in my face. No longer craves a warm embrace
Now I'm rolling in the dirt. She took the car keys and my shirts
Left me frightened of a kick-start."

The lyrics seize my attention and I look, really look, at Luc. The beat becomes stronger, two more guitars and a keyboard upping the ante.

"Petrified of passion, petrified of pain
Petrified that reason will evacuate my brain
Turn the throttle off a kick-start
Make excuses, all the reasons I can find
To stall a kick-start."

283

The audience have begun lifting their knees on the word 'kick', then stamping them down onto the floor in time to the drum beat and every 'start'. *He explodes with charisma when he sings, comes alive. Yes, OK, Jude, admit it – he's raw sexy.* Emma begins pulling at my arm: I am dance averse, I am not going to budge and besides, I want to know the tale in the lyrics, to know what happens to him, to watch the tilt of his jaw, the efficiency of each finger, fast and sure on strings. Mesmerised, I have no intention of dragging my eyes away.

I yell, "Bloody hell, he's Bruce Springsteen's doppelganger." Emma emits a beery hiccup within inches of my face, forcing me to turn. Her stare is unfocused; her eyelids resemble partly drawn blinds.

"What did you say? A doodle-ganger?" Gently, I push her back towards the dancefloor.

"No, Emma. A doppelganger. Off you go and dance."

More verses come and go, swirling like the wind in a gale into every empty space: between the audience, above their heads or bouncing off the hard surfaces. A grey-rinse granny in her seventies is dancing beside her younger-version fifty-year-old daughter, their pendants swinging left, right, left, right in time to the rhythm. Beads of sweat are trickling from the brow of a Clarke Kent lookalike. He is grinding hip to hip, cheek to cheek with a strikingly beautiful woman. His hands appear to be permanently restless, unable to prioritise between holding her pliant, svelte waist and a need to stop his glasses sliding off his nose.

> "Stick the jump leads on my heart
> I can breathe now we're apart
> Yes, I'm searching for a kick-start."

A roar of voices join in the chorus amid shoes banging to the beat and a sea of upstretched arms. I stand up straight, let rip with the throng to pelt out a final,

"There's gotta be a kick-start."

Chapter 25

Luc's exit kept being interrupted by well-wishers – an over-zealous handshake from Emma's man; a "Wow, your band is great," from the treasurer of the Toilet Fund Raising Committee; an air kiss to his cheek from a complete stranger as she pointedly pressed a small piece of paper into his shirt pocket and whispered in his ear,

"I love your style. Would like to hire you for a private party? Call me."

He brushed off more compliments but decided, first things first, he wanted to get his precious Fender Stratocaster tucked away safely. He had to lift it above his head several times as he navigated his way through stray elbows and waving wine glasses. Eventually, he managed to escape and his eyes adjusted to the murky half-light outside. He headed across the paddock adjoining the car park and unlocked his Land Rover. Lovingly, he zipped the guitar into its case and wrapped a blanket around it, then placed it under a plastic sheet in the back. He shivered – a stiff October wind was scudding clouds in front of a huge full-circle moon. He felt an urge to reach out and touch it, convinced his hand would disappear inside. Cackles of high-pitched female laughter intermittently broke the air. Between them, he felt that special quietness which descends at night in the countryside, mammals tucked up asleep, only a pipistrelle bat flitting past his ear. Thick clouds heaved their way across the sky, obliterating the joyous moon.

Standing, twisting, leaning extra weight on his good leg for two hours, it always took its toll. *I could leave. The band isn't going on again. I'm getting too old for this, get so damned tired. Do I want to stay and subject myself to disco beat and a raffle?* But then he decided, *What I really need right now is an Adnams.* He had just clicked the key in the door lock when a sixth sense told him he wasn't alone. Something in his peripheral vision had definitely moved. He readjusted his focus to squint at the distant hedge, then scanned in a half-circle around the empty field. *Yes, the merest hint of movement about forty metres away under the canopy of that huge oak tree. A person, the frame of a tall, really thin man in biker leggings, sideways on and facing towards the tree. Very odd; perhaps he's having a slash?*

What Luc had imagined was part of the trunk stepped forward one stride – another

figure, slightly smaller, short hair. He thought, *Must be a woman, although there is something about the set of the shoulders and neck which is not at all feminine. So hard to tell in this light.* He deduced by the erratic hand movements that the couple must be having a conversation but Luc couldn't quite hear the words. The smaller figure melded again into the trunk. Luc was just about to turn and head back to the boisterous gathering when the biker leant in to kiss the spot where Luc knew the woman's lips must be. The corners of Luc's mouth crinkled briefly. *A moonlit tryst. I shall sneak away and leave them in peace.*

Without warning the transient clouds parted and a heavenly beam of moonlight hit the ethereal scene. Luc felt an instant pang of guilt; he hadn't intended to be a voyeur. They had seen him, and he could now see them properly. The recognition of *that* profile hit Luc's consciousness like a sledgehammer and his teeth clenched in a spontaneous reaction. Another excruciating three seconds passed. They stared at Luc, Luc stared at them. Then Jeremy melded back into the tree again. Luc became aware of a warm tang of blood creeping around his lower teeth. He swivelled sharply on his good leg and walked briskly away.

Fuckin' hell. I never, ever would have guessed! Now I really must have a beer.

* * *

Luc barely registered the loud calls of, "Yellow 158. Yellow 158 – yes gentleman at the back, you are the lucky winner of our star prize this evening. Dinner for four at The Angel Hotel."

He hurried across the empty middle-ground of the hall heading for the huge glass double doors flung open on the far wall. The fresh breeze ruffled and parted the streamers of tacky silver cabaret tinsel hanging from the pelmet above the door frame, and he misjudged his step out onto the paving. Instinctively his free hand caught the frame but he couldn't stop half his beer sloshing down the back of a white blouse. The wearer screeched and, caught off guard, spouted her rebuke as she turned around.

"What the hell?"

Luc was still half bent over in mid-recovery when he blurted out, "Oh sorry," then rose to his proper height to establish who the wearer of said blouse might be. They both hesitated a split second, then spoke in unison.

"Oh, it's you."

Judith dropped her eyes, unexpectedly shy. Luc plonked his beer glass on the nearest plastic table and snatched at a redundant paper serviette.

"Turn around, Judith." He felt the warmth of her shoulders in the tips of his fingers as he guided her twist, then pressed the serviette onto the damp patch of cotton sticking to her backbone. She fidgeted as if to move away.

"*C'est la vie.* It's one of my favourite blouses." He gently pulled her closer again, savouring the intimacy.

"Stand still, for goodness' sake. Should I add a little water to dilute the stain?"

A good ten seconds passed and he realised that they were both dithering, before her brain clearly reconnected its neural pathways to her tongue. Rather irritably, she snapped,

"Please, don't worry about it. I'll spray Vanish on it as soon as I get home."

A crush of lanky teenagers were all hovering outside, exchanging broken chat and prodding their smartphones. Luc, unsure what kind of small talk was appropriate, gulped down the remaining beer left in his glass. Judith mirrored, polished off the remnants of liquid in her bottle of J2O. Luc broke the silence first.

"Are you here alone?" He had a sudden urge to chastise her. She was screwing up her eyebrows. He could hear his own mother scolding his sister for the same kind of rude frown. She seemed to gather herself, regain control over the truculent rebels and manage a token smile with her reply.

"Oh, I've been with my friend Emma. You may remember her from Thetford Forest and her partner Max. But I haven't been able to find them to say goodbye."

Luc waved his arm towards some empty tables and dared himself to turn the full force of his special Melt the Polar Icecaps beam in her direction.

"Bit crowded here. I don't think either of us wants to join in with chat about Ed Sheeran's latest single or who said what on Twitter. Shall we sit over there for a few minutes till you spot them?" She hesitated and he sensed a thaw.

"Hopefully, my company is preferable to feeling like a spare part. At least for the moment."

The less-than-stable chair bent a little as Luc sat down. She appeared to flick a 'polite' switch to 'on' in her attitude fuse box.

"This evening seems to have been a sell-out. I imagine the Village Committee will have raised more than enough money to install the new facilities. And, by the way, Damage are extremely good."

Luc was struggling to concentrate. The revelation – Jeremy's moonlit profile – was flashing up in his mind's eye.

"Thank you. I'll pass on the compliment to the boys. What kind of music is your thing?" He didn't listen to her answer at all, nodded in what he assumed was the right place now and then. His head was in a whirr. Jeremy and Judith? Were they still an item or not? What was the latest he'd heard? He'd lost track. It hadn't been of any great interest to him. Jeremy had told Robert, Robert had told Isaac, Isaac had shouted something at the gym several months ago in the middle of a seriously heavy workout. He seemed to remember Isaac's final comment being that Judith had been rather upset. She was prattling on, mentioning Hall & Oates and how she'd never actually attended a pop festival. As she spoke, she fiddled about extricating several items from her handbag till eventually she retrieved a small purse. She spotted his quizzical stare at a pair of tatty leather riding gloves flattened under the handbag.

"I know, not a normal item for a woman's handbag."

Luc began studying her face, her soft seashore eyes. *Should I squeal on Jeremy? Clearly, Jeremy must have batted her away. But did she know he was batting for the other side. Or does he bat for both sides? Hmm, that would fit."*

"Luc. Luc." She was halfway to rising from the chair, her voice suddenly insistent enough to wrench his attention. "What would you like to drink?" He graciously accepted Judith's offer. When she returned with the drinks she sat down, simultaneously handing him the beer glass and speaking at the same time. Her casual question, felt to him as if she'd flung a spark into a box of kindling.

She said. "May I pick your brains on a rather tricky subject?"

He nodded. "Feel free. Fire away." Judith tipped back her head, took a long swig at the fruit juice.

"I had an absolutely terrifying near-miss on the road when I was riding only last week. If Rommel wasn't such a rock-solid mount, I could easily have ended up in the morgue. I'm thinking that perhaps it's about time we horse-riders helped to educate bikers a bit more."

She furrowed her brow in such an earnest look, Luc's reaction was to take a sudden swig of beer. Could he hide the sense of outrage with which her throwaway comment was filling him? Instead, he tempered his reply to a flippant "If you really want my opinion, I think perhaps the boot would fit best on the other foot?" He felt a sweet satisfaction in seeing her cheeks flush before she spat out a reply.

"Hardly. What are you suggesting? That riders are in the habit of endangering the lives and limbs of other road users by travelling at breakneck speeds?"

Somehow, she'd managed so quickly to press his Intolerance Button. This time he allowed the sarcasm to drip through his words.

"It was a purely rhetorical question. Explain to me exactly what happened, then I can give you an informed reply."

She put her drink down carefully on the table and fixed him with a quizzical look, then launched into her yarn. It was long-

291

winded and graphic, but he realised that he didn't mind at all, because he loved following the tale her hands told. They moved with the pitch of her voice, gesticulating one minute, pressing together in a praying shape another.

"That's certainly a riveting story. I have to applaud your tenacity and ability not to panic. However, I have a very short reply to your original question and that is…" He paused, drew his thumb and index finger around the stubble on his chin, leant back against the chair. "Road Tax." His palms were outstretched, his lips in a pucker. He revelled in laying it on, schoolmaster thick. Judith remained quiet so he repeated the question, stared straight at her. "Do horse owners pay road tax? Answer. No."

He leant forward a little closer to her, a strategy he'd been taught in the army. When you want to unnerve a person, get closer. A visual stand-off ensued as he elaborated.

"We have to pay nearly £50 a year before we can put rubber to tarmac. You have that privilege free of charge, so who has the greater right to use the roads, tell me?"

He had to concede that she was good, very good at concealing any reaction. Not a single muscle in her alabaster face twitched in any way, but a stray lock of walnut-coloured hair slipped across her cheek and as her breathing quickened, the swaying of the soft hairs was a giveaway.

"Fair comment. However, that also applies to cyclists and bloody joggers and none of those wear down the roads in the same way that cars, lorries and motorbikes do!"

Luc was tickled with himself; he'd managed to get her hook, line and sinker. *Her eyes are flashing with fire. I'll keep her going just a little bit longer.*

"True, very true. You are determined to expostulate about motorbikes but what about the issue of dung? The sloppy, green kind that horses are prone to deposit on the very same blind bend that nearly caused your demise. Half a bucket of poo dropped by one of your precious ponies in the wrong spot can be as slippery as a patch of ice! Have you thought about that? Littering. You're littering the road with a hazardous waste product. There should be a law against it."

By now the skin from Judith's cleavage to below her chin had turned into blotchy patches of heat but Luc knew he hadn't had this much fun in ages.

"Why the hell can't riders pop along after a hack and sweep up their excrement?" Her look of hurt sent a pang of momentary remorse through him. She turned away from his mocking jibe and her voice quivered a little.

"That is an absolutely absurd suggestion, Luc."

He knew he'd tipped from tease into cruel and that's when he decided – *time to fess up*. As she jerked herself up out of the chair, chin proud in the air, twisting to swing her handbag over her shoulder, he caught her wrist, adding his other hand to pull her closer.

"Apologies. There is something you should know about me and my relationship with motorbikes." Suspicious resignation pulsed through her forearm but, still seated, he didn't let go. "I happen to agree with you wholeheartedly about bikers riding at lunatic speeds on public roads. What you don't know is that's why I've stuck to off-roading for over ten years now."

Judith's eyes doubled in roundness.

"You mean that you are actually on the same side of the fence as me? You've been dragging all my anti-biker arguments out of me for the past twenty minutes and intentionally stoking me up?" The full force of her swinging handbag hit his shoulder then continued as the buckle clipped his earlobe, but her expression was alive. She pointed her finger at his nose and wailed, "You bastard. You, absolute bastard."

Once she let rip with the profanity, he knew he'd cracked the veneer. She even managed to play him at his own game. Spotting his Achilles heel, she feigned a doe-eyed love of country and western music, especially Dolly Parton! And because he'd already been so mean to her, she managed to reel him in before collapsing in a fit of the giggles and squealing,

"Gotcha. I wish you could see your face, Luc. Classic. Dolly Parton? Do I look like a Dolly kind of fan?"

After that he watched layer upon layer of her propriety slowly peeling away. She gripped his thigh and launched into her next question with a genuine hunger for knowledge.

"I have to say, going back to my dalliance with death last week, the bikers had no space to slow down immediately after the blind corner and before flying past Rommel, so I understand that none of them could have ridden any differently. It was just bloody bad timing so please explain to me why the hell they have to ride so close to the white line? Surely, if they lean over on a bend, they're likely to hit an oncoming car. Whereas if they kept to the left, they'd be safer?" Luc took a deep breath and began.

"The accepted rules of road positioning are basically that as you take a right-hand bend you should be riding over to the left of your lane; as you take a left-hand bend you should be over to the right; and if you're going along a straight piece of road you should be just to the right on the crown of the road. That gives you the best line of vision through a corner or along a road. But we don't live in an ideal world, do we? People drive much faster out here in the countryside than they do in towns and open A roads, where the safety gurus dream up their recommendations. In short, it depends which way the bend is going, whether it's on the brow of a hill, and whether you fancy becoming a hood ornament on the bonnet of a nineteen-year-old's Polo."

Judith then voiced a curious question.

"I now know that you don't dally with death on the open road, Luc. Surely you must get a kick of some sort from off-roading? I mean you're ex-army. Boys and their toys and all that, horsepower is king. I can't imagine you pootling along the grassy lanes on a little 250cc?"

He puffed himself up, raising his bent arms and biceps Tarzan fashion.

"Of course, I love power just as much as the next man. The big difference with off-roading is that you also need something which can handle the surfaces as well as being the right weight. For example, a will o' the wisp eight-and-a-half-stone woman hasn't got the muscles to manage a really heavy bike. There's also absolutely no point in owning a bloody tiger of a bike if you haven't got the know-how to handle it."

"Never thought about it before. You bikers have exactly the same problems as we do! Give an inexperienced rider a hot, fast thoroughbred or a powerhouse of a warmblood and they'll have their face in the dirt in no time." Luc's mind flashed back to their log-cabin weekend.

"Is that why Emma, a grown woman, sticks to a feisty pony rather than a proper horse like the rest of you?"

"Absolutely. Her little Rocket is probably the equivalent of a 250cc. If she rode anything bigger, not only would she get flattened at some point in the stable but she'd be a cert to end up in a wheelchair from a predestined fall. Classic mistake so many inexperienced or over-confident riders make – buying something too big or too sophisticated for their capabilities."

"Proper horsepower dilemma by the sound of it. Which are

you, Judith? Are you a pootle-around-the-lanes-at-5mph kind of rider or a hurtle-over-rock-solid-telegraph-pole-fences-at-30mph kind of rider?"

"What do you think, Luc?"

Luc stretched out his legs. His trousers were suddenly feeling uncomfortable and tight. He fidgeted a little in his seat before a very considered reply.

"You're an adrenalin junkie, for sure. Cool as a cucumber on the surface, disguising a need for speed underneath. Am I right?"

Neither of them had noticed that the village hall had gradually become devoid of people. Flashing lights had been packed away, crisp packets and debris swept up until eventually a helper balancing a stack of three chairs one on top of the other tersely warned,

"I'll need those chairs in another five minutes. Some of us have got beds to get home to."

Then Judith caught him totally off guard. She pulled her leather gloves out from under her handbag, fixed him with an incredibly impertinent smile and slapped the gloves with a dramatic flourish down onto the table.

"I'm throwing down my gauntlet to you, Luc. A challenge from one adrenalin junkie to another. I want you to take me off-roading in Thetford Forest. Are you up for it?"

There it was. He suspected his – "If you're serious, then yes, I'd be happy to" – was possibly in hindsight a foolish one. Time would tell.

He walked Judith to her car. He knew the uneven, dimly lit surface was exaggerating his limp and spotted her fleeting sideways look before she casually enquired,

"War wound?"

He measured his off-pat reply by pausing briefly, reaching out to touch her shoulder and looking deep into those summery hazel

296

eyes. Sand dunes came to mind. The scent of her skin, cinnamon-dusted brioche, imprinted in his memory.

"No. A disastrous encounter between a 4 x 4 and the motorbike I was riding. Long story... I'll tell you another day."

* * *

Luc rolled over, kicked at the duvet. His thoughts always struggled to settle post-performance. He felt rather smug: he'd stuck to beer when Judith offered to buy his drink. He'd stopped at three. In fact, he'd also avoided his usual habit of sliding into gloom the moment he stepped over the threshold and into the lull of his solitary existence. Tonight, the whisky bottle temptation, his tonic for the low after the bright lights and buzz of a gig, simply passed him by. He tugged the duvet in tight up around his neck, curled in a foetal position around his own stomach, his mind a muddle of dissected, half-remembered images and filtered conversation. What had gone down this evening? He couldn't quite decide.

Luc felt the tendrils of tiredness permeating deeper and deeper. He rolled over, fingered his nails in a delicious scratching motion along the edges of the scar tissue. *Need to test her sense of humour, she dated Jeremy for goodness sake! Find out whether she's a rigid stick-in-the-mud.* His fertile imagination was already in overdrive, brewing a plan. He chuckled, visualised the whole scene. *Thetford Forest is perfect. She will either scream, become livid at the joke and run for the hills immediately, or she will 'get it'.* His near and far memory banks continued drifting backwards and forwards. *I don't know, I just don't know – a Hooray Horse Henrietta. Rather attractive, but deep down privileged and intrinsically conservative?*

Chalk and cheese.

Juliet and Judith.

Past and present.

Memories versus the future. Can I be happy again?

He was drifting. Drifting into sleep, flowing into the music. The song, their song. His song to her – 'Romeo and Juliet.'

Husky lyrics whispered into the pillow. Old sorrows swallowed into the dark.

Chapter 26

The layer of fly corpses stacked against the windowpane had thickened over the summer months. Luc didn't like to interfere in Isaac's housekeeping arrangements, but the prevalence of hordes of flies landing on handles, mats and light fittings needed seeing to. Besides, the squeak each time Isaac pressed the pec deck together was grating on Luc's nerves. Luc was acutely aware that his only contribution to his use of all the kit was a once-yearly booking for Isaac to take his missus to Maison Bleu for a slap-up meal. He wondered, should he take matters into his own hands, arrange a close encounter with either Jif or WD40 in all the appropriate places?

The knots in his shoulders were sore. Twenty pull-ups later and his session was finished. Isaac had begun winding down with his stretching exercises so Luc joined him to stand side by side on the rubber mats in the middle of the garage.

"I've got a free morning tomorrow, Isaac. Shall I give this place a good spring clean before the winter sets in?" Isaac briefly stopped swinging his arm up over his head, eying his mate with quizzical disbelief.

"Things must be slow if you're offering to put a pair of rubber gloves on." Luc reached down with his hand to make a manly adjustment through his shorts to his undercarriage.

"Not really. But I do appreciate that you and Fiona are rushed off your feet with the pub *and* the children. Just offering to do my bit." Isaac propped his left foot rigid against the bench, then leant down to touch his toes.

"Decent love life lately?"

Luc decided that he must be mellowing in his old age when his answer to this question was a simple "Quiet," and yet he recognised his own ambivalence.

Isaac scooped up his sweatshirt and opened the back door of the garage.

"See you in the bar in five."

* * *

As Luc ambled into the pub, Robert threw a sideways wink in Isaac's direction before he hailed Luc from his bar stool.

"You missed a cracking ride this morning."

Luc ignored Robert; he waited till Isaac had finished drawing the pump handle towards his chest, watched him add the glass of beer to a full tray of drinks then raised his eyebrows briefly as he met Isaac's look. He nodded when he spoke.

"Adnams."

Robert dug in again. "Sure we can't persuade you to join us for the ride next Sunday? Should get the chance for a proper burn-up. Eight of us doing the run from Earl Soham to Sizewell."

Luc braced himself, taking a moment. His normal reaction to Robert's scab-picking comment would have been a rebuff but, instead, he was distracted by the arrival of Jeremy. In the twelve footsteps it took Jeremy to approach his biker cohorts, Luc spotted two anomalies in him: one, he had a carrier bag hooked over his wrist and two, the lack of his normal constrained air of confident entitlement. To add to Luc's consternation, Jeremy also didn't utter his usual, rather formal, "Hello, Luc. Work been busy lately?" or "How's the Honda running these days?" Instead, Jeremy waved his arm towards the pint which Isaac was placing beside Luc's elbow.

"I'll get that for Luc."

Robert scowled momentarily, appearing determined to press home his own hospitality first. "I fancied ringing the changes and Isaac's got a new Malbec in. Shall I pour one for you?"

Jeremy barely managed a distracted, "Yes, whatever you're drinking is good."

Robert continued with a mocking drawl in his voice. "Waitrose bag. Not your usual style!"

Jeremy ignored the slight and raised the laden plastic bag towards Luc. "I've been having a sort-out and thought you might like these magazines. The July issue's got a great article on some Asian overland rides which is right up your street."

Luc took the bag, opened it, graciously poking his nose in a little to peer at the cover picture on *Motorbiker* before catching the handles of the bag over a hook by his side.

"Thanks, Jerry. Much appreciated."

From the corner of his eye, Luc saw a bland expression of shock appear on Robert's face, and a bell began tolling in his own head. *Curious. Wonder how many times I can pull off the 'Jerry' short form before Robert chokes on his own consternation? And the drinks ordering protocol has changed: Jeremy offering to buy my drink before he's even reached the bar? Think I should possibly pinch myself but Robert is watching Jeremy, and Jeremy is stroking his fingers casually down his cheek. Twitch imminent? No, it's not in me to make him suffer.*

The basic metaphysics of the group had changed; no one had planned it, no one had anticipated it and Luc didn't like the way

Robert appeared to be analysing his every move. Robert's modus operandi was normally some jovial story about his business shenanigans during the previous week but, uncharacteristically, he fell silent. Luc realised that if he looked at Jeremy, then Jeremy immediately dropped his eyes submissively, then Robert would look suspiciously at both him and Jeremy. The looks flicked around in a three-way circle several times. For a split second Luc found himself tempted (alarmingly) to make a game of this new pecking order.

Robert broke the spell first. He picked up his bottle of red and swivelled on his stool then cleared his throat, appearing to trip over his own tongue in his haste to speak.

"I was just about to tell Luc about our run this morning and see if he has the bottle to come with us next Sunday." With that, he playfully gave Luc a thumbs up sign and Jeremy immediately grabbed at the lifeline of a familiar subject, launching into a full-on description of each curve and hill of their one-and-a-half-hour journey.

"Sunday by mid-morning though is an absolute 'no go' for you, Luc. You'd have to be up at the crack of dawn and home again before all the churchgoers, family picnickers and Lycra brigade are cluttering the highway." Isaac stopped rubbing the teacloth around the inside of a clean tumbler. He chipped in excitedly.

"Yah – remember that silly woman dithering about at the crossroads with her pony and trap?" Luc stopped mid-gulp of beer, swivelling his eyes in Isaac's direction. Isaac clapped his hands together, a look of exasperation furrowing his brow.

"Best stretch of straight road all morning when we were about to hit 90 and…"

Luc couldn't contain himself, snapped irritably at his best mate.

"I hope to God you lot slowed down to 25, perhaps 30 mph – Yes?" Isaac didn't flinch but his fists were frantically squeaking another glass dry.

"Fucking hell, of course we did. By the time we passed her on the intersection, her passenger had time to jump off and grab the pony's head. We crawled past and the woman at the reins even waved to us."

Robert looked quizzically at Luc. "Since when did you become a lover of equine welfare, Luc?"

Luc smirked back at him but elected, instead, to turn and speak directly to Jeremy.

"By the way. Have you got the final figure on how much money we made at Walmsley Band Night?"

He noticed Jeremy's Adam's apple bob up and down as if swallowing a knot in his throat. The topic of the village hall bogs came and went and Robert eventually excused himself to head for the pub's own facilities. Robert gone, and Isaac out of earshot in the other bar, Jeremy grabbed his chance. He dived in with a stricken sincerity which pulled at Luc's innards.

"About the other night, will you…?" Luc took in the droop of Jeremy's posture, the grey hollows under his cheekbones. Abject defeat, he recognised it – that kind of emotional surrender. Too common in men who have worn fatigues; in men who have stalked the desert, the snipers and the deceit of war. Jeremy was still staring at Luc's hand resting on the bar. He tried again with a little more volume:

"Will you… did you see?" Luc stood up to his full height, held out his arm at a right angle, square, rigid, palm vertical.

"What about the other night? I didn't see anything. I was too busy putting my guitar in the Landy." He waited a moment, expecting Jeremy to resuscitate his own courage. It didn't happen.

"Nowadays, it's not a big deal who anyone chooses to be with. Don't beat yourself up, society really has moved on." He saw the relief and peace which flooded in as Jeremy shook on their unspoken agreement, their entente cordiale.

"Thanks, mate. I didn't expect you to understand. I'm in your debt."

Luc suddenly spotted Robert only feet away and moved a step backwards. He retracted his hand before nonchalantly sliding it into his pocket. Robert strode forward, directed his query at both of them, lingering over the words.

"Did I miss something?" Luc made sure his reply was unexpectedly firm and left no room for any further fishing.

"Not really. Jerry and I had a bit of business to sort out."

Luc noticed the skin popping in and out on Robert's temple, knew his curiosity gauge must be close to detonation. But a yoke appeared to have been lifted from Jeremy's shoulders and the errant muscle above his cheek was no longer contracting.

Chapter 27

Judith

I yell in the direction of Mother's kitchen. "I'm off now."

Branston appears through the half-open hall door, sits down, begins licking his paw and swiping it in huge circles from chin to cheek, cheek to chin, and back again. In between he adds extra saliva but keeps missing the telltale remnants of milk sticking to his chin. Seconds later and Mother follows her feline shadow into the hall.

"Oh, I made you a tea, dear. You're always in a rush and you don't drink anywhere near enough liquids. I watched a programme the other evening which said you should drink a minimum of two litres of water a day."

With her spare hand, she begins waving the swollen knuckles of an arthritic finger at me and tut-tutting. I am late as usual but take the four long strides across the flagstones and wrap her with a gentle hug. I breathe in the oh-so-familiar scent of camomile which rises, comforting, from her skin.

"And *you* know that Branston will be leaving runny brown stains on your carpet again if you insist on giving him milk, Mother!" I can feel the fur of Branston's body winding a figure of eight through our stationery legs. Mother presses a mug into my hand.

"Don't spill it, you ninny," she chides in my ear. I feel a sharp shock at noticing that Mother's cheeks seem much hollower than I remembered and her once thickly covered scalp now has visible gaps between the hair roots. I grasp the mug.

"I promise I shall drink it en route. Now, your lunch is beside the microwave and remember not to overcook it. No more risking your crowns on sausages cooked till they're solid as gun shells." Mother taps me on the nose with the tip of her finger, a hark back to my youth.

"Stop nagging and get on your way. Off you go." Extricating my ankles from the cat, I head for the front door.

"Won't be back till about three-ish. Bye."

Climbing in behind the steering wheel I type 'Two Mile Bottom, Santon Downham' into the satnav and register a brief pang of guilt. A rare occurrence for me to fib to my own mother, but I know her reaction would have run something along the lines of: 'You get enough excitement doing what you do well – which is riding. Why on earth would you want to try out something as dangerous as a motorbike at your age?'

Lizzie knows what I'm up to.

* * *

As I edge the Shogun over the potholed entrance to the rest area just off the A134, I can see the large blue van and trailer parked exactly where Luc had described. The offloading ramp is already dropped to the ground. A smattering of anticipation is already kicking off in my body – in my case more like heartburn than any romantic butterflies-in-the-stomach kind of feeling. *Mental note to self – perhaps Gaviscon is the answer?*

The rush of summer dog-walkers, hikers and cyclists has

declined in time with the autumn temperatures. It's a weekday in term-time so the car park is empty except for us. I stuff my handbag and mobile under a blanket in the footwell. As I get out of the car, I'm wondering where on earth Luc is, then spot him a little way off in the distance on the edge of the trees, busy propping a bright green-and-white motorbike on its stand.

He yells, "Well done. You got here. Women and maps don't normally work well together."

Even from a distance, I can feel his smile weaving its fingers like the warm weft of a favourite jumper. I have to throw my voice a little to reply.

"And you should know that sarcasm is the lowest form of wit."

A friendly sparring already and we're not even within five feet of each other. It feels incredibly natural. Love it. No pretence, no shallow correctness in the name of civility. Clearly, what you see is what you get with Luc Stockdale.

As I approach, he stands up, watching me with an unnerving scrutiny as I get closer. He opens both his arms wide, gallantly kisses each of my cheeks and before I know it, I'm encircled by a full-blown bear hug. I cannot resist the chance, rest my head for three seconds against his collar bone. I can imagine the flavour of his skin. Then the essence of the thought is gone again as quickly as it arrives and Luc is suddenly all efficiency and tutor.

"Right, Judith. We're here on a mission and I expect you to listen properly to my instructions. OK? Then I think you will have a corking good ride. The Green Lane route we are going to follow takes about three quarters of an hour and skirts in and out through the periphery of the forest. But if you're struggling, you must be honest. No grand gestures of false resilience allowed today. You'll be using totally different muscles to riding a horse and the last thing I want is for you to have an accident. We can turn back at any time."

A bitter tang of regurgitated scrambled egg lurches up the back of my throat followed by a light burning sensation. I wince as I press the palm of my hand between my breasts. Luc looks concerned.

"Are you OK?"

"No problem. Just ate a belated brunch after riding. Fret not, I've been looking forward to our little challenge all week."

"Right. Well, first things first. Let's get you kitted out. No changing facilities I'm afraid."

We walk back to the van and Luc pulls out a large black plastic bin liner and a helmet from the front seat. My curiosity is getting the better of me as he loads my arms.

"Handy that you have spare protective clothing. Do you often take women out on the back of your bike?" I'm adding a cheeky upward inflection and I detect the tiniest pinking of his cheeks. He refuses to be drawn and gives a very flat response.

"An old flame. Juliet. Luckily you are roughly the same height and build as her. Said she didn't want to keep her stuff when she left."

Note to self. Don't tease him about Juliet, whoever she was.

I watch as Luc walks up the metal trailer ramp, one foot carefully placed in front of the other. The narrowness of the space and the incline of the ramp creates a very lopsided effect. It feels wrong to stare. *I wonder what exactly his injury is – what should I say?*

"Is there anything I can do to help unload the other bike?" He looks down at me from above and nods his head off to the left.

"Leave this to me. I'll change once both you and the bikes are ready. You won't be seen from the road if you go to the far side of the van. I promise to be a gentleman and not peek over my shoulder. Oh, and don't leave your jeans on. You'll get far too hot. I'm sure you can work out which are the knee pads and which are the arm pads."

Disappearing around the back of the van, I notice that the forest in autumn is strangely mute, the joyous breeding birdsong of earlier months having gone. I am soon preoccupied with the task in hand – grappling with overly tight denim while hopping about on one leg; standing to display my knickers to the wide world while strapping on knee pads; pulling on bright lime-green leggings and last but not least, stuffing my feet into rigid boots. That's just the bottom half. I fish about in the black bin liner again. Next, arm pads and a kidney protector. Finally, I pull the matching green-and-white shirt on over my top half. *Ready – I think.* I grab the helmet strap and put it over my wrist and stuff the scrunched-up bag under my other armpit.

I realise that I'm walking in a slightly ungainly, self-conscious fashion and waddle out to find Luc. I spy him by the forest track about ten metres away on the far side of the smaller bike, facing towards me and waiting patiently. He is leaning his elbows on the saddle and as I approach, he stands up. I feel slightly embarrassed.

"Sorry. I seem to be all fingers and thumbs today." Luc then casually steps forward two strides from behind the bike as if to meet me. That's when my jaw drops.

Terribly predictable comment, but that's exactly what happened.
Because my eyes must be deceiving me.
Have I been hit on the head and I don't know it?
Am I not really here? Am I in the middle of a very odd dream instead?
Shi-i-i-it. One of his feet is definitely facing backwards!

A shiver ricochets through my shoulders. I go to take one more step closer to him... My leg freezes, part raised in a (ceasing to walk forward) disbelief. Luc is stationary, he is still sideways on and his right trainer-clad foot (the nearest to me) is facing in the opposite direction to his left foot. His face is blank. I can feel my eyeballs move from Luc's feet to his face and back again. There is a dull clunk of teeth on teeth when my mouth shuts. I stand square again and manage only one word.

"*But...*"

Luc's lips suddenly spread into an immense smile.

"I thought you knew," and he pauses for the most irritatingly dramatic five seconds I have ever experienced in my entire life before adding, "I have a prosthetic leg."

It feels as though I am watching my own self from some weird parallel universe. I can see the thunderous frown hitting my very own face with a vengeance, feel my fingers rigid, splayed, touched by an electric fence of exasperation. I can hear my own guttural voice verging on a scream.

"*No, I didn't!*"

Luc can clearly contain himself no longer. He has planted both his hands firmly on his hips and is emitting a howl of laughter.

"Your face. A charging rhinoceros would look friendly compared to you!" The fury burning in my chest begins to rise in a sweeping tide up my neck to my tongue.

"Sodding hell. That's not funny. You absolute *bastard.*" Sucking in a second lungful of air in preparation for a further volley of expletives, I am outside myself again. A further wave of emotion comes pounding in, hot on the heels of the first, only this time it is pure, unadulterated relief. Then it hits me smack in the face. *Wow, he's funny. That foot is utterly ridiculous.* I know I'm biting my top lip to kill the snigger that's bubbling through.

310

He's close now and my eyes connect electrically with his. I am blurting out, "Have you ever seen one of those sketches with a three-legged man? I'll create some words especially for you. Just give me a minute to prepare ..."

My wits have returned at last from outer space. I need a prop. I spy a small mound of woody debris close by. Dropping the helmet and bin liner on the spot, I spontaneously grab a thick two-and-a-half-foot-long piece of timber from the pile. Luc looks perplexed. I carefully place the short branch at a twenty-degree angle from my crotch to the ground and gripping it with one hand, begin mimicking a stiff three-legged walk. To Luc's consternation I start to turn in circles while singing.

> "I'm Luc the Boot, fiddle-diddle-diddle-dum
> Got a wonky foot, fiddle-diddle-diddle-dum
> Whenever I try to make it stay
> It wants to go the other way
> I'm Luc the Boot, fiddle-diddle-diddle-dum
> With his wonky foot."

Coming to a three-legged halt in front of Luc with a dramatic upward flourish of the third leg, unfortunately my decision to attempt showmanship is foiled. I tip forward into a bow and accidentally hit myself on the nose with the branch. Luc starts clapping enthusiastically and cheering.

"Bravo. Bravo." Then adds, "I might steer clear of ever asking you for assistance with lyrics though!"

Unceremoniously, I drop the log to the ground, but when I look up into those bluest of blue eyes, the sparkle of fun is tinged with confusion.

"Right. We'd better stop pratting around now," and he strokes his index finger for a mere whisper of a moment on my cheek, smiles his designer stubble smile. His intense gaze is turning my innards into soup, a hot spicy liquid which melts me to the core. Eventually he breaks away with a gruff,

"Give me ten minutes to put my leg back together properly and we'll get going."

"Was that a party trick you've done before? Or was it pure spur of the moment to put your leg on back to front?"

"Guilty, guilty. I only ever do it for very special people though."

Perhaps I have been blind, perhaps I have been slow, perhaps I have been too self-obsessed, but then why didn't anyone tell me earlier? Why hasn't anyone mentioned it? Does it really matter? There it was, I thought, as we set to with our preparations. *His Achilles heel. His infirmity.* Without hesitation my next words come from nowhere.

"Luc, I'm staggered. How the hell did you do that? May I help putting your leg back together?"

Apparently, the human mind is the fastest computer in existence. In the next fraction of a second, mine is processing hard. *Is it actually relevant to how I view him as a person, as a man? Answer – no. Would I write off a perfectly good horse just because I have to apply an extra bandage to its leg whenever it needs to work? Answer, most emphatically – no.*

His look of suspicious surprise evaporates with the practicalities of showing me how exactly the prosthetic leg fits snugly onto his own upper calf and knee. His back propped against the van and hidden from prying eyes, Luc is soon both trouser-less and legless in only a pair of workmanlike, paint-splattered shorts and a long-sleeved T-shirt. Within minutes he has deftly donned his outer biker trousers and with each new instruction a richness is creeping into his tone.

"For goodness' sake stop prodding and poking my attachments and make yourself useful. Pass me the leg. Good. Now just stand next to me so I can grab you if I lose my balance." Deftly, he slips the pale pink moulding on over his stump and knee. He quickly rolls the leg of his bike trousers down, carefully pulls his protective boot on over the sock and foot and, hey presto, stands upright, tall and proud.

Tutor again, Luc's instructions and final preparations fly by and without further ado, my helmet is on and I am astride the bike. I am sitting too far back and he grabs me firmly by the waist and shunts me forward on the seat. *Two hands around my waist. Does he have any idea how good that feels? Note to self – pay attention.*

"OK, Judith, muscle memory. It will all return once you're up and running. Right, put the bike into neutral." Luc's voice is muffled, helmet thickness. My cheeks are pressed claustrophobically inside the padded sphere. "You can kick-start it now."

I hit the pedal hard with my right foot. Satisfaction – it whines into life first time.

"Pull the clutch in – yes, left hand." My left foot is already there clicking into gear; my right hand brings up the throttle a tad.

"OK. You're ready to roll. Off you go". Fingers ever so slowly stretching out, biting point is reached, my knees bend as my feet leave terra firma. I lurch forward six feet, clench both fists wildly, over-rev, let go of both levers and splutter to a tragic stop only ten feet away from where I'd started.

"Bollocks!" I yell inside the sphere. *I can do better than this.* I fire up again.

Luc is yelling from behind, "Square up your elbows and stop leaning back so far."

And it does come back, in dribs and drabs, then in bursts of recollection. Circling slowly around the perimeter of the car park, bravery growing, including some twists in and out of the wooden picnic tables. Seeing Luc's thumbs up when I pull up with confidence.

Luc pooh-poohs my girly need for warmth when I insist on grabbing my puffer jacket from the car. We set off on this grey October day, initially along a dirt track and I start to drift outside myself. I am watching from afar as the speed of the trees gradually changes in my world. They become a kind of trunkometer, a visual indication of my progress, my journey, this day in Thetford Forest. It starts tentatively, the solid dark brown of coniferous bark interspersed occasionally by the sparse branches of a stray beech or silver birch. Everything is muffled save my acute attention to the sound of the engine. Nothing else matters, the revs tell me everything.

We stop briefly. Luc checks I'm OK then we're off again. A little faster, Luc's back bouncing along twenty feet away, a whiff of burnt oil shooting up my nostrils. His words are on repeat. *Elbows out, cut off the throttle, leg forward, roll around the corner, throttle up again, change gear faster, a bit faster. Trunks are beginning to blur. Smattering of sand in my face. Adrenalin high. Slow down, brake gently, mind the rut, revs up again.*

No idea how far we've gone. Shoulders cramped, fists aching. Luc is way ahead now, must be at least sixty metres.

In the movies, a catastrophe always happens in slow motion. Not here, not today. I am still viewing as an observer, but I am given no split second in which I can press the pause button on the remote. There is no rewind or stop. I see the transient mass of brown hair, legs and horns certainly before Luc, because I am well back.

The roe deer lands from the covering trees – half a second.

It's already into its next stride – half a second.

Luc spots it – half a second.

One stride and it's already cutting across his path and I watch Luc react – half a second.

His front wheel is flung sharp right, a thin strip of hide and hairs is embedded into the tyre – half a second.

Startled, head low, the stag is already on its next stride on grass again – half a second.

Luc and his bike plough into the ground – half a second.

The stag, the runaway jaywalker, an unpredictable brain encased in a body of living muscle, bone and skin. The guilty party is gone as fast as he arrived.

I become a strange observing participant, an oxymoron, a 'me' who is also someone else. And again, in the movies, I would grind to an immediate halt, flinging my bike unhindered to the ground. Rush to my friend's side with screams of, 'Luc – are you all right? Luc, speak to me.' In the real world, self-preservation kicks in first. My mind processes, my limbs follow the instructions. *Don't grip, you'll go faster. Don't crash into him and for Christ's sake, don't fall off.*

Luc's body is under the bike. *Fingers towards me, off the throttle. Brake. Clutch. Engine still.*

Luc isn't moving. *Feet down. Brace your arms, Judith. Don't let it fall over on you. Damn, it's heavy. Down, it's down.*

Luc is stirring, a long, drawn-out groan gurgling through the air as my clumsy biker footwear threatens to trip my urgent strides. *No flinging myself, damsel-in-distress, or wailing in earnest. You know better than that, Judith, but I can hear the blood pumping in my ears. Whoosh, whoosh, whoosh. First aid rule number one, Judith – stay calm.*

I sink to my knees behind Luc's shoulders, lean over to be in his eyeline. His body is pinned to the ground with the full weight of the bike resting on his right leg and hip. His right arm is buckled under his back.

"Don't try to move." His low moaning is interrupted by his reply from between strands of grass tussock.

"Do I look like I can move?" His eyes flutter closed so I drop to speak within inches of his cheek.

"I'm going to lift the bike off you. I shall do it as gently as possible. OK?"

"Mmmm," is all he can manage.

Problem. It's going to be… heavy. Plan best position, Judith. Use your loaf, woman, use your loaf. Dropping as close to Luc's body as I can get without actually touching, I have to crouch in a kneeling position with my elbows resting on the ground. Bracing my back, I put one hand on the handlebar, the other on the saddle and heave. *Shit. This is heavy.*

The bike lifts a couple of inches. *Don't let go now, not now. The weight will rest back on his leg.* Luc throws in a strained, unhelpful "Put your back into it, woman."

I shuffle my knees and shoulders in tight and heave again. The bike rises, a little more, then a little more again until I am suddenly standing and with a triumphant last shove, the bike topples in the opposite direction.

First aid rule number two, Judith – assess the patient's injuries. At ground level again, I twist my head horizontal in order to look properly into Luc's face. His eyes are wide open now.

"What hurts, Luc? Can you move at all?" He tries to lift his head, but as I then go to lift his left arm he barks.

"*Don't* try to move anything. It's my right side that's the problem. I don't know. Hip, pelvis, something horrendously painful like that."

I raise one hand to point in the general direction of his legs and add, "Can you feel your feet and toes?"

"What all five toes and one foot?" My palm shoots up to my lips and I stutter hurriedly,

"Ooh, sorry. Really sorry. Foot in mouth... Oh no, *even* worse."

Getting in a fluster now. Not good. Stay calm. Too hot, too hot. I quickly wrench off my gloves, then grapple with the chin strap for what seems an eternity. Clarity returns to my thinking as the numbing effect of both is removed. *What to do next?*

"Luc. Where is your mobile?" I notice a horrible pallor to his skin accentuated by the blackness of the shiny helmet.

"In the pocket of my shorts." Bending to my knees yet again, I begin trying to wriggle my hand under the waist of his leggings. My face is up close and personal at his ribcage. Luc's voice is quivering:

"I don't know. Some women will go to any lengths in order to grope my groin." I have to turn and smile.

"Oy. You're not in a position to be cheeky. Now let me concentrate for goodness' sake." I become acutely aware, with proximity, of a warm hint of male pheromones laced with Lynx Africa invading my nostrils. At last my fingers locate the square shape of his mobile next to his thigh pocket. I pull it out with glee only to exclaim in angst once I turn the mobile over,

"Oh no. The screen is smashed." And I can feel the bile rising when I step a little away and give the mobile a pointless shake. I prod and swipe at the lifeless gadget.

Luc is watching me from the corner of his eye and mutters, "Surely you can use your phone? Why didn't you get yours in the first place?"

My cool is evaporating. Don't show it, Jude.

"It's back at the car. I know I can never get a signal here in Thetford Forest."

Step outside yourself and act the part. Think of this as a movie. A sudden moment of lucidity hits me and my confident reply is a surprise even to myself.

"No point in wishing for a mobile. Or waiting here for assistance in the form of some random passing person. I shall have to go and find help."

First aid rule number three – make the patient as warm and comfortable as possible. As I carefully lay my own coat over his body, I notice just how chilled the ground is. I chatter to him as I busy myself with preparations – taking his unworn windcheater from under the bungee strap on the back of his bike; folding and stuffing it gingerly under his helmet to support his head; trying to move his free left leg to prop him roughly in a recovery position; hearing his yelp with pain when I have to bend his knee.

"I recognised one of the intersections we crossed not far back from here. I'm certain I've ridden close to here before. I should be able to find my way to a little house which sits right in the middle of the forest. If I can't get help there, I'll ride on till I get to the main road."

I am down close to Luc's face again. His sighed "OK" simply accentuates his resignation.

Chapter 28

Judith

'Let the movie begin' – and it does with a vengeance. My sense of urgency mounting with each called question or command from Luc.

"How are you going to find your way back here?"

Brain in a whirl, brain on speed dial. Don't let on. I start rummaging in my puffer jacket pocket to retrieve a fistful of pink and yellow strips of material. With a flourish and a triumphant, "Ta-dah. Easy – I shall lay a trail," I wave some of the tassels aloft.

Luc lets out a sudden cough, followed by a guttural moan. His following and valiant attempt at cheerfulness comes out in uneven fits and starts:

"I dare not ask why on earth you have a pocketful of such an odd item!"

First aid rule number… oh fiddlesticks, I've lost count. Whatever it is – keep the patient talking and reassured.

"No, I must admit these are an obscure item. I was tying some of them to a new section of electric fence a couple of weeks ago. It helps the horses see the thin wire so they won't accidentally run into it."

I quickly stuff as many bits of material as possible down the front of my shirt and tug on my gloves. By the time I'm up and ready for the off, Luc has fallen into near silence and an ominous, steel-coloured cloud is hanging overhead. As I straddle the bike, Luc gives no real acknowledgement when I manage a successful kick-start. The engine splutters a couple of times as it crawls away under me. *Do not look back. Think ahead. Let the movie begin.*

A dull *whirr* inside my helmet. A dull *whirr* inside my thoughts. A dull pitch and whine of the engine. An engine that quickly becomes my friend, my mentor. It sings a crazy song – a tune of grinding struggle through patches of deep sand. A tune of humming speed on the straight. Everything becomes blotted out bar the constant bouncing motion and my need to concentrate.

Down the straight here, turn left. Stop carefully, keep the engine idling, fling a pink strip onto the ground. Remember cross-section 246. Go again. Trees flying by. A labyrinth of squares within the forest, some numbered, most not. Slow, slow. Foot out hard. Right here, I think. Is it right? Clutch, brake. Nothing to distinguish this turn so fling a couple of yellow strips. Off again. Drizzle cloying at my shirt. I bump along past a felled patch of open space, huge symmetrical rows of branches piled high to decay discreetly. Another strip flung asunder. Hurry, Judith, hurry. Startled, a blackbird shoots across my path. It's here, it's not here. A fleeting winged distraction. Trees, after trees, after more trees. At last a hardcore track – yes, this is it. I've ridden along here with the girls. But which bloody way were we facing? Is it this way, or that way? If only I was riding Rommel right now, he'd have known… Follow your instinct. Go with your gut.

Suddenly, the movie has come good – there it is, just a stone's throw away. The little dwelling with its fringes of thatch drooping down over the upper windows and its neat inviting gate. The sign hanging there, a bright beacon of fresh light against the brownness of the world around reads: 'Rose Cottage'. The heroine has arrived in one piece and she is going to save the day. I can see her get off her stationary mechanical steed and pushing at the little gate. I know her breathing is coming short and sharp, I see her rattling the gate frantically, spotting the chain holding it shut. I know she worries briefly: *Mesh fencing. Big dog? Little dog?* She calls out.

"Hello. Anyone in? Hello." And I watch her judge the height of the fence before swinging first one leg, then another over the top. She is running down the path, she pulls a glove off with her teeth and raps her knuckles, bang, bang, bang, against that door.

Nothing happens. She reverses eight feet, stands back, her eyes flitting from window to window in search of any light, any telltale sign of occupancy. She has already backed away again in readiness to leave when the door slowly swings open. The darkness of the backdrop, the dim confines of the porch mean she struggles to form a picture of the face which she assumes is speaking to her.

Impatiently she barks, "There's been an accident in the forest. My friend needs help urgently."

I see her squashed, misshapen features as her fingers struggle against the suction keeping her helmet in place. I see the waif-like man move forward into the daylight. I hear the shock in their respective voices.

He says, "Judith, isn't it? Judith from Table Talk. You wore a green blouse."

And her reply, "Umm. Oh umm. Yes," and she hesitates. "Oh, I remember. Yes, you're right. Hello, Stanley. I'm *so* sorry. I didn't recognise you in the poor light."

The clapper-board in her mind begins to bang shut at regular intervals from the moment the steady voice on the other end of the phone begins a trained interrogation. The urgent questions are thrown at her as if she is sitting in the Mastermind chair, her chosen subject being: 'Decisions in an emergency'. She can see herself in each shot as it unfolds; the hesitancy in her voice when there are questions about air ambulance versus standard ambulance; her rising panic at the protracted discussions on the whys and wherefores of a rescue; placing her hand over the phone and throwing a heartfelt, "Do you have a grid reference for this place," at Stanley, "one ending in TL or it's useless."

The visual frames continue to flash by relentlessly: The elfin man shaking his head. This woman, this Judith on a big cinema screen, this 'I'm not really here, therefore this isn't really happening' Judith. Them relying on her information as being accurate. Having to make it her call. This woman swallowing the need to cry with her reply to the operator, "I cannot be absolutely certain whether that patch of cleared forest is due west or more like north-west. I'm sorry. It's probably best if you send a normal ambulance. It can at least go some of the way on the track." Placing the unwieldy, old-fashioned receiver back in its place.

Then I come crashing back into my own very real world with a sudden awareness of Stanley's unblinking stare and a leisurely tick, tock, tick, tock sound caressing my ears. *What next?*

"They said it's important I stay here, so I can help them locate the right place. I'll wait outside for the ambulance." Stanley, however, becomes rather insistent.

"You probably need a cup of tea. All this excitement. I'll go and make one."

I try to protest but it would seem rude and the reasoning in his final comment is sound. "No point in getting even wetter. They won't get here for at least twenty minutes." The merest wrinkle at each corner of his mouth is the one and only and most subtle of messages in an otherwise unreadable face.

I find myself shown through to his sitting room. I slump into a high-backed chair close to the window and become the one occupant in the room. I tug with two fingers at my green-

and-white sleeves; the polyester returns cloying to my skin. *Will I leave a wet bottom shape whenever I decide to rise?* I can just hear a cupboard door clunk shut, the rattle of china upon china, the clink of a teaspoon sliding into place. *The kitchen must be next door.*

My eyes have adjusted to the verging-on-nocturnal interior light and it feels as though I have stepped into a time warp. A mock-up of a front room in a 1940s working-class home. Taking up pride of place and at least a fifth of the limited wall space is a piano. I rest my head back onto the chair and realise I can see right past the garden gate and out down the track. *Good. Excellent vantage point, Judith.* My stomach lets out a low growl, then silence falls again. The kind of total silence that one rarely experiences in a world of constant background interference. *Odd. Tea seems to be taking a long time.* Then I hear it. A scuttling above my head, in the ceiling. I crane my head upwards, concentrate harder. The sound repeats a little further over. *Rats, mice. Stanley has a rodent problem.* Quiet falls again. *Where is that man?* My gaze wanders out of the window. Then a muffled thud, thud, thud breaks the air immediately above me. *Did a picture fall off the wall perhaps? But it was too solid a sound and it was definitely three times. Who is upstairs now? Because I can hear a cupboard door closing in the kitchen?*

I realise I am holding my breath and force myself to exhale. *Stop being utterly stupid, Judith, you're tired. In fact, my wrists are aching. Must have been holding the throttle too tight.* I tip forward to cup my chin in one palm and begin massaging along the back of my neck with the other hand. My inner safety gauge rises without warning and I jolt upright against the chair again. Momentarily not sure, then quickly pinpointing Stanley's head peering around the door. *Was he watching me?*

"Sugar?" he croons.

"Just milk, thank you," and he disappears as silent as a cat.

Within seconds, he sidles in carrying a tray of sage-green crockery reminiscent of hundreds of village halls in post-war Britain. He busies himself carefully pouring from the matching teapot. He places the saucer and generous triangular cup on a tiny occasional table near my elbow and, devoid of any politeness, I pounce. As I clutch the cup and saucer between my weary fingers, they rattle violently, forcing me to plonk them back on the table in haste. Stanley's nose twitches the tiniest of movements, he shoots me a sympathetic smile then stops a plate of biscuits halfway to being offered.

"It will be the shock setting in. I'm sure. Leave the saucer, pick up the cup. It will warm your hands."

I down the first cup in one and Stanley carefully pours a second. He presses me to add some sugar and I reluctantly concede. My unsettled thoughts are stumbling around making any protracted interaction low on my wish list. Instead I stir my tea unnecessarily. *Luc will be chilled to the bone by now. Where the hell is that ambulance?*

Stanley catches my longing look at the biscuits. They are stacked in two perfect circles, digestives on the outside, custard creams on the inside. He has used at least half a packet of each in order to create the effect. He appears to read my mind as he holds out the plate.

"You must be ravenous. Pop some in your pocket for later. You're going to have a long day."

I flash a quick look at my watch between mouthfuls of McVitie's best. *Ants in my pants. Can't sit here doing nothing any longer.* I make a point by craning to peer out of the window and Stanley takes the hint.

"Maybe a good idea for you to stand by the garden gate now. Keep an eye out."

* * *

Fifteen minutes later and we are trundling along in the ambulance. Five adults crammed into an interior designed for horizontal patients rather than upright passengers. We are a motley collection. The professionals are made up of Lawrence, a cheerful chappie, at a guess in his mid-fifties. Quite a bit of loose flesh is hidden beneath his uniform, but he has the kindest of kind expressions under his prescription NHS glasses. His co-worker Dawn exudes a 'no messing with me' steely efficiency despite her 5'3" pruned height and long, dark ponytail. The third official member of the crew is a strapping lad of a medical student tagging along in pursuit of experience. Jasper's swinging stethoscope is already in situ around his neck.

The two interlopers are Stanley and myself. A heated discussion before we set off had Dawn firmly trying to put down her Cockney foot with a, "We cannot be a taxi service simply so that Judith is able to retrieve a motorbike from the middle of the forest." I had quickly won the argument with, "I cannot face being left in the forest alone again to find my way back to safety. I'm already pretty exhausted and it will start to get dark very soon. Do you want to end up with another emergency services call for a lost woman?" It was eventually agreed that Stanley should tag along too in order to accompany me back to the cottage.

Up front in the cab I am directing the driver, Lawrence, and explaining my ordeal of the past one and a half hours. I am tipping forward on the cab seat and between left and right sweeps of the windscreen wipers, I am studying each new grassy cross track that passes by. The dryness of my eyeballs has become irritating and I wish that I could pluck my contact lenses out. *No chance. I wouldn't even be able to see far enough in this drizzle to direct a piss-up in a brewery!*

We get as close to Luc's whereabouts as possible without risking a stuck ambulance, then get out. The rescue operation lurches into overdrive the moment we set off on foot. Dawn immediately voices her reservations about my ability to navigate us through the maze of avenues until I quickly explain.

"Hansel and Gretel. You're probably too young to have heard the tale. Hansel fills his pockets with stones and uses them as markers to guide both him and his sister home. That's what gave me the idea." My reward is her nod of approval.

There is a sense of honed urgency and very little chatter as we march along in a line. Trouser legs are soon sodden, especially Jasper's. He appears to have walked straight out of the hospital out-patients with no heed for the inclement weather. The stretcher is hooked under his arm and he is bending his head low into the oncoming wetness. His shoes occasionally slip on the grass and he has no coat at all, just a jumper and a woolly scarf wrapped around his neck. I am the lucky one with my impermeable footwear. At the front, I am striding out as briskly as my followers will allow. Occasionally, I point with excitement whenever I spot another tassel marker. After what seems like an eternity but in reality is probably twenty minutes, I spot the low burgundy-red puffer jacket atop the mound that is Luc's body and call out while I run.

"Luc. Luc. We're here. We're here."

* * *

If this was a movie, there would be a close-up shot of me cradling Luc's head in my arms while whispering assurances and encouragement. The camera would follow one single tear as it descends to stop at the corner edge of my (incredibly) lush lips. I would mouth the words "I love you" and the scene would fade to notes from a full orchestra!

C'est la vie – Judith McBride you are not in a movie.

In reality, I am told quite firmly by Dawn to

"Stand back a little, Judith. You've done great getting us here. Let the experts do their job now."

And I watch, suddenly superfluous but also fascinated with the procedures. It's staggering how much practical medical kit is packed into two small backpacks. Luc becomes amazingly chipper once the Pethidine kicks in but cannot stop a proper yowl when he is rolled onto the special Scoop stretcher. My coat is still wrapped over Luc's chest and straps are holding him secure. I crouch down hurriedly attempting a chance to catch his attention. There is strain etched in tiny wrinkles across his brow, but he manages to throw out a final playful barb at me.

"It strikes me that whenever I go anywhere near both you and Thetford Forest at the same time, I end up in a heap under my own motorbike."

Unable to stop myself, I ignore the proximity of Dawn and her latent impatience and reach over to press the back of my curled fist briefly against his forehead. There is a distant 'other world' edge to Luc's voice with his earnest, simple request.

"Don't try to ride my bike back. It's far too powerful. Please don't."

"Fret not. That's why Stanley is here. We're going to push it."

In the movies the heroine would walk beside her man, holding his hand all the way. My own alter ego is desperate to do exactly that, but then remember. *I am not writing the story. I am merely a participant.* Instead, the world around us becomes mournfully still again. I turn to Stanley who is barely visible beneath his knee-length waterproof mac and flat cap and, with more confidence than credibility, I announce, "OK. Let's get this bike back."

* * *

I can smell the crushed pine needles as I watch us up there on the big-screen version of our very own story. Stanley and the woman, a bedraggled pair slogging their way through the relentless drizzle. She in a borrowed anorak, two sizes too small for her, the motocross garb and boots underneath no complement. Him a feeble outline.

Positioned either side of the Honda, each with one hand on the saddle, the other on a handlebar, they lean into the weight. At other times they have to struggle to balance the heaviness and simultaneously steer around a corner. Every now and then the brunette glances across at Stanley's grim visage. Very quickly the sweat is mingling with the raindrops running down his cheeks and he scrunches his cap up and stuffs it in a pocket. This action sets free his comb-over to flop this way and that in time to his movements.

She finds herself having to dig incredibly deep. Her tank of energy running on near empty, they stop for a moment and she suggests,

"We could leave the bike here. Luc's friend Isaac can retrieve it tomorrow."

Stanley makes her feel guilty with his answer.

"No. Daren't leave it out here overnight. All sorts of weird, thieving sorts. We'll keep going."

And they do make it back to the cottage sanctuary in the middle of the forest. It's 5.30pm and the clouds have drawn a curtain of impermeable darkness over the land. I see the weary pair make one final shove as they wheel the motorbike over the threshold of a large shed. I am pleasantly surprised to feel a unity, a battle fought together and won, portrayed when Stanley announces simply,

"We did it."

* * *

Me, the audience in my own story, is shocked to feel a soppy warm glow as the final scene unfolds – Lizzie is sitting in her car outside Rose Cottage, the engine is running, the wipers are wiping, the headlights are casting out towards the blackness. This woman, this Judith, is thanking Stanley as they part in the murk and the moisture and she sees the way his world has come alive. The flourishing or scrunching of his cap tight in his hands, the animation in his parting words thrown at her as she gets into the car:

"I've never had this much excitement before. It's really quite invigorating."

The orchestral theme music grows as his solitary figure is seen waving at the receding car.

Chapter 29

A purple bobble hat travelling at approximately 25mph along the Upper Melling road marked the progress of Lizzie along her usual route. Bemoaning the arrival of an early freeze, she pulled the hat snugly down over her ears. The sharp, dry air hit the back of her throat when she sucked in quick breaths going up Clay Hill. She shut her mouth to coast down the hill.

The further she cycled, the more light-headed she felt. The further she cycled, the more acute became the pangs of mild nausea. She forgot to stand up on the pedals and a twinge of pain shot up her neck when she hit the east side speed bump. *Ooh, that's sore. Haven't even got the energy to curse.* One-handed, she pulled the scarf too tight around her neck; the bike wobbled a little around pothole number one before she grabbed the handlebars properly again. *Far too much wine yesterday evening. Jude is to blame. Haven't ever seen her let go quite like that before. Booze probably helped, I'm sure, but she seems lighter, focused, energised. Can't quite put my finger on it.*

Lizzie passed the old boy's garden. She noticed that all the greenery had gone; he had already dug over most of the soil and only a few rows of frost-dusted Brussels sprout plants remained – determined sentinels of an approaching winter. Lizzie stopped at the intersection and tried to look right. It hurt – she had to twist her whole body to peer down the side street. She frowned as she pushed off again and pondered, *Why exactly was I trying to do a handstand against the wall in the pub at 11pm? I remember a lot of cheering and clapping before my arms gave out.*

In the past few weeks, she had taken to pedalling with absolute venom in order to shoot past My House in as few seconds as possible. She strictly avoided any eye contact with the 'Sold' sign, but this morning was different. This unloved wreck was clearly being given a makeover. The hedge had been slashed, chopped and trimmed into a naked version of its former shape and the front façade of the house was partly hidden by a high-sided U-Drive van and two ladders.

As her wheels revolved along the lane, Lizzie became preoccupied with rubbernecking and, too late, she spotted a smattering of stray hedge detritus littering the tarmac. *Blackthorn all across the road. Damn it – my tyres!* The pain which shot from her shoulders and up through her neck matched the sudden swerves she had to make left, right and right again, to avoid the small heaps of offending twigs. The west side speed bump jolted a final jarring wrench, it seemed just for good measure.

It was a good hour later that Lizzie set off to trudge back up the track from the livery yard. The heavy squidginess of the now seriously flat tyre made pushing harder than she had anticipated and only served to aggravate her existing aches even more. *I should just make it home in time for lunch. An hour. Any other calamities in mind for my world, God? Jude's answer would be – sing. Should I, shouldn't I?* She stopped her less-than-resolute walking and cast a cursory backward look down the road. *What the hell. No one can hear me. Cheer yourself up, Lizzie. Go on. Be a devil. Something nice and simple.* And she began to speak rather than sing in time to her own footfall.

"Jingle bells, jingle bells, jingle all the way.
Oh what fun it is to ride in a one-horse open sleigh – hey.
Jingle Bells, jingle bells, jingle all the way."

She reached the end of the drive and began walking towards the offending section of road which was still covered in patches of wood shards and thorns. Her confidence had begun rising with the tune and she started to throw a little volume into her chant. A minor insurgence against life's revolving door tendencies.

"Oh, jingle bells, jingle bells, jingle all the way.
Oh what fun it is to ride in a one-horse open sleigh."

At the point where she passed the double gates to My House, she was verging on singing, of sorts. She was unexpectedly startled out of her introspective march by a male voice, which arrived from on high.

"Santa will ne'er venture into this coonty."

Lizzie stopped immediately and turned, her eyes roving around the My House drive, garage and garden in search of the source of the interruption. The baritone spoke again.

"A caterwauling wuman like that will scare him awa for at least two Christmases te cum."

At last Lizzie pinpointed the rude joker. Her focus in her vision readjusted and, in between the cross pieces of linear metal and ladder rungs, she could make out the shape of a man. He was leaning out of an upstairs window, his expression indifferent. *Is that white paint above his mouth or has he been eating whipped cream? Wits, wits, wits. They have abandoned me. What the hell kind of reply do I give to that?*

"Smart arse," is what came out. Followed by, "What else is a girl supposed to do when she's having a bad day?" She was about to resume her trek when The Voice interrupted again.

"Have ye far te gay? Would ye like te leave yay bike here?" In order to be able to shout yet again, Lizzie took in a deep breath, but her reply was quickly pre-empted as The Voice waved a spare hand and yelled,

"Hang on a minute, I'll cum doon."

Fifteen seconds passed until eventually the man came out of the house with a dachshund close on his heels. His checked lumberjack-style shirt was loose above grubby jeans and he was dabbing at his upper lip with a hand towel as he bounced rather than walked across the gravel. There were telling white hairs running through his otherwise dark brown head of hair and Lizzie observed: *Spritely for someone who must be what, at least fifty-four years old?*

"You do realise this is your fault, don't you?" she exploded and pointed at her deflated tyre. "You haven't swept the road since your scalping of that hedge!"

The wire-haired bundle of canine enthusiasm arrived at Lizzie's side first and immediately jumped up to rest his two front paws on her knee. *Not a breed I would have expected for a man.*

"Sorry, but Aa didne cut the hedge and this hoose isne mine."

Lizzie automatically freed a hand to reach down and fondle the soft ears as The Voice stopped in front of her. She was surprised when he swept away her already disagreeable first impression of him by saying,

"Ye appear te have already made friends wi me ferocious hund. May Aa introduce masell?"

His handshake was vigorous, it matched his walk. He wrapped his two builder-strength hands around her one and continued shaking for three seconds longer than one would expect. "A'm

Douglas. And this is Dougal. Or Doug and Doog if you prefer?"

Tired. Want to get home. Need a hot bath. Lizzie ignored his niceties, instead she pointed at his face.

"Shaving foam. You missed a bit." *Let's get this over with as quickly as possible please.* "Can you at least relay to the plonker owner of this place, how irresponsible it is to leave cuttings all over the road." Lizzie dropped down onto her haunches in order to continue scratching Dougal behind his ears, only to have The Voice follow suit and come down to the same level.

He asked quizzically, "Goon?" then made a rabbit's nose shape of his top lip. They were both still squatting above Dougal; to the outside world, a picture of intimacy, but Lizzie's daggers-at-dawn look provoked a hurried reply from The Voice. "A'm hoose-sitting for a week for ma pal, the new owner, so A'll mak sure he noos. In fact, Aa shall find a broom and brush awar every wee bit masell. How's that?"

"I have to cycle along here several times a week so the sooner the better. Thank you."

Hang on, I didn't invite you to join me down here. Back off, mate. Lizzie straightened up again.

"Lovely family dog," is what came out.

She noticed a fleeting sudden sadness when The Voice added, "We're ne a wee family. No... Dougie and Aa are simply bachelors united."

Lizzie's inside-outness with her day meant that she didn't really notice him tracking her every move, his tallness or his neat goatee. All she registered was his ugly Roman nose. The joint efforts at friendliness which the two strangers had made hit an awkwardness so Douglas resorted to a prop and scooped his dog up in his arms. He looked guiltily at the ground.

"Can Aa start our conversation again. Firstly, te say sorry

fer the ribbing when ye were minding yuse own business. And secondly te offer ma assistance should ye wish to accept it."

Lizzie's inner grump took a moment to think. *Man and small dog – endearing but I cannot understand half of what he's saying.* She pressed a couple of fingers gently against her temple, rubbed them in a small circle but the heavy thudding behind her eyes continued.

"Apology accepted. I know I'm not *X-Factor* material. Anyway, I really must be getting this bike home and pushing it is my only option." She placed her fists on the handlebars again, resignedly adding, "Nice to have met you."

Douglas remained undaunted by this striking anathema of a woman with her riveting green eyes and purple hat.

"Strange wee straw accessories sticking te ye scarf, but ye really dene strike me as being a farmer's wife. Am Aa right? Perhaps Aa could un-besmirch yuse first impressions of me. If ye leave yuse bike, Aa could drop it off fer ye tomorrow when Aa have ma pick-up here. Wud it be a help?"

Lizzie smiled wanly back at Douglas. *Nosy bugger,* was her immediate thought.

"The answer to your first question is, no. The answer to your second question is, yes, that would be great. I wonder though… may I have a glass of water before I set off home?"

* * *

Addictive habits, Lizzie knew, could rear their ugly heads in multitudinous forms, but hers she also suspected was plain and simple – a need to browse, to check out the selection; to fill a fundamental need to receive some praise; to feel attractive; to be 'chosen' by someone. A Sunday habit, after her morning stable duties were complete, to flick through any new profiles which had been added since her last visit. A frivolous treat to herself at the end of a fraught week in the clinic. To receive a blown kiss emoji could lift her spirits more thoroughly than any packet of biscuits and, unlike alcohol, avoided an ugly hangover. She had no problem kicking the habit whenever she had a fully-fledged relationship on the go, but right now she was bored. She made herself a frothy cappuccino, double-checked Douglas's text message and noted that he hadn't been specific about exactly what time he would arrive with her bike.

She settled into her favourite spot in her conservatory, her reclining chair facing out towards an assortment of barns, lean-to buildings and land to the rear of the house. For several minutes, she sat and gazed into the middle distance, occasionally taking a sip of her coffee. A dozen Texel sheep broke up the greenness of the grass, pottering about like portable woollen extras in a framed watercolour. *Some people*, she thought, *have an ability to see beauty in absolutely any type of weather, but for me a drizzle-enhanced October landscape just doesn't cut it.*

The first few drips landed, cool on her head. Drip, pause, drip, pause, drip, pause. She didn't move because she wanted to be absolutely sure. She felt each droplet spread a little over her scalp and warm, until another one fell, irritatingly persistent. She sighed, then stood up and grudgingly began shifting everything around. The glass-topped coffee table was heavy and had to be moved carefully – a favourite piece of furniture made from sun-bleached driftwood with each individual branch in the base cleverly held together in a spiral. Eventually she sat down again, comfortable and ready, her laptop fitting neatly on top of her Auntie Bettie's TV tray. The flex stretched perilously tight from the socket under the rim of the table to her chair so she shunted herself forward a few inches.

CLICK **Website:**   Dancing in The Moonlight

CLICK **Inbox/New Messages:** "Spartacus"+"Dream Boy"

CLICK **Spartacus**

Oh dear, he only has one photo.

CLICK **Dream Boy**

Such a little poppet, but he obviously hasn't put in a mileage limit on his search. Brighton is a little too far, methinks!

CLICK **Newest Members**

The screen slowly populated with pictures of male faces and Lizzie impatiently moved the cursor along the rows. After a couple of minutes she froze and stared.

CLICK **Highland Husky**

OH SHIT. It's Douglas and Dougal! Smart suit in that photo. Not very enamoured with that Roman nose though.

She scrolled on to another photo.

Wow, love the huskies. Is that him driving them?

The loud buzzing of the doorbell startled Lizzie and she had to lurch to grab the laptop and tray as they slid off her knees. Fast-forward one minute and by the time she hastily flung open the front door for Douglas, she was feeling decidedly cross.

"Come through, come through. This way. Um… I've just had a bit of a calamity."

His footsteps clattered a little on the wooden floor as she

hustled him through to the kitchen-diner, but she was in too much of a tizz to stop and stress about hobnailed boots. She felt the satisfying scratch of her fingernails as she ran them roughly through her hair near her forehead, struggled to create a half-smile.

"Would you like a coffee? It might stop raining if we wait before unloading the bike."

She waved her arm in the direction of the open conservatory doors and followed him into the chaotic scene. She saw his eyes investigate the room, absorbing information about each individual item: a mishmash of overturned coffee table, its glass top separated from its base and perilously balanced as if it might roll away of its own accord any minute; her lime-green art deco reclining chair; the TV tray with its fussy, floral rose picture, stranded half on, half off the ottoman; the laptop open and wedged on its side against the wall, its cable trailing. His concern when he spoke sounded genuine.

"Oh goodness, Aa see what ye mean. Shall Aa right a few things fer ye while ye sort out the coffee?"

"No, no. It's my mess. Just give me a moment." She moved as if to push past him.

He turned, momentarily polite in a strange house, and for a couple of slow-motion seconds she was certain she could get to the laptop first, but he was nearer than her and over-zealous in his rush to be gallant. Lizzie disliked the tingle of distressed energy which prickled in the skin at the back of her neck. She had to flatten her urge to barge past him, hurl herself at the laptop – on which the incriminating husky photo was clear to see – and snap the lid shut. Douglas quickly picked up the device but remained bent over as if ready to place it on the sill. Lizzie noticed his wallet threatening to escape from his back pocket; she willed him not to look at the screen. She spoke with urgency.

"You've gone to enough trouble returning my bike."

His movements suddenly became very precise, almost ceremonious, as he absorbed the content on the screen before him and his right-hand fingers lingered on the lid. The seconds crawled, seeming endless to Lizzie, till Douglas rose again and eventually faced her. In order to avoid any embarrassing acknowledgement on either part, she made a point of concentrating on the shape of his Adam's apple. He spoke first, until Lizzie was finally forced to look straight at him. His eyes appeared to be about to pop, his irises enlarged and black, the mischief bursting to get out. Instead, it sparkled, cryptic through his every consonant and vowel.

"A-hah – a fellow scroller. Ha ye spotted anyone in particular that tickles ye fancy?"

She had to concede, game set and match to Douglas. She paused, but the silence simply encouraged him to be even bolder.

"Wud ye like te gay through aw the official channels and exchange messages via the wee website first? Or are ye happy to skip aw that palaaver?" She looked at the laughter lines, three on each side, fanning out from the corner of his irreverent eyes.

"I think we can dispense with the formalities. I might still check out your credentials, though. After you leave!"

* * *

His movements, she noticed, always appeared measured, as if he had all the time in the world, and his accent was proving a source of great hilarity for both of them. 'Gooin doon the rood' – he'd made her practise it several times throughout coffee and she was still saying it when they spilled out of the front door. She continued her piss-taking. He seemed to like being the butt of her jibes and she chanted as she crossed the drive, "Doug and Doog, gooin doon the rood."

As she got closer to the garage, she spotted the white perm of 'The Wig'. It kept bobbing about on the far side of the dividing hedge. Thankfully, Tracey Bannister could only ever peek over the top by standing on her tiptoes.

The drizzle had stopped and Dougal scurried about from the flowerbeds to the gravel, frantically gathering as much vital sniff information as his nostrils could take. Lizzie unlocked her garage door and waited. Once Douglas had extricated the bike from his van, he propped it against the hedge and began reloading his toolboxes and containers. Standing at her full height, Lizzie was able to see Tracey leaning towards the hedge, strangely still. No more clip, clip, clip, shrub-trimming noises. Lizzie's preoccupation with her own nosiness meant she didn't see Dougal lifting his leg on the wheel of her bike... until it was too late. She rushed to shoo him off, yelling as she ran.

"Dougal. *Dougal.* Get off. Go pee somewhere else."

The dog shot a hurried glance in Lizzie direction, stopped his disrespectful widdling and galloped across to his master. Lizzie stood with both hands planted on her hips. She could see the funny side of the misdemeanour and quickly threw her light-hearted reaction loudly at Douglas.

"Don't they say that dogs learn from their owners?" Douglas raised his hand in a grand circle to indicate the edges of her garden. She decided she liked his tendency towards showmanship.

"He's markin his wee new territory."

She giggled as she replied,

"Should I be worried?" As she started marching towards the van, she could see The Wig elevate a little more. *Practicing up on our ballet points are we by any chance, Tracey?*

Lizzie jolted her head backwards at the hedge. Douglas got the message and winked at her then continued by performing as if to a theatre audience:

"Perhaps on ma next visit. If ye be a really good girl?" They both spotted the slight movement of the buddleia bush in Tracey's garden and heard the click of her front door shutting. Douglas turned to face her and spoke again, "Will yuse be making me wait a wee while afore a second visit?"

It arrived, his kiss, immediately after they stopped laughing, catching her off guard. The ends of the bristles in his goatee brushed against her chin a split second before his lips planted demanding on hers. *Ooh Douglas, forward or what! My antennae are normally hypersensitive when it comes to men and their advances. Am I pleased or offended at his presumption?*

Chapter 30

Judith

The flames in the grate curl around the birch logs, hugging the contours before shooting up, ferocious and orange. I watch a sliver of bark which has broken free. It warps in the intensity of the heat, crackles, throwing out sparklers of light then falls, a charcoal ending. The solitude and serenity of this space, bathed only in firelight, warms my bones. In the recesses of the sitting room and behind each chair, the blackness is solid only until I study it more closely. As my eyes adjust, there is a pixilated soft sepia of individual squares and slowly my vision manages to formulate the shapes – the chest, the lampstand, the vase.

How long till Mother detects my hiding place, I wonder? When I tap the screen of my mobile, the harshness of its white light is vulgar, like a profanity let loose in a library. I feel the need to occupy my fingers while I wait for Luc to answer his phone, so I begin scraping cat hairs into a tiny ridge at the edge of the cushion, stroking in the same direction as the weave.

Brr, brr. Brr, brr. Brr, brr. Brr, brr. Brr, brr. Brr, brr. Brr, brr.

Is he OK? There could be post-operative complications, a blood clot, anything!

Brr, brr. Brr, brr. Brr,brr.

He said to phone this evening. Perhaps he's still recovering from the anaesthetic.

I press the red 'X' button, close the phone and place it on the sofa beside me, staring into the flickering heat of my own thoughts. Can I stop wading through historic treacle? It's sticking to my hands, leaving messy patches of distrust and uncertainty on the exposed surfaces of my self-esteem.

When I pounce on the flashing phone I make a spontaneous decision – there is no excuse for regret. I can picture Luc as we chat, propped up with pillows, probably driving the nurses nuts. One minute all charm and humour, the next caustic jibes, a form of pain barometer. The fluid texture of Luc's voice, I realise, seeps into me as it gradually becomes quiet, more intimate, and the waning glow from the fire suggests how easily an hour can tick by. It's as if we are here on the sofa together, my head in the crook of his shoulder encouraging me to be bold so that, when I delve, he is honest. I discover that he is struggling in the same way as I am to wash away the black treacle smudges of old wounds – Juliet remains on the shirtsleeves of his bruised memories.

A loud, steady rattling purr just the other side of the door suddenly distracts me from the bubble of my conversation with Luc. I remain silent for a few moments while Luc continues talking. Mother, I decide, must be in the hall with Branston. The feline shadow will be weaving his way through her legs, while he continues his appreciative drone. He wouldn't stay in the hall if he was alone. As I whisper a goodbye to Luc, my smile feels sensual and as downy as the delicate cocoon of ginger hairs rolling in my palm.

* * *

The strength of my need to see Luc surfaces without warning when I find myself hitting the ticket machine in the hospital car park and a trickle of blood quickly begins oozing from my thumb. Physical violence: I abhore it as a form of expression – inexcusable. My reprisal on an inanimate object finishes with a vehemently screeched,

"Damn, damn and effing damn. You stupid machine, just give me a ticket! I haven't got time for this."

Placing the bloodstained ticket on the dashboard, I have to waste more precious visiting time rummaging about in my handbag for a plaster. *It's the radiators in the hospital, that's all,* I tell myself as I leap three steps at a time up the stairs. *My tension, the heat. It's the radiators, Jude.*

How unsettling it is, arriving in the ward. I am acutely aware that I am the one solitary visitor to this section. Two geriatric male patients appear to be deep in slumber, another is pottering about reorganising his bedside cupboard and the two other middle-aged patients have their noses in books. *Privacy is going to be impossible.*

I have been wrenched out of my normal comfort zones. No turf underfoot, instead, thoroughly polished lino; no petrol exhaust fumes, just mildly scented hand sanitiser; no rustle of dried leaves and an occasional blackbird's call. I know that I am smiling excessively as I walk boldly up to Luc, but I can sense that neither of us is quite sure how to behave. The school-teacher in me announces,

"Wasn't easy trying to guess whether you are a healthy-eating fanatic or a decadent lover of all things sweet, so I've brought both – some grapes and a man-size bar of Cadbury's."

A safe course of action, that's what I need. I quickly press two forefingers to my lips then tap them onto Luc's while my other hand unceremoniously plonks the Sainsbury's bag onto his table.

I cannot do gushing, never have been of that disposition, and the only words I manage to muster come out on the horribly awkward side of flippant.

"How's the hip?"

What the hell is wrong with me? Such a shoddy attempt at empathy. Is it surprising that he is poe-faced, disinclined to look at me. We haven't touched. Is it me, is it him? Buck yourself up, Jude!

"Strapped up," is his reply and he scrunches his hands into the bed and lifts his body a few inches to one side then mutters, "How's the horse?"

"Rommel, he's bandaged up, confined to barracks. Cantered up to the gate in the wet two days ago, slid straight into it."

"Oh dear, bummer for you. Will he take long to recover?"

"Six weeks, if I'm lucky – who knows? Done his check ligament."

This is ridiculous. I cannot read him. What a fool I've been. He feels nothing. Pie in the sky romantic ideas whispered into the phone, that's all they were. And anyway, he's totally unsuitable for me. I manage another thirty seconds of avoiding a direct one-to-one look, by trying to stop my handbag strap from sliding off the top of the chair. I sit down. *Why is Luc so fascinated with folding his sheet neatly over the edge of the blanket?*

I spot that one trainer lace is dangling unevenly loose compared to its other end. I lean down, start tightening the lace, anything to busy my fingers, my mind, a fidgety need to avoid any unsolicited familiarity. As my shoulders come up past the level of Luc's feet, I notice that the man in the next bed is wearing silk pyjamas. *Businessman perhaps?*

When my hand rests on the bed blanket for a moment, Luc touches it and I flinch. But his reflex is much quicker and he holds my fingers firm, safe, suddenly soothed under his; in an instant all my fretting evaporates. The stone-blue colour of his eyes is highlighted by the directness of his stare, verging on defiant. I get a fleeting sense of a challenge when he smirkes a little then shoots a question, true and straight, right at me,

"Might he end up as glue?" My brows, a law unto themselves I know, have come together.

"Pardon?" He still doesn't blink and repeats the question.

"I said, if the worst comes to the worst, will Rommel possibly go to the glue factory?"

Flummoxed, is he or isn't he winding me up? I retrieve my hand from under his.

"What *are* you talking about?"

Hot, my ears are too hot. I notice that Pyjama Man has put his book down; I stare at him for a couple of seconds, trying to claw together my thoughts. Luc casts a sly sideways smirk towards Pyjama Man before continuing.

"Surely you know that the crushed bones and cartilage of horses are used in the making of glue?"

"Don't be ridiculous. Of course they aren't."

I look hard at him; the tiny dimple in his chin has gone crooked and I can see the merest hint of a tremble.

"*Yes* they are."

I keep my lips closed and breathe out noisily through my nose.

"All right, all right. You're winding me up."

"*No*, I'm not."

"Yes, you are."

"I promise, I'm not."

A clear, concise, male voice interupts from close by. "No, he isn't."

The room is suddenly quiet, our bickering stopped dead in its tracks. Both Luc and I swivel our attention in the direction of the bed next door, then both men laugh out loud and Luc points at me gleefully.

"Gotcha, Jude!" My clenched-fist wollop of his arm is less than playful even as I throw it.

"*Bastard.*"

"No hitting allowed while I'm incapacitated. Give me a kiss instead. In fact you didn't give me the kiss of life in the forest so I want one now."

Laughter lines seem to multiply all over his face and I see his look of sweet expectation as I come closer, then chagrin as my mouth brushes past his lips and deftly lands on his cheek. For a whole five teasing seconds I remain leaning in, bent over his pillow, floating in the blue sky around his pupils, breathing in the fresh bread and eucalyptus scent of his skin. Then the stark white frame of the hospital bed behind his ear comes into focus. I shift away a little, half-turn ready to steady myself on the arm of the chair, feel a brief smugness at being in control... It is short-lived. Luc's fist shoots out, and well before my bottom has got anywhere near the seat, he is grasping my shirt-collar. The over-zealous tug and a misjudgement of distance means our teeth collide before our lips. I tip my head back a little, exclaiming:

"Ow, slow down." And he does – walks the most gentle, tickling walk of mini kisses along first my top, then my bottom lip before asking, "All better now?"

The skipping is here, under my left breast, a fast-paced rhythmical strumming and I know, without even looking down, that my shirt is rising and falling. I wonder, *Has my heaving bosom been cast for a leading role in* Pride and Prejudice?

A pointed clearing-of-throat noise breaks the spell and Pyjama Man's well-spoken voice follows the interuption.

"He is right, you know. Dead or dying horses were often referred to as being 'sent to the glue factory.' Horses have a lot of collagen in their tendons and ligaments, their bones and even their hides. And collagen is the key ingredient in glue."

I reluctantly sit down and look in the direction of the next bed. Pyjama man is relishing having an audience.

"In fact, the word collagen actually derives from the Greek word *kolla*, meaning glue and the suffix *gen*, meaning producer. Of course, more recently other substitutes have been used."

Luc reaches forward, just managing to touch the end of his fingers with mine. We both politely continue to pretend to listen, but I keep the tips of my fingers unmoved from Luc's. The trickle of energy, a capillary of certainty, a knowledge between us. The bland drone of syllables floats past me in a breeze. Every now and then I glance sideways and catch Luc gazing at me.

This feels right. This feels good.

Chapter 31

Judith

"Slow down, Jude, for goodness' sake. Where's the fire?"

Caroline screeches at me as I negotiate the Shogun in an erratic line around potholes. The track is littered with shards of light and shade, the pines filtering a striking horizontal icicle pattern across the ground. We are in high spirits. Our drive to Thetford Forest has been a never-ending series of girl talk and updating: Caroline quizzing me about my fateful bike ride; Lizzie and I creating a dramatic bubble of intrigue around Stanley and how shocked we'd been to discover that the recluse of the forest was one and the same person as Lizzie's computer geek. Ours is a mish-mash of disjointed and incoherent conversation going three-ways and something like this:

"Do they think Luc will make a full recovery?"

"All being well, but he'll be on crutches for at least six weeks."

"Doesn't Stanley have the tiniest feet and hands you've ever seen on a full-grown man?"

"Caroline, where did you say you got your new horse from?"

"Funny you should say that, but yes, he struggled to get his fist around the handlebars of the bike. I'd forgotten I noticed that."

"Mind that bump, Jude. The cake is slipping off the plate."

"I had to go all the way to Lincoln. Lovely set-up. Money no object."

"So there must be some romance in the air after your heroic efforts – surely?"

"Did you make the carrot cake? Or your mum?"

"Ask me no questions and I shall tell you no lies."

"Is that the answer to the romance or the cake question, Jude?"

"Both. I prefer to remain a woman of mystery!"

The latter reply brings a volley of "Oh no. Come on, Jude" from both Caroline and Lizzie, but my four-wheel drive has arrived outside Rose Cottage so our happy trio duly pile out. I am pleased to see that there is no chain on the gate and I begin briefing the the girls in earnest as we make our way along the path. My words are hushed.

"You know I didn't fancy coming alone and we don't have to stay long, but Stanley was an absolute trooper. Remember, he's not the most outgoing of personalities, so you must keep things toned down while we're here."

I have already raised my fist to knock on the little olive-coloured door when it opens without warning and I only just arrest what would have been an extremely embarassing whack of Stanley's nose. A rush of circulation up my neck heralds a hot flush and Caroline's snigger just behind my shoulder is barely restrained. Stanley smiles at me.

"Ladies. Do come in, won't you?"

Ducking as we step one by one into the narrow hallway, Lizzie, ever the professional, immediately engrosses our host in a series of courteous comments and platitudes. Stanley has politely taken our coats and is carefully hanging them one by one on the hall stand. No casual throwing and crushing, instead each movement measured to its frugal minimum. The heavily engraved oak stand includes a mirror with four wrought-iron hooks positioned either side. The bottom half of the stand is a bench and this rather grand piece of furniture reaches from floor to ceiling. The overall effect is that it may well actually be holding up the ceiling! Caroline runs her fingertips casually over the dark wood and offers a considered opinion.

"Nineteenth-century Renaissance. Hand carved. Very nice."

Stanley visibly puffs up with pride and replies, "Thank you. Three women in my house at once. A first."

I notice our framed reflection, our statuesque forms appearing giant beside Stanley. He is wearing a white cotton shirt and his navy tie is knotted as neat as a pin. He gestures with his outstretched arm to guide us into his sitting room. The warmth and wafts of woodsmoke hit me as I enter. My mind wanders back. *Such a stark contrast. Is it only five days since I was last here? And he's switched the light on. I can see so much more.* Today, my mind is present in the room, not creating vivid imaginings of Luc drifting into hypothermia. It gives me a chance to scan my surroundings properly. There is an addition: a table covered with a well-worn but immaculately clean tablecloth. The green crockery is back and has been laid out in four place settings with cubes of sugar stacked ready in a small bowl.

"Make yourselves comfortable. Please sit down." Stanley graciously offers to make tea and excuses himself.

The second we are alone, Caroline and Lizzie simultaneously turn to me, both squashing their foreheads into wrinkles. Lizzie is the first to whisper.

"He's certainly unusual. I'm guilty of having thrown him onto the oblivion stack in my memory box the last time we met at my office."

I have already nabbed the chair in the window. Lizzie is painstakingly trying to remove clingfilm from the cake but her fingers are quickly sticking to bits of cream cheese topping and plastic. My comment comes out tetchily.

"Stop faffing around, will you?"

Lizzie looks from her hand to me, then back again and is just about to lick the offending goo off, when I see her cock her head to one side as though she's listening to something. Statue still, her mouth wide, thumb within inches of her lips, she stares at Caroline.

"Did you hear that... that scuttling noise above our heads?"

Caroline has been counting the number of wattle upstruts in each wall and studying the daub which is coming away in small chunks. She pokes at a loose bit of clay and straw hanging on by a few horsehairs to the wall. I feel no urge to pay much attention to Lizzie's imaginings because a heavy fog of tiredness has crept up on me. I rub half-cupped hands into my eyesockets.

Caroline chimes up, "What, Lizzie?"

On cue there is the sound of a distant and confused skirmishing of clawed feet on floorboards, then a distinct – thump, thump, pause – and again – thump, thump. Lizzie swivels her eyes, lunatic fashion, in circles and answers very slowly,

"*That* noise."

I watch the door to the kitchen swing open and, with a gentle bang, it hits the corner of the table. Stanley enters in a crab-like sideways motion to allow for the teapot in one hand and a small milk jug in the other. His eyes do their characteristic narrowing to slits, the second he appears to feel the loaded atmosphere in the room. So he quietly places the teapot on the table mat and the jug beside it. I jump in first, but there is a momentary catch in my throat mid sentence.

"We're wondering whether there may be something upstairs, Stanley? We've heard a sort of thrashing around noise above this room."

Stanley remains silent, rock-like, so I feel the need to press again.

"Perhaps a bird came in through the window or down a chimney?" My new-found elfin friend then steps a little closer to my chair. His top lip folds in slightly, then he whispers as if a state secret is about to be revealed.

"Ah, that's only Thumper." He takes a breath. "My rabbit, Thumper."

And this, I always remember afterwards, is the pivotal moment at which we become bound together as a group. I watch the surprised but delighted shock which turns into smiles, then ribald laughter, as Stanley explains.

"There are three guinea pigs and Thumper. I keep them all inside during the colder months. Buried two little corpses the winter before last in the freezing snap. Put them in a shoebox side by side, poor mites. Not their fault, entirely mine – too cold it was. I just didn't think. So now the others are living in my mother's old room."

Within minutes, tea is forgotten and we are all piling up the spiral staircase, asking incessant questions. We reach the landing and Stanley halts us with a raised hand.

"You will have to be calm and move slowly, ladies, otherwise you will frighten them. We don't normally have visitors."

The babble of female voices ceases and Stanley leads us into the room. A rodent heaven, nirvana for rabbits, happy valley for South American cavies, call it what you like. Stanley has installed a rabbit hutch with a ramp in one corner. We become a rapt audience, watching as Mr. Chortle with his swirly rosetted coat frolics up and down over a mini-hill in the middle of the room. All created with Stanley's fair hands, he explains that the old carpet tacked onto the hardboard is there to stop tiny feet slipping. Underneath the artificial hill is an archway which, according to Stanley, is

"Thumper's favourite spot. He hoards carrot pieces under there."

When Lizzie makes a sudden move to drop to her haunches, the startled rodents panic as one, sawdust flick-back and scratching claws evidence of their fright. Thumper is no longer visible bar the tips of his two ears at the edge of the underpass. A sharp thump, thump, thump, thump rings out again. Stanley chips in.

"You startled him. That's his rabbit-to-rabbit warning signal, sends them all rushing to their burrow in the wild. If we keep still for a couple of minutes, they will come out again."

Sure enough, within a few minutes, the furry quartet bravely appear again. Stanley expertly picks up two of the guinea pigs and hands one each to Lizzie and Caroline. The two women squat side by side, oohing and aahing, Caroline at the delights of Hermione's tortoiseshell and white patches while Lizzie uses her thumb as a measuring stick for Pippa's whiskers.

Mesmerised as I am by this obscure and precious moment of ridiculousness, I am struggling to stay focused. A little light-headed, I steady myself, placing one hand on the wall for support.

"Stanley. May I pop downstairs now and pour myself some tea? You stay up here."

I sidle out carefully. Downstairs, the heat hits me again when I enter the sitting room. Cup of tea in hand, I am about to sit down when the antimacassar on the back of the chair catches my eye. The eighteen-inch square of white linen is so in keeping with the whole room and I run my fingers over the bobbliness of the detailed embroidery. The colours in the silk thread are fading, but the ornate stitchwork is still secure. A classic depiction of daisies, roses and pale blue forget-me-nots, probably sewn to a template and I know I've seen it before. A sharp and unexpected stab of guilty memory reminds me of a tearful scene and my own harsh words to Mother: "It's old and worn out, Mother. For goodness' sake. It really is time to bin it." *A lost art. Another era. Time marches on.*

I pop another log on the embers of the fire and slump gratefully into the high-backed chair. I purse my lips and slurp; the hot stream of Darjeeling burns all the way down to my innards. The occasional creaking of a floorboard and muffled conversation from upstairs is continuing, so I rest my head onto the antimacassar and close my lids against the beams of light.

Odd, very odd. Two visits and I already I know this is my favourite seat!

Five days – *since I last sat here.*

Four days – *since Luc's first phone call from the hospital.*

I open my eyes for a second; the door is still shut. I decide to wander back to my daydream and the clinical confines of my visit to the hospital.

Three days – since I visited him and goodness, there are only two words that pop into my mind to describe our reunion – weird and wonderful. The horrible weirdness of the first fifteen minutes in each other's company – the relief when a nurse arrived wielding a bedpan like a weapon and pulled the curtains around Pyjama Man.

In the shadows of my hazy slumber I become vaguely aware of people tiptoeing around the room. The gentle click of a door latch, the sound of a far-off kettle boiling, the scrape of knife on plate. A prickling sensation in my upper arm is suddenly too much so I move it floppily from behind my head, down onto my lap, feel no particular need to open my eyes.

Two Days – *since I bought the Elbow CD.*

Luc insisted I should listen to a song called 'Starlings'; he hoped it might become 'our song'. I want to drift into the precious lyrics, hum the tune, float in a cloud of silver words.

The soft timpani beginning so silky, draping itself luscious. Words of flattery, words of poetry.

The tender way the music creeps over my skin. Words about the selfishness that comes with age.

The crashing thunder of raucous trumpets. Words about a horse destined for glue.

The chorals, the feeling, the slow rise of it. Words of orange groves and lunches.

The rhythm of the timpani repeating. Confessional words, a man who is true,

To the words that promise of listening and dreaming. Till we fall, a wave of starlings.

I move my hand, prop it against my cheek then crook my knee up and snuggle deeper into an ephemeral comfort zone all my own. My thoughts continue meandering.

This year has been so strange. This year has been quite scary. This, my year of serendipity. We pigeon-hole or squash the people we meet into boxes of our own choice, often within a nanosecond of the first sighting, the first chat, the first perfunctory meeting and yet, so often we are wrong, I am wrong. *The man beneath the face that is Stanley: who would have guessed? The man beneath the façade that is Luc Stockdale: I never guessed – till now.*

Singledom – we search, we fall, we search, we fall again. Hope – it gets picked up, trodden on, dusted off, then slung in the hedge again. It can be a dangerous ally or a fickle friend. Some people really only want an escort for the evening, a friendly warm smile on the end of their arm to whom they can spew out their woes with no fear of mockery or retribution. The essence of being human is to crave companionship, to mourn loves lost, but in the end all we really desire is an audience with hope.

Weary, so very weary. Sleep delicious, sleep…

Shaken, why am I being shaken? Let go of my arm!

Blearily I drag myself into conciousness. I look into the emerald eyes of my best friend, spot a shred of carrot wedged between her teeth, mumble playfully,

"Cake good was it?"

I hear her kind words in response:

"Jude… time to go."

Acknowledgements

Many people have helped me with both the research and writing of this book. Some have been especially patient with a fledgling novelist. My heartfelt thanks go to :-

Clair, Rachel and Helen – the inspiration for all the forest tales and female banter.

Lesley – for her bookworm skills.

Dan, Andy and George – for their motorbike expertise.

Roger and Fiona Clarke for their invaluable anecdotes and knowledge of bloodhounds.

The Blue Pencil Agency and Pat McHugh – for their vital critiques along the way.

And last, but not least, thank you to all the Troubador staff for helping me to avoid falling at the intimidating hurdle called "publishing".

About the Author

Debut author Lorna Roth grew up with her roots firmly planted in the countryside. She quickly spread her wings to live and work in both Australia and Los Angeles; the latter giving her a career in the unusual world of international horse transport. Post career, she returned to the UK where a sense of humour was essential when combining the demands of motherhood with the rigours of living on a small Suffolk council farm.

Her creative bent draws on a quirky mixture of her experiences with the unpredictability of people, life and animals. The plot for Kick-Start took shape after she was regaled with the escapades of her less than young, single friends. Lorna prides herself on funny, outside the box humour to describe complicated emotional situations. Her mission is to relay the joys, vivid characters and graphic realities which go hand-in-hand with living in rural East Anglia.